REBOOTS

REBOOTS

UNDEAD CAN DANCE

MERCEDES LACKEY & CODY MARTIN

This is a work of fiction.

Cover art by Christina P. Myrvold; artstation.com/christinapm

Portions of this book have appeared previously in *Reboots* and *Reboots: Diabolical Streak*.

ISBN: 978-1-64710-022-3

First Edition. 1st Printing. November 2021
1 2 3 4 5 6 7 8 9 10

An imprint of Arc Manor LLC

www.CaezikSF.com

CONTENTS

PART ONE

BAD MOON RISING

You know what they said in that ancient movie, about being in space? Well here's a news flash for you: in space no one gives a shit if you scream. Especially not your shipmates. Oh, you'd think your shipmates would care, right? I mean, it's just all of you against all of the dark and vacuum and whatever crap the universe has dreamed up to kill you? Another news flash: no. Especially if your shipmates are a bunch of sociopathic dirtbags that think dead puppy jokes are a laugh riot.

So the screaming and cursing in the aft drain chamber was pretty much "Tuesday."

So much for the glamour and excitement of interstellar travel.

We'd strapped Fred down for the blood-drain again, and since he was human, it was going well aside from all the noise. That would be me, standing in the corner, doing my best to look like an appliance, while Fred screamed and ranted. That would be the High and Mighty, watching, and occasionally changing out a blood-bag, since I wasn't to be trusted with something as important as their property. Three pints down, two to go, and Fred was still in fine voice. That was the thing about Fred being a Fur (ah, excuse me, I should be more sensitive, a "Were-person"); he regenerated the blood he was losing almost immediately. A couple spinach salads and a slab of beef and he'd be fine. Turn him loose under this planet's moons to let him feast on whatever he could catch and kill and he'd be more than fine. I never could figure out how it was that he could eat anything remotely living and carbon-based when he wolfed out, even if it would have poisoned him in human shape. Miracles of Were physiology,

3

I guess, but hey, no one pays me to be the brains—hardy har har. Come to think of it, no one pays me at all.

"We," had him strapped down, by which I mean "me," since the Fangs (and I will be damned all over again if I call Our Vampiric Lords and Masters anything but Fangs) never got their lily-like hands dirty if they could help it. They were the "mission specialists." Meaning they had an excuse to be divas, or figured they did. It was up to me and the others to do all the work. And Fred, because he was lowest on this particular food chain. So yeah, that's the shipmates. Three Fangs and a Fur, and the hate and contempt was so thick most of the time it's like a fog in the air.

Barnabus was in charge today. Oh Barnabus, who really got the short end of the Vampiric stick. Someone had bit him late in life, and as you are when you get Turned, so you stay. So there he was in all his sagging, jowly glory, looking like a basset hound in a tailored jumpsuit. Can't really wonder why he's a douche; he has to look at the others, who may not be the supermodels of the Fang world but certainly are not coyote-ugly, and at himself, and grind his fangs. Even their jumpsuits look good on them, while his looks … like a janitor uniform. Yes, here we are, hopping stars, and the attire de rigueur for space travelers is still the jumpsuit, go figure. Must drive the Fangs crazy, with their obsessive-compulsive fashion sense; it's kind of hard to get designer labels hundreds of light-years from the nearest retailer.

The rest of the Fangs were lined up, waiting for their liquid lunch, and Barny was making them wait, which was not exactly *quelle surprise*. Barny was his usual patronizing self. He smiled snarkily down at Fred, who glared up at him. "Good boy, Fred. Nice doggie." He patted the top of Fred's head, then quickly pulled his hand out of reach when Fred snarled. Granted he was in human form, but some of the Wolf carried over, and he'd been known to bite.

"Shut up, Barnabus," Fred said, then told Barnabus what he could do with himself and where he could put that hand in long, loving and profane detail, using only Barnabus's full name. Ol' "Barny" hated his full name; believe it or not, in the Before time there'd been some sort of soap opera with a Vampire in it by that name, and … well, let's just say for the aristocratic Fangs, a soap opera was to the Grand

4

High Literature of their kind (snork) as Mexican *lucha libre* wrestling was to the Olympics. Fred and the others chose to use Barny's full name as often as the occasion warranted to get under his skin, which happened pretty often, because he was really easy to aggravate. But with Barny sticking the verbal knife in and rotating it, as well as being none-too-gentle about the drain, *and* being parked on a world where he mostly couldn't go outside the ship, Fred was not happy at all and he was really heaping on the verbal abuse today. Not that I blamed him.

This particular dirt-ball must have had a dozen moons, maybe more, I hadn't counted. It wasn't my job to count things, just like it wasn't my job to think; I was just the guy they got to sweep up the shed fur and whatever the Fangs discarded and the crap that got tracked in, strap Fred down in case he wolfed out in the middle of a drain, fix the ship's systems occasionally under strict supervision, and rehydrate the dehydrated cattle brains and stick 'em in the feeding chute so the rest of the Zombies didn't waste away to nothing but bones. I mean, they could still do the job as bones except they tended to fall apart when they tried to pick up anything heavy, or were backhanded by a pissed off Fang-face. Inconvenient. God knows the Fangs shouldn't be inconvenienced by anything. Dicks. Oh, had I not mentioned this before? Yeah. I'm a Zombie too, which is why nobody gives a shit what I think, because I'm not supposed to be able to think. More on that later. Everybody has rude names for us. Reboots. Shambler. Deadhead. Bone Bags. Rotpot. Corpsicle. Mikey Jerkson and Chiller Thriller … you know, I never did figure out where those two came from. Only the older Fangs seemed to use those two terms.

The Fangs—who really, really hate that name for our Vampiric Lords and Masters—got their rations from Barny, finished up the drain time on Fred and took their time in turning him loose. He did his usual ritual of pissing and moaning, cursing their families and hoping all the demons in the universe chose to pay them a visit, but he put more feeling into it today than usual.

"Someone woke up on the wrong side of the kennel this morning." The Fangs never, never lost a chance to get in a dog-reference. The few Furs I'd run into before this cruise all seemed really self-conscious about their animal sides, and Fred was no exception. Maybe it was because when they morphed out, they were pretty much ravening, mindless beasts on steroids. Poor Fred. All those moons meant he was wolfed out most of the time if he went outside or got near an unshuttered viewport. It wasn't that he had any choice in the matter; it was just automatic, as much of a physical necessity as the Fangs' need for blood, or a person's need to breathe. When he did go all wild-eyed and hairy, it was best not to be anywhere nearby. Imagine a five foot four accountant-looking guy turning into an eight-foot-tall unholy terror that basically wants to rip apart and eat anything that looks like it might be made of meat; that's what Fred becomes whenever he gets hit with the light of any moons, if they were full. You would think that the moon phase wouldn't matter on a spaceship; hell, conversely, you'd think that *being* in a spaceship wouldn't matter if the moon was full. What do I know? Maybe the Norms figured out how to put anti-moon-phase shielding on the hull—but it didn't work on the open viewports. I'm just the janitor, and I wasn't exactly a rocket scientist when I was alive. Besides, in a 'verse where Vampires, Werewolves, and Zombies exist as a matter of fact, some things just are and it doesn't matter that they don't make sense.

Fred was going on with his cussing for longer than usual too, his tirade becoming less profane and more inventive as time went on. "I'll tear you in half and throw you out of the airlock. When we're parked next to a yellow star." That was new. Death threats are not anything that this lot hasn't already made before, but when you start working in the specific weaknesses, it strikes a chord. Fred's idea would probably work, too. G-class yellow stars and those close to them in stellar classification are deadly to Fangs; the light crisps them nicely, and if they are out in it long enough, it reduces them to ash. One bit of trivia I can verify: there actually *was* a coating on the viewports that prevented yellow sunlight from hurting the Fangs, probably some kind of UV coating. I was supposed to paint a new coat of it on the inside once every three weeks. That vulnerability was what had kept the Norms on top against Fangs when the Great Uncloseting happened. Norms were top-notch at finding and exploiting weaknesses.

Antonio sneered. Antonio *loved* his full name. Antonio della Contani, supposedly some sort of Venetian royalty, right? I'm laying bets on him actually being plain old Tony Conti from Brooklyn who was Turned in the 50s, based on his taste in music and the fact that he acts like a punk thug in nice clothes. "Promises, promises. Puppy didn't get his walkies."

As usual, they were at each other's throats, verbally if not actually. Not that it mattered if they did tear pieces out of each other, they'd just regenerate, heal, both. The same wasn't true for the likes of me; I'd stay in a not-so-neat pile, with my parts wriggling around until my brain got tired, unless my bits got shoved into a recycling unit or someone was kind enough to stitch me up. And this wasn't exactly a kind bunch, if you get my drift. Besides, Zombies are a dime a dozen; we're nothing more than part of the inventory.

Yeah, that's the other thing about being a Zombie. Being Undead is totally rad unless you're one of *us*. Vampires are strong and fast and persuasive. Werewolves are giant hairy woodchippers on legs. Zombies are janitors. Smelly janitors. Disposable janitors. Whenever one of us breaks, they just shove the bits into the recycler and grab another one out of the hold. I used to have a name, forever ago. I don't remember those days all that well. Now I just go by Skinny Jim, when there's someone that bothers to speak to me. Which, let me tell you, isn't all that often. Zombies are not exactly what you would call stellar conversationalists, so why would they?

That's another thing. Not a lot of Zombies can talk. Most of us really are mindless—burnt out or burnt up by whatever made us the way we are. We can do simple tasks, sure, especially if shown what to do a few dozen times. But there's not a lot of intellectual stimulation amongst Zombies, if you don't count munching on the occasional rehydrated brain. You don't find us sitting around discussing Kierkegaard. So, I'm special in that regard; I've got some of my mind left, but no opportunity to show it. And no incentive, to tell the truth. The Norms—well there were no Norms out here in any great numbers so that was moot—still, what the Norms would do, I didn't like to think about. Not after the Zombie Wars. And the other Undead don't like the manual labor to be too bright, and I'm not sure what *they'd* do if they found out I was different. They'd probably do what the Norms would do, and sad as my existence is, it beats the alternative.

"Fuckin' elitist bastiches," Fred muttered under his breath. Fangs. Thought they were the kings of the universe. Ask any of them, and they'd tell you. Not a one of them was ever some wino that got rolled for Type O-Pos in an alley, or would at least admit to it. Oh no. All of them had longer pedigrees than the winner of the Kennel Club trophy. And they *all* had the goofiest names you've ever heard of. Always something faux-fancy or exotic sounding. You never met a Bob the Vampire. He hated them, this ship and—well not the job, exactly, but after the first few new planets it had gotten … routine. But this was a paying gig. Not the greatest gig in the universe, *except* for the pay, but it'd do for now. Now, of course, being quite a stretch; he'd signed on for three hundred years for this tour, give or take a decade. They were about halfway through their supply of Reboots, with the other consumables—spare parts for the hardware, mostly—at about the same level.

But it was at times like this … most of the time, lately … he asked himself: why would a bunch of monsters from ancient fairy tales and B-movies be out roaming the stars, anyways?

He knew the answer though: why else—the ones that had the power and the money made the rules.

And that would be the Norms.

It was because the Norms were the real kings of the universe, or at least, of Earth. They had the lock on the stakes, the silver bullets, the SunGuns. Oh, poor Norms, who just didn't have the weaknesses of the Undead. The light of yellow suns didn't make them fall into a coma at low levels of exposure or burn up at high levels. They weren't terminally allergic to silver, or garlic. And they could run faster than any Zombie *and* they had flamethrowers. Only thing they didn't have were long life spans, long enough to do serious space exploration. Fangs, Furs, and Reboots though, they did, and there wasn't much out here that could actually kill a Fang or a Fur if it didn't already know the weaknesses.

The pay for a long cruise was excellent, and without having to worry about dodging religious fanatics, or wolfing out and maybe hurting someone or worse—or, for the Fangs, going comatose and vulnerable once the yellow sun came up—so, for the ones out of the broom closet, exploration was the mainstream place to be. There were more volunteers than there were ships.

So, things got along pretty smoothly, for the most part, back home, at least for the Paranormals that wanted to just get along with Norm society. Personally, Fred thought that a lot of them were sellouts. You could still find a measure of freedom on some of the colony worlds, and a lot of the Paras that didn't get exploration gigs had shipped out for those, or so he'd heard. But back on Earth? Stuck kowtowing to the whims of the Norms, never daring to even stick a toe over the line, always afraid of setting a "bad example" for the rest of your kind? To hell with that noise. The Fangs and Furs (the ones that weren't Underground and actually had some moxie) all cued up for their shots at a ship as first choice, colony as second. Fangs for crew, a Wolf or two for the fresh blood for the Fangs, and crew too, and the Zombies—the Reboots—for menial labor. Neither Fang nor Fur needed to worry about the Reboots chowing down on their brains, the Reboots ignored them both so far as feeding went. So the Norms on Earth got rid of their problems, everything was one humming happy assembly-line, and that didn't matter for crap out here. Because once you got out here you found out what the real pecking order was, and you were looking at three hundred years locked up in the same tin can as the creatures that considered you Lunch That Talks. And they'd really rather you didn't talk, just grovel and do what you were told.

It was Fred's job to make sure that the Reboots were sent to the right places and made to do the right jobs. He was a supervisor, for the most part, only taking care of the most sensitive jobs personally. At least he wasn't *just* the Fang cafeteria; he'd been an engineer before he got bitten, and he still was an engineer now. Today, he had a sensitive job to take care of. The ship's main drive was being finicky, so Fred had to eat some rads and fix it. On any vessel that held Norms, and there were a few, mostly Earth-system stuff, there were dozens of safeguards with redundancies and contingencies and so on. Not so for a ship like this. Paranormals didn't get hurt the same way that Norms did, so it was more acceptable to cut corners, and thus costs. Ah the joys of space exploration.

He'd take some Reboots along to hold lights and pass him tools. A few extra sets of hands never hurt, even if the hands were prone to falling off at the worst possible time. Antonio still hadn't let him live down the time a Reboot's finger had snapped off and shorted the grav generator.

Fred pointed at the three nearest ones. "Command phrase: come with me. You, you, and you."

They didn't bother naming the Reboots; they all were dressed in cheap red coveralls—which he thought was a nice touch—and all responded to "you" so long as they noticed someone was talking to them. One of the ghoulies looked somewhat startled—or at least as startled as a decayed corpse can look—when Fred spoke to him, but Fred shrugged it off and started marching them all to the lift that would take him to the reactor. It was probably nothing more than a nerve twitch. You never knew with the Reboots. Once he thought he'd caught the one that looked like a desiccated surfer dude trying to skateboard. He chalked it up to the Fangs trying to fuck with him. It wouldn't have been that hard to stick a piece of insulation board on some casters and tell the Reboot to stand on it.

Were all the crews this dysfunctional? How could they be? How would anything get done if they were? Then again … paranoia set it. Because it was true that it wasn't paranoia if "they" actually were out to get you, and there was no doubt that the minute the Norms thought the Paras just *might* get the upper hand, out would come all the stockpiled weapons, the stake—and SunGuns, the garlic spray, the silver-coated *everything*, and lots and lots of flamethrowers. The Norms just preferred things to not be chaotic and messy and dangerous. So …. *Maybe that was the plan; send our Kinds out in the stars to kill each other. And meanwhile, find some planets the Norms could use—y'know, as a "nice if it happens" bonus. That would just figure. Have the bad luck to get Turned, and as a Were no less, only to get shipped off to the stars to deal with Larry, Curly, and Shithead for however long it took until one of you snapped and you all killed each other. The way these lowest-bidder ships are built, the Norms could probably afford that, and it wouldn't be nearly as messy as a Norm versus Para war.* He shook his head; thinking in circles like this was sure to drive him mad.

Or maybe this all was just paranoia, and the other crews all got along just fine, and the universe had decided to stick Fred with the most petty, vain, and antagonistic bunch of bloodsuckers ever created. Given how his luck usually went … yeah, that would be about par for the course. It made more sense than some enormous Norm plot. Right?

Not that it mattered to him at this point anyway. Because whether it was part of a huge plot against the Paras, or whether it was just bad luck, he was stuck here with the Divas of the Damned for the foreseeable future. He muttered more curses as he made his way to the engineering section, thinking of all of the different ways he'd like to kill his shipmates. Well, re-kill. Actually, all things considered, he wouldn't feel unhappy if he got to re-kill all of them three or four times before finishing them off for good. *A Wolf can dream ….*

Man, Fred had it bad. Me, it didn't matter, the Fangs couldn't get a kick out of verbally tormenting me, and when they were in a bad mood, I could just make sure I wasn't the one within reach of their claws. It might get different later, when the numbers of us Reboots started getting a lot lower, but for now, I was just one more tree in the forest. Thing is, the Fangs could get all the reaction their hard little flintlike hearts desired out of Fred. The poor sap was a great big hairy ball of reaction, and the longer the trip went on, the shorter his fuse got. Reboots didn't have any brains except the ones we were munching on—har har—so we didn't notice and didn't react. Fred though, he was the only Fur on the ship, and the only one who acted with resentment when they were looking for someone to verbally abuse that wasn't one of them.

And the Fangs *loved* to make people squirm. I don't get it. I never had much to do with any of the other Para races before I got herded up with the rest of the Zombies I was with, shoved into a red jumpsuit and stuck in the hold, so … were all Fangs like this? I don't know. But this lot really took the "fun" out of "dysfunctional." When Fred wasn't around, they fought with each other. When he was around, they ganged up on him. It was like they weren't happy unless they were spreading pain to something other than themselves. Maybe it was part of the pecking-order thing that Fangs always seemed to establish, and maybe they figured they each had to be the Alpha, Fearless Leader Supremo, at least over someone; maybe that sort of thing came with being Turned. Or, maybe, we just got stuck with the biggest assholes the Fangs ever produced and the powers that be lumped all of them together to keep all the grief in one place.

We arrived at the section where the malfunction was. Fred started pointing at each of us Reboots, positioning us where he needed us, and then went about the task of fixing what was wrong. I was just supposed to flip a switch whenever he told me to. Looked like something dealing with the ship's coolant systems; a lot of heat got generated by the drives, and it needed some way to safely bleed off into space. I played along, allowing Fred to do his part and treat me like the others. It was boring, but it was better than … well, what? Rehydrating brains, I guess. Waiting to get broken beyond repair, like the others? Like just another replaceable component on this ship? Or standing around and thinking. There's nothing much around here that makes for comfortable thinking.

Then things got even more "entertaining." Grigoire decided to make his entrance, when we were about halfway through and the ship was running on the APU—which meant no one got to do anything that wasn't absolutely necessary. Grigoire took special pleasure in torturing Fred; he really, really hated Werewolves, more than the average Fang. Before Paras were outed to the entire world, Fangs and Furs were already at each other's throats in some kind of eternal holy war, or something. When us Zombies started causing enough trouble for the Norms, both sides came to a truce to try and "save the herd," as it were. Didn't seem to do much to quell the resentment and hatred that immortal beings can harbor in the long run though; a grudge seemed to age like fine wine with some of them.

Grigoire was the vessel's astrophysicist, which meant on a scale of one to ten on "Uptight Asshole-ness," he scored a whopping seventy-three. He was probably the same when he was a Norm, if the near-ancient vids we have onboard of *The Big Bang Theory* are to be believed.

Oh right. Yeah we've got an entire shipload worth of anachronisms. You'll find that most Fang/Fur culture is based on the years between 1875 and just about 1990. Those were the Golden Ages for them. Before that, Norms were scarce enough that when enough Norms went missing, people noticed, and went hunting. After that, there were cell phones and computer networks, and when Norms went missing, the information got passed around the damn world in less than a day, and Norms went hunting. In between that, there were plenty of people around, enough so that you got runaways and misfits, and other types that would vanish, and no one would notice much of a pattern or really care, mostly because there was kind of an attitude that if you didn't march in lockstep with every other Norm, you deserved whatever terrible fate came to you. So that's when most of them got Turned. And that's where their cultural tastes got stuck.

And for those that weren't from that time? Well, Home Services supplied us with all the entertainment we were ever likely to get—as long as it was long out of copyright. So that meant a whole lot of twentieth and twenty-first century stuff and not much else, and absolutely nothing from the *House of Mouse*, because of the special copyright exception. What you see that much of tends to become part of you, and that's about all we see out here.

"Hey, Fuzzy Wuzzy. How's it going with the repairs? Try not to get any dog hair in the components; it's a pain to get out, you know?" Grigoire slapped on his best smile, which looked fake and painful stretched across perfect and blemish-free dead skin. "Oh wait, that's right, *you're* going to be the one to clean them out!" He laughed at his own humor. "Never mind then, carry on."

"Grigoire, not now. Think of it like this: if I don't do my job correctly, then the ship falls apart. If the ship falls apart, you'll be getting really cozy with a couple of red dwarfs. And I'm not talking the Snow White kind either, sucker." Fred was pissed. Poor bastard. In another unlife, I would've really had my withered heart go out to him. Here, he was just another prisoner that might end up busting me to pieces. "I don't come tell you dirty jokes while you're piddling with your equations, so how about you go brood about the unfairness of unlife, pine over the women you aren't getting to bite, or write Goth poetry or something while I do my job?"

"That's really funny, fleabag. Make sure to comb some insect killer into that hair."

I'm not sure why, because it's no worse than any of the other shit they call him, but there was something about that name that always got to Fred. He put up with a lot of crap from the Fangs; but what other choice did he have? But whenever they called him that, he got mean. Fred put down his tools with a loud clang and turned to face Grigoire, an ugly smirk on his face.

"At least I still have all my hair. Must suck—hardy har—that you got bitten so late in life you were stuck with a comb-over. Tony said you were looking lighter around the North, by the way. You been picking at yourself again? You should know better than that. You haven't got anything to spare up there." Fred twirled a finger around the very top of his cranium, grinning evilly the entire time. And that was all that Grigoire needed. It's an interesting thing, to see one of the Fangs really vamp out. It's not too unlike the Weres, but a little more subtle. Grigoire's eyes filled with murder and a cold fury that always unsettled me. Something happened that seemed to make the shadows deeper around him, calling on the infernal whatever-the-hell that animated Fangs, I suppose. He bared his terrible canines and leapt for Fred, claws extended. Fred partially transformed; his features became more bestial, with his hair growing longer and his muscles rippling and growing under-neath his skin. He can do that half-transformation at will; he just can't completely wolf out. He still has full control over himself in the half-state, which was good; if the wrong stuff was busted in this room, the ship had a fairly decent chance of exploding. Ah, lowest-bidder contracts ....

There was about sixty seconds of ultraviolence and way-too-fast ruckus, which was fortunately confined to a relatively robust part of the engine room; then Antonio appeared in the door, yelling at the top of his lungs. *"Knock it off, morons!"*

They froze. Antonio is the Captain. Top of the Fang food chain. I *think* there's something in their instincts that makes the other Fangs obey him. Maybe he's been Undead the longest, or he was born or Turned with a certain *whatever* that just made the others obey. Didn't matter; they jumped when he said to. A good thing, too, since otherwise this would have been a hulk floating in space about three months into the mission, inhabited only by us decayed types until the brains ran out. Not so much because they knew how to kill each other without helpful tools like wooden stakes and silver, but because they'd probably have blown something up and gone through a bulkhead, with the end result being the lot of them sucked out into deep space to form a fighting ball until they all froze solid, or Fred ran out of air. The Fangs didn't need air, but they wore suits to protect themselves from the cold and to be able to talk to the ship and each other. At near-zero Kelvin even a Fang will freeze solid and be unable to move. Fred, however, needed air, though he would last longer than a Norm would.

"You!" Antonio said to Fred, pointing. "Back to work. I want a hot shower and *La Traviata*. And you—" he pointed to Grigoire. "Act like a civilized noble, and not a thug. You can always be demoted if I choose. As far down the chain as I care to put you." Antonio always tried to play at being sophisticated and a part of "Undead royalty." I always thought it was a heaping pile of bullshit, personally. "So behave as if you deserve your position, or you'll be second in command to Fido." Tony got a wicked look on his face. "And I'll let him tell *you* when you can eat."

Grigoire hated being talked down to by Tony, even though it was his place in the chain of command, but that was just a whole new level of insult. I don't think it was my imagination, what there was left of such a thing; matters were escalating around here. He shrieked a terrible and piercing wail, and then went to work on us Reboots. I've been around when either the Fangs go woolly, or Fred has his moon phases going on. But never in such close quarters. He ripped through us, pulling Zombies apart with his hands, tearing at us with teeth. It was horrible to watch, but I couldn't move. He was working his way toward me, and I didn't dare run. To run would be to show that I knew what was coming—and that would show I could still think. I was dead either way. Well, dead again. Perma-dead. If I could have closed my eyes, I would have, but my eyelids are sort of glued in the open position.

"*Grigoire!*" Tony used a worse voice than before. It was the sort of voice that you used with a dog that just took a dump on the carpet in front of you. The tone ... I can't describe it. If I'd had blood, it would have been frozen. More Fang powers. Even Fred went statue-still. Grigoire stopped with one clawed hand raised to rend me from stem to sternum.

Tony was really pissed now. "Not in front of the help, fool of a child," he hissed. "Back to your quarters! Now!" Grigoire fumed, shooting another savage look at Fred before he finally retreated. I tracked my eyes the barest few centimeters to look at Fred, then to Tony, trying to keep my face uninterested in the happenings around me. Kind of hard to be any more deadpan when you're already dead.

Fred cocked his head to the side. "That Zombie looked at me funny."

Tony sighed heavily, squeezing the bridge of his nose with his fingers as if to stave off a migraine. I think that's just another affectation on his part; I don't think the Fangs have such human concerns as headaches. "That's because you're funny-looking, Fred. Go take a flea bath or lick your ass or something. Just get the drives fixed first." If I could still evacuate my bowels, that would've been the moment for me to do so. That had been ... way too close. And dusty wheels had started to turn in my head.

"Pete, what other choice do we have? We're coming apart at the seams, here, literally." I pointed at Pete's left shoulder; he had been wedged between a mainframe core and its housing while trying to install some new wiring, and one of our less-than-awake Reboot brothers decided to push anyways. I was sewing him back up. "Nobody ever tries to fix us, because we're disposable!"

"Dude, what's the point? We go back home, and we're just more Deadheads. You know what they do to us, especially if they think we can talk and think and feel. Well, feel kinda, at least." Every conscious Reboot remembered what happened to Xavier, the short-unlived "Lord of Zombies" and his Zombie War. It hadn't been pretty even by Reboot standards, which you had to admit, were somewhere in the sub-sub-basement. Get out of the gutter, so those of us in the sewer can get some sun, sorta thing. Xavier had been the reason why the Fangs and the Furs came out of the broom closet to help the

Norms in the first place. Zombies on their own can be dealt with pretty easily, if a Norm has a lick of common sense. But, when you have one that can think and command all of his rotting brethren? One that can plan, make strategy, and has an almost endless army that doesn't care what parts get blown off while constantly replenishing itself? It was almost the end of the Earth. I wasn't there to see it; I was Turned years after. Doesn't stop me from still getting hives thinking about it.

I wasn't going to give up on *my* plan, however, because I didn't see how we had anything to lose. If we did nothing, we were consumables anyway, and eventually they'd be down to just me and Pete. "Do you want to get flushed out of an airlock? Our brothers and sisters can't tell the difference; they'd just float along, hungry as ever and not knowing the difference. But we're awake, man. If we're not insane now, think about what an eternity floating in nothing would do to you. Or if you got ripped apart—there you are, conscious and watching your bits get shoved into the recycler."

"Dude, listen." Pete had been a professional surfer, or so he claimed, before he had become a Reboot. He retained the sometimes annoying habit of reverting back to his former speech patterns when he was perturbed. "I get what you're saying, man, really I do. But look at us. We're just a couple of stiffs, man. They're Fangs and a Fur. What do we got against all five of them, dude? Seriously."

Then it hit me. The last piece of the puzzle fell into place. Not only did we need to ensure we weren't in line for the next temper tantrum, we needed an ally. And it wasn't going to be a Fang. "Fred."

"Fred, what?" Sometimes Pete can be so dense. I mean, dense even for a Reboot. It clicked for him a few seconds later, and realization shone through his milky-white eyes. "Dude. You're fucking insane already. You know that?" But that wasn't disbelief I heard in his voice. It was cautious admiration.

"Yeah? Who else gets a shorter, shittier stick than us? Fred. Who's got as many brains as Grigoire, and gets treated like the third-world hired help? Fred. Who would give anything to see every Fang on this ship turned into corpsicles? Fred."

Pete rubbed his stomach woefully. "Man, you know better than to say brains around me. I still got the urges, dude."

17

I smacked him lightly. "Focus, butthead. Fred hates them worse than we do. And—" I paused for effect. "—Fred can pilot this boat."

"Yeah but ... oh, dude. If we come outta the closet ...." He shook his head—carefully, to avoid dislodging anything. "Even if he's okay with it ... that can't be taken back, like, there's no do-over, and he has that any time he needs to pull something out for the Fangs, turn on us."

I laced my rotten fingers behind the patchy scalp at the back of my head. "Pete, sometimes ... you've just got to look at the bigger picture."

Whenever it was scut work that had to be done outside, it was Fred that did it. Usually. He was actually getting out of most of it in this star system; with six *visible* moons dirtside for the planet they were orbiting at any one time, there was a lot of "full moon" time—during which he was pretty useless. Inside the ship, he could stay human as long as he didn't get mad and decide to go half-Wolf. Outside? All bets were off.

Though, just before the "drive incident," Grigoire had locked him out to get back at him for some other petty damn thing, leaving him out for half a day. He'd pounded on the airlock door for an hour, screaming at them.

"Come on guys, will you let me in already? I've had like five minutes of me-time since you—HROOOOOOOOOOO!"

"Someone turn Fred loose again?"

Yeah. Real funny. Wolfing out wasn't any fun for Fred; "he" got lost in the animal and he damn well didn't like it. After it ended, it was mostly a blur of images for him. Back on Earth? Lots of blood and terrible memories. Here, in deep space with nothing but Undead that he hated worse than the Dark Prince? Promises of dreams to come, and as a sort of compensation he could plant the Fang-faces over the vague images of whatever it was he'd ripped into. Still, he didn't like being out of control like that. Well, now they could tote their own barges and lift their own bales. He got to stay in the ship.

Which of course meant ... he had to stay in the ship. Inside the same walls, breathing the same canned air, watching the Reboots.

Reading. Watching the Reboots. Rewatching the vid library. Watching the Reboots. It was getting so he was even considering cracking into the opera collection that only Tony ever watched. The best thing about being able to get outside was the air on the planets that had them—even when he was human, his sense of smell was better than a Norm's. So even with the CO_2 and air scrubbers, there was always this faint stench in the back of his nose from the Reboots. The Fangs wouldn't notice, of course. He didn't think they actually had a sense of smell anymore; most of them didn't need to breathe, outside of speech. As far as he could tell, all they could smell was blood; and the only one with the fresh stuff was Fred. But Fred's sense of smell extended outside the bounds of known science; he could compartmentalize a million different scents, and discriminate among them. Almost all of them were disgusting on this cruise. That made the times of being able to get out on a planet all the more important.

So he was stuck in here, which only made him think more, about a lot of uncomfortable things. There were only so many new deaths that he could imagine for his shipmates, so even that grew boring eventually. Ugly notions kept intruding. He knew the Reboots were expendable, but what if they all were? What if Home Services actually expected them to kill each other out here? That might explain the fantastic rate of pay; if they weren't expected to make it back, it wouldn't matter how much the pay rate was because no one would ever collect.

He shook his head, hoping to banish the ominous implications of his line of thought. There was work to be done, and it seemed like more than usual. The ship was always malfunctioning these days, but now that he was feeling irritable all the time, even the ship seemed to be trying to torment him. Such an idea, of course, was at odds with his logical brain; it was just the nature of such a sophisticated piece of machinery, just like it was in his nature to go berserk with a full moon and for the Fangs to be assholes. More so, really—the ship might be sophisticated in design, but she was still built by the lowest bidder. Still … things had been happening that just were not in the list of "malfunctions."

For instance, the lighting. It was never, never, never to have a UV component except in his personal quarters, or for the onboard hydroponics garden; a garden that was for his sole benefit. He had to eat after all, and though Wolf might live by frozen steak alone, man did not, and this thing supplied all the needs: veggies, algae, and this fish called tilapia that bred like rabbits and sucked up seasoning so at least it didn't taste the same all the time. Some of the bulbs had gone missing not long ago; he suspected at the time that one of his crewmates were going to be playing a particularly painful prank on each other. So, naturally, as soon as one of the Fangs got a sunburn from a replaced bulb, he was the first one blamed.

Not a malfunction, and not an "accident." More like an "on purpose." But the Fangs all claimed innocence, and he knew that *he* hadn't done it—not that he could prove otherwise. It was almost as if there was a third party around here. Which, of course, was impossible. He'd heard of haunted ships before, though those were all Gremlin-haunted, but this one had been vetted back in dry-dock as Gremlin free—one of the few things that Home Services seemed to have done correctly on this flight. Could a Gremlin have somehow hitched a ride? But how? There weren't supposed to be Gremlins out here, and they hadn't taken on anything new. Besides, he knew Gremlins, and he'd booted all the Gremlins out on their shakedown run as he was supposed to do; that'd been three days of nonstop fun, crawling through wiring ducts, Jeffries tubes, and hydraulics.

Hell, maybe he was sleepwalking, and he really *had* done it.

Just one more charming item to add to his list of aggravations.

"He's dead, Jim." We were in the engineering section again. Whenever the Fangs or Fred didn't need us, those of us Reboots left outside of the holding pen were free to roam around, weighed down with tool belts. Kind of like free-floating tool chests with limited maintenance ability; if something minor was wrong, just point at one, give it the command, and have it do a job. If we got busted wandering around it wasn't as if it mattered.

One of our brethren had just that happen to him. I stared down at what was left of him. It wasn't even remotely pretty, and even as distant as my own emotions now were, I felt sick. "Must've been one of those damned Fangs; Fred doesn't really knock us around, unless he's wolfed out and can't tell the difference."

He was in pieces, some of which were still squirmy and half-attached. I looked down at him and felt a dim desperation. Pete stared down at the bits too. He made a grunt that sounded uneasy, but before he could voice any objections, I cut him off. So to speak. "Pete, we *can't* stop now. Do you remember what happened when you died the first time? Before you came back?"

Pete shook his head. "Naw, man. I do remember I had caught a killer wave the day I died, and had found some good herb, too, but that's about it."

What I half-remembered woke the one emotion I could really feel well: fear. "Well, I remember. I didn't see any Pearly Gates, or fiery brimstone, or a light at the end of the tunnel. I sure as hell didn't get reincarnated, unless someone stole my spot in line. I just remember darkness before waking up again." I played with a frayed tatter of the broken Reboot's red jumpsuit. It had been … well, empty, a void, a nothingness that is hard for me to describe now, and I doubt I could have described when I was alive. All I know is it was negation. The absence of life, the absence of *me*. It's what I imagined regular Reboots were like, all the time. Blank, empty on the inside, no purpose. "That scares the crap outta me, Pete. I didn't do much when I was alive, and I don't want to waste this second chance, such as it is."

Sighing out of habit rather than because I actually had breath, I took out a screwdriver from my coveralls, and plunged it through the eye of the ruined Reboot. Destroying what's left of the brain does destroy us permanently. It's about the only thing that does, other than incineration. Getting ripped to shreds will leave us helpless, but still "conscious" as long as the brain is mostly intact. Killing the shredded Reboot was a small kindness, all things considered.

Good old Barny decided to get revenge on Fred *and* his fellow Fangs.

Someone reported a landing-strut sensor misread. Fred went out to check it, during the twenty or so minutes when there were no moons up. And … tried to get back in, only to discover the airlock door mysteriously sealed, and he spent another forty-eight hours wolfed out and locked out. Barny wasn't too good at figuring consequences, however, because he'd locked Fred out under the moons with only a day's worth of stored blood left. Bad timing. Antonio was not happy. Come to think of it, he never was. This had pushed him from "glowering and miserable" to "glowering and furious."

The Fangs had been forced to go hungry for almost twenty-four hours, and once they got an exhausted (but well-fed!) Fred back on the ship, Tony had ordered them up into orbit to keep it from happening again. Fred was not a happy puppy, and that was not the only reason. Today sucked, and in more ways than one. It seemed that the ship was being extremely touchy; there were a number of subsystem failures that, while not serious, were time-consuming. Not only did he have to deal with the aggravation of having his crewmates bitch and moan to him about all of it, and "Why wasn't this fixed already?" it was also a feeding day. He was due to report to the medical bay in fifteen minutes; and at the last minute, Tony evidently decided that this was enough time for Fred to check out a potential atmosphere leak on the observation deck, so that everyone didn't suddenly decompress. Not that decompression would bother the Fangs or even the Reboots, but *he* would die, and that would leave the Fangs without food. At this point, Fred thought that dying quick and easy like that would be better than continuing on this trip; he wouldn't have to listen to them anymore, and his own last thoughts would be of how nice it was that they would die slowly and painfully of starvation, or much more slowly and not so painfully of starvation while sleeping. Bad things happened to Fangs that don't feed and then stay awake too long, and it wasn't much better for the ones that went into hibernation when food got scarce.

Grumbling loudly and cursing his lot in life, he stepped into the anteroom to the observation deck. Something that caught his attention was that the doors leading from the other sections were all locked, for some reason. He mentally shrugged, probably just another bullshit prank by one of the Fangs. Grigoire again, more than likely. Tony had come damn near to demoting Grigoire to "Fred's helper," and he'd only been talked down from it by the rest of the Fangs pointing out it would be a bad precedent.

Fred finally reached the observation deck—and immediately sensed that something was off. Next to one of the doors was a Reboot, and it was looking directly at him. Somewhere in the back of his mind, he recognized it as the one he'd caught on a skateboard.

And it talked.

"Sorry, bro. This'll only last a couple of minutes."

The Zombie flicked a switch, and closed the door between the two of them. Before Fred could even register what had happened, the outer shutters for the observation canopy slid open, letting the cold light of three full moons in through the viewport.

"Goddamnit, Tony. Fred was supposed to be here five minutes ago. I'm hungry!" Hephaestus, the ship's navigator, was the whiniest of the Fangs. Whining was irritating to everyone, and only aggravated all the worst traits of the inborn jerk in each of the rest of the Fangs.

Not that any of them were going to win Miss Congeniality. Even *Fangs* considered all other Fangs jerks.

Tony scowled, and made a quick revision in the feeding order. "You'll get your share, Hephaestus, just like the rest of us. Today, you're going last, though, and if you make another single peep about it I swear to all the dark and sharp things of the Underworld that you'll be floating home."

Hephaestus looked down, cowed by his superior. Grigoire and Barnabus shared a nasty grin. Any suffering was good suffering, as far as they were concerned, and for Barnabus, this meant he got to move up one in the queue.

The intercom started up with a pop and a crackle. Tony rolled his eyes. Another malfunction. They'd stopped using the intercom on his orders because they were all playing "dueling DJ" on the damn thing for the first six years of the trip. Grigoire was the first to look up and cock his head to the side. "I know this song …."

"I see the bad moon arising.

I see trouble on the way …."

Tony had particularly keen hearing, and he was the first one to hear the main doors for the medical bay open, even above the music. He turned away from Heph toward the door. "About time, Fred. The

23

damn intercom is on the fritz again. Besides, this Vampire likes his room service prompt—" Tony didn't even have to take the milliseconds to sweep his eyes to the door to know what was wrong. He heard it, and smelled it. Fred was a monster, and bigger than ever; the more moonlight he took in, the more powerful he became when he wolfed out. All Weres were that way; luckily, Earth only had one moon to shed its light on all the dark creatures she possessed. Fred had become a nightmare of eight feet of hair, claws, and jaws, and had murder in his dark eyes.

They were running, but not nearly fast enough.

Fangs and Weres were both blessed with many dark gifts. Strength enough to topple buildings, supernatural senses, and in the Fangs' case remarkable powers of persuasion; provided, of course, the individual Fang trying to do the persuasion wasn't a complete douchebag. There are some things not even supernatural manipulation can overcome.

Like being a douchebag. Or an enraged and moonlight-drunk Werewolf in full form.

They were also inhumanly fast. Of the two species, though, the Weres were faster, and Tony cursed this racial difference more than ever. Fred had been on top of the group before anyone could even bare his fangs. They had been in the medical bay for blood, and blood there had been; it was splattered messily on every surface. Some of it was Fred's, but most of it was his Vampiric compatriots.

Fred regenerated at an incredible rate; they could have, as well, if they were supplied with fresh blood, but the only fresh blood was in Fred's veins and … he wasn't exactly cooperating.

So they had run; Fred's Change could only last so long, if he didn't come in contact with moonlight.

For some reason, though, every single viewport shutter was wide open. Due to the way the ship was positioned above the planet they were supposed to be surveying and evaluating, they had visible moons on almost every side—three completely full ones above them, in relation to the ship's rotation. Fred kept getting stronger, and they kept running. There was no silver on the entire ship.

The Mission Planners from Home Services reasoned that Fangs or Weres killing each other would be suicide; without food, the Fangs would wither and sleep and maybe die before they could get back to Earth. So no silver.

As for the Fangs, the planners counted on "safety in numbers," or so the brochure said. A single Were couldn't hope to overpower the rest of the crew by his (or her, though female Weres were much rarer) self. That *should* have kept the Fangs in control. Obviously, the planners hadn't counted on a situation like this one—multiple moons, all the viewports wide open, ship in orbit, and no way to get the ports shut without getting torn into tiny pieces. Well, someone *might* have been able to get the ports shut in one section, if he volunteered to be the one that would end up shredded. Right. *That* was never going to happen. An altruistic, self-sacrificing Vampire? Get real. One of the reasons they made it through getting Turned in the first place, rather than ending up another messy victim on a slab, was the fierce determination to *live* no matter what it cost. Which was, when you thought about it, more or less the definition of being self-centered.

So they ran, desperately.

"He's right behind us, we've got to move!" Grigoire's voice was a shrill scream; he had lost his left arm in one of the running battles, and it was only now starting to regenerate. Barnabus looked worse, almost as bad as a fresh Reboot; cuts and grievous wounds covered his entire body. He was holding his guts in with both arms and hobbling pitifully on a leg that had been twisted completely around in its socket. They all felt so weak. They were past due for their blood ration from Fred; it didn't help that he was spilling their claret, expending their life force with each swipe of his claws or flashing of his horrid jaws. They also were looking to each other with hunger; they could drain one of their own, replenish their strength ... but Fred was chomping at their heels and they didn't even have time for that.

"I know, goddamnit, but we can't stop to open any of the doors, or he'll catch up with us!" Beneath the panic and terror clouding his mind—two sensations that Tony had not experienced in millennia—an analytical part of him wondered why most of the doors they came to were locked. It was almost as if they were being herded somewhere, driven ever forward by the beast at their backs.

"What're we going to do, Tony? Oh fuck!—" Hephaestus went flying ahead of the group, tossed bodily by Fred. He slammed into a bulkhead with a sickening and wet crunch, his ribs protruding from his back from the force of the blow. Recognition clicked for Tony; they were at the airlock! Without thinking, he shoved the other two Fangs into it, then kicked Hephaestus inside, while hitting the activation relay so hard that the housing around it bent and creaked. In a split-second, the inner airlock doors closed with a snap-hiss. Fred barreled into the door, his fury fueling strike after strike against it. His claws raked against the metal to fruitlessly send showers of sparks into the air, and he howled impotently at having his prey so close but out of reach at the same time. Even if he'd had the mind to use controls, they weren't where he could get at them. Shipside door airlock controls were all on the inside of the airlocks for a reason. Nobody could get shoved inside unconscious and spaced that way, or at least, not easily. You *could* override from the main control room, but that would take some significant planning, and Fred was not exactly thinking in this state.

Tony put his back against the bulkhead. He was in better shape than the others, but only marginally.

They were safe. Tony automatically began to plan. They could put on suits to keep from getting cold-damaged and protect them from sunlight. Grigoire could get to either the control room or the aux control from outside and override the viewports. Without moonlight, Fred would change back to human form eventually no matter where in the ship he was. Or, they could just wait him out, hoping he'd stay in this section.

They all began to chuckle, which broke down into full-out uproarious laughter. They didn't really breathe, but it was a stress reaction that their dead bodies still remembered. It was a ghastly sight, in truth; four broken bodies, dead in most ways that counted, laughing and spilling more blood all over the deck. Tony had to wipe blood-tears from his eyes, he was laughing so hard. Fred continued to rage outside of the door, pounding against it relentlessly with his impossibly powerful fists.

Their laughter died as one when one of the space suits that was stored in a wall alcove stood up straight. The blast visor flipped up to reveal a Reboot inside of it, illuminated by the harsh helmet lights.

The grav kicked off, right on schedule, as I raised the blast shield on the suit. I looked at them through the visor, and all they could do was look at me in stunned silence as they rose slightly from the floor. I knew that this made no sense to them, that this was so out of character for a Reboot even their lightning reflexes would not be able to save them, especially without footing. So, baring my busted teeth through my patchwork lips in the most evil Bond-villain grin I could manage, I said, "Adios, suckers." In two smooth motions, I flipped them "the bird" and then snapped up the safety for the outer airlock doors. In the old movies, they used to show people getting sucked into space in a rush of atmosphere, trying to scrabble and hang onto anything they could. It doesn't really work like that, though, not when no one is ready for it, anyway. One second, the Fangs were there. The next, I felt a slight jolt against my restraint harness, and they were gone into the blackness, like darts out of a blowgun. There was nothing in the airlock but me and my suit; it was like Tony and the rest of his bastard brethren never even existed.

Then I waited; being a Reboot, I'm pretty good at that. When the banging from the other side of the door subsided, I waited some more. Couldn't hurt to be too careful, and, besides, we had a plan. Stick to the plan. In movies, it was when you didn't stick to the plan that things went off the rails. So, I just floated there, whistling some old commercial jingles to myself. Funny how that stuff sticks in your mind. I don't drink anything, but there I was, rattling the words to a cola commercial around in my head, or what was left of it. Halfway through it, the outer doors closed and the chamber repressurized, and the grav came back on again. I unhooked myself from the restraint harness, looking to the door. There was a flash of hazard lights, and the heavy blast doors opened. On the other side, as planned, was Pete.

"Dude … is that you?"

"No, it's Hannibal Lecter. I've come for you, Clarice." I trotted forward, enjoying the feeling of the artificial gravity again; weightlessness isn't my thing, even though my stomach doesn't really get queasy anymore. "Where's Fred?"

"Probably sleeping it off somewhere, man. When he trips bad like that, he usually gets a killer headache afterwards. Dude, are you sure that we can trust him?"

"Pete, we've gotten this far. Time to take it the last mile." Besides, he was the only one who knew how to fly this boat. While we could probably sit up here for a while, eventually orbit would decay and then … a very fancy cremation. It was now, or never.

Fred woke up with a monumental headache. If he had been cognizant enough through the immense pain to think about it, he would have declared that this was the worst headache in the history of man, living or unliving. Once the pain went from mind-blanking to merely Olympic, he started to remember—or notice—a few things.

Like the fact that his clothing was in pieces, which meant he'd almost certainly Changed. And that his last real memory—before the usual flash of blood and screaming and then nothing but red, red rage—was of three full moons staring down at him, as if they were laughing at what would come next. And … and a Reboot opening the ports.

While *talking*?

No, that part had to be a hallucination. His mind did that sometimes, right at the Change, as if it was trying to protect him from what was coming.

Looking around, he took stock of his situation. He was in a storeroom for tools. Sometimes when he wolfed out, the others would corral him into a room and lock him in until his Change wore off. Then he noticed that the door was torn inwards, and that there was blood all over it.

"What the hell is going on?" His voice was thick and scratched; even though he regenerated constantly, roaring and howling a lot took its toll on his human-again vocal cords. "Grigoire? Antonio?

28

Anyone?" His eyes caught movement in the hallway beyond the door—a person-shaped smudge of shadow against shadows. Probably one of the Fangs here to chew him out for busting the door.

"Hey, which one of you assholes made a Reboot open the shutters in the observation deck? There were three goddamned full moons out there!" The figure stepped through the ruined door; it was dressed in a space suit, obscuring the identity.

"Oh, that was me. Sorry about that, friend." Friend? He'd been called plenty while on this flight, with some of it so off-color that the Dark Prince, hell-red bastard that he was, would've blushed upon hearing it. But he'd never been called friend.

"Seriously, who is that in there?" That voice wasn't familiar either. Had they—no, surely they hadn't been intercepted by another ship! Okay, there'd been rumors of FTL in the works but nothing but rumors ....

The figure seemed to look down at itself.

"Oh, the suit." The suited figure took off its helmet; beneath was the Reboot that had looked at Fred funny-like a few days ago. It grinned. A Reboot grinning ....

"I'm the local Sheriff," it drawled. "Heard there was some trouble. Looked like you could use a hand, pard."

He felt exactly the way he'd felt when he'd been taze-stunned at the end of his first Change by the Norm cops. "All the demons of hell, it talks!"

Could a Reboot look sheepish? This one shrugged, anyway. "Uh, yeah. About that. Name's Skinny Jim. Pleased to meet you, Fred."

Fred was so flabbergasted by this turn of events, that he found himself deep in a conversation before the "stunned" wore off. Oh, he had heard about the "intelligent" Reboots, but he'd always thought they were an urban legend. The entire "Zombie uprising" had occurred decades before Fred was even born, after all, and the general consensus among people of his generation had been that the "King of the Zombies" had been nothing more than a figment of the fevered imaginations of the authorities. Either that, or a manufactured "threat" to give them the power to do pretty much what they wanted to do with the Paras.

Joke was on him, it seemed.

Then the Reboot told him what had happened to his four crewmates.

Joke was—even more so—on the Fangs, who were drifting in a decaying orbit right now, and who would, if not rescued, eventually come to a fiery end, conscious and starving most of the way. *Serves the bastards right, all said and done. Just wish I could see it.*

They spent a good long while talking. The Reboot explained his plight, and what he had done about it. Fred wanted to be angry, wanted to be filled with righteous fury for being used. He knew that he should destroy the Reboot, and flush the rest out of the pen and into space, then report back to Home Services immediately.

But he couldn't bring himself to do any of these things. It didn't take him long to decide that things had just become a lot more interesting on the UES Cenotaph, and he suspected ... a lot more peaceful, too. No more getting drained to feed evil bastard Fangs. No more orders from Tony, needling from Grigoire, bitching from Hephaestus, or dueling with Barnabas. Taking stock of everything, Fred was suddenly happier than he had been in over a century and a half.

"Well, how about that. You know, Jim, I'd shake your hand, but—" He shrugged uneasily, looking at the deck.

Skinny Jim didn't have much in the way of an expressive face, what with the sunken eyes, retracted lips displaying broken teeth, and shriveled-taut skin, but somehow he conveyed resignation. "Yeah, I know, I'm a Zombie."

"Hey, it could come off!"

They both shared a laugh, although the Reboot's was kind of wheezy. It was the first real laugh that Fred had had for many, many years. One not tainted by *schadenfreude*, or at the expense of someone else. It felt good, and it felt clean. Fred also noticed that it was as if a weight was off of his shoulders, and that was also good, welcome.

A smile broke out over his face; he didn't immediately notice when another Reboot trudged up behind Jim.

"Oh, Fred, I want you to meet Pete. Fred, Pete. Pete, Fred."

The skateboarding one! Fred goggled. He felt his eyes bulging when it opened its mouth. "Yo, dude. 'Sup?"

"Ye gods, two of them! I mean ... two of ... you ...." It wasn't every day that a Werewolf met a talking Zombie, much less two of them. The shock wore off quickly, though; after the roller coaster of emotions, combined with his still monstrously bad headache, he didn't have the energy to stay stunned and stupid for too long. "So, why didn't you guys talk earlier? Why didn't you flush me out of the airlock with the rest of those scum-suckers?"

Jim stepped forward. "You remember Xavier. Right? The 'Zombie Emperor'? After that, any of us that seemed to possess any greater cognitive ability than your average jar of mayo were exterminated. Being anything but another mindless deader didn't do much for anyone's survival chances."

"Yeah, but that still doesn't answer why you didn't flush me out of the ship, also. If I weren't cool with this, I could take the ship back to Earth. Or just re-kill you myself and save Home Services the trouble." Fred placed his hands on the hips of his tattered jumpsuit, trying to present a strong front, even though he wasn't truly feeling it.

"Honestly, that was the weakest part of the plan. But, you suffered just as much as we had under the Fangs, if not more; they actively hated you, while we were just scenery and mildly useful furniture. So, I—I mean, we—took a chance. It was worth it to see Tony's face when all the atmo got sucked out into the ether and them with it."

A fiendish smile crept across Fred's face. "Damn, I wish I could've seen that, actually."

"Good news is, I recorded it via the ship's security system. Wanna see it?"

"Bet your ass I do." He paused, thinking for a moment. "Well, what do we do now? We can't really go back to Earth, which isn't that big of a loss. Place is a hole, or at least it was when I left."

Skinny Jim nodded. "Me and Pete thought about that. We figured that finding a decent planet with lots of yellow sun would be a good start, one that can bake us nice and leathery. High UV to sterilize the bacteria. Kill the rot, and a little oil solves most of our problems. For you, well, pick one with no moons and plenty of stuff for you to munch on, or only one moon and stuff the Were can eat, and when you go human again you've got the ship's garden. As for everything else—" he pulled out a deck of playing cards from his pocket, "—have you ever played poker?"

It took us a while, but we found pretty much what we were looking for. Yellow-phase star, no moons and not a lot of exploitable resources. Someplace that wouldn't offhand look too attractive to Home Services. We called it "Planet Hawaii," since it was mostly islands, mostly tropical, and contrary to what you are probably thinking, "island paradise" planets are not on the top of the list for places to go. Home Services wants *commercially viable* resources, and the number of people that can afford to take offworld trips to tropical islands that vary only from the same kind you find on Earth by the exotic flora and fauna are … well, you're not going to be able to find enough to support a single trip, much less a resort. Never mind that none of them would ever live long enough to get here, even with hyper-sleep tubes. You still age some, even when you sleep.

So this was our little pocket paradise. Screw the non-contamination directive, our seeds would grow here, so besides the hydroponic garden, we figured we'd have the Reboots out there doing the slave labor for a little plantation for Fred, and what with the place being mostly ocean and all, the water wasn't salt, so we just needed a nice big lagoon we could cut off from the rest of the oceanic biosphere. We'd find an island that had one, sterilize it, and seed it with algae. Once that got started we could transplant more tilapia, and bingo. Fred would be set forever. We did all that, and settled down, happy as beach bums can be.

As for us, all we needed was that nice hot sun and oil. Fish and some of the peanuts that the greenhouse had in it provided oil. We Reboots really didn't *need* to eat brains to keep going, so we saved the freeze-dried stuff for me and Pete for kicks, and let the others do without. They wouldn't touch Fred—more of the Para influence than anything—so although they moaned a lot, it was no big deal.

In six months, we were self-sustaining. Then it got better, because even the moaning stopped, and I found the Reboots scrounging some sort of fungus that they seemed happy to munch on. At least, I think it was a fungus. It was spongy, neon-orange, and when

I tasted it, it was actually better than the freeze-dried crap we sub-sisted on. I figured I would wait and see what happened to them in the long term before I moved the stuff onto *my* dinner plate, but it looked like a viable option for the others now.

I kind of hoped it wasn't sentient, whatever it was, but hey. Survival of the fittest and we were only harvesting one island, so screw it. If it wanted to survive here, it could evolve a mouth and talk to us, or grow some legs and run for it.

Naturally, Pete didn't hold any of my reservations, and started chowing down as soon as he tasted it. Whatever, while I dimly liked him for our mutual plight of Undead sentience, if he wanted to risk himself, I wasn't going to stop him, and I could watch *him* for signs of lapsing into the usual Reboot coma due to his new diet.

Fred and I could always change over to chess from poker if that happened.

So, Pete and I baked to a nice, healthy, flexible brown in the tropical sun. Fred got a tan. Pete taught us both to surf, such surfing as there was on a planet with no moons, and we all settled down to a pretty nice and quiet life. Even if I did smell like Planters Best from the peanut oil. Fred said it was a much appreciated change from perma-rot. Me, I never had noticed.

"Ante up, sucker," I said, pushing my chips across the table. I had a good hand. A really good hand. Which meant that when Fred lost, he'd have to do my bidding, muwahaha. I was trying to decide what that would be. I was powerfully inclined to an external speaker system, so we could play some music out here. I was pretty sure he could rig it, and reasonably sure we could weatherproof it. We didn't have crazy tides due to lacking a moon, but we did have some powerful weather systems and seriously impressive storms.

Fred scratched the back of his head. "I feel like I'm forgetting something." It was our third year on the planet, and things had been humming along fairly smoothly for awhile. The other Reboots were all doing their thing, we had the luxuries we wanted, and there wasn't anyone to bother us in this corner of the galaxy. The orange sponge hadn't evolved a mouth, and Pete hadn't turned into a wandering corpse, so I'd added the tasty stuff to my menu. We hadn't bothered to check on the subspace radio for news for over two years, since it was all more of the same. So-and-so tin-pot dictator was toppled, new government rises, such and such planet was annexed for whoever corporation, Home Services celebrates the whatever. Those of us in the ships might have been taking the long and slow route, but communication was still at real-time speeds. It mattered little to us; we were separate, insular and sufficient unto ourselves. The *only* thing we got from the rest of the civilized galaxy was that we'd set up the computer to continue the automatic downloads of entertainment stuff, which flooded in faster than we could watch or listen to it. Home Services did that much for the ships, probably because otherwise the crews would kill each other from boredom—providing they'd been less like ours had been, that is. Life was good.

I should have realized it was too good. But, when you're on top, after having been in the gutter for so long ....

So here we were, at our usual game. We had a comfortable table and lounges pulled out of the ship, set up under what passed for trees—more like giant ferns, but they kept the sun off. Since there wasn't a breeze at the moment, a couple of the Reboots were working one of those overhead pulley-fans they used to have in India in the bungalows the English overlords lived in. Fred had a storage-closet-brewed beer next to him. Trust humans, once you get past basic food and shelter the next thing we think about is booze. About a hundred yards away, little waves lapped on the black sand—this was a volcanic beach. Behind us was the ship, Nestled up against a cliff. I had to laugh when I thought about our landing.

"*Y'know ... I'm not sure that that was much of a landing.*"

"*What?*"

"*Well, you did shear off a quarter ton of rock off of that cliff ....*"

"*Y'know what they say? Any landing you can walk away from, is a good landing. So, stuff it, wrinkles.*"

We could still lift the ship if we had to. Like, oh, if one of the really *big* hurricanes decided to bear down on us. The fish and the veggies could survive one—better we got the hell out of Dodge if one of those things put a target on our island. So ... screw it. Fred had been right. It had been a good enough landing.

I grinned, staring at him. I could grin, now. The last time Fred lost to me, he made me—well, I guess you'd call them tooth veneers—to give me something that looked human-ish again, and the oil had given me nice, flexible lips, even if they were a bit thin. "You're stalling. Even Pete has folded already."

"No, it's not that." A perplexed look crossed Fred's face. "It feels like there's something I should have remembered. Something important. I just can't place my finger on it." I could tell that whatever it was that Fred was thinking about, it was bugging him immensely. I decided to take his mind off of it.

"No use, *compadre*. I'm not letting you out of this hand. I've got plans for my winnings, and you can't get off that easy." I gave him my best "gotcha" look. He was an aggressive player, normally. That *should* have gotten him back in the game, but it didn't.

I put my cards facedown on the table. "Okay, if it bothers you that much. Did you leave your lunch on the stove?"

He shook his head. "No, it's not that. It feels … important."

"Is there an experiment you started and forgot to check on?"

Fred scoffed. "I haven't done an important experiment after the time I tried to stick three Reboots together for that—"

"I know, I remember!" If I slept, it would have given me nightmares. "Was there a news alert? Have you checked for one lately?"

He shook his head again, looking down at his cards. "No, I've scanned for our names, the ship's name, the Fangs' names, everything. Got it on automatic for the ship's computer, set up in a way so we don't get traced. Nothing on any of us, so far as I can tell. It's not that."

"Forget to check the weather?" That had happened once. It hadn't been drastic, but three of the Reboots had gotten washed out to sea, never to be seen again. No clue what happened to them. We hadn't exactly been vigilant about checking for aquatic monsters. We'd pretty much figured that if something couldn't crawl up on land to get us, we were good.

Suddenly, we all heard the whine of an extraplanetary booster engine powering up, quickly building to a frantic roar. All of us turned to look at the ship; even the Reboots craned their leathery necks in that direction.

"The *hell*?" I said. A single streak of fiery exhaust burst away from the top of the ship, with the bright point of light at the end of it blinking out of sight quickly leaving only the thick plume of smoke pointing like a finger, upwards.

A big, fat, middle finger to our entwined destinies.

"Oh," said Fred, guilt plastered over his face. "Shit."

"What?" I asked, sharply. Then even more sharply, *"What?"*

"That's what I forgot." He laid his cards on the table, face up— nothing at all but stray cards. "Ship's emergency beacon. Launches automatically if the ship's captain doesn't check in after a predeter-mined amount of time. It's so Home Services can recover the ship and any assets that are left. Tony was the only one supposed to know about it." Fred looked up to meet my gaze. "I discovered it while I was bored and poking around some of the auxiliary systems one night. I kept meaning to deactivate it, but I never got around to it." He looked down at his hand. "So … y'all got your bags packed?"

Oh hell. But … no point in making a deal about it. If there is one thing I am at this point, it's pragmatic. So Fred screwed up. Right now screaming about it wasn't going to change anything; the Fangs had tried that often enough, and look where they were now. "Any more of those things onboard?"

"Just the one that I remember finding."

"Should we change islands, or whole planets?"

"With Home Services involved? If we could scoot out of this galaxy, it'd be just barely far enough."

Bugger. Oh well. We could dump some Reboots to leave room for food for Fred, harvest what we had, and be off here in a reason-able amount of time. The Dark Gods in charge of our fate only knew how far we would have to go to get out of reach. Or if we could.

Right. "Let's check the news. See how close they are to here." That would let us know how long we had to get a good head start. Twenty years would be nice. I could scream at Fred all I liked once we were on the run.

Then again, given the guilt on Fred's face, maybe I should just let him stew on his own. Without him, we'd have probably been drifting forever, and our plan never would have worked. Still, it was a colossal, colossal fuck up. *Deal with what you can, while you can.*

We ran for the ship, and started the computer scanning through the news. I checked the "colonized planets" list, Pete for the "messages from near-space" and Fred for stuff that needed a little more hands-on than what we were doing.

Fred made a strange noise. I looked over at him. Under his tan, he was pale. "Uh … looks like things have changed while we've been going with drive on full for the past century and change. We've got new neighbors. And they didn't get there by the long haul, like us."

Oh, I did not like the way that sounded. My brain might not have been the best in the world, but …. "Please tell me that doesn't mean what I think it means."

"We've got not a whole lot of room to run, and we're a lot slower than the competition." He grimaced. "That's the long and short of it, as it were."

Oh … *hell*. The Dark Gods above *and* below were laughing at us. That rocket's contrail had been a middle finger after all. "No. FTL? Portal tech?" I begged him to say no with my beady little eyes. Fred merely shrugged. A lot changes in one hundred and some odd years. And we hadn't been looking for it until now. And that was *my* fuckup. Fred was the techy, I was the one that had told the computer what to watch for in the feeds. But … damn it, when we left, *everyone* said FTL was impossible, and the most anyone could manage would be near-light!

So everyone was wrong. Okay, fine. Now we could both wallow in guilt. Wallow later, move now. Definitely abandon some of the Reboots. Run a couple of wires into the lagoon, stun the fish, flash-freeze. We'd been taking care of the hydroponics garden in the ship instead of letting it go to pot, so Fred was set.

"Dude. I'll get the Reboots harvesting brain-balls," Pete said, and headed out of the ship. I looked at Fred.

"Ship's mine," he said. "If you guys can handle everything else."

It was hard to think this fast. I hadn't needed to in a long time. "Can we decide where we're going once we're up?" I asked. That would take one thing off the list.

"Yes," he said instantly. "If you guys can get everything loaded back in, and whatever consumables—"

It had just occurred to me that there was something else we could leave behind … all the crap we'd needed for the Fangs. Best thing to do would be to sink it, so no one knew we'd lost them. The more we could confuse the issue, the better.

The blood storeroom could hold a lot of brain-balls ....

"Have I got determination on what to dump?" I asked. Fred just nodded. He was already busy with what I assumed was preflight, pre-readiness stuff.

"As long as it isn't me," he added, jumping to another set of controls.

Right. Stun the fish and harvest. Harvest what we could from the garden and the rest of the island. Strip out the Fang crap. Sink it in the ocean. Would it be possible to simulate a wreck? Probably not, damn it.

I realized I was wasting time. I could think and plan while I did the first stages.

That, and curse all the Dark Gods.

PART TWO

JUST THE RIGHT BULLETS

eamus Murtaugh Ian ap Llowynn, who answered to "Ian Lonagan" so far as Home Services was concerned, sauntered back to his office in an exceedingly contented frame of mind. A delightful three-hour lunch in the presence of the equally delightful Sharice from Planetary Resources Accounting, coupled with the high probability that he would be completely idle this afternoon, made this Pucca one happy puppy. Oh sure, *technically* he wasn't supposed to be fraternizing with other employees except under very specific and Home Services-sponsored circumstances, but she was Planetary Resources and *he* was Extraplanetary Exploration Incidents (aka, "oh fuck, we got a beacon") and it wasn't *really* fraternizing when they weren't even working in the same mega-block, much less building, much less department, now, was it?

Ian was on his three thousandth game of Spider Solitaire for the day when the e-mail came. This job was virtually perfect for him; lost in the bureaucracy of Home Services, there was very little work he was actually expected to do.

Besides, he worked hard enough chasing after tasty tidbits like Sharice.

Home Services just didn't appreciate that sort of thing; heaven knew he'd petitioned to open a new position that would let him get paid directly for just that. How else was she supposed to stay content in her dead-end, soul-sucking accounting job, unless someone like him made her life exciting? Parahumans were always a hundred times more attractive than Norms, a thousand times better at evading actual commitments—Home Services would be annoyed if

Sharice actually *got married* and had a real life and real responsi-bilities, as opposed to the illusory life and very real thrills Ian was giving her. Home Services would have been even more annoyed if someone like a Fang had moved in on her, and possibly even Turned her. Whereas, with a Pucca, she was safe from Turning into anything, and Ian had several hundred years' worth of experience at ditching someone if she somehow did begin to want more out of him than she was ever going to get.

Annoyed at the distraction from his diversion, Ian closed the game and opened his e-mail. "Well, *this* is depressingly different."

It was an automatic notification from a broadcast repeater satellite on the edge of the solar system's frontier. It was dated as having been sent three months ago, which was strange until he read further into the e-mail; usually any beacons that came in were within minutes of "Special Circumstances." Those circumstances usually being that an-other crew had gone batshit insane and torn itself to pieces, or that a ship had pancaked into a rogue asteroid or some other such cosmic mishap. Lowest bidder, after all, and it was difficult to find *competent* Fangs or Fur engineers. Paras still made up most of the crews, even with third-generation FTL. They were still the toughest things around, and with what was out there, you wanted a crew that was hard to kill.

"That explains it." The e-mail listed that the beacon was one hun-dred and forty-eight years old, launched four months prior; the older generation ships were very bare-bones affairs, and the tech capabilities were almost literally light-years behind what was available now. He hadn't seen a beacon from one of these babies in ... well, more than a year. He checked the ship list; this one hadn't been heard from in three years. Plenty of reasons for that, really, so no one had checked on it.

What was interesting was the partial log recovered from the bea-con. The ship had *landed*. And had stayed that way, while still receiv-ing Galaxy Net feeder streams.

"Keeping an ear to the ground for the cavalry, huh?"

No moon. Lots of sun. Looked as if the onboard Fur had done the impossible, overcome the Fang crew, and hijacked the ship.

I seriously don't have the time or patience for a Wolf hunt. Who'll wine and dine Sharice in the meantime? He'd have to check out a scouter from Home Services—oh the paperwork!—put in an appropriations request for ship, cash, and supplies, head out to that backwater, look for the ship—

And unless the Fur in question was a terrible pilot and the ship had been so damaged in landing it couldn't take off again, it was unlikely that the ship would still *be* there. Which meant *another* round of paperwork, getting authorization to search the galactic neighborhood ....

"A fracking snipe hunt," he said aloud with disgust. It could be months. Years! And at the end of it he'd have to try to wrangle a pissed off Werewolf. A pissed off *old* Werewolf, which compounded the problem. The older a Fur got, the tougher he got. And meaner. And this one had dispatched a full Fang crew, which argued that he was very tough and very mean, indeed.

It was the same for many Parahumans, granted. Still, far more aggravation than Ian wanted to deal with. And no prospects for romancing tasty females, human *or* Para. What to do? How to avoid this? He'd been hired to deal with dead ships, not rogue ones. This was *not* his skill set!

Inspiration struck Ian like a ton of bricks. Why not just do what he always did when responsibility came a knockin'?

He opened up the Rolodex—an antique novelty gift from one of his exes—and started flipping through it. *Someone reliable, but replaceable. No one from in-house. Inexpensive is a plus ... there!* Ian punched up the ident number into the vidphone, which picked up on the first ring.

"HB Investigations." The face was male, and rather forgettable, the sort of face that could get lost in any crowd. It was also not the face of a receptionist, which meant the Boggart in question was not in a financial position to hire anyone. Good. Lean and hungry; he'd probably jump at the chance to get a case from Home Services.

Ian licked his lips, smiling. "Mr. Boggart, I represent Home Services, Extraplanetary Exploration Incidents division. It seems that I have a job for you."

The Boggart cut the connection, and wondered if he had been a little too hasty ... but a completely unnecessary check of his credit balance and the sure and certain knowledge that there were several bills coming due soon made him shake his head a little. The fee was probably woefully small by the standards of that smartly dressed Pucca on the other end of the connection, but he *had* wrangled half up front and a per diem *and* a finder's fee if he actually discovered the ship in standard salvageable shape. The half up front would cover all those bills and then some. Home Services could certainly afford it. And what neither the Pucca nor Home Services knew, of course, was that he wasn't exactly going to have what you would call "traveling expenses" even though he was charging the per diem for them. A little extra cash for greasing palms never hurt, though. He'd pad that in later as "itemized expenses," but he'd need the cash up front. He drummed his fingers on his old desk; he'd had it a long, long time, and it was an antique at this point. Real wood. Not worth trying to sell, though, they'd made a crap-ton of these things back in the day, and they'd been made to last, so there were still a lot of them around, most in much better shape than his. It was scuffed and battered, and the top had more coffee rings than he had ever bothered to count. There were two chairs in here, an ancient sofa that he slept on when he actually slept, big built-in bookcases full of battered old-fashioned paper books, and two giant old wardrobes that held clothing and other things necessary in his job. No one ever gave them a second glance since hardly anyone but an antiquarian knew what a wardrobe was anymore. Through the only other door was the reason he'd rented and held onto this particular office, although it was in a far from convenient part of town: the full bathroom, from back when this whole building had been owned by a single firm, and this had been one of the executive's offices. He lived here. Not that the landlord was aware of that. There was no good reason to have an apartment, really, not with food stalls within walking distance, and a perfectly good couch.

His mail pinged, and he pulled up the file from Home Services. *UES Cenotaph*. Har har. Had to have been an early ship, they'd run out of graveyard humor names for the exploration vessels pretty early on in the process and just started assigning the names of old hurricanes; start with a name book at one end of the alphabet, and work your way down. So, standard crew, hold full of Reboots, one Fur, four Fangs.

Well, the *obvious* first-cause would be the Fang Council of Elders; the Nests had their fingers into every little dirty enterprise imaginable, just like the old Norm mobs, so chopping up a ship was small time for them. Before he even opened the file, that was his assumption. It was vanishingly unlikely the Fur had taken the thing over, but the proximity of the ship going missing to when FTL went commercial was just too much to be a coincidence. There had been quite a few ships that went down that way—more than the Home Services was ever going to admit. A little private subspace radio exchange, spacing your resident Fur twenty-four hours before rendezvous with an Elder Corsair, and Bob's your uncle. It was easy enough for the Fangs to manufacture new IDs for the mutineering crew, and even easier for them to vanish into the Fang Nests once they'd gotten themselves the "dowry" of one-fourth of a ship. Strip the ship for parts, or refit her and pull all the ID, and sell her to an Indie spacer or pirate fleet who wouldn't ask any questions—standard MO for the Elder Nests.

The Pucca's notes, though ....

Ship reported being landed under control on a no-moon, G-class sun and water world. Huh. *Unlikely as it seems, this would point to a takeover by the Were engineer.* Beacon goes up, and no big shock, Home Services didn't even do a lookie-loo, figuring by the time they got there the ship would be gone. No wonder the Pucca had contracted this out. *He* didn't want to have to charter something from a settled system, then go out to nowhere to find nothing and a cold trail. On the other hand ... it wasn't as if the Boggart had anything pressing on his desk. He could put up with a lot of tedium for a per diem.

Curiouser and curiouser. And it stayed put for three years. In fact the beacon had gone up while it was on-planet in the same place it had landed. Three years? What was the Fur-face waiting for? Furs were almost as well organized as the Fangs were; aggressive, territorial, and strong as hell when they wanted to be, they had expanded hard and fast on the early exploratory crews, and even more so once FTL became commonplace. Could it be that he was able to call up a Pack to hijack the ship, even the odds with the Fangs?

What if it was ... both? "Rendezvous with a Corsair and let us off with—" What? Well maybe they'd found something valuable, had dumped the Reboots and packed the hold with it. Call it Un-obtanium. "—let us off with the Unobtanium, you get the ship and your choice of worlds." No moon, and an island paradise to call your own ... might not appeal to an Alpha Fur, but a Zeta, maybe. Point being, maybe there was some MacGuffin that made the deal attractive to the Were. That could complicate things.

Or ... if the Boggart had had hair, it might have stood up on the back of his neck. Or it might be a Lone Wolf. Lones were rare, and rightly so. The Pack generally did not tolerate any member that unsocial; and their intolerance was generally lethal. Lones were therefore that much more unpredictable and smart. Most of the strongest ones got out on the early flights, over a hundred years ago. Nowadays you found them on border worlds, or scamping through freighter lines.

Work the latter two theories then. Hijacking by Pack or Nest, because Nest Elders were smart enough to set a ship down on auto just to confuse the issue, or collusion between the Elders and a Loner. He shook his head; speculation without more evidence was worthless at this point. It was time to track down what few leads he had.

In the ancient days a PI would have hit the pavement. The Boggart flexed his fingers. There was still shoe-leather involved, but the first step these days was to hit the net. *See what I can dig up on the turkeys they had on this crew.*

Hours later, the Boggart emerged from the sea of information with some nuggets. He leaned back in the chair; its elderly mechanism complained faintly. "Down lights," he ordered; the office AI obeyed. He thought better in the dark. Fred Stewart had had no real Pack to speak of. The Fangs had all been from different Nests with different Elders. The Boggart shook his head. There didn't seem to be enough of a connection to suggest that some Elders had cooked up a plot to hijack the ship. He very much doubted that the Fangs had colluded to do it on their own. What in hell had Home Services been thinking, back then? Well, maybe that was the point, they hadn't actually been thinking at all.

Or maybe that had been long enough ago that the old, clandestine "attrition policy" had been active. There had been plenty in Home Services that had figured the best way to be rid of the Paras on Old Earth was to ship them out and let them tear each other to small, bloody bits. Stupid, of course. All you got out of *that* was a hijacked ship and one or two *really* powerful Paras with a hankering to taste Home Service's blood. But, that's how things had been done back then. Stupid, and wasteful, which seemed to be par for the course even nowadays (just the current wastefulness was in a different direction), but that was beside the point. Stewart did, however, have a "cousin"; someone Turned by the same Pack Leader. As good a place as any to start. He was currently on the edge of the solar system, working a mining platform in the Kuiper Belt—an interesting oddity there, because it was honest work, albeit dirty and extremely dangerous.

He did a little more data mining and poking, but couldn't come up with any other connections. Even the Fang Nests that the four Fangs had come from didn't seem particularly interested in seeing them home again, and that had been *before* the ship went missing. That settled it; he'd book himself as freight for the next tramp freighter scheduled for that sector, and see what he could shake from the bushes. From there, it'd be onward to the planet Fred had landed on for his three-year vacation. Who knew? The ship might still be there, case solved, or at least, solved to the point Home Services wanted; he could collect his check and look for another gig. Home Services cared more about the equipment than the personnel; his term would be completed, and they'd send some bounty hunter after whatever was left of the crew. If there was anything, it was barely possible he'd find a bunch of Reboots wandering around and the withered remains of Fur and Fangs; space accident was still a valid explanation for this whole mess.

This was going to mean ... well, he was going to end up in some places that weren't exactly "modern," more like twentieth century. The companies that ran the working parts of the galaxy had their sights set on one thing and one thing only: profit. Which meant that when they installed a mine, say, they sent down a workforce and a lot of 3D printers, from little ones that printed parts, to big ones that printed walls and roofs. And what got built and installed was whatever was cheapest to slap together and more importantly, cheapest to run. So you'd have capsule hotels that could have come from 2010 Japan, fusion furnaces that were the latest and greatest, and the grunts that were cheap to hire (because AI workbots were buggy as hell and the "I" part was still mighty iffy), went to their jobs on 'vators, or even cheaper, paternoster lifts. Yet those grunts might well be using state-of-the-art exoskeletons to manhandle heavy objects.

He put together his traveling crate. He was not, after all, a creature that required very much in the way of resources. A little water, a little food, and air—and that was only on the front- and back-end of the trip. For the rest ... baggage class. That was why he was going to bill as if he was a paying passenger on these boats, but end up paying for nothing but a crate mostly full of nothing. Fey spirits of his sort didn't need anything but their anchors. In his case, the anchor was a busted pocket watch. Air bottle, check. Water bottle, check and full. "Food," well, he wasn't fussy, and that was bars of the "one-bar, one-meal" stuff they fed military grunts. The bars tasted like lemon-flavored chalk, but it was better than nothing. Gun. Oh yes, the gun.

An old-fashioned .455 Webley-Fosbery, an antique, actually, like the PIs in ancient films carried. It was as heavy as an anvil, and as accurate as any laser gun he'd ever fired. It had a history, and was definitely not all that it seemed. He could have sold it for a small fortune, and would sooner have sold his soul, assuming he had a soul to sell. No one expected a Para to carry a slug-thrower, especially not an antique. Swords, knives, bows, sure. In the case of Fangs, whatever was newest, shiniest, and expensive. Not a gun. Something about a lot of Paras being unable to fully adapt to the times; immortality did that to some. And some were just plain allergic to iron and steel; the Pucca was probably one of those. It wasn't just the gun, though, it was the bullets. You had to have just the right bullets for a job like this one.

All was in order. All he had to do was make the call and the pay the shipping fee, seal himself inside, and the pickup bots would do the rest. It wasn't the first time his chosen shipping company had gotten the crate from a seemingly empty office, or delivered it back to the same office, and it wouldn't be the last. The bots didn't care as long as they had the lock code for the door and the fee had cleared the bank.

He always preferred dealing with bots. They had no curiosity, which suited this Boggart just fine.

The Boggart slipped in ethereal form outside the crate several times during the trip, just to check on the progress, but never long enough to trip the Gremlin-sensors. The very last thing he needed was some freighter-bull coming in the back to check for hitchhikers. The Boggart wondered if there was ever a minotaur stuck in that gig; it'd have a nice bit of symmetry. And if there was one thing that the Home Services *did* show from time to time, it was the odd moment of whimsy. Flunkies like Ian had to keep themselves entertained somehow, and the Home Services cube-farm staff was about ten percent Paras. Which only went to show that there were bureaucrats everywhere. There was a rumor that Home Services had even considered hiring demons, because they were so *good* at bureaucracy, but in a rare moment of good sense, they'd decided against it.

Tempting as it was to swap briefly to a solid body and snitch something from the galley, that would be a dead giveaway of his presence, and the Boggart confined himself to checking on their ship's progress. Slow but steady. He'd pre-booked a bunk at the hostel—there were two kinds of housing at these mines, capsule hotels like the hostel, which were basically self-contained bunks, and company housing, which was basically a capsule in a shipping container that gave about the same amount of space as a prison cell, with slightly better amenities. Some outfits still used open-hold barracks housing, but that hardly ever turned out well nowadays; too many "special needs" employees, whether it be need for blood, UV intolerance, weakness to cold iron, or a violent reaction to garlic. His shipping crate would be delivered to the hostel, he could climb out of it and check in. It was bot-run, he'd checked on that, so there would be no questions about where he came from or how he got there. Once checked in, he'd use the uplink in his capsule to place a call to the Pucca, confirming his presence at the mine. Helped to create a paper trail; when he made out his expense report he would need to be able to prove he'd gone where he said he had. *Have to justify everything for the bean counters back at Home Services.* In between progress checks there was just a lot of waiting. The hold was pressurized, but not climate-controlled, and it was quarantined. Some ships just loaded everything into bigger shipping containers and strapped it all to naked frames exposed to space, but this was a smaller, older model that carried stuff that couldn't take hard vacuum.

Mind, even hard vacuum didn't get rid of Gremlins; no such thing as a perfect vacuum, after all, and Gremlins would latch onto anything. But that wasn't his problem. The point was, he had to pretty much stay ethereal so he wouldn't use up his consumables. But a PI job had always involved a lot of waiting, whether it was staking out a wandering spouse, or drowsing away a long wait to get to where you were going. One reason why he was in this job; he was good at waiting.

The trip was boring and uneventful, the docking routine, the delivery—by which time he was in corporeal form again, and using his air and food and water—also routine. The automated desk asked no questions at the hostel, and within an hour of checking in he was sealed in his pod and placing that call. After making sure it was office hours for the Pucca, of course. Wouldn't do to inconvenience the meal ticket. Most of the trip had been made at sublight, with the second half traveling "backward" as the ship slowed itself. Without too much time dilation, there was still a stretch that had put him out of sync, star-lagged.

"Ah," the creature said, then blinked at something he read on his end. "Where in all the hells of Earth are you? A *mine?*" *Dumb bunny doesn't know how this sort of thing shakes out.*

"Fur had bloodline kin here," the Boggart said shortly.

"Oh." The Pucca leaned in to look at the screen. "Are you in a *pod?* What kind of shithole—"

"They don't exactly have five-star accommodations out here," the Boggart pointed out. His contact shuddered. Anything less than executive suites and room service on call were foreign to the company man. "I'm just checking in, per the contract. I'll let you know one way or the other after I contact the other Fur."

"And Home Services appreciates your exactitude. I'll expect your call; if I don't take it, leave it for my message service." The Pucca terminated the connection, not wanting to waste a cent more on it, no doubt. *Home Services appreciates your exactitude … what's he do, spend his time memorizing a dictionary? Probably one of those "word a day" calendars; it'd fit for his type of office drone.*

He spent the next few minutes stowing what few belongings he had with him. The pod was just over eight feet long, four high, four wide. The bed conformed to whatever configuration you put it in; the climate control meant linens were not necessary. An entertainment and 'puter-pad workstation swung out of the wall on an arm, and there was a built-in light just over his head. Everything was a matte cream color. The slide-down side could take a bullet, and Dark Gods forbid this section had a blowout, it would seal and the pod would become a life-pod in which you could last as long as you didn't die from lack of water. Croaking the customers gave a chain a bad rep.

His next course of action would be to hit up the local watering hole; every place like this had one as a matter of necessity. When beings were engaged in hard and dangerous work, they needed a designated place to unwind; otherwise, they found other—and often more destructive—ways to release the tension. And it had to be some place that was *not* owned by the company they worked for, or by Home Services. If such a place didn't exist when an outpost was established, someone would create it, off the books, clandestinely, in warehouse space or even a ventilation shaft if one was big enough. Off the books meant home-brewed swill that could poison people as often as not, and worse, so far as the companies were concerned, was not something they could charge duties or taxes on. So after a brief time of trying to fight such places, the companies now planned in spots and leased them, collected their bit, and looked the other way. A much tidier solution.

"Where's the bar?" he asked the desk-bot. They hadn't wasted any money on this one; it was basically a screen, an electronic slate and fingerprinter, both set into the wall. The entire set-up was covered with crude graffiti, most of it directed toward Home Services or the bot. The tinny speaker crackled to life.

"Please follow the directions on the screen, and have a nice day!"

The bar was called, imaginatively, *Bar*. The instructions were fairly simple. It was nowhere near the hostel, which was port side, and beside the admin housing. It was tucked right in between the miners' housing and the dockworkers' housing, and as far from admin and the port as it was possible to get. Gave the drudge workers easy access, and allowed the VIPs to go slumming when they wanted to.

Well right now he'd fit right in. Deep down inside, some part of him wanted, desperately, to cruise into the place in a fedora, trench coat with the collar up, and a snub-nosed stogie in hand. But do that, and he was just begging for trouble; more than usual, at least. So … old coveralls that had once been a sort of yellow-brown and were now mostly gray-brown with oil and wear, baggy and saggy enough to hide the gun, over a T-shirt and cheap pants. Face-shaped face, slightly unkempt, slightly graying dark hair, stubble. He'd found that the face was one of the less important details, so he had a few that he used regularly as templates. Never mind the fact that most Norms looked all the same to Paras, and vice versa. And if any company goon questioned his being at the hostel instead of assigned housing, he'd flash his Home Services temp ID and his permanent PI license, and say something like he was "looking into irregularities." That always made company men sweat, because there were *always* irregularities, and it was their nightly prayer that no one ever looked into *theirs*. Graft and corruption were the hallmarks of civilization.

He didn't encounter anyone though, at least, not on the way down. It *was* down, too; at least as this mining base counted things. Waste not—as they hollowed out the rock, they had taken the surface constructions down and rebuilt them inside. Cubic space was cubic space, after all. Smart, really; things were safer under a skin of rock.

It did mean that there wasn't exactly a view, however.

To keep people from feeling as if they were living in a hamster maze, the corridors all had two-story ceilings, with faux sky panels over the lights. Since this wasn't an exactly top-tier operation, it was all low-grade and poorly fitted. Right now, it seemed to be designated "night," so the faux-sky showed lots of blotches that were supposed to be stars, and the lighting was subdued. Which meant that the garish red light-tube *BAR* set into the wall beside a door was visible from the lift. Otherwise it was just blank gray walls with doors, some with plaques telling what they were for the rest of the way. Not even an attempt to make it look like a regular city street.

He pushed open the door; it wasn't powered like you'd find on any decent setup. A few raggedy pool tables tucked into the corner, even more raggedy beings crowded around them, and dim lights. The actual bar top took up most of the space. It was lit from below, which cast everyone's faces into sinister and jagged shadows. Two bartenders to deal with the volume of customers; the Boggart got the impression that this place was probably constantly packed, as different shifts went on and off duty. Rank smoke from cheap smokables filled the space, which no doubt gave the air scrubbers fits, assuming that they even bothered with them. No one looked up or noticed him coming in; he was just another miner, beaten down and ready to forget his shift over a few libations. Funny word, that. It *meant* an offering poured out for the gods. Except this looked like a place, and people, the gods had forgotten, and they knew it.

The Boggart trudged up to an open spot at the bar, putting just the right amount of weary shuffle into his gait; he'd found that getting the walk right helped sell a disguise as much as anything. He bought a beer. He drank it, and listened. People thought that being a PI was all about asking questions. It wasn't. It was all about listening unobtrusively. *Then* asking the *right* questions to the right people. One of the bartenders was a Norm, the other was a Para—and you didn't have to be a Para to pick that out. The customers had neatly segregated themselves in front of their respective barkeeps. Like keeps with like, and that was the rule even out here. Well, except for the groupies. There were always groupies, at least for the attractive Paras. You saw them in the fancy high-priced Para hangouts, the kind that Pucca probably frequented. Lots of kids wearing black and too much makeup for the Fangs, lots of kids all primitive and tribal for the Furs (even though the rate of Turning was a *lot* lower for the Furs), and a crap-ton of kids all done up in weird pseudo-medieval or what he liked to call "magic-slut" getups for the … Others … even though there was no way in anyone's 'verse you could get Turned into one of the Others. But no one was winning any beauty contests out here, and no one was going to become the poster boy for the trendy lifestyle of the Urban Para.

The Boggart was carefully situated right at the division between Para and Norm customers. The Norm barkeep had served him first,

but as his beer emptied, it was the Para that approached him, rec-
ognizing him for being, at least, *not* Norm. "What'll it be? And I'll
be serving you from now on, pal; don't want my tips going to the
Normie." Close up, the remains of horn buds and the goat eyes betrayed the barkeep as a Satyr. Figured. There wasn't anything that
Satyrs didn't know about booze, and the beings that imbibed it. He'd
probably had his horns freeze-burned off so he'd fit in a standard
space helmet; custom jobs were expensive. The goat legs wouldn't
matter; most Satyrs just padded the toes of human boots and shoved
their hooves inside. They had to wear pants and shoes pretty much
everywhere, local laws being what they were, though they generally
groused about it whenever anyone would listen.

"Shot of rye and another beer." The Boggart waited while his
drinks were fetched, scanning the other patrons; nothing but disinterested stares terminating at the walls. "Thanks. Wondering if you
could point me in the direction of a friend of mine. Just hired on
here. I owe him some creds, and I wanted to settle the debt before it
got any bigger."

"Depends on who y'friend is, now doesn't it?" The 'tender leaned
forward on the bar, putting his blunt face close to the Boggart's. His
breath smelled like hay. Must have cost a small fortune to import out
here, unless he grew his own.

"Leroy McCandless. A Were, hard to miss. Know of him?" The
Boggart had done some research in between his ethereal jaunts in
the cargo hold, mostly from the collected files he'd received from
Ian. The Fur's "cousin" seemed to be the North American redneck
variety of Were. While there were other Pack variants, the majority
of North American Packs, for some reason, seemed to be rednecks.
Punks and skinheads in Europe, familial clans with more blood ties
in part of Asia. All of it got mixed together in the great melting
pot of space, though some kept to type. Seldom did a Pack member
go out alone; there were generally at least three of any one Pack in
any single place, even if they might not work the same shifts. They
Denned together and generally socialized together, and made basic
Pack alliances with other Furs.

"Ha! That's a first, Leroy *being owed* money. Usually the other way
around." The Satyr sized him up for a moment, then nodded. "He's

over in the corner there. He's on the shit list with the local Den, so I'd be careful 'bout asso-see-atin' with him too much. Don't wanna become puppy chow." The Satyr gave a gap-toothed grin, and then moved on down the bar to higher-paying customers.

Sounded like Leroy and his Pack-cousin were two of a kind. The Boggart slowly turned his back to the bar, putting his elbows up. He made sure to try to keep his face disinterested, his expression as beaten down as the deck below the miners' feet. Slowly, he let his gaze pass over the area the bartender had indicated. *Bingo*. The scruffy miner matched Leroy's picture; strangely, he looked cleaner than his picture did. He had his back to the wall, and was hunched over his drink. He sure didn't look like a Loner; Loners generally looked like Alphas on drugs—big, dangerous, and a bit crazy. *Don't want anyone sneaking up on you, huh? I wouldn't either, not in this hole.* The Boggart finished his shot, but held onto his beer to sip; it looked more natural for a man to be holding a drink in a bar than not. Handy weapon in a pinch, if it came to that. He shuffled off from the bar lazily, weaving his way indirectly through the crowd toward Leroy. The Boggart was doing his best to be casual, diffident. Nothing to set off any aggression signals. There was at least one other lupine Fur in here, and two big cats; hard to tell for sure since they were in human form, but he reckoned from the fact that one was black and the other Asian that they were a Leopard and a Tiger, respectively. Probably both low-level supervisors, still low enough to not be welcome in the management club, wherever it was. Crew bosses, more than likely. Half a dozen Tommyknockers, which you'd figure for a mine. A couple Goblins, a couple Kobolds, ditto. No Dwarves. They specialized in precious stuff, and this was plain old materials mining. And two dozen Norms.

The Boggart must've made a misstep, however; probably the eye contact at the last moment as the crowd parted. Leroy looked up from his drink, and his eyes instantly locked onto the Boggart. He sniffed once, his eyes got big, and even though he was fully human, so far as the Boggart could tell, the hair on the back of his neck moved on its own; hackles rising.

Oh hell. Without a word, Leroy flipped the table at the Boggart; it went sailing through the air, narrowly missing his head and crashing into the patrons behind him as he ducked under it. Leroy was already up and out the door before the splinters had hit the ground.

Time to hoof it.

As the Boggart had expected, Leroy headed for the elevators. Likeliest would be for him to make a break for the levels below this, engineering and the mine itself. But Leroy surprised him. Instead of grabbing one of the constantly moving chains and hopping on a platform, he bypassed the elevators altogether and plunged down an access tube beside them. By the time the Boggart reached it, the hatch had been jammed closed from the inside, a wrench wedged into the access bar.

He turned his attention to the slow-moving elevators. They were the crudest possible interpretation of the concept; a continuously moving loop of one-man platforms; you reached in, grabbed the "chain" that connected platform to platform, hopped on and rode to your destination. Cheap, certainly. Dangerous, absolutely. But the companies didn't waste money on amenities for grunts. And compared to the dangers of the mines, this was trivial. Probably killed a couple of miners a year, and with all such fatalities, the company would pay the next of kin—if there were any to begin with—a truly generous "survivor benefit" and move on. A couple of those a year was nothing beside the cost of "real" elevators and maintenance. The savings were enormous. Same went for accidents in the mines themselves. It was cheaper to pay off the relatives than install safety equipment.

The elevators moved at a glacial rate; the Boggart now had two options. Use the elevator, or try and figure out where Leroy was going and find another way down and cut him off. But this wasn't his first time on a mining colony; he checked for a service panel.

There was one, unsealed, right next to the access tube. And the password and ID of "guest" worked just fine. *Morons never do learn to change those.* A little poking at the screen got him a set of cams in the tube Leroy had just thrown himself into. The companies might be laissez-faire when it came to safety, but never when it came to security. *Come on, come to Papa ... there!* He saw the exit for the access tube that Leroy had taken; since most of these mines were all based off of the same modular units, he knew exactly what to do.

Another couple of pokes showed him the layout of the next floor, and there was only one way that Leroy could go from that tube exit. So where to cut him off before he got to some place branching off in more than one direction?

There. Not another tube, but a mail chute, an easy way to chuck deliverables from this floor to engineering. Advantage: it was a straight line down. Disadvantage: nothing human-size would fit in it.

Ha.

The Boggart ran, putting on a burst of supernatural speed. Speed Leroy would probably not try to match; he'd figure the Boggart was going to take the first 'vator down, and he'd have plenty of time to hide, since the exit for that tube was on the other side of the hollowed-out rock. He made a baseball pitch with his watch, sending it clanking down the chute; as soon as it went out of sight, he went to the Nowhere-Space, the Between, and manifested himself where the watch was. Little tricks like that could save your life, and the Boggart had a six-demon bag full of them.

Something went *squish* when he rematerialized; too small to be anything but an Imp or a Gnome. Lucky break; it wasn't anything alive; he'd only landed on someone's lunch, probably pitched down the tube by a spouse. But it wasn't damp, so he didn't worry about it; he just grabbed the watch, shoved it back in the pocket it belonged in, and pelted to intercept Leroy. They met at an intersection just before a bulkhead; the Boggart was expecting it, so he lowered his shoulder and threw his weight into Leroy. The Were crumpled and followed the Boggart's momentum into a wall toward the bulkhead; he was cornered, now. The Boggart felt what was coming before he even knew what was happening; he leaped back a pace, giving Leroy some room.

"You done pissed off the wrong set of teeth and claws this time, asshole!" Leroy had gone partway Changed; wicked claws had burst from his nails, and his teeth and hair had elongated to cast his features in a feral light. Leroy roared mightily—until the Boggart busted him right in the mug, hard. Letting the Fur posture and build up steam would only work against his purpose, after all. He kept it up, smacking him hard in the face with an open palm and alternating it with slugs to the gut. Leroy was forced to back up, drawing his arms—and thus those too-dangerous claws—in close to protect his body and face. Leroy was definitely not a Loner Alpha; too much ground given, too fast. But, he still had the Wolf buried under his skin. Once his back hit the bulkhead, he got some more fight in him. Slashing both arms down and outward with a roar, he forced the Boggart to retreat a step.

"Don't force this any further than it is, Leroy. It'll only end hard for you." Leroy didn't seem very inclined to listen. He howled loud enough to shake the dust off of the overhead pipes, and then lowered his head to charge. In one smooth motion, the Boggart drew the Webley-Fosbery and fired the large-caliber round at a pipe several feet in front and above Leroy. It burst spectacularly with the impact, spraying coolant directly into the Were's face. Leroy yelped and jumped back, temporarily blinded and definitely startled. That was all the Boggart needed, just enough time to slip his hand into the overall's hip pocket and get out the silver-plated brass knuckles.

Time to get to work.

He started with Leroy's face, and didn't stop; he just kept working his jaw, over and over. Leroy would try to push himself up, but the Boggart would just kick his legs out and do it all over again. That was one thing about beating the monkey-shit out of a Para; it took a lot of goddamned work, sometimes. The Boggart kept going until Leroy's face looked like a tenderized steak; one of his eyes was closed up and he was spitting out blood and more than a couple of teeth. *He's had it,* the Boggart thought as he raised his fist a final time.

"Hold it, hold it! I'll talk, I'll go wit'cha! Whatever! Just don't hit me anymore, man!" There was a canine whine under his words, the sort of pitiful whimper a dog made after getting whipped for shitting on the carpet—a good sign. *Now* the Boggart could get some goddamn cooperation.

"Talkative, now? Hell, I thought we were both going to get our workout over, first. Another time, maybe." The Boggart grabbed Leroy by the lapel of his jumpsuit, lifting him up. "Got some questions about a cousin of yours, and a certain ship he was on. Name of Fred, went out on one of the early voyages. Ring any bells?

Leroy whined, and cringed. "I don't—lemme think! Cousin? Pack-cousin, ya mean?"

"Yeah, Pack-cousin. About a cen-and-a-half ago. Engineer." The Boggart kept a tight grip on the lapel, and shook it a little.

"Ya mean Fred the Squint?" Leroy shook like a cocker spaniel about to pee in submission. *I've got him beat, now. Used the stick on him, time to use the carrot.* The Boggart backed down a little, the last thing he wanted to do was get whizzed on.

"Listen, I just need some information. You help me, I help you. It's not like I'm doing this for free, after all. No reason for you not to see some of the creds, right?"

The mention of creds turned off the last of the Fur's reluctance. Just like that, the sap's entire life story came pouring out in one great torrent of uninteresting crap. He was so sorry for this, terribly ashamed of that, and so on. What little pertained to Fred only amounted to a hill of beans that the Boggart could've figured out for himself. Fred was a Loner, that was the first thing that the Boggart had gotten right, driven out because of his technical aptitude in a demographic that was big on muscle and short on brains. He got tough because of it, but decided to try his hand at spacefaring to escape the bullshit anyways. And that's all that the file—or good ol' Leroy here—knew or could infer. Once Fred hit space, that was the last his former Pack had heard from him. He hadn't even arranged to bank his pay with the Pack credit union, which was a bit of a grievance, often repeated over the years, it seemed.

The Boggart knew that he wouldn't get anything else useful out of Leroy; the Were had been cowed, and had already spilled his guts. The Boggart dropped him to the deck, dropped a small packet of folded credits on his chest, then turned to walk away.

And was stopped.

What he met was a wall of meat and anger; the local Pack had decided to show up, maybe attracted by Leroy's howls, and led by the Asian Were.

The Boggart took his real form, sort of like a giant-sized lawn gnome from hell. Pointed ears, dark-gray skin, black beard, and a lot of pointed teeth. "Something I can do for you, gents?" he asked, in a warning tone.

59

The Fur snarled, just a little. Lifted lip, showing dominance. "Step aside; we've got business with this whelp, now that you're done with it. Yeah?"

He moved to one side and made a sweeping gesture toward the beaten Leroy. "Be my guest."

The Boggart didn't look back as he walked away, despite Leroy's insistent whines turning to yelps of pain. Owed money? Insulted a Pack leader? Stole someone's bitch?

Not this Boggart's problem.

As he trudged back to the hostel, he made a lightning decision. So, he'd found out that the Fur was a Loner. That made it all the more likely he'd colluded *with* the Fangs. So before he went and chased any more wild hares, it made sense to check out the Fang angle first.

And he wouldn't find any of the movers and shakers in the Fang world here.

He smirked to himself. The Pucca wasn't going to like this.

The Pucca could bite him.

There was an old saying in the Norm military: "It's easier to ask forgiveness than get permission," and the Boggart wasn't planning even on asking for forgiveness. No matter what happened, he'd get better results than the Pucca; he knew it, the Pucca knew it, and besides, the Pucca didn't want to be bothered, so the Pucca could justify the next expenses to the higher-ups himself.

But he did check very carefully to make sure that the Pucca was going to be out of the office before placing his call and leaving his message.

"Dead end, except that the Were is alleged to be a Loner, so that makes collusion with the Vampires likely. Pursuing that with my sources. Will report when I arrive."

Once again, the Boggart booked freight out—this time the only ship leaving was faster than the one he'd come in on, a fast courier in fact, mostly carrying data storage. His crate would take up very little space, and a fast courier likes to fill every bit of space it has. There was room. He booked it, booked into another hostel on the other side, checked his supplies, checked out of the hostel, and parked the watch inside the crate. Once he saw the 'bots come fetch the crate, he joined the watch. This time the wait would be much shorter, and no need to check progress.

Besides, only the crate would be occupying that bunk in the hostel when he got there. He was going where the Elite met, and at least for a little while, he'd have to pass as one of them.

Fangs and Furs both *loved* deep-space stations. For the Fangs, well, eternal night and complete control over who and what came and went, what was there not to like? And for the Furs, while they'd have preferred a sunny no-moon planet, well, one out of three wasn't bad, and the control aspect fed right into Pack mentality. Norms needed the stations as waypoints to greener pastures. They were expensive to build and maintain, but Norms hated staffing them. And the Fangs, at least, knew everything there was to know about luxury, and were happy to turn their stations into tourist traps overflowing with people who wanted to toy with the danger of a Fang bite— one that they were guaranteed in the contract wasn't going to be fatal. Everybody won.

With the chance that the Norms were going to hit the place with theoretical torches and stakes approaching zero, the Fangs turned the stations they ran into pleasure palaces. Once FTL was finally working, they were exactly the sorts of places that Norms with a lot of money liked to visit. They were also the sorts of places that groupies liked to live in. That attracted a sprinkling of other sorts of Paras as well.

The stations had real names, but the Fangs always renamed them, and those were the names that stuck. This one was The Tenderloin.

Not a pun on steak/stake as most assumed, it was named after the notoriously lawless pleasure district in the city of San Francisco in Old Earth's late 1800s. The Boggart recalled the place very well, with mingled pleasure and revulsion. He regarded its namesake with the same mixed feelings.

Once again, the hostel was 'bot-tended, with a sprinkling of Reboots. No one to pay attention when he sprung the crate, checked himself in, got what he needed and shoved the crate into the bunk

61

and sealed it—and stepped out into the lights-and-shadow-play that was The Tenderloin.

First thing he needed was a *real* hotel room. Those were not hard to come by. The station itself had private housing for the Nests and Dens, and their hangers-on, storage for the Reboots, and lots and lots of hotels, which ranged from the luxurious to—well, *he'd* never had the money for anything past the lower end, but if rumors were true, genuine fur bedspreads and hot-and-cold-running vices were just the start. The only people who ever used the hostels were crews from the ships and transients. The Boggart reckoned he'd find himself a place just a hair below midrange. He didn't want to make the Black Dog turn white-haired overnight.

Wardrobe would be important too. Fortunately around here, unless you *lived* here, you could get by, in fact, you were encouraged to get by, with temporary clothing that just washed down the drain when you showered. So once he got himself situated, he got himself a couple of appropriate outfits.

First stop: the Den where he had a contact.

Nearly all of the Packs, and certainly all the Nests, had their own front clubs. These helped pay the bills, and were what the tourists came to see; to get to the Den or Nest proper, you always had to go through the club, running the gauntlet of bouncers and less-obvious security. Lots of flash and plenty of distractions to keep the looky-loos occupied. Costume de rigueur for a Den front club was always more-or-less rough trade. Punk, "tribal," and industrial styles predominated; but of course here in The Tenderloin it had to look expensive. So the Boggart strolled out of the hotel in an outfit that looked a lot like a couture version of mining gear, minus the safety helmet.

Fangs and Furs both had light-sensitive eyes, so the hallways—two-story hallways, in an odd reflection of the mine—were shadowy. It helped play up the image, as well. But unlike the miner "town," these walls were alive with advertisements and images of what was behind them. It made the hallways seem more crowded than they already were. And there were a lot of people here. Most of them were tourists, often wearing outfits that would have made a stripper blush, or costumes that made them look as if they had just come from some alien party. Which … they likely had. With the most wealthy were their guards, in sober black, not even trying to blend in; oftentimes the hired help that one carted around with them was as much of a status symbol as one's clothes. Occasionally some of the Fang Thralls or Pack Pups wafted through the crowds, on their way to somewhere. The groupies. This was heaven for them.

There were Reboots here, and a lot of them, but you would never see them. They were all behind the scenes, doing the crap work it took to keep a place like this running. Way more Reboots than bots—Reboots were cheap, bots were expensive. Eventually that game would dry up; couldn't be more than a couple billion Reboots left from the ol' Outbreak, and they weren't getting replaced at anywhere near the rate they were breaking. It was legal … and considered highly desirable by some … to get Turned into Fur or Fang, but no one that was sane wanted zombification—no payoff. But by the time the Reboots ran out, someone would probably figure out how to make cheaper bots. Or they'd discover a planet full of stupid aliens and turn them into the next exploited class. If there was a resource out there, Home Services and the Norms in charge of it would make sure to squeeze every last drop of usefulness out of it.

The "Den of Iniquity" was where the Boggart was headed; most Fur clubs called themselves "Den of" something or other. The place wasn't any more "iniquitous" than any other Den, and considerably less so than the Fang "Lounges," but he supposed it made the Beinn Bhan Pack feel tough and wicked. They'd originated in Scotland, but if there was a single Pack member here with so much as a patch of Scottish hair on his carcass, the Boggart would be shocked and amazed. Still, they all assumed Scottish names, and his contact was Fergus MacDubh. *Time to rattle ol' Fergie's cage.*

The shadow play outside the Den of Iniquity was of wolves running over hills in the full moon, then meeting up with what looked like a porn-vid idea of a witch's coven, morphing into half-state and grabbing them and the whole thing dissolved into mist before anything graphic occurred, leaving the onlooker to make up his own mind about whether the Furs tore them to bits or merely tore their clothes off. Always classy at these sorts of establishments. The Boggart nodded at the bouncer at the door, and made his way inside.

At a Fang Lounge you'd probably be hit with a wall of sound with whatever electro trash music was popular this decade, but Fur ears were very sensitive. Still, the zen-thrashno made him wince. The first bar was pretty crowded with a mix of Pack Pups (mostly male, as the Fang Thralls were mostly female) and tourists. The decor was pseudo-hunting-lodge, all faux unfinished logs and hides with the hair on, light fixtures made of faux antlers and mounted trophies on the wall, which were themselves probably holograms. The only Furs he spotted right away were a couple at the bar, and they weren't wearing Beinn Bhan colors. And as he got closer to them, he realized they weren't Wolves anyway; both were Tigers.

He headed for the next room; same decor, it was still a public room, but there was another bouncer at the door who eyeballed him carefully before letting him pass. The outfit and his Para status would let him that far without a challenge—or a bribe, for that matter.

The next room was more of the same, but quieter; same music, but dropped down a couple notches. Fewer tourists, more Pack Pups, and now, more Furs. All of them were Wolf except for a Panther and a Leopard who were shooting an old-fashioned game of pool against a pair of Beinn Bhan Furs. It appeared to be a friendly challenge match. The Boggart always found it curious that there was less hot-blooded rivalry between the feline and canine Furs than there was between the various canine Packs. Would've made for an interesting study for the sociologically inclined.

A careful survey of the room showed him what he was looking for: a Fur in Beinn Bhan colors of dark green and charcoal gray, leaning up against the wall by the bar, but not drinking. This would be the one that a would-be Pack Puppy would come to in order to apply for entrance. And this would be the one a stranger like the Boggart would come to if he happened to be looking for a Pack member. A "gift" would be expected in either case.

With Wolves you were expected to be direct; with the Cats and the Foxes, you had to dance around the subject a good bit. With Coyotes ... you never got a straight answer. Ever. Bears ... well the Boggart hadn't met any Bears yet, but he'd heard you had to be even more direct than with the Wolves. So he just strolled up to the contact and laid it out. "Need to talk to one of your Pack, brother."

The Fur eyed him. "Law?"

The Boggart shook his head. "Home Services. But not interested in him. Looking for a Loner gone AWOL." He was wearing one of his "professional" human faces, but when he grinned all of his very sharp teeth were exposed. "Let's just say I'm the kinder, gentler version. If they send one of their own ...." He let the sentence trail off. They both knew the punch line. Home Services didn't care about anything but the bottom line, and if they sent an agent—a real agent, and not a pen pusher like that Pucca—there'd be raiding squads and interrogation rooms involved.

"Info is a fin. Access is a Benjamin." Strange how the old nicknames for money had stuck long past the time when "dollars" were something no one saw outside of a museum. But, there you had it. The vast majority of the Alphas had been Turned during the "Golden Ages," when pickings were much easier, and a solid majority of those had been in the half-century between 1920 and 1970. You tended to stick with the things you knew then, when you were a Para that got Turned.

Ah the lupines. So easy. The Boggart passed over a fin. "Fergus MacDubh in the Den?"

The Fur consulted his data-cuff. "Not yet. Due in five." He held out his hand. The Boggart crossed his palm with the Benjamin. And how many people knew that name was actually the name of the man whose face had been on that denomination of bill? Damn few, outside the Paras.

A door behind the contact slid open, and the Fur stood aside long enough to let the Boggart enter a third bar. "I'll let him know you're looking," the Fur said, as the door slid closed again. The Boggart could literally *feel* the envious glances of the wannabe Cubs burning holes in his back as the door closed them out.

This was a bar set for the sensitive eyes and ears of full Furs. Not faux hunting-lodge this time, this was the real deal. Furs liked real wood and real hide around them. Even the trophies were real, and probably harvested by the current Alpha or his immediate predecessor. The Boggart had to chuckle at the memory of how many anti-hunting and vegetarian societies had dried up and blown away once all the Paras came out of the broom closet. It was one thing to throw fake blood on a mink-wearing woman who'd never lifted anything heavier than her handbag. It was quite another to confront seven or eight feet of snarling muscle when you picketed his favorite raw-meat restaurant. And the Fur Packs took the idea of cutting into the food supply ... personally.

The music was down to a whisper, the lights no brighter than moonlight. It suited him just fine; immortals tended to have similar tastes after a time. This was where the She-Furs were, but one look at him told them he wasn't their kind, so they ignored him; that also suited him. All of them were Wolves, though not all were in Beinn Bhan colors; She-Furs had a bit more inter-Pack mobility than the boys did. The Wolves all had a similar sort of look, though—fashionably scruffy, tough, and muscled. Not elegant. Not particularly pretty by human standards. Your Cats, now ... *those* oozed glamour and sex appeal. The Boggart's eyes darted around the room. *If I know ol' Fergie ... there; the knot of women vying for attention.*

Fergie was the Pack Beta. The Alpha was the Fur that enforced the rules and the pecking order, and did (or led) the fighting when it needed to be done. The Alpha was generally monogamous with the Female Alpha, the Beta got all the rest of the women. That was particularly true of Fergie, who was a politician, never mind whatever scams he was running on the side. Not the kind that got elected to office—the kind that *ran* the office, kept everything running smoothly, knew where all the skeletons were.

The Boggart worked his way over to the knot of She-Furs who had converged on someone just entering the bar from the Den side. Under the mock growls and teeth-bared play threats, the Boggart heard Fergie greeting each of the girls by name, and the occasional *smack* of a play-slap on the rump, followed by the obligatory squeal and teeth-snap. A human feminist would have been outraged, but there wasn't one of these women that couldn't—or wouldn't—take on any of the boys in this bar in a straight-on Fur fight. This wasn't macho chauvinism; this was pure Fur instinct translated into human behavior. Sniffing asses in public just wasn't done ... unless you were in Fur form. Fergie immediately picked the Boggart out from the crowd. Not a big deal for a Fur; the Boggart wouldn't smell anything like anyone else in this room. And, of course, he'd been warned by the contact. It wouldn't have surprised the Boggart if Fergie knew about him the moment he set foot on the station, despite all of his precautions; the Fur was just that sort of Wolf.

But Fergie being Fergie, he couldn't just manage a simple greeting. He made an elaborate thing of throwing his head in the air, sniffing loudly, and exclaiming, "Och weell! Be that one of the Fae I scent?" Then peering between two of his She-Furs and exclaiming, "Boggie! Faith, and I'd know that particular English leather-and-heather smell anywhere! How's my favorite Sassanach?" As if his data-cuff hadn't been buzzing all along.

The Boggart simply nodded. "Fergie. I see you're still doing well on your particular rung on the ladder."

"Now, is that any way to talk to an old mate?" Fergie feigned a hangdog look. "An' after all we've done for each other too."

"Oh, I remember all we've done for each other, Fergus. I've still got the scars from some of the things you've *done* for me. Last I recall, you burned me, Fergie. Which means you owe me."

"Burned ye, lad? Only thing I recall burnin' was London Bridge ...." Fergus grinned toothily. "Oh now, don't tell me ye were holed up in some tart shop or other when I did that." He tsk'd. "That sweet tooth'll be th' death of ye, lad. Ye should stick t' the Water of Life." To underscore the comment, Fergus downed a double shot of what passed for single malt around here.

"Funnily enough, someone said the same thing 'bout you and precious metals." The Boggart patted his jumpsuit lightly where his revolver rested in a pocket. "We need words, private-like."

Fergus's eyes narrowed, though he kept his jovial tone. "All right lasses. The boys need t'be talkin' borin' business. Not Pack, just a wee bit of palaverin' regardin' our corporate would-be leash holders. Off wi' ye." There was more butt-slapping and squealing and giggling— She-Furs were easily overcome by hormones and instinct in the presence of a strong Beta—and Fergus led the way to a booth that he quickly privatized.

And as quickly dropped the accent. "Hamish said you're tracking a Lone for Home Services. What's that got to do with us?"

The Boggart snorted. "What do you think? There are two currencies that you deal in, Fergie: favors and information. You owe me a favor, and I want information."

Fergie shook his head. "You're not helping here. I need a little more data on *what* you're looking for. I'm not going to spew random Pack info at an outsider."

The Boggart relaxed, and steepled his hands together in front of him, clearly signing that he wouldn't be reaching for the gun any time soon. "You've got your fingers stuck in a lot of pies out here and beyond, Fergie. The Lone I'm looking for is a probable hijacker. Evidence, what scant little there is of it, says he might be working with Fangs, since he's not affiliated. Since your business doesn't really care about species loyalties, I figured you were the guy to see."

Fergus pursed his lips, and nodded slowly. "Last 'jacking I heard of was a Nest. And that was a good six months ago. Since there's no love lost 'tween us and the Fangs, I'm happy to tell you it was four Fangs out of the Le Fevre Nest and they spaced their Lone and all the Reboots as soon as they realized FTL was a going proposition. Of course, good luck to the company trying to prove that or track the ship down. She's parts now."

"Got a ship name attached to that gig?" It almost certainly wasn't the one the Boggart was looking for, but after having spent enough time as a PI, one learned to fish out extra creds from information wherever one could.

"Mourning Glory." Fergus grinned. "With a 'U.' From what I heard on the jungle telegraph, she was parted out and the skeleton fired into a red dwarf in just under a week. Le Fevre set a new record."

The Boggart allowed himself a small smile. "They are getting better an' better with each passing year. Sure you're not just fishing to have me help you take out some competition, Fergie?"

Fergus clasped his hand to his heart. "I am pained. *Pained*, I tell you. You strike me to the heart to even suggest I would consider such a thing!"

"Uh huh. You got anything else for me? Or ought I come back here again sometime to keep you company?" The Boggart raised an eyebrow, inviting a little more—if there was any more.

Fergus snorted. "Seriously, Boggie, 'jacking those old pre-FTL ships—not a lot of that anymore. Most of the ones still missing weren't 'jacked, they're out there floating dead thanks to crews that went medieval on each other. That's where I'd look if I were you."

"Yeah, I'll keep your tip in mind." The Boggart stood up and got out of the booth, and turned on his heel before calling over his shoulder, "Until next time, Fergus."

Fergie was already heading for his Shes. "Only if I don't smell you coming first, Boggie me lad."

At least he wasn't in the hostel. And the "budget" tourist digs were pretty plush for a Were-run establishment. The real money was made in the clubs, on booze and drugs and the careful taste of the Fang and other vices, so the Boggart figured the hotel rooms were intended to make sure you were well rested so you could run right out and repeat all of them as often as possible. This of course didn't apply to high rollers; they were milked of every cred they had in as many ways as possible. It was as much status as it was privilege for that sort to spend all they could.

The Boggart had to focus. He needed to at least seem profession-al for this part. *Time to check in with the nanny.*

He checked his sidereal time; benefit number one, the Pucca would be in the office. Oh well. Might as well give him something other than a message to listen to. Benefit number two: the call went through lightning fast. Evidently they wanted folks here to be able to brag about the good time they were having to the folks back home as quickly and often as possible to entice other full pockets and empty heads to try the fleshpots as soon as their vacation days came up.

The call connected with a flicker after the third ring. So the Puc-ca had him on forward-direct rather than talk-to-the-secretary bot. *Interesting. Fewer records that way.* There was probably a grift with this entire deal; he'd suspected it in the beginning, but hadn't seen the angle and still couldn't. Not yet. There was *always* a grift, in his experience, when you got close and personal attention from whom-ever was passing out the creds.

He nodded at the Pucca's image. "It's me. Ready for the update? There's not terribly much, yet."

"Looks like you're coming up in the world. You actually have a room, and not a coffin wired for net." The Pucca smirked.

"Needed to justify the expense account you gave me, after all. Besides, places like this require certain behavior in order for somebody like me not to stand out more than necessary." The Boggart glanced at his pocket watch absently before looking back to the Pucca's visage on the screen. "Anything new on your end of the wire, before we get into what I uncovered?"

"Sorry. The *Cenotaph* is still missing, and the crew hasn't turned up anywhere that there are facial scans. So?" The Pucca didn't look terribly sorry. But then, by his standards, this room was probably on the scale of a no-tell motel. He probably thought the Boggart was still slumming.

"Kicked over some rocks, had words with some beings that I know. The line is quiet on this one." The Boggart scratched the bridge of his nose, and looked thoughtful. "If it was a 'jacking, then they've done really well and really shitty at hiding it."

The Pucca looked confused. "I beg your pardon?"

"Look at it like this. Whatever crew was in on this, they were dumb enough to trip up with the emergency beacon, after setting down on a planet for a good long while." He waited while the Pucca nodded. "Should've been an easy pickup for some unhappy men with heavy weaponry by that point. Duck soup. Yet they're able to skate through all the possible scans, information nets, and gossips without a peep. It's strange, and hijackings are usually pretty straightforward affairs in my experience." Time to drop the bomb. "Like the *Mourning Glory*; soon as the crew found out FTL was up and running, that ship vanished from all the radar." There. If the Pucca looked that one up and found out it was still listed as "missing," he might figure the Boggart knew where and how it went missing. And that would mean another check.

And if the dope didn't ... the Boggart could still sell the info, later.

The Pucca nodded, brows creased. "Hmm. Put that way ... they sound like the unluckiest wise guys, or the luckiest idiots in the universe."

The Boggart shrugged. "Won't know until I find out more. I haven't run out of options yet, but I'm going to need you to put down creds for a rented skiff."

"I'd already assumed you'd need one. Home Services has a franchise operation and you have a rental option wherever they are. Schultz Wrentals, with a 'W'. Don't ask me why." From the sly look on the Pucca's face, Humph actually had a good idea why. With a 'W' because what they were "wrenting" were "wrecks." Oh well, as long as it got him there and back. It couldn't be *too* bad here, though if he'd been back at that mining colony, all bets were off. Here? Well it didn't do to kill the customer because the customers had families and anyone who could afford to come here could also afford a very expensive lawyer. But one thing *was* certain. Whatever he got wouldn't be new, it wouldn't be fast, and it wouldn't be pretty. "By the way, in order to do that I had to look up your file. For your full legal name and all …."

The Boggart waited. He knew what was coming. And he really wished this was a face-to-face so he could grab that smarmy bastard by the throat. With his teeth.

"Really, now. *Humphrey?* Humphrey … *Boggart?*" The snickers started.

"Yeah … and?" There were plenty of choice curses that some of the old gods, the ones that hadn't died out yet, could probably grant him; the only thing that stopped the Boggart from uttering them was the fact that he still needed to be paid. A dead HS Pucca can't very well issue a check.

But the only thing that would have mollified him at this point would have been the knowledge that whoever had first summoned the Pucca had named him Harvey. Which, of course, wasn't likely. Damned Norms. He hadn't known anything about Old Earth vids and actors when *he'd* been summoned, or he likely would have found a way to get past the protections and swap his summoner's face with his ass. All the hells, he'd gone millennia without a Norm name! It wasn't as if *he'd* chosen it!

He waited for the Pucca to finish snickering and wipe his eyes. "Ah, that was good. Best laugh I've had all day. Your chariot will await you, *Humphrey.* I'd say 'pick it up any time' but we both know that time is money, and Home Services is particular about getting their money's worth."

A not-so-subtle hint that he was being watched and would not be allowed to linger on at a luxury station on Home Services' dime. This place wasn't his style, but the Pucca wouldn't know that or even care. "Yeah, I hear you. We'll be in touch, wabbit." Oh and time for a not-so-subtle hint of his own. "Remember, I don't get to break the rental and I *do* get paid per diem for transit time." The Pucca pursed his lips, gave a curt nod, and then broke the connection.

Maybe that would at least ensure him that the wreck would be fast, if not new and pretty.

Five minutes later, when he checked the Schultz client site on the station's intranet, he smiled crookedly.

A former long-distance racing skiff. The frame wasn't warped, which meant it hadn't been in any crashes. Everything else looked pretty beat up, but he wasn't interested in the boat's cosmetics. *Yeah. That'll do.* He reached into one of his back pockets, producing a small round flask. *A little whiskey for the night, and come standard dawn, we'll ride out for a day on the beach.*

Without needing to be in ethereal form for this transit—or at least, part of it—he'd had the crate humped to the skiff without being in it. The skiff had been modified for idiots, of course. Manual override happened only if the automatics broke down. He could have by-passed it easily enough if he had cared to; knowing how to do such things proficiently were infinitely handy in his line of work. He just didn't care to take the time to do it, for now.

He did go ethereal just because it was more comfortable once the skiff launched on its automatic path—the Pucca had supplied the rental firm with the coordinates, probably to make sure he didn't make any side trips while on Home Services' dime. From the smell that was pricking at his nose, someone had been sick in this thing, a lot, and a hint of the stink was still in the air scrubbers. And he knew why someone had been sick in this thing. It was fast. And it was not at all delicate in its vector transfers. Well, it was a racing skiff after all, and you didn't expect the same smooth ride out of one of these bastards that you got from your standard skiff. The inertial dampeners had been turned low, to give racers a better feel for the handling;

it made for somewhat rough riding, however. The oversized engines that they had strapped to it were designed to run system courses almost as fast as military boats, which suited the Boggart just fine. The faster he got to the planet, the sooner he'd finish this job and be on to the next one.

No room for creature comforts either, just the one cramped little cabin with the barest of amenities necessary to biological life in space. But he didn't need anything at all when he was ethereal, so that was how he stayed except between course changes. When he was in the Nowhere-Space of the ethereal, he was still somewhat aware of what was happening to his pocket watch; after a time, he heard the ship's alert blaring.

Must be there.

He slipped back into the corporeal world, and oriented himself as he absently stuffed the watch into his pocket. Keying up the viewscreen, he saw his destination hanging there against the blackness of space; it was an uninteresting water-covered rock of a planet, with a few islands dotting the surface from long-ago volcanic activity. *Might be profitable for somebody to drop a claim on this place, develop it as a luxury planet, if it weren't so damned far out here in the ass-end of space.* He set his scans to wideband, looking for any satellites or other early warning devices; hell, if he was lucky, the *Cenotaph* would show up as a dead hulk in orbit, waiting for him like a pot of gold at the end of the rainbow. That would certainly solve everything and he could go home and collect his check.

Of course, he was never lucky. Just some metallic particles and other light debris that all ships shed normally whenever entering or leaving atmosphere.

It wasn't hard to pinpoint where the ship had been when it launched the emergency beacon. The beacons hadn't been made by the lowest bidder. They were the one item on the ships that was mil-spec. So he followed the coordinates down to one of the eleventy-million little islands that comprised this place, and the skiff bumped itself down right on the spot that the *Cenotaph* had vacated. Good thing it wasn't still there; the skiff was made for speed, not sturdiness, and would've crunched quite nicely against the hull of a big science cruiser.

Scan showed that the air was good—so he cracked the outer door and had a look outside. It looked like any other beach back on Earth: silicates, water, the usual. The plants were all relatively simple, with a few Earth analogues. Wrong sort of green, a lot of blue and red. Looked like prehistoric stuff, Jurassic, Mesozoic, but without the giant bugs or monster reptiles.

Something seemed off, though.

The Boggart looked closer; there were definite signs that the area had been carefully worked over to look like it'd been untouched by sentient hands. He wandered around for a couple of hours, kicking things over, ranging the coast, looking for anything that might have been left behind to indicate what was going on at this beach for three years. The Boggart was about to give up and head back to the skiff when his ears pricked up on his skull; something was moving in the underbrush. Not stealthily, either. Something native?

He took the big revolver from its oiled leather holster, and waited. *No cover out here—just gonna have to face whatever is coming head on.*

"Come out nice and slow-like, and it'll go easier on you," he growled.

Whatever was in there stopped for a moment, and then seemed to change direction; it was definitely coming closer to him, now. It sounded bipedal. And slow. And clumsy.

He had settled the sights of the revolver on a patch of under-brush directly in front of him that was thrashing as something tried to force its way through. His clawed finger was slowly tightening on the trigger when it emerged.

"Rurh?"

A Zombie stood in front of him, with its head cocked to the side in dim curiosity.

The Boggart was taken aback—almost enough to drop his revolver—by what it was wearing. The Zombie had been fitted with a grass skirt and what passed for a coconut bra, with a string of spongy flowers, long dead, draped around its neck. It picked up a frond of the local flora, and stalked toward him ponderously. When it was close enough, it stood up straight as it could, and started to fan the Boggart.

It took him several seconds to realize his jaw was open, and close it with a loud click. He looked past the Reboot, and saw several other humanoid shapes shuffling through the bush. More of the same;

some were still dressed in the HS-issue red jumpsuits, and others were similarly garbed as the first, grass skirts and all. He sat down on the sand, and just stared for a few minutes while his brain did its best to reset from the shock.

This'll do somethin' special to the Pucca, for certain. He holstered the revolver, and got out his minivid camera. He just knew that if he didn't shoot some vid, the Pucca would never believe him. He was puzzling over his next move as he got as much footage as he cared to.

Who the hell would put Reboots in grass skirts and teach them to fan people? Not 'jackers. This was putting an entirely different complexion on the problem. And ... reluctantly ... he was beginning to like these guys.

Which was another problem, because he was *supposed* to catch them and turn them over to the company; he was contracted to find the ship, but it had been implied since then that he was taking on the job of finding this Fred character and whatever accomplices he had. He shook his head; the Boggart *always* finished a job, and by all the hells of the universe, he was going to finish this one.

Two things were for sure here. This was a yellow-sun world, and anyone who put Reboots into grass skirts had a hell of a sense of humor, so there was no way it had been the Fangs who grounded the ship here. Most Fangs had about as much of a sense of humor as a chunk of ice.

It had to be Fred, and that meant he was one dangerous Fur, because he'd somehow overcome *four* Fangs, one of which was likely an elder Vamp. Whenever the beacon went up, he had to have known his goose was cooked—probably did a quick cleanup job on the site, and then made tracks for the stars. A pre-FTL boat, so it'd have been slow going, and he'd want to get to the closest bit of civilization so that he could blend in, the Boggart wagered.

Well, that would give him his next stop: whatever was nearest. He sighed. "Time to check the charts and draw up the anchor," he told the Reboot.

It, of course, said nothing.

The Boggart decided to go ethereal for the trip to the next station. It was a short hop by translight, and he was bored. After a while, interstellar flight did that to you; it wasn't as if it was scenic by any means, and if you weren't going from here to there on some fancy luxury boat that had a myriad of things to entertain the passengers, you might just as well be sealed in a box with crap food and minimal comfort. He was already docked at the station on autopilot, then he became aware that an alarm had gone off; he recognized that the alarm *only* indicated that the ship had dumped the cockpit's atmo. You know, the important stuff for the continued functioning of most living beings. And in a skiff ... well, by the time he checked, it was too late to go corporeal and try and fix the malfunction.

Mentally cursing the Pucca, the company that had rented him this almost death trap, and the Fates, he retreated into the No-where-Space to wait for the station to repressurize the skiff and investigate. Eventually they would have to do both. You couldn't have a boat tying up a dock indefinitely.

After a length of time, he felt that his pocket watch was still in zero atmo, but moving.

The hells?

I got a bad feeling about this ....

But it wasn't as if he could do anything about it. He was one of the Paras that needed to breathe. Vacuum wasn't good for him, and that was entirely aside from inhibiting his ability to imbibe whiskey. That "malfunction" was beginning to look like an "on purpose"—but who would know about the watch? Or had this just been a simple "purge and grab"? He'd heard of those ... not many, because people who had the ability to even rent something that could go translight were wealthy, and wealthy people had heirs, and heirs asked questions ... but it did happen.

Well if that was the case, someone was going to get a rude surprise. He might not have his revolver with him when he came out of Nowhere-Space, but he was something of a weapon all by himself.

The watch went into a dark, small place. Also in a vacuum. After a while, he sensed the hiss of air returning to wherever the watch was. And there was light, and heat, and what felt like enough room to fit his frame. He was tempted to erupt into the area like a Bog-gart-shaped jack-in-the-box from Hell, but native caution made him go corporeal ... carefully.

It was a good thing he had. There were many, many weapons pointed at him.

The lighting was subdued, which was what you would expect, seeing that the people holding the weapons were either Fangs or in Clan colors, though he didn't recognize the Nest. Silver and dusky lavender? Not one he knew. But this wasn't some over-the-top bordello-style "reception" room, crowded with expensive baroque furniture and trinkets, nor was it the angsty, gothic, blacker-than-black trite room out of some old vid. This room would not have been out of place in the home office of a major executive. Everything was sleek, stylish; there was a lot of high-end equipment in here, and most people would never even recognize it as equipment in the first place, because it had been styled to be unobtrusive. The chair that the watch—and now he—were sitting on probably cost more than he'd ever made in his long life. The piece of sculpture functioning as a desk across from him cost ... well, his brain went into meltdown trying to figure it out. And the woman behind the desk, as sleek and stylish as the room ...

... had not been that expensive when he'd last known her.

"Hello, Claire." She'd been beautiful then, by human standards. Now she was a work of art. Every platinum hair in her chin-length bob was in place, her pale complexion was flawless, and she had not gone the route of so many Fang women by painting her lips whore-red. Tasteful. Very tasteful. As was the two-piece, asymmetrical, steel-gray suit she wore. No surprise that she had a lot of equally expensive boy-thralls holding those weapons on him. And they looked competent. Pretty boys who were also well-trained bodyguards—either she'd had pretty boys trained, or she'd had bodyguards sent out to whole-body-sculptors and either way, it would have made a big hole in most people's bank accounts. Well, she'd learned about the need for competence from him. "Been what, thirty years? You don't look all that much worse for wear." He appraised her again. "Little bit on the pale side, though."

"I have an iron deficiency," she deadpanned. "And there's just no sun up here."

"Shame, that. You used to kill in a bikini."

She smiled. He didn't like that smile. There was a nasty edge to it. "Oh," she said. "I still do. Easier to clean up that way."

He felt a chill. This was a woman with a grudge—one who had nursed that grudge, cherished it, and given it a name. "I can see you're doing well for yourself. It's been nice chatting, but I'm not here on a social call; work, you see."

She surprised him. He'd halfway expected some sort of dramatic scene. Instead, she sat back in her chair, and with a touch of a finger on the armrest, a large screen opened up on the formerly blank wall. "Let's see. Working for Home Services. Skip-tracing? Or would you call yourself a repo-man?" A copy of his contract and the image of the Pucca came up on the screen. "Really, Boggie, is that all you can do? I thought you had more ambition than that."

He shrugged the slight off. "A gig is a gig, darling."

"Ah. A 'gig,' like I was a 'gig'?" Her expression didn't change, but he could feel the acid in her voice. Still cool and collected in front of her underlings, though.

The Boggart stared at her hard. "You know what I meant. Don't make one thing about the other."

"You can't have your argument both ways, *darling*. Either I was just a gig, and easy to leave behind, or you are a lying rat bastard with the morals of a tomcat." Perfectly manicured nails tapped lightly on the polished surface of the desk. "In a way I have you to thank for my success. If you hadn't dumped me like yesterday's leftovers, I wouldn't be in this chair today. You taught me all about looking out for Number One, Boggie, *darling*."

"Thirty-some-odd years is a long time to hold a grudge, don't you think?" He bit his lip, then shook his head. "You want something, Claire, and it isn't revenge for what went on back in Cleveland. If you wanted me dead, you could've had me spaced and had a shiatsu massage by now."

"What's thirty years when you're immortal?" she countered. "But yes. You owe me, and I intend to collect. And I have your watch." One of the drones snatched it off the chair and handed it to her. She dropped it into a box, a small, but very heavy-looking box. She closed the lid. "Now," she continued, her voice taking on the hard and chill quality of a diamond. "This is how it is going to be. I—well, my Nest—own this station. Everything is all on the up-and-up so far as anyone is aware. But you know my kind. You know I have other deals going. Things that the Norms would rather not know about. There is a bad man, who wants me to pay him money not to tell the Norms. I wouldn't mind this, blackmail is factored into the balance sheets, but he's also demanding permanent docking and repair privileges. Sanctuary, so to speak. This is not a privateer station. I often have military, corporate, and Home Services' ships here. Granting him his request would make things very difficult for us. He knows all my thralls, all my drones, and everyone I might go to in order to make him go away. But he doesn't know about you." Her fingers tapped on the surface of the box. "You are going to make him go away, remove him permanently from the universe. If you do, you get the watch back and we are even. If you don't, the contents of this box will be vaporized. That means you cease to exist, as far as the universe is concerned, if you don't keep to the deal. Are we clear?"

This is getting worse by the minute, the Boggart cursed to himself. "Crystal, Claire. I suppose I'm taking my ship; I'll need my gear back, naturally." He looked at all of the weapons, still pointed directly at his head.

"I'm not an unreasonable woman, Boggie. Your gear is already on something better than that beast you came in. And I wouldn't want your leash holder to know you were taking a side job." Her lips curved into something that was a parody of her old smile; more predatory. "I'll even make arrangements for you so that you can report back to him as if you were working on his errand."

"And the man? Who is he? I ought to know who he is exactly if I'm going to be killing him, don't you think?"

"Captain of the vessel, an old Ojibwa. Nathan Runner is what he goes by. He's taken to piracy these last few decades, and recently traded up for a retrofitted science barge." She looked down her elegant nose at him. "I believe it used to be called the *UES Cenotaph.*" The little smirk on her face told him that she knew very well this was the ship he was looking for. "Now, be a good little Boggart and take care of this for me. Then you can go back to whatever mundane chore the HS is paying you a pittance for."

This "Runner" had to be something out of the ordinary. What, the Boggart couldn't even begin to guess, since his knowledge of most Native American customs was limited to what he'd picked up rather than any serious study. He had the gut feeling that Claire was screwing him over somehow … he just didn't know how yet. All he knew for certain was that if someone with as many obvious resources as Claire had was not able to come up with a solution for her problem, then things were going to get ugly for *him*. But what choice did he have?

"There's really only one answer you can give me, Boggie," she said, with chilly, false sweetness. "So you might as well say 'Yes, Claire, I'll take care of your problem' and get it over with."

The Boggart sighed. "Yes, Claire, I'll take care of your problem."

"Now was that so hard?" She picked up the box … and by the way she picked it up, the sucker was even heavier than it looked … and handed it to one of the thralls, who in turn took it to the Boggart. When he got it, he reckoned it probably weighed a good twenty pounds.

"Triple redundancy, *darling*. Tamper with it, and it vaporizes the watch. Wait too long, and it vaporizes the watch. Run too far with it, and it vaporizes the watch." She smirked and wiggled her fingers at him. Her nails were long, and painted steel gray to match her suit. "Ta-ta, Boggie. Come back soon."

One of the thralls made a little gesture with the barrel of his weapon. The Boggart took this as the sign that they were taking him elsewhere—maybe that transport she'd mentioned—and stood up, the box under his arm.

"You want to know something funny, Claire?" He turned toward the door and started to walk away. He looked over his shoulder slightly as he walked. "You were prettier when you were alive."

She stiffened, and for a moment looked exactly like one of those Uncanny Valley super-real 'bots that some high-end execs had as receptionists (and were rumored to have as "recreation" as well). Cold, moving, but no one would ever mistake her for something that was—or had been—living.

But she didn't retort, although he'd expected her to. She merely made a dismissive movement of one hand, and deliberately turned her attention to something on her desk.

The thralls ushered him out. *Guess I struck a nerve.*

He had to admit, once the thralls had closed the airlock door on him and his box, that Claire hadn't done him wrong in the way of transportation. This was a sweet little boat. Hell, for all he knew, it was her personal little runabout. Just as fast as the skiff, but far more expensive. And certainly safer to fly in. It was decked out in the same style as her office—sleek, modern, expensive. Luxurious. Things that looked hard—like the captain/pilot chair, which appeared to be molded from solid chromed steel—were often made of materials that would mold to you and cradle you like a warm hand. With massage, should you desire it.

In a way, that feature was just a little creepy.

As Claire had said, his equipment had been carefully stowed aboard; there wasn't much, granted, because the Boggart had always been a light traveler. Reflexively, he checked the revolver and its ammo. Everything was right there, minus the round he'd expended. Even the wooden bullets, which he found a little surprising, all things considered. With everything in order, he set the ship to leave the docking bay and start on a course toward the coordinates that Claire had provided him with. She knew the pirate captain's planned routes in this system, so it shouldn't have been too much of a hassle to find him. The only real question was how the Boggart was going to get aboard and kill the dumb bastard. This boat didn't have any offensive weaponry of any sort, and the pirate ship was more than likely retrofitted with all of the usual variety of things that make other ships stop working or go boom. Besides, he was fairly certain that the Pucca wouldn't appreciate it if he blew up the ship that he was contractually obligated to track down.

And neither he nor Claire would be happy if her pretty little runabout got trashed.

How do you best draw in a predator? With easy prey.

Ugly, but it would work. He just had to hope that no one on this privateer knew about Boggarts. *We're pretty rare … I just hope we're rare enough.*

It was a very expensive runabout, just off the usual flight paths, floating, apparently without power. There was a distress beacon calling, but weakly—so weakly that the broadcast probably wouldn't get past near-space. When the *Requisition* neared and tried to raise the crew, there was no answer.

"Whatdya think, boss?" asked the navigator.

"I think we've found a tasty morsel in need of our loving care." Captain Runner leaned forward on the console. "Circle around and get in close, and scan it again. I don't want any surprises."

Vids to the contrary, there was no way to scan for "life signs." What there was—you can scan for heat signatures, signs the engines are up, and sometimes hack into a ship's computers to find out what the state of things aboard her are. The crew of the *Requisition* were good at all of those things, and what they had to report was enough to gratify the heart of any privateer. Engines were cold. Ship was cold. And airless. Ship's computers reported a malfunction that had vented the air, which had probably killed the pilot and any passengers. Or if not—it was equally possible the pilot had ditched in a life-pod, expecting to get picked up and come back after her. That would be why he had left the distress beacon going. But out here, he'd die of dehydration, or his pod would run out of life-support power before he got picked up. Too bad, so sad, rich boy goes out roaming and discovers the universe is a bad place with very sharp teeth.

"Send out a man in a suit, and get what he can out of the cockpit and cabin, set up a tow line on it. Then we make tracks for the nearest space yard; Hollis has been giving us good coin for ship carcasses, lately." He licked his cracked lips greedily as he looked to the navigator. "If they find any bodies, have 'em bring that, too. My cabin."

"Aye, boss." The navigator was too used to the Captain by now to shudder, but the comm-and-systems man looked green—which was not his natural color. They were both new hires, picked up only a few stops ago, before they had taken this ship. They would get used to how the Captain ran things ... or they wouldn't, and might find themselves requested to "dine" with the Captain in his quarters. The Captain had a unique way of dealing with troublemakers. Like people who mistook him for a Reboot, which he most assuredly was not.

It was some time before the Boggart felt that his pocket watch was back in atmosphere. He waited what felt like several hours, just to be sure; wouldn't do to go corporeal in front of the entire crew as they divvied up the spoils from his borrowed ship, what little there were. When he felt it was safe, he eased himself into the here and now, and found himself, and the box with the watch, and the gun case with his revolver and ammo, all in what looked like a storage closet. There were other things on the shelves; he didn't pay a lot of attention to them.

The *Cenotaph* had been a big ship; it had to be, to hold all the Reboots, their food, the food for Fred, the fish tank for Fred, and the hydroponics for Fred. Then there was all the exploration and analysis equipment. The Boggart assumed all of that storage had been cleared out along with the E and A stuff—probably sold on the black market faster than you could blink. That would make for a lot of crew space. *Captain probably took the old captain's quarters, though, so that narrows it down. They built these boats to spec, mass-produced them back when deep-space exploration ramped up. If he's not there, though ... I'm screwed.* He opened the storage-closet door a crack, peering into the hallway beyond and listening. There was some shouting and jeering, but it was far off. *Gotta draw most of them away if I'm going to have a chance at this.*

The biggest storage area had been the food-storage hold—freeze-dried brains for the Reboots, and freezers for the Fur. Odds were, that had been turned into a cargo hold. He made his way through the corridors slowly, keeping low and stopping every few meters to perform a listening check. The Boggart stopped once more outside the hatch for where he had figured the cargo hold was; silence was the only thing that greeted him. He keyed the hatch, and stepped through the portal as it swung inwards. As it swung closed with a loud clank behind him, two crew members stepped out from behind a crate, both holding mugs of something foul smelling. They were both human, or near-human, and as surprised as the Boggart was.

Everyone stood stock still for several beats.

The Boggart spoke first. "So, a Fur, a Fang, and a Priest walk into a bar—"

The crewmen did a double take. That gave the Boggart all the time he needed. He rushed forward, staying on his toes as he charged them. The one on the left had the presence of mind to try to swing his mug at him, but the Boggart ducked under it and leveled his shoulder into the man's midsection. He gave a quiet *whuff* as he staggered backward, his air gone out of his lungs. The other one finally reacted, dropping his mug and slapping his hand to the holster on his hip. The Boggart placed his left hand over the pirate's, and squeezed, digging claws through leather glove and into flesh. The pirate screamed, and tried swinging a haymaker at the Boggart's head with his off hand. The Boggart easily leaned out of the way, the wind from the pirate's punch brushing his face. His fist was a lot more accurate than his assailant's, crashing into the side of the man's jaw. The Boggart didn't waste a moment; he slammed the crown of his head forward sharply, shattering the nose of the man he was holding. The pirate reeled back, blood leaking through his fingers as he clutched a hand to his face. The Boggart, almost as gently as a concerned brother, pulled the man's hand back and then proceeded to jab him three more times with his right fist. The man's eyes rolled back in his head, and he fell to the floor in a messy heap.

The Boggart turned to the other pirate, who was just now starting to recover from his blows. "Sure you don't want to lay down, me ducky?" The pirate shook his head to clear it, then glanced at the mug still in his hand, throwing it away angrily.

The Boggart shook his head. "You're gonna die, an' badly. The Captain'll have you, once I'm done, and I expect he's not a gentle sort of leader."

The pirate led with a strong right hook, but the Boggart blocked it with his arm, and slapped him hard enough to send a trickle of blood from his lip in response. Another punch came sailing for his face, and the Boggart pushed it aside, sending the pirate off balance. He grabbed and twisted the man's arm, bending the hand at the wrist until he was certain it was near the breaking point; the Boggart forced him to his knees, pressing his arm up. The pirate looked up with pain creasing his brow.

"Raise your chin a little." The pirate was breathing raggedly, and did so. The Boggart reared back with his free hand, and brought it down savagely, square on the point of the pirate's jaw. He slumped to the deck, out cold.

The Boggart released him as he fell, then reflexively dusted off his hands, grimacing. Well, that was a complication he hadn't needed. He dragged both of the limp bodies toward a storage container.

Best not to leave these two where their pals can find them easily.

He made sure they were both bound and gagged properly before he closed the container's doors.

Time for the next bit of this moronic plan.

He gathered up as many boxes as he could, nothing too large or anything that he needed to drag. After that, he dumped out all of their contents in a pile, sorted out what would burn, and with an unhappy grimace, poured most of the contents of his flask over them.

The Boggart didn't use a lot of magic, but he had a few, small tricks up his sleeve. He stared at the pile, then snapped his fingers.

It went up in a *whoosh* of blue flame and whiskey-smell.

Poor waste of good whiskey. Right-oh. Part three. And if I'm lucky, the Captain has better booze than I did.

It had been hard going getting to the Captain's cabin, but the Boggart had finally made it there. Most of the crew was busy running down to the cargo hold where his little fire was burning merrily, which left him a fairly clear path to his destination. Ancient ship or spaceship, the one thing no sailor takes lightly is a fire.

He'd had a few close calls, but had managed to avoid any further violence. The Boggart didn't waste time when he was faced with the door to the Captain's quarters. He knocked brusquely, and was greeted with a rough shout of "Enter! And ya'd better have word that fire's out. Otherwise, I might'n just figure that I'm hungry."

The Boggart had donned the face of one of the crewmen he'd knocked out; his dirty jumpsuit could have passed as the standard garb for any pirate or dockworker in dozens of systems.

"Fire's been contained, Captain. We've got men in the hold assessing the damage, just came from there myself."

It took all his control not to show his reaction to the full sight of Captain Runner.

He'd half-expected a lot of things.

This wasn't one of them.

The Captain looked like a Reboot—sort of—but obviously wasn't the usual Zombie. He stood about eight feet tall, and was skeletally thin, emaciated; his dark skin was patchy, his face cadaverous, his eyes an unholy scarlet. Literally unholy—the Boggart could sense the demonic energy in him, something ancient and evil coiling in on itself behind those eyes. His black, unkempt hair was pulled back in a rough braid. There were raw, oozing places on him … not exactly sores, more like places where the skin had stretched too far and torn and now was … sort of … healing. His lips, like a Reboot's, had pulled back from his teeth, giving him a permanent skull-like "grin." To make things even more macabre, he wore what looked like a fancy blue uniform. And not just any uniform. An ancient US Cavalry uniform from centuries ago, in design at least; it even had the faded golden crossed sabers.

There was no way a real uniform would have survived this long. Would it? And why was he wearing it in the first place?

The jacket hung open to show his chest … which was not a pretty sight.

What in the name of all things dark and pointy is this bastard?

The Captain grinned at him, pausing for a few moments before he spoke. "Good, good. So, *Renly*, would you grace your Captain a further moment of your time? I haven't supped with any of the crew in a long while. I fancy a bit of company."

The Captain recognized the crewman's face that he was wearing, and by name at that. *Not good. Going to have to bullshit this as much as possible.*

The Boggart paused, uncertain for a scant moment, then replied. "Certainly, Captain." Well, what else could he do?

He stepped farther into the cabin, closing the door and quietly setting the lock on it behind him.

Runner was sitting at a desk that was as big as any man could expect, but the pirate captain dwarfed it with his size.

Nice of Claire to conveniently forget to mention that this guy is a fucking Monster. If the Boggart got off of this ship alive, he swore that he was going to do something to repay Claire for her kindness.

"So Renly … as y'know, I'm a big man, hard to move in this cabin. What say ya get down some of that whiskey for the two of us." The Captain nodded to some place behind the Boggart; he half turned and saw a well-stocked series of bar shelves built into the wall. He walked over hesitantly, searching for a moment before finding the bottle the Captain had referred to; he held it up for inspection. "That's the one; fetch down the glasses too."

There were only two shot glasses. One was twice the size of the other. Pretty obvious which one was the Captain's. The Boggart brought them both to the desk, put them down, and without being asked, poured.

The thing reached over the desk—giving the Boggart a good idea of its reach—and took the bigger glass. He tossed the contents down, and cocked one of those devilish eyes at the Boggart. The Boggart drained his small glass, never taking his eyes off of the Captain.

Something is off.

"Siddown, Renly." He did so. " Have another." The pirate leader poured them both stiff glasses of the whiskey; the Boggart had far better than this blended swill, but he couldn't rightly refuse while playing the part of the obedient crewman. "So, Renly, how long have ya been with this crew?"

Oh shit.

"Long enough, Cap'n. If it pleases you, I need to get back to my duties." *Run now, regroup, do anything but stay here.* His gut turned to water, and a feeling of dread was growing with each passing second. He'd survived as long as he had in his profession by trusting his instincts, and they were all screaming at him now to save his hide.

"Yer duties are what I say they are, Renly. An' I say they're t' sit right here an have another drink." The Captain didn't seem angry ... more ... amused.

Which in the Boggart's estimation was not a good sign.

" 'Course, we both know you ain't Renly. Ya might be wearin' his face, but you ain't Renly." The red eyes bored into his. "So now, I got two questions. The first one bein', did ya kill him? If so, I hope ya stashed the body. When I'm done with *you*, I'll want some dessert. And the second bein', what are ya, an how do ya taste with steak sauce, stranger?"

Runner stood up faster than the Boggart thought he could for his size, and *flipped* the desk like it was made of balsa wood instead of steel and heavy composite. The Boggart fell sideways in his chair to avoid it; he felt the crash as it slammed into the door. He rolled, narrowly avoiding the Captain's following stomp, and then sprang to his feet. He dropped the mask of Renly, opting to concentrate on keeping his skin attached to his bones instead of holding up the useless guise.

"Well, yer lively enough," the Captain taunted. "Why don't ya try the door?" The way was blocked by the desk leaning at a crazy angle in front of it, not to mention that he'd locked it himself on the way in. He'd meant to keep out anyone that would interfere with the bloody work he had come to do, not to trap himself.

All the fires of all the hells on Claire.

The Captain lunged then, his big ropey arms trying to grasp the Boggart. He ducked under and rushed forward, trying to get past the pirate. Runner was quicker than he thought, however; the giant monster spun, catching the Boggart between the shoulder blades with a huge elbow. He crashed into the liquor cabinet's doors, shattering bottles and glasses.

"I like to tenderize my meat a little, y'see." He barked a short laugh. "An' marinate it in booze."

The Boggart came up with a shard from a bottle, slashing in quick arcs at the Captain. The glass bit into his fingers and hand, but he ignored the pain. The Captain chuckled and took a bold step forward; the Boggart met him, slicing the pirate open from midsection to his sternum before stabbing his side a half dozen times.

The Captain roared with laughter. "Is that all ya got? Yer a piss-poor excuse fer an assassin, much less a Para." Almost carelessly, Runner backhanded the Boggart, causing him to fly hard into the far corner and force stars into his vision.

But damn *he's strong.* He shook his head to clear his vision, and came up in a crouch, the glass shiv still in his hand. The Boggart feinted left, then right before rolling between the Captain's legs. He sprang to his feet again, wrapping his left arm around the pirate's waist as he stabbed the upper side of his foe's rib cage with his right hand. No blood came from the wound, only a foul-smelling ooze that filled the room with its stench of corruption.

The Captain plucked the Boggart easily from his side before flinging him into the air again. This time the Boggart didn't land nearly as well. Something popped in his left shoulder, and the world exploded in a wash of pain. It was everything that he could do to prop himself up on his good arm, glass shiv still in hand.

Need to stay conscious. If I black out, I'm done. He fought back the blackness, and won … though not by much.

The Captain stalked closer casually, stooped over in a room too small to fit his frame. As he reached down, the Boggart slashed up again desperately, separating the flesh from the ribs under the Captain's left arm. The skin was laid open in a flap, exposing bone and shriveled organs beneath.

"Ya've got some fight in ya, I'll say that. Yer makin' this pretty entertaining. And that's sayin' somethin'. I'm gonna enjoy eatin' ya, that's fer sure." He leaned in, grinning wide to show his terrible jagged yellow teeth, blood seeping through his gums. "Yer better than them pissants I got fer a crew. Bad for morale to eat them too often or without cause, anyways. Yer gonna make me strong. But how about we dance a little more first? I like t' work up an appetite." He picked up the Boggart by the scruff of his neck, lifting him off of the floor as easily as if he was a rag doll.

The Boggart slashed at the Captain's wrist, splitting tendons and cartilage from bone. The pirate's grip never wavered or weakened.

I'm gonna make him strong? He's going to goddamn eat *me?* The Boggart punished his memory, trying to beat something out of it. His head was pounding, and he could see his vision going dark around the edges as blood leaked between his pointed teeth. This all sounded vaguely familiar, but what—

"What in hell are you?" he gasped, not really believing that the monster would give itself away. What could he lose in the asking, though? It bought him a moment to breathe, if nothing else.

The Captain roared with laughter. "Vamp bitch didn't tell ya? Ya never fought a Wendigo before? Well, first an' last time, then."

It all clicked at once for the Boggart. He knew what he had to do; he only hoped he'd live long enough to pull it off. The Captain slammed him against the wall, then threw him once more, this time at the rear of the cabin. The Boggart hit the wall and slid down, holding onto consciousness as hard as he could. The Captain loped toward him again, picking up the Boggart by the throat, leaving him scarcely enough room in his grip to breathe.

His massive fingers wrapped fully around the Boggart's neck. "I've enjoyed this, assassin, but all games come to an end."

In response, the Boggart flipped the glass shiv in his hand, then swung his fist down and hard into the Wendigo's left eye. The pirate simply laughed, gripping the Boggart's fist in his own hand of iron; then he slowly *pulled* the shiv out, before tightening his fist and crushing the glass in the Boggart's hand. The eye—unlike the rest of him—was intact. Still like a glowing coal in the socket.

"I take it the Fang bitch sent you personal, insteada gettin' 'nother of her flunkies?" the Captain asked, casually. "Had t' space the first dozen boy-toys she sent after me. Fang infection spoils t' meat, sours it. Not very good eatin.'" He laughed. "I reckon this is her best, last shot. Yer not bad. Not *good*, but not bad." He let go of the Boggart's right hand, still grinning. "So, take *your* best, last shot, assassin. I'm hungry." No fear there; clearly he didn't think there was anything the Boggart could do to change the outcome.

"Alright." In a single deft motion, the Boggart unholstered his revolver and shoved it into the wound he had caused on the pirate's left flank. For a frantic half-second he wiggled the barrel around until he found what he was looking for. *The heart!* Looking into the Captain's eyes, he pulled the trigger.

A muted *whumph* was the only sound the heavy pistol made as the solid-silver bullet and all of the expanding gases from the shot vaporized the pirate captain's heart and other nearby organs.

Runner's eyes went wide, and for a moment his grip tightened around the Boggart's throat, threatening to squeeze the life out of him.

Just as quickly as it had come the strength fled from the grip, depositing the Boggart onto the deck in a heap.

Then the Captain toppled over like a dead tree. He hit the deck with a heavy *thud*, and did not move, the hell-light gone from his eyes, which were now only empty, dark sockets.

The Boggart could only lie there, panting, waiting for his wounds to heal. This had been sheer luck; he'd kept the revolver loaded with what was left of his silver bullets, figuring that since this Captain was putting pressure on Fangs, he had to be a Fur—especially since most privateer crews were Furs. A pirate made as much sense, though; plenty of loot and bodies to feast on. This was the first time he had ever seen one; he hoped it would be the last. At least his own curiosity and the nature of his job had made him research every Para there had ever been reported since the time of the Zombie Uprising. Otherwise ... he'd have been dead.

Of course, he could have gone ethereal as soon as the Wendigo tried to eat him, but he would still have been stuck on the ship with no way off while the Captain and crew were actively looking for him.

Which meant eventually the timer on that box would run out.

And then he *would* have been dead. And he'd have been spending every one of those last minutes either in the Nowhere-Space agonizing about it, or popping in and out, trying to figure a way out.

The Boggart opened the cylinder on his revolver, counting the remaining rounds. *Four left. Should be enough for this job, barring any more ... complications.* He flicked his wrist, closing the cylinder with a loud snap. His head was swimming, and his left arm was still refusing to work—probably dislocated at the shoulder. He needed a little bit of rest, at least. It was going to be a stone bitch putting that shoulder back in.

He couldn't stick around here, either. Eventually someone would come calling on the Captain—the *late* Captain, he reminded himself—and would find the grisly results of the melee.

Besides, the Boggart still had more work to do before he could leave.

He took a deep, pain-filled breath, and went ethereal, jaunting to his watch, back in the hold.

It was a shock going from feeling "blissful nothing" back into "agonizing pain" again. He nearly blacked out. This must have been the worst fight he'd had in ... well, a long time. He put his back against the wall and slid down it, then, gritting his teeth, grabbed his "bad" wrist with his good hand, and pulled, and rotated slowly, until the shoulder snapped back into place with an audible *pop*, and a stab of agony that put spots in front of his eyes. He could have used more whiskey ... and a rare steak ... and a bed. Maybe a nice woman to massage him while he healed ... yeah, that'd be the ticket.

Too bad what he got was a storage closet that still smelled of smoke from the air recyclers, and a cold bulkhead. Life sucked. But it beat the alternative. Like being the blue-plate special for a Wendigo or dying in a puff of vapor. He did his best to patch himself up, cleaning up the cuts and draining the very last dregs from his flask to dull down the pain. It didn't work nearly as well as he had hoped.

He'd have to find an EVA suit to get over to the runabout. Once he was in there, he could first call the Pucca and give the bastard the coordinates of what used to be the *Cenotaph*. Then he could call Claire. Then he'd drink the runabout's bar dry. First, however, he still had a little bit more of the ol' skullduggery to perform.

He looked up at the shelf that held the watch-box and something occurred to him. There just might be some loot in the closet that would be small enough for him to pocket. By damn, he deserved it, and why should Home Services get it?

He dragged himself to his feet and looked over the shelves, pocketing a few things that looked expensive, high-tech, or both. It was a little hard to figure out what might be good; Paras, except for maybe the Fangs, weren't particularly good with tech. The Boggart had kept current with the advances of late, but like others of his kind was still slow compared to Norms. That Fur he was after, Fred, had been a rarity; he had taken to tech and engineering like a fish to water. Maybe because he'd been an engineer before he was Turned. The Boggart was a far more ancient thing, all told.

While he searched, he became aware that things outside this closet were getting … noisy. Very. Alarms went off—that would be when the Captain's body was discovered, he reckoned—but shortly after that, the noises got more chaotic. The whine of energy-weapons, the sound of old-fashioned gunshots, screams, yelling … it appeared that the only thing holding the crew together had been fear of the Captain. With that gone, it was chaos.

Which was good and bad. Good, because no one would be looking specifically for him. Bad, because anyone he met was going to assume he was someone to kill.

Well, he'd just have to be sneak—

The door to his closet opened. Before he could react, a Reboot darted in, and slammed and locked the door behind himself. The Boggart turned around slowly. The Reboot had its hands placed against the door, as if to hold it against whatever fighting was raging outside. "Man, this is a *bad* scene. Vibes all wrong, everything gone to hell …."

The Reboot turned around, and only then did it notice the Boggart. "Oh."

Before the Reboot could react, the Boggart had his right hand around its throat, his left going to its mouth; a good twist, and he figured that its decayed head would come off. The Reboot's eyes grew wide in their sockets, and it held its hands up slowly.

The Boggart took a moment, nothing but shared silence in the closet. Carefully, he let his left hand move away from the Reboot's mouth. "You're a Zombie."

"No shit? Hadn't noticed." The Reboot checked himself. "Dude …." the Reboot said weakly. "Dude, don't, like … do anything rash. Okay?"

For a moment, the Boggart wondered if he'd hit his head a little too hard. "How can you talk? Are you part of the crew?"

"Dude, I dunno how I can talk. One day I was catchin' waves and partaking of some killer Maui Wowie, the next thing I know, I'm a walking stiff." The Reboot flailed a hand. "I *told* Fred we shouldn't head for any place with people in it, but noooooo, he just had to go to the nearest station, and we get there, and it's *ass deep* in Fangs, man!"

The Boggart slapped the Reboot hard, and ignored that some flakes of skin came off. "Hey, slow down. Get your head straight. Who are you? And how do you know Fred?"

"Fred?" Belatedly the Reboot seemed to realize he'd spilled a name. "Fred who, man?"

The Boggart held up a single claw in front of the Reboot's face, cocking an eyebrow.

The Reboot folded. "Dude, don't, dude, I dunno who you are but … look, we were on this ship, see? *This* ship, actually, before it went to hell. And we spaced the Fangs, cause they were, like total douches. Breaking Reboots, only a matter of time before they got us, and Fred was sick of it, too. Y'know, being lunch and taking their shit. And we found a sweet spot to park, and then the stupid ship sent up some dingus or other and called for help and Fred, Fred, he was the engineer, he said we had to get ourselves lost someplace where there were lots of people and I said no, but he wouldn't listen, man, and we headed for the nearest big station and it was full, I mean *packed* with Fangs, and Fred got off to look around and by then I'd figured out how to fly this thing and I took off and then these guys found the ship so I played like a dumb Reboot and they took it to a refit yard and that's all I know man!" All the information spilled past his tattered lips in a rush, and the Boggart absorbed it all. It included the interesting fact that as far as he knew, the renegade Fur was still back on "the station."

"And that would be what station, exactly?" the Boggart asked, in a little growl.

The Reboot could not have been happier to babble on. "The one with all the Fangs, run by the Fang bitch, dude, Fred was figuring he'd head for the nearest Fur station an' try an' hide, or Norms, but there ain't a lot of Norms out here in this corner of space, but he figured a Norm station was better 'cause no Norm would ever be able to sniff him out, he was gonna sell the ship for scrap an' use that t' run off, an I figured he'd just ditch me, cause man, who cares about a dumb Reboot, so that was why I took the ship an' booked, an' the Captain, he picked up the ship not long after I left the station, I figured I had more chance hiding with the other Reboots so I hid for a while."

If the Reboot had had working lungs, he would have run out of breath before that sentence was over. Everything started falling into place for the Boggart, though. This Reboot, the beach planet, the pirates, the whole shebang. The Reboot had outlined it very nicely. He couldn't help but smile. "That's good, much better. You still haven't told me your name." His outstretched claw twitched once, just a little closer to the Reboot's eye.

"Pete," squeaked the Reboot.

"Well Pete. This is what you are going to do. If you enjoy keeping your brains inside your skull, you're going to show me where the engine room is. From there, we're gonna get a nice EVA kit. And then you are going to come back here to this closet and you are going to lock yourself in. And you are not going to move for at least a couple of days; probably safer for your wrinkled hide with all the fighting outside, anyways. Savvy?"

"Yes," the Reboot squeaked. "Sir."

"All right then." The Boggart let go of the Reboot, smiling. "After you."

Did Reboots tremble with fear? Could they? The Zombie seemed steady enough to the Boggart as he shambled along the corridors. The Boggart was not entirely sure that he trusted this thing; after all, a Zombie that could talk was a Zombie that could lie. Everyone remembered what the last famous "talking Zombie" was capable of. And there wasn't much left of him to take body-language readings from. He kept his hand on his revolver and his eyes trained on the Reboot. They could still clearly hear the fighting, no matter how far they ventured into the ship. From what the Boggart remembered of older ship layouts, they should be heading in the right direction.

"Any of the other crew know that you're smarter than the average bear?" He grinned, pushing the Reboot ahead of him.

"Uh, what?" The Reboot stopped and turned to stare at him. "What's that mean, dude?"

He knows what it means, and he's going to lie, the Boggart decided. But he figured he'd give it a try anyway.

"Any of the crew know you can think? And talk?" he said, with exaggerated patience.

"Dude! Why would I, like—*gurk!*" The last came as the Boggart closed his unwounded hand tight around the Reboot's throat.

"Don't lie," he said, gently. "I've got centuries worth of figuring out how to tell when people lie. And, if you couldn't tell, I'm not in the best of moods right now. Also, I know exactly how to take you Reboots apart and scatter the pieces so you can never get back together again. So if you don't want to spend the rest of however long with your head crammed in a wallspace staring at nothing, don't lie." He released a little tension from his grip, just enough for the Reboot to speak.

"Yes," squeaked the Reboot. "I figgered, the Captain being … they'd take anything." He looked sullenly at the floor. "I think he might have been planning on selling me, down the road, anyways."

"See how easy that was?" the Boggart said, releasing him. "Now I know. And now you know I know. So you know not to try anything really, truly stupid, like leading me into an ambush. Right?" Pete nodded vigorously. The Boggart gave him another shove, and the Reboot started to shuffle forward. "And make sure you don't lead me in circles hoping we'll run into someone. I am pretty good at finding my way around a ship."

95

The Reboot's meanderings became a bit more direct after that, with the only obvious detours being to avoid obvious hot spots (as evidenced by the increased volume in fighting sounds—weapons firing, screaming, crashing, and the moans of the dying, usually). Finally he stopped at a closed door.

"This is the new engine room." The Boggart gave him a look. "I mean, dude, it's like the old engine room but there's new engines in it. FTL stuff, now, instead of the 'slug drives,' like the Captain called them, man. He made me go in there a lot … uh, there's lotsa rads. I guess they weren't too careful with the refit."

Peachy. "Then you'll know your way around." He gestured. "After you."

If the Reboot had been hoping the information would keep the Boggart out, well … too bad. Because it wouldn't. Fey didn't give a crap about rads. The only problem was, they might trigger the box holding the watch, and he didn't want his revolver and clothing to suddenly start triggering rad alarms elsewhere. The Boggart stripped out of his jumpsuit, piling it in a corner outside of the hatch to the engine room, with his revolver and the box with the watch safely buried under it. He could get to it quickly enough, if need be, and it was unlikely anyone was going to bother looking under a dirty, torn, bloody jumpsuit during all the fighting.

The Reboot averted his eyes, and fumbled with the access lock. To the Boggart's eyes, it didn't look like stalling, it looked like Reboot clumsiness. The outer door slid open, revealing a small safety chamber, adequate for two. "When we get in there, show me where *this* will do the most damage." The Reboot saw what the Boggart was holding, and his eyes went wide. "Just to disable the engines; don't want to send you to the dark below in a radioactive puff, Zombie, have no fear." He imagined that Pete was having a very hard time not fearing, right now. "Think about it. I can't have you morons chasing me once I get to my boat. Right?"

"Uh. Right dude. Whatever you say." Pete did as he was told, looking over his shoulder at the Boggart every few seconds to make sure that the Para hadn't changed his mind and decided to blow them both to Hell right there and then.

Let him think I'm crazy; makes it easier to get this done faster.

Once it was done they crammed into the safety chamber, Pete closed the inner hatch, then opened the outer one into the corridor. The Boggart dressed and gathered his belongings, checking the cylinder of the Webley out of habit. Still four bullets. And the watchbox seemed unchanged. "Now all I need is an EVA suit, one with full air and propulsion cylinders, and yes, I can tell. You bring me to that, and you and I can part company, Pete."

"EVA suits are at the airlock, dude, you can take your pick." Pete's gait now was a lot faster, it seemed he couldn't be rid of the Boggart quickly enough. *And just when we were beginning to become such fast friends.* Which suited the Boggart just fine.

After a few more twists, turns, and a couple of tense moments when they had to hide and let a running battle pass them, the Boggart and Pete had reached the airlock. The Boggart checked all of the equipment that Pete selected for him; the suit's integrity was in the green, the propulsion system read as being okay if a little on the weak side, and the air canisters were topped off. When the Boggart was ready, with his revolver hidden away and the box tucked under his arm, he flipped down his visor and closed the inner airlock door. Pete watched from the other side, still looking nervous; well, as nervous as a Reboot could manage to look.

"Get out of here, Pete. Run and hide; it'll probably give you the best chance of surviving." Without another word, the Boggart saluted and then cycled the airlock to depressurize. Pete wasted no time, turning and bolting as fast as his rotted limbs could carry him.

Once the outer airlock doors were open, the Boggart activated his mag boots and made his way toward the aft of the ship. After that it was a simple matter to use the propulsion unit that the EVA came with to get back to the ship's own airlock, which the pirates had conveniently left without any sort of security on it. No added security lock, no change to the entry pad, no nothing. *Morons.* Then again, with what appeared to be a crew fathered by the Three Stooges from Hell, maybe the Captain had figured they'd screw up any sort of security that was put on it, and lock them all out of their prize. As soon as the main cabin was back up to full atmo, he popped off his suit helmet and settled down at the controls. With a few tapped commands, his own engines thrummed back to life; a little thrust, and the tether between his ship and the pirate vessel snapped. Someone must have been at the helm of the former *Cenotaph*, because it quickly swung around to see what had happened to their captured prey. That's when the Boggart flipped the safety off of the detonator, and mashed his thumb on the activation stud.

It was a little anticlimactic; the pirate ship shuddered, and kept drifting in the same direction it had been taking before he killed the engines. Which basically meant it was now rotating, slowly, in about the same space. Good thing they hadn't actually been traveling anywhere; from what he heard, an abrupt translation from FTL to sublight could be pretty rough for passengers. As in, "crew becomes wet paste against the wall" sort of rough.

The Boggart set his course on the autopilot before leaning back in his chair. He was in dire need of a drink, and there was an entire minibar to raid. But, first, the grim necessities of his profession. "Time to call this in to the Pucca."

"You did *what?*" The Pucca was agape on the vidlink. The Boggart was making sure he took a few screencaps of this conversation; he'd want to revisit the look on the Pucca's face often.

"Tracked down the ship," the Boggart repeated. "She'd been refitted for a privateer. Had a little talk with the Captain, who wouldn't see reason, so I eliminated him and shut down the drives. Explosively, I'm afraid, but she'll still be worth what the original was."

"No no no, *no.*" The Pucca shook his head viciously. "I meant about the goddamned *bomb!*"

"Quit getting your panties in a wad. The old drives were worthless, and you know it. So what if I took out the new ones? You still have a ship with most of the retrofit done for you. It was the hull that was valuable." The Boggart snorted.

"Gods, the bosses are going to have my freakin' head for this. Maybe my job, too." He buried his face in his hands, disconsolate. "This was supposed to be simple, nice and quiet, *easy* even. Hell, I didn't half-expect that you'd find it, really; just have you quit after awhile and write it off, nice and tidy without me ever having to leave my desk."

"Whatever. We still have a contract. You remember, the one you made sure we had down in triplicate?" *No weaseling out of paying me, you bastard. Whatever scam you were hoping to run probably just got shot to shit, too.* "Dunno why they'd be pissed off about it. They got the ship with a three-fourths retrofit, they got a buncha privateers they can either hang themselves or turn over for bounty, all's well that ends well. Don't BS me about my fee being more than even a bare hull, bucko, I know what this shit's worth down to the last rivet." The last part was a bit of a stretch, but it sounded good.

The Pucca threw up his hands in exasperation. "Fine, fine. Christ, you really screwed me on this. Just find that goddamn Fur and finish this rotten mess."

"Have it your way. Out." The Boggart cut the connection, then called Claire.

Or rather, got her secretary. Looked like a thrall, and like most of Claire's boys, pretty, but competent. He'd have to give Claire this much; it didn't look as if she kept anyone useless around. *Maybe she got rid all of the useless ones by sending them up against Runner. If nothing else, she's an efficient bitch.*

"Tell *your* boss her little problem is taken care of, and I'm on my way back. This time, I don't want a room full of guns in my face when I arrive. Got it?"

"We will need independent verification of that, Boggart," said the pretty boy, looking down his nose, as if the Boggart was something green he'd found in the bottom of a coffee cup left in the sink.

"Just check Home Services' outgoing tugs. They're going to retrieve what's left of the *Cenotaph* any second now." The Boggart didn't really care what the pretty boy thought, but he gave the thrall a grin that showed all of his teeth. *All* of them. Even if the flunky didn't believe him, he knew Claire would; if there was one thing about the Boggart, it was that he kept his promises. That would probably get him killed one day. On the other hand, it kept his enemies wary. Part of the reason why he even got this lousy gig was because it was fairly well known that "*The Boggart always delivers.*"

"I'll be doing that," said the thrall, and looked away; the Boggart saw the young man shiver at the sight of his teeth. "You'll have docking bay 27. Try not to damage anything coming in." He cut the connection a picosecond before the Boggart could, getting in one last little snub.

"Little self-important prick," the Boggart muttered, and put the ship on auto so he could make some serious inroads on the stocked bar. He needed it, he deserved it and by all the dark below, he had earned it. He had time to kill, and wanted to at least look a little bit better by the time he got to the station. The booze and sleep would both help with that. Nothing he could do about his wardrobe though. He was going to invoice Home Services for a new coat at least; "expenses" covered a wide range of things when you were on the HS dime, and they had plenty of coin to spare. Good thing for him that most of the Fey healed fast.

One bottle of very good single malt, one bottle of reasonable blended, and one bottle of bourbon later, followed by a good long nap and a sonic shower ... and the Boggart was feeling a good deal better. At least well enough to make himself a triple martini to pass the time while the boat docked itself. Letting a ship autodock was always a time-wasting proposition, because the stupid boats would make as many corrections as a fussy maiden aunt on her first driving test. If there was one thing that engineers took to heart, it was safety, followed very closely by redundancy; in these plea-sure yachts, there were safeties aplenty to keep rich morons from becoming dead rich morons. Too bad, in the Boggart's opinion, though he supposed someone had to pay the bills. There was a lot of money in finding the lost heirs of rich morons. Or *not* finding them, depending on who was hiring. It was a deep, dark galaxy, and credits to be had on both sides of things.

Much sooner than he would have liked, but at least after he had finished his martini and started on a second, the ship had finished all of the tedious autodocking procedures, and was finally at rest on Claire's station. The Boggart strolled out of the docking bay still carrying his martini in one hand, the box in the other, and in all his slashed, bloodstained, and torn-up glory.

Most days he preferred to look anonymous, and not make an entrance.

Today was not that day.

He was wearing his own face. All of the docking-bay personnel looked at him like he had grown a horn in the middle of his forehead. Then they moved carefully aside.

He grinned at them—helped to remind people that Boggarts had *teeth* as well as claws—and sauntered in the direction of Claire's office. He figured sooner or later he'd get an escort. She couldn't allow him to wander all over the station on his own after all. He might frighten the tourists; probably another reason why she had stuck him at the very end row of the docking bays. When the bodyguards came, they tried their best to slip in silently behind him and beside him, but the Boggart knew all the right tricks and had spotted them the moment he entered the concourse.

He toasted them. "Evening, gents. Take me to your leader."

They all looked to each other, uncertain what to make of the Boggart, but kept walking, guiding him. These weren't thralls; probably hired guns. *Needed some extra muscle after you fed the stupid and weak—or perhaps inconvenient—to Runner, Claire?*

To their credit, these guys were neither stupid, nor weak. The rest of them gave a quick glance at one of their number, a man with a close-cropped goatee. *That'd be their "occifer," pardon me, "officer."* He gave an abrupt nod and fell in next to the Boggart; the others formed up behind.

"If you'll come with me, Mr. Boggart." There was no question there; it was a statement. The Boggart nodded back, and ambled along beside him.

There was no particular reason for a station to be cylindrical or circular anymore, not with artificial grav having become more widespread in recent years. As a consequence, stations had retrofitted and spread out like fat spiders in a web. Claire's station was no exception. It would have been a long, long walk to the hub, but the tourists would have complained. At the end of the first leg was a transport system; the goons waved him into a car, which he shared with the head goon and four others. The rest took another car. He finished his martini and handed the empty glass to the head goon, who looked nonplussed at finding himself holding the empty glass. The head goon then handed it back to one of the others. The Boggart snickered to himself, the booze still affecting him some. *What's the point if I can't mess with them at least a little bit?*

The car stopped at what was obviously the administration floor of the hub. The Boggart got out, followed by his escort.

It was pretty obvious where he should go now: the imposing double doors of incised silver metal at the end of the corridor he was looking down. He marched straight for them. He'd have *liked* to straight-arm them both open just for effect, but they opened before he got there.

And there was Claire at her desk as if she'd never left it. "Hi, honey," he said, tossing the box so it landed on the desk with a crash, sending smartpads and desktop trinkets flying. "I'm home."

"So I see," she said dryly. The doors closed behind him, leaving the hired guns in the hall. Evidently they weren't good enough to step on the carpet in the office.

He was likely a sight—his jumpsuit, bloody and torn in a dozen places, had the top half-wrapped around his waist. The cuts and bruises he'd suffered weren't completely gone yet, though they didn't show up as much against his charcoal-black skin. Still, he looked battered, and had wanted her to see how much that wasn't stopping him.

"I assume you want me to open the box now? Darling?" she asked. As if that was an option.

"I did what was asked," he spat. "Though you conveniently left out a few key facts. Like it was a goddamn Wendigo I was supposed to kill." He gestured at himself. "He didn't go easily, as you can imagine. He probably made chopped liver out of your own guys. So yes, I want you to open the box and give me back my goddamned pocket watch." He looked down at her, his dark eyes glinting. "Don't make this difficult."

"Oh. Really." Her fingertip made little circles on the top of the box. "After you've proved so very useful? I'm sure I can think of some other things for you to do."

"Don't play, Claire. A deal's a deal, and you know what they say 'bout me."

She said nothing. She only nodded to the four guards in the room with her. One reached for his shoulder, but the Boggart knew that it was coming. He grabbed the thrall's wrist, wrenched it, and then put all of his strength in sending the man forward over his shoulder. The Boggart didn't wait to see what happened to that man; the next one was already upon him, from his left. For that one, he kicked the man's knee, hyperextending it; the thrall screamed shrilly, but the wail was quickly cut off by three quick jabs and an uppercut from the Boggart. The man's teeth clicked loudly as he tumbled backward.

There were still two thralls left standing, however. They were far more wary; they spaced themselves out, trying to flank the Boggart from the front and back. The one in front of him was a broad-shouldered bull of a man with a pug face. His eyes were what betrayed him, though; the Boggart saw them widen suddenly, a scant breath before the thrall lunged forward.

The Boggart fell to his left side, catching himself with his hands and leaving his right leg thrust out. The large man was already committed in his charge, and tripped across the Boggart's out-thrust leg. He went sprawling face-first into the man that had been behind the Boggart; they collided in a messy pile, cursing.

The Boggart recovered first, and began kicking both men as hard as he could, aiming for their kidneys and bellies. Suddenly, arms had wrapped around his chest and arms—the first guard that he had thrown. He was dragged backward, away from the two guards on the ground in front of him.

Alright, fella. We'll just take a little bit longer, is all. He sunk his claws into the forearms of the man that had grasped him, eliciting a scream from his captor. Lifting one arm up to his face, the Boggart took a bite out of it, wrenching his head to the side suddenly. He felt blood dripping down his chin.

One of the guards on the ground had disentangled himself, and came running for the Boggart with an upraised fist.

He was handicapped. He didn't actually want to kill any of these fools. It wasn't *their* fault they had fallen for that treacherous bitch, and been dumb enough to submit themselves as thralls to her blood. It didn't mean he was going to cut them too much slack, but he understood the *why* of it all, at least. This was how the Fangs worked. It was instinct for them to gather thralls, it was instinct for them to use their amped-up sex appeal to do so, and when testosterone and Fang pheromones hit the human male, the brains went right out the window. But he was too tired and too beat up to give too much of a shit for whose fault it was. He was pissed off, and would *not* tolerate this nonsense. Even from Claire. *Keep telling yourself that, champ. It's bound to come true eventually.*

The Boggart threw his head back, breaking the nose of the man whom he'd taken a bite out of. He heard the man fall to the floor with a weighty *thunk*, and knew that one was out of the fight. *Two more.* One had dragged himself upright, meaning to come straight on to face the Boggart.

Bad move. You should have waited for your pal to right himself.

The Boggart spat the chunk of flesh still in his teeth; it flew right into the bodyguard's face, causing him to throw his hands up in disgust to get the bit of gore out of his eyes. The Boggart kicked hard, driving his shin into the man's stomach; he could feel the wind as the air escaped the thrall's lungs, bending him over double. The Boggart took a half step forward, bringing him abreast of the bodyguard; he brought his right elbow down on the man's neck hard, sending him to the floor hard.

And then there was one.

The Boggart glanced at the lone conscious thrall, on his knees now from where he'd been knocked down. The Boggart glared murder at him. He could tell that the man was beaten.

"Enough!" the thrall gasped. "Truce!"

The Boggart simply walked past, shoving the man roughly down, not even sparing a backward glance.

In a few strides, he was next to Claire. She gasped sharply; for the first time, her expression actually demonstrating something—a mingling of fear and uncertainty. She had no idea what was about to happen to her. She was a Vampire, but only of some thirty years; not yet as terribly strong as the Elders. She could have fought him, and maybe won, but she didn't move a single muscle. The Boggart brought his clawed hand up to her face ... and took her chin between his fingers gently. "I'm not anybody's pet, Claire. You keep making that mistake about me. We had a deal, darling." He looked down for a moment before meeting her eyes again. "You know how

I am about those. Like I said earlier." At that moment, dozens of thralls burst into the room, all of them pointing very large guns directly at the Boggart's head.

The fear left her eyes, but not the uncertainty. It was hard to read a Fang, but he thought … just for a second, she looked like the old Claire, before she had become possessive and the fact that he was immortal and she wasn't had started to make her a little crazy and he had to cut things short.

He'd been told, hellfire, he *knew*, that anything but a casual fling didn't work between Fey and Norms. For his part, he'd tried to keep it light. Well … yeah, tried, that was the kicker. Maybe he hadn't tried hard enough. Maybe he hadn't *wanted* to try hard enough. Maybe … he was no shrink, he didn't know. All he did know was that it got messy, and sad.

Thirty years ago ….

Just for a second, there was that old spark there. And it faded … but it didn't entirely leave her eyes.

And maybe if he'd been what he was back then ….

But that was a long time ago. And she wasn't the old Claire. No matter what was underneath it all, she was a Fang now, and Fangs didn't have lovers. Fangs only had drones and thralls, and the Boggart would become neither for anyone. That was her Hell, now, he realized; she had become what she was, ultimately, to find him again. His immortality had driven them apart. Now hers would drive them away from each other yet again. It was heartbreaking, even for his old soul … but he had a job to do, and the Boggart always delivered.

"You're right, Boggie," she said, quietly. "A deal's a deal." She traced another couple of circles on the top of the box; there was a hum, and the top irised open. "Go ahead. Take the watch." She laughed a little, bitterly. "Don't worry, you won't lose any fingers."

He reached in gingerly, still staring at her eyes. They used to be a tender green like the forests he remembered from his homeland, in a face the soft pink of an apple blossom, but now they were cold emerald against ivory. He still saw something of her old fire there, though, behind it all.

"Damned if we do, and damned if we don't," she said.

"There might be another time, Claire ... in another life. But it isn't now. I've got my job, and you've got your life." He smiled, reluctantly. "It's a small galaxy, though. Doubtless I'll run into you again."

"Not if I see you first," she said, with a brittle laugh. "Time for you to go back to your leash holder. I have a station to see to."

He could tell that she wanted nothing more than for him to take her into his arms, to erase the past thirty years in a single embrace ... but that's not who he was.

The Boggart always kept his word.

Without saying anything else, he turned away from her, striding past the guards and the mess and out the door.

Sometimes ... he really hated his job.

As much as I wish it wasn't, this is one of those times, the Boggart reflected as he made his way to his skiff.

Home Services was probably not going to be entirely happy about the bill they were going to get from "Bert's Men's Outfitters." On the other hand, if they bothered to look at what the bill *might* have been from the upper fifty percent of the stores on Claire's station, they'd figure out that it could have been much worse. The Boggart had a kind of melancholy pleasure out of his new duds; it seemed that *retro was in* for this decade, and he was outfitted in classic *film noir* style.

Only fitting, you dirty rotten sentimentalist. If he was going to walk out on the dame, he might as well look the part. He shoved his hands into the pockets of his trench coat, and pulled the completely useless fedora down over his eyes, and slouched into that piece of crap the Pucca had rented for him.

Of course what the Pucca didn't know was that he'd hocked one of the knickknacks he'd purloined from the pirate, and there was some very nice single malt indeed that was going to help him ease his sorrows and discomfort. As the skiff pulled away from the station, he cracked the first bottle, never bothering with a glass.

To Claire; what could've been, what will never *come to pass.*

The Boggart passed the time in silence, drifting toward his next destination—one he hoped would wrap this case up. He was tired. And that little pissant Pete had better have given him the straight dope. He wasn't at all sure he had the steam to tail-chase this Fred much farther. *Vampires, talking Reboots, a freakin' Wendigo, and one wily Werewolf. It sure can be a strange universe, sometimes.* He had time and then some to contemplate all of those mysteries; the station he was bound for was another backwater, and even worse it was a *Norm*-run backwater. It was also his last shot; it was going to take him days to get out there, and once there he had no more moves or clues to go on.

On the other hand, where else would Fred go? It would be one thing if he still had Pack connections, but he didn't, no Pack would trust a Lone from another Pack even creeping in like a Zeta with his tail between his legs, and he probably didn't even know where to contact any of his bloodline to see if his old Pack would take him in.

And unless I miss my guess, he's running out of money. He knows he can't tap his owed wages, not after pulling the stunt he did, so all he's got is whatever he scrounged up on the first station. In fact ... wonder if he didn't work his way over there on a freighter ... which means ....

Ha. Fred's gonna have to find a job. Running was easy when you had time, friends, and credits. Time Fred had had. He certainly didn't have any friends anymore, and the last the Boggart had already guessed the truth of.

This might be the first decent break he was going to have in this case.

This was a working station; none of the flash of the first tourist trap the Boggart had visited, and none of the polish of Claire's station, which catered to a much higher clientele. The thing was huge. It had to be. Entire arms were leased by various companies. It might be a backwater as far as the tourist trade was concerned, but as far as the mercantile and industrial trade went it was a hotspot. Right in the "sweet spot" where several sorts of raw materials could come together for manufacturing, and positioned perfectly as a refueling depot for short-run transports. Ninety percent of the traffic here was commercial, not tourist, with the odd smattering of colonists, researchers, and religious pilgrims from every and any faith.

But it was a lot higher on the food chain than the mining colony had been. Pretty much everyone here was skilled labor, even the stevedores. Operating transfer equipment took a lot more brains and better reflexes than digging and blasting rock. This translated to better pay and more safety. Still what in the old, old days would have been called "blue-collar" work, but skilled and specialized.

And it took tough creatures to do it. Every time you worked industrial, things went wrong, and they usually required brute force to put them right, which is why it was even stranger that this was mostly a Norm facility.

The Boggart got the vibe as soon as he disembarked. There was no effort here to make things sleek, or shiny, or pretty—but they were military-clean, big, and hard to break. Solid. As a tiny little boat, he got put as far in toward the hub as they could get him, which suited him just fine. Berths far out on the arm were reserved for huge transports. And the berths on this section of the docks were as physically close together as they could be and still dock safely. There was a wide variety of little, working ships crowded in here. Tugs, short-haul messengers and delivery service for small, extremely expensive things, a few skiffs like his, probably owned by wildcatter explorers, even a couple military and Home Services couriers.

The corridors were strictly segregated: people on two narrow walkways on either side, middle reserved for a light-rail system that zipped heavy and bulky items to the ships. Compared to the meandering throngs of tourists on the last two stations, these corridors of industrial-beige bulkheads and floors seemed sparsely populated. And everyone in them was very purposefully going *somewhere*. This was no place to meander.

Good thing the Boggart had a destination. Another transient hostel. There were plenty of them: for crewmen of ships waiting to be loaded or unloaded, for laborers that weren't in company quarters. From there, he figured his next option would be to pick up short, casual jobs from the pool if he needed to, and meanwhile, sniff around without being obvious. He had the skills, he had the brawn, and most importantly, he had the union card. There were times when that came in handy, and this was going to be one of them. Since this was a working station, he didn't have to wait very long for an "application process" at any of the jobs he took up there; out this far, there was always a labor shortage, so if your credentials checked out and you showed up, you could start working immediately in most places. And that's just what the Boggart did.

Most of it simply involved showing up and listening to people, just as he'd done in the mine-colony bar. He'd found out early on in his profession that most people will spill their entire life story with very little prompting; everyone wanted to be heard, to be recognized for who they were and what they'd done. It was when you started getting too probing and pushy that they all clammed up. The Boggart also took in a lot of gossip; who was going where, doing what to whom, birthday plans and vacation trips, torrid romances and crushes. The first job he took was as a one-shot unloading/reloading gig for a transport that had just docked; get the goods off, don't drop any of them, and put new goods on. These were jobs that moved things like his crate, only heavier—too heavy for an unassisted human, not bulky enough for an AI-assist mass-loader or a powered exoskeleton. Luckily, he was a rated power-exo driver, which is what he moved up to after the first job. The union card said "longshoreman" which covered a lot of jobs like that; kind of funny when you came to think about it, since there wasn't a shore to be seen around here. He almost dropped a crate on the deck supervisor's foot when he laughed at the memory of the Reboot he had found on the beach planet, wearing its grass skirt and coconut bra.

The creds had been plentiful for the gig, comparatively, but that's not what he was here for. He needed information, a lead to follow, and using a power-exo on a landing deck bustling with activity wasn't exactly the best way to dredge up information, so he quickly dropped it. Now, the good thing about having a "longshoreman" card on a station like this, especially one that was still a bit understaffed, was that both the union and the bosses were pretty loose about just what a "longshoreman" could do. He was pretty certain after the first couple of gigs that wherever Fred was, it wasn't on the dock crews. So when a maintenance job showed up in the work-detail pool, he applied for it and got it. More hot, heavy work, stuff bots were just not good at and Reboots would break trying to do, never mind that the profusion of Norms made Reboots unviable for most of the station. The bots with an AI robust enough to be able to discriminate between "piece of debris" and "slightly misplaced piece of vital equipment" were either too large or too fragile for the environment in the Jeffries tubes, whereas a sentient organic would recognize in an instant that a damn power cable had come loose and was dangling on the floor waiting to fry him, or the critical circuit junction had spontaneously jumped out of its slot and was now in that pile of miscellaneous flotsam that had collected in the corner. Despite the Gremlin sensors, the damn things were still periodically reinfesting the station every time someone whose protocol was less than up to par docked.

In between jobs, he always made a point of hitting the cafeterias and local watering holes whenever they were the most crowded, usually on shift change. A station like this one worked around the clock, so there was always a shift coming on and going off, depending on which job he was focusing on. It played merry hell with his already abused sleep schedule, but he toughed it out, adjusting so that he got to as many different points on the station as he could with the largest variety of crowds. He had to admit one thing, whoever had bankrolled this outfit was one of the best overall employers he'd ever seen. The pay was decent, the food at the company-owned cafeterias wasn't big on variety but it was nutritious and cheap, and even his bunk at the hostel was the size of a walk-in closet and not just the standard eight-by-four bunk. From what he heard through the grapevine the benefits were good, too. And as a result, people worked well, and hard, and more quickly than they would have if there'd been supers busting their asses all the time.

He was wearing a different human face whenever he went in to a new job, but he kept all of the faces vaguely similar so they more or less matched the ID; it helped for people to recognize him from being around without really being able to place where they had seen him last. Whenever he was questioned, which was rarely, he allowed others to fill in the blanks for him.

"Hey, you're that guy that just came over from admin, right? Been down on the docks for a few days? Pull up a chair, man; we've always got space at this table."

"Not as much space as you have between your ears, Jack." The second worker pointed a fork at the Boggart. "Obviously it's what's-his-name from electrical. He can grab a seat all the same, just don't insult the man, huh?"

"Hell, it's okay. I get mistook for that admin guy all the time. Name's Skip. Skip Morgan." And that was usually all it took to get in. This bunch was particularly chatty; all of them were older Norms, and seemed to have taken up permanent residence on the station. He didn't blame them; as places to live in the wide galaxy went, this was above average for regular Joes. And for his purposes, this was exactly the group he needed to get closer to. Regulars noticed the new guys. They treated him like an old friend, which meant sharing all of the gossip; they didn't mind that he didn't put in his own opinion at all. It just gave them more of a chance to air their own.

"And what about those pilgrims that just got in a couple of cycles ago? You know, the ones with the bells and the chanting? They're just sitting in the corridor in Section 3 … waiting." The third member of the group was the one that had spoken up. "They creep me out," he said, giving a theatrical shiver.

"Everything creeps you out, Jeff. Being creeped out is your natural state of being."

"Yeah, well … I don't know, man. Bells and chanting …."

That was how the conversations went; Jeff, Jack, and Monty, the Boggart found, actually had a great deal of knowledge about the goings-on in the station at any one time. They were some of the "oldest" workers here; they'd been here since the station went live twenty years ago. Naturally, he had to wade through seas of bullshit to find anything, but he liked listening to them all the same. Unfortunately, work had to come before leisure, so he continued to pick up different jobs. After he was sure that he was blending in well enough to be invisible with his regular set of faces—excluding the one he always wore when around his new "lunch and a beer" buddies—he set off around the station to deal with some of the grittier aspects of detective work. Mostly it involved greasing palms. A few creds here to take a look at a work log, a handful more there to see employee files, and so on. It was all taken out of the expense account, of course, but nothing that the Boggart found seemed to be of any use. If Fred was on the station, he had done just as good of a job of staying inconspicuous as the Boggart had. The Boggart was beginning to lose hope of resolving the case when his next big break came.

Almost literally.

Every place where there were sentient beings, there was gambling. No matter how you tried to make it illegal, gamblers found a way around it. The best you could hope to do was keep it under control. Like drinking. The brains behind this station realized that, so there were bars. There was official entertainment in some of the bars, and in others, if someone wanted to start a crap or card game, or bet on something, well, that was fine. They even had tables set up for it, but no staff manning them; the bigwigs left that up to whoever wanted to play. In theory, it worked well.

In practice, of course ... well, there is always someone willing to prey on the unsuspecting. The Boggart found one such instance as he was making his way back to his room in the hostel from the bar that Jeff, Jack, and Monty frequented the most. He was walking his usual route when he took a different corridor on a whim. The bars around this station had more imaginative names than the one on the mining colony; his usual watering hole was "The Library." He noticed this one because it was a variation on the theme of "places I tell the wife/partner/parents where I'm going that doesn't sound like a bar." This one was "The Laundry." He chuckled a little, then, because he'd never been here before, decided to check it out.

It was virtually identical to "The Library," which made him think it had the same owners. Same sports memorabilia from some obscure teams and sports (high-grav soccer, zero-gee handball), same layout, even the same slightly oddball colors in the decoration (Morocco red and chestnut brown). Some different faces, which made him decide to go for one more boilermaker and hang around and listen. He changed his face to accommodate the change in venue, as well.

He saw one person he actually knew from The Library and from working on a crew with him. Josh Stills, a tough little electrician who had a bit of a gambling addiction. The guys at The Library all knew this, and would cut him off before he lost the rent. But it appeared that the big bruiser he was going head-to-head with in a game of Texas Hold 'Em wasn't being so accommodating, because he was sweating. His normally fine mousy-blond hair was plastered to his skull.

The big guy was new; head like a bucket, bald, no neck, and the sort of build a Norm could only get when he was from a plus-gee world. He had deft hands, though ... too deft ....

The Boggart watched him closely. *There it is, you slick bastard.* The man was dealing from the bottom of the deck, and using a few other dirty tricks when he thought he could. The end result was that he was going to clean poor Josh out ... and from the look on his face, he seemed to be expecting to use more than a friendly word to exact his winnings from the electrician. For a moment, the Boggart figured he'd just turn around and get back to his room at the hostel ... save for that little niggling voice in the back of his head. That inconvenient thing that passed for a conscience, that said "you know Josh, and you know this guy is cheating, how can you walk away?" *Last thing I need is* another *complication.* "Sure," said his conscience. "And then what do you do when Josh gets thrown out of his bunk, or goes without food, or both?" His conscience won. *What the hell, let's go for it.* The Boggart sat down at the table, making sure that the tool belt that he was wearing cleared the seat. Both players looked up at the same time, but the bruiser was the first one to speak. "Closed game, and almost finished. Find another table, chump."

The Boggart shrugged, leaning forward. "Naw, I'm fine here. Just want to enjoy the spectacle. Still a free galaxy, right?" A few of the other patrons had begun to take notice; the big guy didn't have any choice but to accept him.

"Fine, whatever." The Boggart watched the rest of the game intently, ordering a drink but never so much as touching it. Finally, the game came to a close; Josh was out for everything he had, and it was the final hand. "You know what's going to happen to you if you can't pay up, right?" The stevedore leaned in, grinning with huge horsey teeth. "No one likes dumb bastards that renege on a fairly wagered bet." Josh was close to breaking down, at that point; he knew just how screwed he was.

The big moose was dealing out the final hand when the Boggart suddenly snatched a wrench—the largest he had—from where it hung on his tool belt, and brought it down with a sharp *crack* on top of the bruiser's dealing hand. The man screamed, but the Boggart shut him up quickly enough by splashing his drink in the man's face. As he was blubbering, the wrench came up to catch him on the point of his chin, sending him backward and out of his seat.

"Check the security vid footage, Josh," the Boggart said, hoarsely. "He was dealing from the bottom of the deck, holding an ace and a king in his left, stacking the deck, and I am pretty damn sure marking cards with a pin on the inside of his ring." He looked at the man on the floor, weakly cradling his shattered hand. *Won't be using that hand to beat a debt out of Josh, or cheating any time soon.* "That's three kinds of cheating. Seems to me you won these games."

Josh smiled weakly, and was quick-witted enough to scoop up the pot before answering—meanwhile the barkeep was calling security and a good selection of the barflies surrounding the bruiser so he couldn't run. "Uh ... do I know you?"

The Boggart had just enough time to shout over his shoulder as he made his escape. "Nope." He was out the door and had just finished changing his glamour when security came bustling past him, crowding into the bar. *Alright, that's your good deed done for this century, Boggart. Get back on the case, now.*

The Boggart found his usual spot among the three old-timers the next day after he had finished his shift at a new job. *They're the oldest workers here ... but I'm not exactly sure I've ever seen them do any work other than gossiping and eating, come to think of it.*

"... I tell you, there's a ghost on this station. No lie!" Jeff was pretty vehement about it. The others exchanged looks.

"Another ghost, Jeff? You sure that this one isn't the same one that turned off the air-conditioning in your pod last month and flickered the lights?" Monty snickered.

"I heard it straight from Margie, and she heard it from what's-his-face down at The Laundry, the skinny bartender. He said he saw the whole thing with Josh. Dude came in, busted up one of the new hires that was cheating, and then *vanished*." He nodded up and down vigorously. "Big as life on the vid footage in the bar, and gone on the vid footage from the corridors outside. Creepy, right?"

"It's a big station, it's not like it's that hard to disappear, Jeff." This time it was Jack, rolling his eyes in exasperation.

"*Exactly!* Big station ... but not that many people here, either. Someone no one has seen before or since, comes in and bops a guy with a wrench? Things have been strange around here, I swear it. All the new guys coming in, it's something with one of them—" Jeff looked guilty, then glanced toward the Boggart.

"Don't mind him; he doesn't usually mean to be an asshole, Skip." Monty cuffed Jeff on the back of his head. "Do ya, jerk?"

Jeff was rubbing his head, putting his other hand up in defense. "Aw, come on, you know I didn't mean it like that! I'm just saying, is all. Things are getting creepy around here. There was that fresh Gremlin Outbreak *right* when those new labcoats were supposed to be doing a critical test in their section. Those pilgrims in the hall-ways, that new weird guy down in engineering that *never* talks to anyone and keeps *sniffing* all the time, and now this 'invisible man'!" The Boggart's ears pricked up suddenly, and he tried to subtly lean in closer to listen.

It was Jack's turn to reproach Jeff. "I swear to god, if you keep up with that pilgrim crap again, I'm never going to buy you another drink, Jeff."

"Okay, okay, fine. But you can't deny the rest of it is pretty creepy—"

The Boggart held up a hand to interrupt Jeff. "What were you saying about that guy down in engineering?" He shrugged as every-one looked at him. "Only curious; I've got a job coming up down there in a day or two. I want to keep an eye out for all of Jeff's ghosts." He smiled, looking to Jack and Monty, who both started to chuckle, but Jeff didn't seem to notice.

"Yeah, man. That guy … he's definitely a weird one. There's not a lot to tell, though. I think he got here a few weeks ago? Don't know, really. He doesn't hit any of the bars, doesn't eat here, and doesn't re-ally talk to anyone. Mostly works alone down in engineering, doing odd jobs I think."

Monty interjected. "Maybe he just likes to work alone. Or he's avoiding you, Jeff."

Jeff blinked. "Why would he avoid me?"

"No reason whatsoever, Jeff, none at all." Monty grinned. "Maybe he thinks you're creepy. Maybe he thinks you're a ghost."

Jeff blinked again, then shook his head. "Anyways, like I was saying about those pilgrims—" A collective groan sounded from everyone else at the table, but the Boggart's mind was somewhere else already. *Works alone, stays down in engineering, does odd jobs and doesn't talk with anyone ... could that be our long-lost Wolf?* After a week and a half working around the station and digging for even the tiniest nugget of information about Fred, the Boggart had turned up nothing. This was the first thing to come his way that had even the faintest smell of a clue.

It was time for the Boggart to get a job in the engineering section.

What was it about engineering that it always involved lifting large and heavy objects? Even when you were supposedly working on software, firmware, midware ... sooner or later, large and heavy objects needed lifting.

The Boggart's union card did it again. He was in a power-exo ... lifting large and heavy objects. He had no idea what they were for, only that they were expensive, and you couldn't replace them easily this far out. So, he was careful, and put the gray metal boxes and components wherever the senior engineers and team leaders told him to, moving just as slowly and exactly as they wanted. None of the ones that he'd worked with resembled Fred, however, nor had he seen the errant Fur anywhere else on the level he was working on. Caution won out against his impatience; he decided not to ask after him among any of the others working down here, for fear that they might alert Fred. The Boggart had spent two days down here, with nothing to show for it so far. He hadn't been everywhere in the section—not in the special docks for instance. Engineering had its very own docks; kept clear most of the time, because when they needed a component, they needed it *now*, and it was probably critical. Ships with their components got priority. But he'd been on most of the levels, and still no sign of a quiet loner who sniffed. *Maybe that's all this is—another dead end. Might be the engineer that Jeff was so creeped out by wasn't Fred, just a guy with a case of the sniffles. But still ....* The Boggart had a gut feeling that he ought to stay for just a little while longer, let it play out. Like any other being worth a damn in his profession, he knew from experience that it paid off to trust your instincts. And from the look of things, he wasn't going to run out of things to move any time soon. All the engineers he worked with were very happy with how careful he was. Really, it was easy; all he had to do was tell himself there was a vial of old-fashioned nitroglycerine inside everything he had to lift, and his instincts did the rest. For all he knew, there could have been far-more volatile substances inside every box and crate, from how some of the engineers fussed over them.

Wearing the exo was hard, though; it might magnify your lifting power, but inside that skeleton, you were still the one doing the lifting. It took a lot of endurance instead of bursts of strength, which is why you usually saw wiry guys that had the higher classifications. When he was done with his shift, he usually felt as if he'd been doing three or four rounds in a sparring ring with a bear. Or one with that blasted, dead Wendigo. Today was certainly no exception. He'd been on his shift for ten hours straight, and it had taken a toll. The Boggart was marching back to the locker room to punch out and change before drinks with Jeff, Monty, and Jack when he was struck with a sudden impulse to do a little exploring. He let his feet carry him through the section, just making sure to look like he was moving somewhere with a purpose as opposed to just wandering; if anyone stopped him, he'd say he was lost and hope that it was left at that. The engineers could be touchy about their turf.

The Boggart was just about sick of his little expedition when he came to a long hallway. It was filled with access panels, pipes, valves, and all of the usual clutter one could expect for a station this large. The one unusual thing in the hallway was the other person walking toward the Boggart. The man was the stereotypical dweeb; his height, maybe an inch or two shorter than the Boggart, say five foot four. Spectacularly average physique and a plain face that looked like it was made to sweat over math problems and the outcomes of baseball games. He looked as if he should have been wearing glasses. Thick, black-rimmed ones. He had all his hair, but it was a mousy brown, and cut military-short.

His face was a perfect match for the portrait of Fred Stewart. And he was a Fur. The Boggart could see that primal aura from yards away. The Boggart did his absolute best to not allow his expression to betray anything. A plan was already forming in his head as they closed the distance between them. *I'll pass by, get around the corner, wait a heartbeat, and then follow him. When I've got him a little farther from here, I'll corner him. Maybe wait until he gets back to wherever he sleeps, stop him there—*

A feeling like a static shock swept over the Boggart just then, stopping him in his tracks. Fred immediately stopped as well, still a good thirty feet away; his eyes narrowed and his nostrils flared, and he was staring *directly* at the Boggart. The Boggart reached a hand up gingerly toward his face—and found it to be *his* face, his real one, not one of his glamours.

Oh, shit.

Fred immediately turned and ran back in the direction he came from, and the Boggart stutter-started for a second before giving chase. *Goddamnit! I forgot about the anti-Gremlin deterrents down here; I must have strayed too close to one, tripped it, and it shut down my glamour. Shitfire!* It was hard to keep up with Fred; there were many connecting hallways, all of them dimly lit and filled with turns. *If I let him get away now, I'll never find him again. I barely found him this time, and it was mostly an accident. How could I get so damned careless?*

Fred was running for the engineering docks; he probably knew the layout pretty well, and it was probably the fastest way for him to get off of this station. There were miles of Jeffries tubes, access hatches a small guy could easily get into, in case he couldn't find a ship that he could stow away on. The Boggart knew that no matter what, he didn't dare lose sight or at least *sense* of him.

He was so intent on keeping track of Fred that at first the alarm klaxons didn't even register. And when they did, he just ignored them, figuring it was part of the anti-Gremlin system or some routine emergency.

It was only when he saw Fred dashing down one of the docking arms and followed him—and saw a vision out of his own worst nightmare—that he realized that what he was hearing was an alarm for an armed boarding party.

Fred had stopped, turned toward the Boggart, and had half wolfed out—the most he could do without a moon. He was easily a foot and a half taller, and leaner; fur had sprouted out from under his engineer's jumpsuit.

"I'm tired of running from the goddamned HS. I'm tired of living like a rat down in this maze. I'm not going to do any of it anymore. I'm not sorry for what happened." He growled low and menacingly, his snout lowered and his eyes fixed on the Boggart.

"That's good, Stewart. I'm tired of chasing you. There's just one problem, though," the Boggart said, a little unsteadily. "Look behind you."

"You really don't think I'm going to fall for that old—" but Fred *did* turn around, and slowly backed away from the thing that had been standing behind him.

"Hi, honey," slurred Captain Runner. "I'm home." The cold fire was back in his eyes, though he still had all of his grisly wounds from his fight with the Boggart. Somehow he looked *bigger*.

"How in the nine hells did you find me?" The Boggart was backing away, sparing a single glance over his shoulder to make sure there weren't any threats behind him.

"Seems there was a piece of rough beef jerky back on my boat, the one *you* slagged. Think his name was Pete." The Boggart noticed that the pirate captain was picking his teeth with a bone: a femur, by the looks of it. "He sang a little about where I might find my next meal. Have to say, he was a bit rough for an appetizer." He spit the bone onto the floor. "Thanks much for sending that Home Services boat to pick us up, though; a fine first course, and a new ride! I ought to have ya over for dinner more often." The monster leered. "Every time I eat, I get stronger. And ya led me to an all-you-can-eat buffet. When I'm done here, I won't need no stinking ship. I can just sit here, an' let the take-away come t' me. An' I must say it's been a little lonely, bein' the only one of me. But my boys here, they got their first taste o' man-flesh, an' pretty soon there'll be five of us. Right boys?"

The four pirates with him just stared. And their eyes looked … all wrong. There was a strange dark-magic aura around them too—not nearly as dense or nasty as the Captain's, but it was there. And—*they look hungry.*

Okay. Run now, just runrunrun.

If there was one place that the entire station would rush to defend, it would be engineering. And if there was one place that was tough enough to survive being the site of a fight, it was probably engineering.

Not *intact* ... but there wouldn't be any bulkhead breeches or other immediately fatal damage ... probably ....

Fred was the first to turn and run, and the Boggart followed on his heels. Fred was running for deep in engineering territory and away from the engineering docks. In that funny way the mind has when you are in panic mode, the Boggart realized that Runner must have taken the HS ship he had hijacked straight to the engineering docks, knowing that was the fastest way to the beating heart of the station, and that it was highly likely most of those docks would be clear. The klaxons must have started when the pirates ignored traffic control and headed there.

The problem was ... he didn't know this part of the ship all that well. Two, maybe three skidding turns ... and he found himself standing next to Fred at a dead end. From the other side of the wall came the steady roar of a furnace. An incinerator, probably; engineering produced a fair amount of waste, and most of it needed to be reduced to ash before it was processed.

They both put their backs to the wall. Runner and his crew ... there were only four of them, but Runner really didn't *need* them ... stopped pelting after him. Instead they stood stock still. Waiting.

"And you, puppy. You just run on back to yer kennel. Mebbe when I'm done here, I'll let ya grab a skiff and skedaddle." The Wendigo leered. The other pirates laughed. Well, it sort of sounded like a laugh. Like someone had stuck a pissed-off rattlesnake in their chests.

Fred just stood his ground, still nearly seven feet of angry Wolfman. The hallway they were in was much more cramped than where they had found Runner near the docks. *This is going to hurt no matter what.* The Boggart unholstered his revolver, holding it out in front in a low, ready position with both hands.

The only good thing was that those four pirates weren't Wendigo yet. They were well on the way to it, but they weren't there yet.

The Wendigo stared at Fred. Fred glared back, growling deep in his throat, and slowly getting hairier. "No? Suit yourself. I needed a new rug fer my quarters, anyways. Get them."

The Boggart brought the revolver to bear on the closest pirate's head, squeezing the trigger just as the front sight was centered with the pirate's eyebrows. The muzzle blast from the Webley-Fosbery was thunderously loud in the tight quarters, partially blinding and deafening the Boggart. He was able to see that there was nothing left of his target's head, however, before a second pirate was upon him. The used-to-be-a-man shouldered into him, knocking the pistol from the Boggart's grasp. They both tumbled to the deck, kicking and punching, each trying to end up on top of the other. The pirate finally gained prime position, and tried to use his knees to pin the Boggart's arms to the decking while raining hammer fists all around his head. He was inhumanly strong—still not nearly as strong as Captain Runner, though—and the Boggart knew he had to get free before he was smashed to a pulp.

Arching his back suddenly, he rocked the pirate forward, sending the man tumbling above the Boggart's head. The Boggart saw another one of those terrible fists lash out, but rolled out of the way before it could crush his head. They were both on their knees now and facing each other. The Boggart feinted, then fully extended himself in a powerful leap, catching the pirate off guard. The man went down under him, but he wouldn't stay there for long; he was simply too strong. The Boggart wasn't going to give him any time to try to counter, this time; he jabbed down quickly with his fingers stiff, claws burying themselves in the pirate's windpipe. Deep brown, foul-smelling blood welled up, and the pirate's eyes went wide. Still, he fought, and wrapped his hands around the Boggart's throat. Everything was going white for the Boggart, blood pounding in his temples as he found that he couldn't breathe. *Won't die! Bastard won't die!* The Boggart tried digging his hand deeper, but he hit the man's spine and could not push his fingers any farther while his other hand was clawing at the hands around his throat. In another few seconds he'd either black out or have his neck crushed in the creature's iron grip. Desperate, the Boggart took his left hand and speared it into the pirate's throat next to his right hand. His claws passed through the back of the man's neck and painfully hit the deck. *Got it!* Grunting with effort, he scissored his hands with as much force as he could muster. The pirate's head separated from his neck, with more of that nasty, not-quite-blood spurting out from the wound. The dead man's hands released their grip, and the Boggart could breathe again, though he was almost gagging from the stench of the tainted blood.

Where the hell is Fred in all of this? Still regaining his composure, and on his hands and knees, the Boggart bent around to see whether Fred was alive. He most certainly was; both of the remaining human pirates were at him with knives, dancing around him and slashing whenever he would lunge, taking turns distracting him. The Werewolf's jumpsuit was shredded and spattered with blood, but his regenerative ability was keeping him alive. It struck the Boggart that Fred was holding back …. *He's biding his time.* Then it happened; Fred slashed viciously at the pirate in front of him, spilling the man's entrails from the jagged tear he had left in his stomach. The disemboweled pirate fell to his knees, trying to push his guts back in. Fred turned and fell upon the second pirate in a flash of fur and blood; the Wendigo-to-be hardly had time to scream before Fred had ripped him completely to pieces. The injured pirate had a knife raised for Fred's exposed back; the Boggart scrambled to his feet, catching the man's knife hand before it could find its target. Twisting, he brought the knife up under the pirate's jaw until the point was sticking through the top of his skull. The Boggart saw the man's eyes roll up into his head, and pushed the fresh corpse to the floor in disgust.

Just as Fred stood up from his murdered pirate, gore dripping from his fangs, Captain Runner began to clap slowly.

"Bravo. The pup's got claws. The Fey's got fight. I'm gonna enjoy eatin' ya both." He began to laugh. "In fact, I think I'll do it slow. Keep ya both around fer a while. Might even get three or four meals offa the pup, if I keep tearin' off bits." He laughed harder. "Cause a pig like that, ya don't eat all at once!"

The Boggart vaguely remembered that being the punch line of a joke, a long time ago. *Hell if I'm going down as a punch line,* he thought savagely. He knew that he had to get to his revolver to have any hope of taking down Runner. Only problem was he didn't know where in this blasted hall it had skittered away to. Runner advanced on both of them, stooped over with hideous arms groping. Fred howled, and then charged to meet the pirate captain. They both embraced, with Fred biting and tearing with tooth and claw; Runner just laughed again before brushing the Werewolf off. Fred fell to the floor, where the Wendigo landed a kick in his belly, punting him toward the Boggart.

But the Boggart got a sudden brainstorm; as Fred hurtled toward him he grabbed the back of the Fur's jumpsuit, whirled with the momentum, and flung him as if he was an athlete and Fred was the "hammer" in a hammer throw. Fred's reflexes were excellent; about halfway through the windup, he'd figured out the Boggart's plan, and as he was launched, he was fully in control of where he was going and how he was going to hit. He held his arms out in front of him like a spear, aimed directly for the Wendigo's chest.

The Boggart didn't wait to see what happened, he followed Fred, ready to defend or follow up, whatever the result was. Fred's hands speared through the Wendigo's ribs, knocking him back a few steps. That's when Fred started to *pull*, spreading his hands to try to open up Runner's rib cage. *If we can just get to his damned heart.* The pirate captain most certainly didn't like that; he grunted, forcing his chest closed again. Somehow he was able to get a knee between himself and Fred, pushing the Werewolf off. Fred landed hard but came up into a roll, this time running on all fours back toward Runner. The Captain met his charge, catching him and throwing him back in the direction of the landing bays. *Shit. This just went from bad to we're screwed.*

Time to get fancy. And the Wendigo hadn't seen this one yet. The Boggart dashed next to Runner before the huge monster could recover, then using some simple sleight of hand he palmed his watch into one of the pockets on the Captain's union cavalry jacket.

The Boggart whistled. "Hey, sunshine." Runner turned his head just in time for the Boggart to shove a clawed thumb through his right eye socket. The Captain grunted, and grasped for the Boggart's arm ... but it suddenly wasn't there. The Boggart became corporeal again, this time on the other side of Runner, slashing the Wendigo's Achilles tendons. Stumbling, the pirate captain turned, spinning and cutting through only the air with his apelike arms. The Boggart had hopped into the ethereal again; now he came out on the Captain's left side, stabbing through ribs and kidneys. Another jaunt into the Nowhere-Space of the ethereal and he was rematerialized on the opposite side, rabbit-punching the Captain three times. On his next jaunt, he spied Fred getting back on his feet.

At that point he yelled as loud as he could. "GUN!" Then he hit the ethereal again as the Wendigo grabbed for him. He reappeared behind the monster, turning his head as he shouldered into Runner's lower back. "Get the damned gun!" The Boggart disappeared and reappeared one more time—and Runner's hand snapped out, nearly taking the Boggart's head off. *Too close. He's anticipating it now. I can't keep this up forever.* Now he only focused on keeping the last pirate's attention, no longer attacking him. He jaunted from the ethereal to reality and back, always random, all of his jumps centered on the watch. Each time, like a strobe going on and off, he would catch a glimpse of Fred; on his feet, unsteadily shaking his head, then scrabbling on the floor, searching, searching ... there! The Werewolf was holding up the revolver triumphantly, howling. The Boggart rematerialized hands outstretched. Fred threw the revolver, and it sailed through the air perfectly, end over end. The grip landed exactly in the Boggart's hand right before the world exploded into stars and pain. The Boggart's entire left side felt like it was on fire, and it took him what seemed like years to realize that he was on his back and staring up at the ceiling. Captain Runner's face loomed into his vision, the massive head seeming to fill the world.

"I've changed my mind," the Captain snarled. "I'm gonna turn ya inta paste an' eat ya on toast." Runner reared back, bringing his foot up to crush the life out of the Boggart. He couldn't get the gun around in time; it was suddenly very heavy in his hand, and he couldn't find the strength to lift it. The foot was coming down when a human-sized blur slammed into the Wendigo's midsection, roaring. *Fred?* The thoughts were coming sluggishly to the Boggart, but he was able to raise his head off of the deck with effort. Fred was crawling all over Runner, biting and tearing, ripping huge chunks of flesh off of the giant. Runner was shouting and cursing, trying to get a handhold on Fred so he could fling him off and finish with the Boggart. The Boggart marshalled his strength, willing himself to lift the revolver. Slowly, it rose off of the floor, still in his hand, swinging toward the two combatants. Fred was on Runner's back, biting deeply into the Captain's neck, but he was about to be pulled off; both of the Wendigo's arms were raised above his head, exposing his chest. *Jackpot.* The Boggart squeezed the trigger on the revolver, and another too-loud explosion filled the hallway. A gout of blood exploded from Runner's mouth before he fell onto his face with a wet *smack*, depositing Fred in a pile next to the Boggart.

"Ow," Fred said, mushily. And not just because it was hard to speak with something that was half mouth and half muzzle. They both slowly got to their feet, hands on their wounds. When they were facing each other, the Boggart brought the muzzle of his revolver to bear on Fred.

"So," he said, panting hard; the Boggart thought that some of his ribs, if they hadn't been broken before, definitely were now.

"Sho," Fred replied, looking steadily at him. " 'Ere we are." The fangs he had in his Wolfman form impeded his speech just slightly; in any other situation, it might have been comical.

"You know why I'm here, right? Why I've come after you?"

"Shenotah," said Fred. "Shpashed Fangsh. Shtole ship. Oo know they wash pricksh, ri?"

"Yeah, well. Who isn't in this screwed up galaxy." He kept the revolver trained on the Werewolf. "I've chased you halfway across this galaxy, you know. From Earth to find your cousin on a mining rig, to backwaters with nothing but grief and a beach planet with nothing but Zombies. I've had to fight pirates, stevedores, pirates, a goddamned *Wendigo*, and Fang treachery. But do you want to know what the worst part of it is?"

"Shucksh t'ee oo?" Fred asked. *Sucks to be you?*

"The absolute worst goddamn part of this entire rotten mess? It was dealing with that goddamned Pucca from Home Services."

"HS can bite me." Fred's muzzle was slowly becoming more human. "I gave them over a hundred years of my life in a tin can that seemed to have been put together by monkeys, it malfunctioned so much, and a crew of the most dysfunctional Fangs the Deep Dark ever created. And I just came back here to save your sorry ass because ...." He fell over and lay on his back. "Because I didn't want a fucking monster to rip you to bits and eat you, because you were just doing a job, and I didn't want it to rip the first *functional* people I'd seen in a century to bits and eat them either. I *like* these people. I know I didn't talk to them, but I kinda forgot how to talk to nice people."

"Kinda makes you an idiot, doesn't it?"

Fred slowly sat up, whimpering a little, and offered a hand to the Boggart. "Yeah. But I'd rather die that kinda idiot than live knowing I ran out on them."

The Boggart kept the revolver trained on him a moment longer ... before holstering it and helping Fred to his feet. "Great, you're a sentimentalist, too. I don't know how we're ever going to work together. I'm guessing it'll take a lot of whiskey."

"Uh ... what?"

The Boggart shrugged. "You got a lot of talent for running; figured you might be able to put it to use helping me find others doing the same. Unless you like skulking around on stations like a rat all the time." He looked around at all the blood and messy bits of bodies strewn about them. "Besides, like I said, I'm tired of chasing you. Especially if it's going to turn out like this all the fuckin' time." This time he offered his hand to Fred. "Whaddya say?"

"I guess I say ...." Fred's eyes suddenly widened, pupils dilating. "... *oh SHIT!*"

The Boggart turned as behind him Runner sprang to his feet, his hands scraping the ceiling as he was about to fall upon them. Faster than he thought he could, the Boggart unholstered the Webley-Fosbery and fired twice point-blank into the Wendigo's chest. The two big .455 Webley silver bullets tore through wool and flesh before finally finding the pirate captain's heart, ripping through it. Behind Runner an incinerator bay door opened as if by magic; Fred wasted no time, gut checking Runner with all of his strength as a half-form Fur. The pirate captain stumbled backward, finally tottering over and falling into the incinerator, sending tongues of flame shooting out. He screamed then, thrashing wildly; the Boggart thought that Runner might just escape and try to kill them both again when the doors closed as inexplicably as they opened. The hiss of the lock closing was the best sound he'd heard in weeks.

"... did you do that?" The Boggart hadn't realized he had been holding his breath, letting ir out in a quick pant.

"No," said a sarcastic-sounding voice. "Gremlins did." Out of the shadows beside a control panel stepped ... a Reboot?

"Did I mention I have a buddy?" Fred said.

"… another talking Zombie?" The Boggart felt dizzy. "I'm not sure I have the constitution for this many shocks in one day."

Fred gave him a knowing look. "Believe me, man, I know exactly how you feel."

The Reboot shrugged. "We come as a set."

The Boggart shook his head to clear it, then looked back to Fred. "So, you never did answer my question. Wanna become a private eye? After this job, I'll be able to expand my offices. And, as you can tell … it's exciting work."

"Well, I guess … wait, what's your name, anyway?" Fred asked. "And what *are* you?"

"Boggart … Humphrey Boggart." He cleared his throat. "And I'm a Boggart."

Fred blinked. "Seriously?"

The Boggart was about to speak, but—

The Reboot made a sound a little like coughing. "That's right. Ignore the talking corpse in the corner that saved the day. Don't mind me. I'll just stand right here. Like a corpse. In the corner. Alone. In the dark."

"Oh. And that's Skinny Jim." Fred smiled sheepishly. If a Wolf could look sheepish. "And he's right. We come as a set. If it hadn't been for him …."

The Boggart threw his hands up. "I'm too tired to argue. I'll take you both. And I think it's time for a whole lot of single malt."

"So … the way I see it," Skinny Jim said, as the Boggart led the way, limping a little, back to his pod. "The Wendigo ate you, Fred. Boggie here heroically and single-handedly threw him in the incinerator."

"Boy, didn't I just." The Boggart shook his head. "Sad about the Fur, though. No trace left; that's how Wendigos operate, never mind Wendigo *pirates*."

"You're a big damn hero, boss," Skinny Jim said. "I don't exist, of course. Whatever happened to that traitorous prick, Pete, anyway? Who also didn't exist, by the way."

"Wendigos have big appetites," Fred put in, helpfully.

"What a dimrod." Jim shook his head. "Okay, so, here's my thinking. We get the outside of an old anthro-bot, see? Weld me inside. That'll keep me from falling apart, and nobody'll know I'm not an

AI. Then we come up with a name ... I like Boggart, Barkes, and Bot ... Fred can change his name to Fred Barkes."

The Boggart could only bury his face in his hands. Finally, after a half dozen steps, he looked up. "Oh, why the hell not. I'm gonna enjoy giving the Pucca his last expense report."

Skinny Jim suddenly stood stock still.

"What?" said Fred, alarmed.

"*What?*" the Boggart echoed, looking around for trouble.

"I ... just remembered," Jim said with wonder. "Who I was. What I did when I was ... alive. I was an accountant. For the *Mob*." He began to laugh, and slapped the Boggart's shoulders. "Oh, boss, you are gonna love me. Let me make out that expense report. When I cook books, I *really* cook books."

For the first time in a very long while, the Boggart felt his mouth stretching into a genuine smile. He put one arm over Fred's shoulders, the other over Skinny Jim's. "Boys," he said, "I think this is the beginning of a beautiful friendship."

PART THREE

DIABOLICAL STREAK

T he universe had changed in some ways, but had stayed the same in many more. At least it seemed that way to the Boggart. He'd been around and actually active longer than most, save for some of the more adaptable Paras, nineteen centuries, give or take a decade. The modern age didn't particularly agree with many creatures of his ilk, what with its abundance of cold iron, lack of superstition from the Norms, and high technology that helped to illuminate the night that all of the dark and scrabbling beings used to inhabit. But then, Boggarts were more closely associated with humans, or "mortals" as the Fey and the Sidhe used to call them, than some of the other creatures that had come tumbling out of the broom closet at the start of the Zombie War.

Humanity first truly found out about the Paranormal when Zombies showed up. No one knew the how or why of Zombies, only that they didn't go after Paras. Paras largely depended on humanity. Mostly for sustenance of one form or another: blood, psychic energy, offerings, whatever. The Zombie War and its outcome changed everything, the entire world turned upside down as Paras were integrated. Paras were integrated because they turned the tide of the war; humanity was losing against the onslaught of the dead. Paras were what tipped things back in favor of mankind, though the goodwill from the Zombie War didn't last long. Misunderstandings, massacres, more conflicts fought. Once humanity knew that Paras existed, well, humanity was creative and very good at destruction, and the Paras were losing the new war, even though it cost the Norms dearly. Then came the advent of deep-space travel and that was the answer to everyone's problems; population pressure decreased by using Para crews, and the Paras could do what humans could not—live for decades, even hundreds of years on the sublight-speed ships. Zombies were rebranded as the politically correct Reboots, and put into useful roles where they weren't a danger to Norms. One politico had anguished at the time, "What in God's name can you do with twenty billion Zombies?" It turned out, if you were a corporation, creative, with no scruples, and had a lot of jobs too simple even for a bot, you could do a helluva lot.

It wasn't all wine and roses. There was a deep rot within the system. Corruption at the highest levels of government and corporate structures, and the fusion of both into Home Services. Still, it worked while it was needed.

But nothing lasts forever, not even a truce. Now there was FTL, and some of the old tensions between Norms and Paras were boiling up again. It was an interesting universe, especially for a Boggart tryin' to make a few bucks.

Or, as the old French saying went, *plus ça change, plus c'est la même chose.* He'd been hunted or exploited in one way or another for much of his long life, but at least in the modern age, he was his own boss. After the last gig he had done for remnant Home Services, he had been able to set up his own firm and bigger office, quickly followed by wiping his hands of anything attached to ol' HS. Part of that was that it was too much hassle working their jobs and running their errands, anymore. With the advent of FTL becoming widespread and affordable, Home Services seemed to think that a PI like Humph could trot from one end of the known 'verse to the other on a whim. That, and Home Services had lost the importance that they had once held. No longer were they in charge of exploratory expeditions and charting unknown systems for settlement, keeping a tight leash on their Para crews. Everything was outsourced to private companies, now, with mixed Human and Para crews that were much less dysfunctional. Well, except for the Fangs. The Fangs put the "fun" in "dysfunctional." Increasingly, Fangs were happy just snuggled down in their Nest Stations and really didn't want "the adventure of space travel," which just meant more jobs for the other Paras. The profit margins were better and the liabilities were lower for everyone involved. In some systems, there was still a "boom town" sort of feeling, with lots of new wealth ready for the taking.

Not that everyone was pleased that Paras were becoming wealthier and more mobile. Political advocacy groups calling for stricter sanctions on specific types of Paras coupled with an increase in high-profile news stories featuring Paras as the villains ....

After the job for HS, Humph had sat down and had a powwow with Fred and Skinny Jim. Earth was too hot for their little gang, and there wasn't nearly enough action there besides the never-ending job of chasing down deadbeat dads and cheating spouses. They had to find a place to set up shop; somewhere that they wouldn't stand out too much, but where they would still be able to sell their services for a decent price. Humph had a reputation for keeping his word and getting the job done, which meant something—namely credits—in a universe where a lot of beings would sell their own grandmother for the time of day. With that commodity, they shopped around. Stations were out, since there was always too much Were and Fang activity on those; the Dens and Nests would always want a slice of the pie, so to speak. Resort or garden worlds never had all that much going on for them; sometimes jobs would land there, but hardly did they ever start there. After mulling over the problem over a few bottles of whiskey and a few pickled brain-fungi for Jim, they finally found their new home—Planet Mildred.

Planet Mildred was perfect for Boggart, Barkes, and Bot. It was a midsized industrial world, with grav that was Earth-Norm and no moon besides one that was tidally locked and never went full. Fred still had to stay indoors on "bad nights," but otherwise was relatively comfortable. As an industrial world, it had more than its fair share of spaceports and orbiting refueling platforms; combined with its location as a waypoint between anywhere someone would want to come from, and anywhere someone would want to go, it was the quintessential travel hub. Everyone came through Mildred on their way to something else. It was never called Mildred by anyone but the locals, of course. The story Humph heard was that some drunken transport captain had named the planet after his waitress girlfriend. Most people just called it the Hub.

133

Basically, in terms of the old *film noir*, this was the Waterfront, the Warehouse/Industrial complex, Skid Row, and the Tenderloin districts from those old movies all combined. Maybe some China-town thrown in. And the whole planet was like that. Perfect for the three of them, they didn't stand out overly much, and there were always new marks with new tidbits of information, new crimes that the victims didn't want the cops to know about, new crimes that the cops couldn't or wouldn't solve, new gossip, and new job opportunities. Lots and lots of smuggling, which always opened up a job or three on a regular basis. And what they got was "petty" by crime standards. That was always good for keeping the money coming in while also keeping their profile low.

Humph had quite the cozy little setup; he had tossed his old place—the only thing he had kept was the ancient wooden desk—and bought a "business suite" near enough to one of the major space-ports that things were just comfortably shabby without being run down enough to scare off customers. Office in front, living quarters behind it—not that he needed much in the way of living quarters. Fred the Werewolf needed a room with no windows and a good, sol-id metal door, period. The few nights out of the year that there was enough moonlight to cause Fred to go all hairy and wild-eyed, he was able to lock himself down in the room without worrying about the door getting busted down. Skinny Jim the Zombie needed a corner; they'd found an old robot, gutted it so there was nothing but a shell and a couple bits to make him look authentic, and installed him inside with a disinfectant system to keep him from rot, and another to keep his skin properly oiled and pliant. When he wasn't at the computer … scratch that, he was always at the computer. And Humph himself needed somewhere to keep some clothes, a shower, and a bed. He'd initially thought having partners would drive him insane, and sometimes the other two did force him to retreat to the Nowhere-Space connected to his pocket watch, but for the most part, they were almost eerily an ideal fit. Maybe it was Fred and Jim. They had spent the better part of a century and a half learning how to tolerate a hell of a lot, cooped up in an exploration ship with some of the biggest douchebag Fangs in the known 'verse, (which was saying something) and by contrast, the firm was Mellowville. And neither of the boys was exactly going to set the world on fire with their looks. Despite the reputation for charisma that oozed from the very pores of Weres, that only applied to Alpha Weres, and Fred wasn't even a Beta, he was a Lone. He looked exactly like what he'd been before he got chomped—a balding, middle-aged engineer, though he had lost a few pounds and bulked up in the muscle department when you compared him to his Home Services' mugshots. As for Jim, well, in disguise he looked like a second-hand bot. And out of disguise he was a Zombie, and an aged one at that.

Or maybe it was a match made in ... wherever such matches were made. Probably someplace where virgin sacrifices were still a tolerated cost of doing business.

On the whole, things were comfortable for the trio. Their expenses were relatively low, and the jobs were steady, or at least they had been until a bit less than two months ago. The planet they were on was like that sometimes; usually an even flow of cheating spouses, embezzling partners, runaway teenagers, something being smuggled gone missing, someone needing something "taken care of" off the books, custody cases, and the odd bounty gig ... the usual thing for a PI, even in the modern age. Humans—and most Paras, for that matter—never changed. Despite that, there had been slim pickings for longer than usual. The office wasn't hurting just yet, but the expense account wasn't as flush as it used to be; regular shipments of scotch, cigars, premium steaks, ammo, and rehydrated brains had been slowly eating away at their funds.

"Woman Claims Gremlin Is Stalker," Humph read aloud from the news-twits. "Wrongful Death Ruled in Fur Silver-Poisoning Case. Self-Defense Verdict Sends Dwarf to Slammer." He shook his head. "Not a damn thing for us in the twit-feed today, and am I just getting paranoid, or are there more stories out there lately about us being the Big Bad Bogeymen?"

Fred and Jim were seemingly lost in their own conversation; something deep and thought-provoking, no doubt.

"... I don't really care what studies you bring up, blondes are where it's at."

"You've got less brains than I do, Fido. Redheads, hands down, any day of the week. If you can come up with one good argument, I'll eat my own hand. No, really!"

The Boggart sighed. Not that either of the boys were going to get within ten nautical miles of a woman. Not by any stretch of the imagination were either of them the answer to a maiden's prayers. Or even a not-so-much-a-maiden. Fred even had trouble getting dates among his own kind. Being crammed in a small ship as the jack-of-all-work with a bunch of Fangs whose idea of a come-on was to just use the Vampiric hypno-power on a gal had not given him any instruction on the fine points of Picking Up Women. Humph had been trying to school him, but Fred was a slow learner on that subject, and pathetically oblivious to body language from the fairer sex. It didn't help that he had been a Lone Wolf for so many decades; apparently female Weres picked up on that, through pheromones or some supernatural ability.

The Boggart relit the stogie that he had going, leaning back in his chair. *Things have gotta pick up soon. I need something to get me out of the office, and to keep these two busy. Not to mention keep all of them in brains, steak, and booze.*

Secretly he'd always wanted to have the sort of shabby *film-noir* detective office that was right out of one of his favorite PI movies. Preferably including the wisecracking, gum-chewing secretary with a great pair of legs. Well, you couldn't have everything. He had the office now … just the secretary wasn't what you'd see in a movie. Instead of a leggy bleach-blonde, Jim served in that capacity, usually sitting in the outer office when he wasn't playing cards with Fred. Humph had the bigger desk of the two in the second room, facing the door. Fred's desk was behind him, facing into the wall, as befitted the "junior partner." Since this was a se-curitized building, you had to phone when you hit the vestibule of the building to get in, which generally gave Jim plenty of time to get back into place.

"Wish that damn phone would ring," Humph grumbled aloud.

As if it had heard him, it did ring.

"Goddamnit boss, why didn't you wish for a lottery win instead? Or a baker's dozen of sexy, sex-starved blondes …." Fred mumbled, as Jim answered the phone. The light on the unit indicated that it was a call from the front door.

"Boggart, Barkes, and Bot, how can I direct your call?" Jim was saying, as he trotted to his place, feet only clanking a little on the bare floor. "Yes, Mister Boggart is in, but he's on the phone with a client. He should be finished by the time you get up to our office, I'll buzz you on through."

"Mister? Been awhile since anyone tried throwing that one at me," Humph said to no one in particular. Glancing around his desk, he saw exactly how cluttered and messy it was, and clumsily began sweeping things off the top of it into drawers and under the chair. Fred watched Humph's efforts, shrugged, and kicked his feet up onto his own desk. Humph sighed. "Classy, jackass."

"It makes you look better, boss. Professional." Fred paused thoughtfully for a second. "Or what *professional* would look like if it were a few hundred years old and pickled in whiskey." Well that was more what he wanted from Fred. Once a Lone Wolf didn't always mean a Lone Wolf; with the right circumstances, Fred could change his position in life, much as he had already done with his former crewmates. Furs preferred to deal with their own kind when things got complicated enough to need the services of a firm like BB&B. Having Fred play chief detective when a Fur case came up could cinch them the job that might have otherwise slipped through their fingers. Now, if only he'd learn all that a little faster ….

"You're a laugh riot, mother—"

The door swung open then, cutting the Boggart off. He had just enough time to snatch up a file folder and open it, posing as if he were casually studying it instead of cleaning off his desk and cussing out his partner moments before.

"Mister Boggart is waiting for you, sir," Jim said brightly. "Go on in."

Somewhere in the back of his mind, the Boggart had pictured the client to be what they always were in the old vids … a curvy blonde with legs up to there, red, red lips and a voice that sounded as if she was always a little out of breath. At least that's what he always hoped for in clients, even if it was exceedingly rarely the case. It certainly wasn't in this instance.

Well, he'd gotten the blond part right, but that was about all. Thin, mousy-blond, with a face that looked as if he was simultaneously eating lemons and thinking about the pineapple someone had recently shoved up his ass. A conservatively cut gray business outfit. This dude wasn't money himself, but Humph's seventh sense told him that he represented money.

"Good afternoon, gentlemen." The suit said that word in such a way that it sounded like it pained him to associate it with Humph and Fred, even if only to keep custom. "My name is Bevins. You may refer to me as Mister Bevins. I represent Ms. Catherine Somerfield, who has requested me to acquire your services." Humph stood up for a moment, gesturing with one hand for Bevins to take a seat. He did not sit down.

Humph put the file he was holding down, casually flipping it so that it was right side up. "Is there a reason why Ms. Somerfield couldn't attend to this herself? Why send you, Mr. Bevins?" Something told Humph that there was big money attached to this case, if it was going to turn into a job he would take. Then again, they could really use any job at the moment. The boys wouldn't be too pleased if he got picky at this stage.

Bevins gave Humph the hairy eyeball. "I cannot say, Mr. Boggart. My employer is not accustomed to divulging her reasons for her actions to her employees, nor are her employees encouraged to speculate on her motives. I'm sure you understand."

"I do, but you have to understand our position as well, Mr. Bevins. We're not your boss's employees, yet. And while a go-between such as yourself might not be privy to her motives," Bevins noticeably bristled at being called a go-between, "it does come as a factor for us." He took a puff on his cigar, regarding the suit. "That said, your boss can rely on our discretion in whatever matter she needs attended to; I imagine that's why she's using you in the first place. Discretion." Humph loved to make guys like this squirm. Just because those people were in service to people with power and influence didn't mean that those people were any better than the rest of the world; Humph took opportunities like this one to subtly remind people like Mr. Bevins of that fact.

Fred was watching the entire exchange with a bemused expression, keeping his feet up on his desk. *Watch and learn, boyo,* the Boggart thought.

"What we need to know here, is fairly simple," the Boggart continued as Bevins's lips tightened. "Is this job going to involve anything skirting legalities?" He held up a hand before Bevins could answer. "Not to say that if it does, we won't take it. It just means that things get a lot more expensive—and if I find out after the fact that it does, you really do not want to consider what the fee will be, unless you can get your hands on something equivalent to the expense account of Home Services back when they still had a few red cents to rub together."

"The job, Mr. Boggart, is simple. I need you to find a man and bring him to me, relatively unharmed. This is above board, but my employer wishes to keep this quiet. Family is involved, you see, and the company cannot be the center of a scandal any time soon." He sneered, looking from Fred to Boggart. "I'm insulted that you would insinuate that my employer would ever be involved in procuring the services of anyone for less than sterling purposes. I've come to you, not for your apparently flexible morals, but because of your reputation of a being that always gets the job done. And that you can keep quiet about it afterwards." His expression softened marginally, as he appraised the Boggart. "Or have I heard incorrectly?"

Humph spread his hands, grinning wide enough to show his sharp teeth. "No, you've heard right, Bevins. Let's get down to particulars."

"The Case of the Missing Heir!" Skinny Jim rubbed his hands together. "With our skills, this should be a—"

"Hold it right there, don't jinx it," the Boggart warned, interrupting him. "We can gloat when it's over and the money's in the account. For now, assume everything that can go wrong, will." *A pessimist is never unpleasantly surprised,* he reminded himself.

"You are just a ray of sunshine, boss," Jim groused. "All right, Fred, I'll do the usual, you check on the company. Last one done, buys the next meal." Which in Jim's case ... could be expensive. Jim could eat the brain fungus he and Fred had found on the planet they'd taken refuge on. It grew just fine in the spare closet, and it would do in a pinch. He preferred the dehydrated animal brains you could get at the Zombie supply shop. But what he wanted was fresh. That got expensive. Even more expensive than Fred's preferred steaks—unless Fred was really treating himself to the beer-fed Kobe-style beef that could only be gotten imported from off-planet.

"Sounds like you two have your end of things well in hand. I'm going to head out, start hitting the pavement. Message me when you have a heading."

From everything Bevins had told him, the Boggart wasn't at all confident that old-fashioned shoe leather applied to cement was going to get him anywhere. But what he *was* sure of, was that he needed to walk in silence for a while. He needed to mull over the interview that had just taken place, and let his instincts see what intel they could extract from it. Because something seemed … off.

Like his namesake, the Boggart did his best thinking when he was shuffling down an empty city street, making his way from pool-of-lamplight to pool-of-lamplight.

On the surface, this looked like a legit job, nothing that Humph would turn his nose up at even when business was good. The blue bloods regularly had guys like him do their dirty work so as not to sully their delicate hands. It was how the universe had worked for time beyond time, and that was just fine with him. If nothing else, it meant that there would always be a job for him. Still, he couldn't place his finger on what it was about this one that bothered him. Bevins was the usual snob that lackeys could be, he saw himself as climbing the ladder to someday reach the lofty heights where his employers sat, never mind how much of a delusion that probably was. The job wasn't unusual, a rich nobody had run off to the embarrassment of some rich somebodies, and needed to be fetched back. Par for the course.

Maybe that's it, he thought. *It's too simple, too normal. Whenever anything looks like it's going according to plan, it's probably not somehow.* Humph tried to shrug the feeling off, but he just couldn't shake it.

Well, all right then. Plan for the worst, hope for the best. Make sure he still had some favors owed, bolt-holes open, options in place.

He pulled a microdot out of a hidden compartment in his watch, stuck it in his PDA, and opened the files. Just to be sure.

He frowned a little. There were fewer options open than he liked; still had some but … he made a note that if this panned out, it was time to spread the love around and buy himself a few more shady operators. It never hurt to have a few more cards to play when the chips were down. A little bail money here, a little bribe money there, and it all added up to favors owed. Favors that one day might mean the difference between nailing a case or ending up in a shallow grave.

Humph's comm unit chirped. He tapped a button, cueing up the earpiece he was wearing. "Boggart here, go ahead."

"It's me, boss. Got a lead for you." Fred was silent for a moment, and there was the sound of shuffling papers and data pads. "Looks like you're headed for the pleasure district on the east side, not too far from where you are now. That's the last place Jim found a cash withdrawal. Big one too. Looks like he was planning to find the original good time that was had by all."

"Wonderful. I'm heading there now. I'll be sure to say hi to your Ma, Fred."

"Don't bother," Fred quipped back. "She's too busy collecting all those nickels."

Humph had spent the next day and a half slogging all through the pleasure district before he finally hit pay dirt. Humph didn't like going through there, even though his work forced him to tramp through often enough. Too many holo advertisements, bright even in full daylight. Too many shills too eager to entice him into their dens of "delight." As much of a city creature as he had become, it was also too crowded. Oxygen stations, brothels and sex clubs, trendy and exclusive bars with lines that stretched around the block, street vendors hawking everything from technological toys to sausages of dubious origin to the mostly legal drugs. All of it was pressed in on itself, commerce and vice squeezing into every crack and crevice that it could. He didn't much care for the crowds either. Too many Norms trying to look like Paras. Too many Paras pretending to like the Norms. Kids too young to be here, decked out in Fur tribal gear.

Jaded adults trying to find something new to jazz themselves, wearing outfits he couldn't afford in a year's worth of jobs. Paras passing as the latter—but he knew them with a single sniff. A very few Paras not even trying to pass, but serving as the exotic shills at the doors of clubs and bars. Furs mostly, a few Satyrs, some things he didn't recognize at first glance. There were a lot of mythologies out there, and it seemed Old Earth was disgorging a little something new out of them all the time, as Norms got the trick of Invocations and Bindings. Not everyone was out of the broom closet voluntarily; some, like Humph, had been dragged out, kicking and screaming, by a Norm who had learned some magic and wanted a Para pet—or slave. You never saw Reboots, of course. They were tidied away behind the scenes where no one would have to look at them. It wasn't as if they had the capacity to care. Intelligent Reboots like Skinny Jim were one in a billion.

It was mostly Norms though; Mildred was hardly an exotic world, there wasn't much here to attract a Para that didn't have to be here.

It had taken a little bit of effort, but not too much; the usual haunts were scoped out, palms of bouncers and madams were liberally greased, bartenders and maître d's at some of the more upscale hotels and casinos were discretely questioned, with credit chips passed along just as discretely. He'd come across just what he was looking for when he bribed a senior bellhop into allowing him into a room that Harry the missing heir frequently reserved when he wasn't on the lam, it turned out that he had been there just the night before, and the room hadn't been turned over yet. Humph found a crumpled receipt printed out from the desk net station. It was a confirmation for a reservation at a different hotel, not nearly as upscale but still way out of Humph's price range, across town. Harry had made it under an assumed name, and it looked like he was paying with a quick-use cred card; it was the sort you could pick up for a preset amount. When bought with cash, they were nearly untraceable; no name was attached to them, and once they were empty you just threw them away and bought another one.

Untraceable, unless, of course, you could winkle out the card number from the receipt and the transaction. Well, he'd leave that to Skinny Jim and Fred if he somehow missed the mark at the new digs.

He gave them a quick heads-up, and a scan of the receipt, and he was off. Rule number one of being a PI: don't be stupid. Rule number two: if you have partners, tell them where you're going. Humph didn't much care for having the starring role in a chump comedy. If he got in a bind that he couldn't handle on his own, having his partners know where he was going would at least give them a heading for where to send the cavalry. Or the coroner, depending.

His destination was The Troposphere Hotel. It was done up to look old-fashioned, somewhere around the early to mid-twentieth century, while still having all of the modern amenities that the rich and shameless could want or need. Harry probably thought that it was a quiet place to lay low at, since it was a couple of rungs down the ladder from his usual accommodations, never mind the fact that it would have taken six months' worth of pay for someone like Humph to even spend a night there. *Monied myopia, sometimes the rich really like to make things easy for me.* Barging in through the front door wasn't going to be that much of an option, not this time; despite the evidence to the contrary, Harry might have been canny enough to bribe someone at the front desk to alert him if anyone suspicious came around. This called for something a lot more subtle, something that would get him quietly and seamlessly past the hotel security—which at this level of things, would have living bodies attached to guns along with the usual electronic surveillance.

First place to look, the service entrances. If there was any way of getting inside without attracting notice, it would be there. At the third one—at a guess, it looked as if it was somewhere around the restaurant area—Humph hit pay dirt. There was a crew of workmen in paint-spattered coveralls loitering there, obviously on break. And from the look of them, this was a bunch hired from a temp-labor outfit, it seemed that none of them knew each other all that well. Easy money. Humph was wearing a general laborer outfit already for just such an occasion. It was the top of the hour, which meant their break was probably almost up; he confirmed it when they all started to put out their non-carcinogenic cigarette butts and get up. Humph was already in similar basic work clothes, old and worn enough that a lack of paint wouldn't be noticed. Invoking some quick and dirty magic and putting on one of his generic faces with his glamour, Humph surreptitiously slipped into the group as they shuffled back inside.

He dropped to the back of the group as soon as they were inside, and kept his nose alert. The smell of hot water and strong bleach told him when they were near the laundry, and he slipped away, following the scent. It was easy enough to find a janitor's coverall—no Reboot janitors for this joint—and sneak it out of the pile waiting for pickup and distribution to the locker room.

Places like this didn't bother with ID tags, which could be duplicated, passed off to a friend, lost, or stolen. For low-level help like housekeeping and janitorial staff, they relied on RFID—radio frequency identification—tags sewn into the uniforms, uniforms which you had to put on when you arrived and take off when you left. Perfect for his purposes. A janitor-tag would allow him access to everything but the high-roller suites without question. He changed faces again; no sense in tipping anyone off as to what he was up to, since there was always the off chance that someone watching a security-cam feed was actually paying attention. Next objective was to find a terminal hooked into the hotel's registry—somewhere near the kitchen ought to work. Following his nose again combined with his knowledge of general hotel layout, it didn't take him long to find what he was looking for. The terminal was set up for the waitstaff so that they could ferry room-service orders promptly to the guests. It was a closed system, which meant that it wasn't connected to any outside net. He was going to need a hand to get the information he needed out of it. Tapping his comm unit, Humph spoke in a whisper. "You still paying attention, boys? I'm in, and need you to actually earn your overly generous wages."

Jim was the first one to reply. "On it, boss. Whaddya need this time?"

The Boggart attached a miniature transceiver to the data link on the side of the terminal, checking over his shoulder as he spoke. "Need you to do a remote hack, find out which room Harry is holed up in under his fake name. Got it? Link is up and ready whenever you are."

"My magic fingers are at your command," Fred quipped, sounding actually chipper. "Oh, this is sad, sad and pathetic. You're gonna need to remember this one, boss, there is no ice and no firewall from this terminal, and they left 'support' as an ID and 'guest' as a password. Amateurs. Room 1210."

"Good work." Humph retrieved the transceiver and was about to cut the comm line when that familiar feeling of unease crept into his belly and up his spine. "Do me a favor, keep digging about our employer and the mark. I've got a feeling on this one; it's been too damned easy so far."

"Bugger. I hate it when you get feelings. Are you sure it wasn't just something you ate?" By this time in their association, Fred knew very well when to trust Humph's gut. He waited a few beats, and then sighed. "Roger. Preparing for excrement to hit rotating blades. Out."

Time to figure out my next move. The room that Harry was staying in was on the high-roller level of suites, which made sense; the play-boy wouldn't be caught dead in anything less, even when he was on the run. This presented a problem for Humph; that level was security-restricted, and the low-security rating RFID tags in his clothing wouldn't grant him access. *Guess I'll have to break out a moldy oldie from my bag of tricks.* Since the terminal was still open, he put in an order for room service to an occupied suite on the same level as Harry. Putting in an order to Mr. Somerfield's room might tip him off, and Humph really didn't want the aggravation of a foot chase this late in the game. Access to the level was really what he needed. Once there, Humph would have more time to observe the situation. Nine times out of ten in his job, roundabout was better than going straight to the objective. Besides, with no idea whether or not Harry was in the room, alone, with companions, or hosting a free-for-all orgy, manifesting right there would be a very bad idea.

After the order was completed and the terminal powered off, Humph made his way to the pickup area and waited. Just as he expected, a snooty-looking waiter arrived soon after, checking the details for the order on the terminal; Humph saw that it was for the order he had put in. Sidling up to the waiter, he used some well-practiced sleight of hand to slip his pocket watch into a pocket on the waiter's jacket; a simple pickpocket brush-by was all it took—that, and a craven apology. The waiter might have looked snooty, but at least he wasn't mean to the help. "Think nothing of it," he murmured, hoisting the heavy tray up over his shoulder.

When he was sure that no one was looking, he slipped into the Nowhere-Space connected to his watch, and waited some more. He had called it the Between. It wasn't "like" anything at all, he had a vague idea of where the watch was going, but other than that, the closest you could come to describing what used to be the Between was that there was literally nothing to describe. But it was a great place for a nap.

Back when he had been a simple Boggart, the Between had been something else entirely. He had been tied, not to an object, his pocket watch, but to the land, and the house on it, and to a certain extent, to the people living there. For some immortals, like the Boggart, there's no concrete Beginning; you just are. That had given him a different nature entirely, and access to more expanded powers. He had been a trickster, but one that confined his mischief to amusing or useful pranks as long as he was given his portion of what the farmer produced—usually in the form of some of the food at meals, and of the drink the farmer brewed. But most importantly, he had access to the energy the land and the people produced. And the Between, his Nowhere-Space, had given him immortality, let him sleep for centuries if he chose, and gave him what was, essentially, his own little world. A repository for his power, what he drew on from the land and the people on it.

Then he'd been summoned and bound, all of his vast being forced into a tiny object, and been cut off from all of that. Now, though he didn't much like to think about it, he was no longer immortal. Long-lived, certainly, but no longer immortal. He was tied to the mortal plane. The Between had become his Nowhere-Space—a place of emptiness, where he could still retreat to, but not for millennia or even decades. His existence had become hollowed and terrestrial all at once. It was something he had learned to live with and, despite everything, was comfortable with now. After all, there was single malt scotch.

There was a sensation of traveling on the same level for a while, followed by the feeling of rising. While in the Nowhere-Space, Humph changed his face again. He was going to need a new one to retrieve the watch. When he felt that the watch was no longer rising, but moving horizontally again, he waited for a moment, then materialized about twenty feet on the back-path, behind the waiter, counting on the fact that the man would be too busy balancing the heavy tray to notice anything going on behind him. He tailed the waiter just long enough for the man to reach the appointed door, and as he started to put the tray down, Humph hurried a few steps. "Here, pal, lemme give you a hand with that," he said, retrieving his watch as he aided the waiter in dropping the tray onto a receiving table beside the door. The waiter nodded thanks, then turned to the door, using his pass-key to get in. On this level, you didn't expect to have to answer the door yourself. Humph hurried on.

That went almost too well. It'd be nice to have good luck instead of no luck to bad luck, and I'm not one to look at easy money askance. But still .... Humph shrugged the feeling off, focusing his thoughts on the job at hand. It didn't take him long to find Harry's room; it was one of the larger suites and was tucked in a corner, which meant it didn't have an abundance of adjacent rooms like the smaller ones did.

Well, now he was here, so this was the sixty-four-million-credit question. Sneak in, or bust in? There was no question but that Humph was going to have to get in, the only real question was how. He tested the door, mostly out of reflex—and found that it swung inside easily. And that could only be bad news for Humph. *Oh, goddamnit all. I hate it when I'm right.* His belly tightened up, and the feeling of uneasiness came back with full force. He hunched down as he pushed the door all the way in, keeping behind the wall and only peeking out enough to see into the room. When no one started shooting or yelling at him, he decided it was safe enough to venture inside.

To put it plainly, the room was a mess. Most of the highly expensive wooden furniture had been overturned, some of it broken to pieces. Brocade upholstery was shredded. One of the crystal light fixtures was hanging out of the socket, flicking on and off unsteadily. The bed was torn up, with stuffing and bits of memory foam showered around it like debris from a bomb's crater. Linens with a thread-count higher than an executive's salary had been reduced to rags. Humph began to poke through the remnants of the room, toeing over piles of scattered papers or ruined silk-velvet drapes. He'd tossed a lot of rooms in his time, looking for clues or hints that would help him finish a job, and he recognized this room for what it was: a setup. Whoever had done this job wanted it to look this way, not because they were looking for anything in particular. It was painting a picture with nice broad strokes; only a critical eye would recognize it as an orchestrated scene. And with a joint with as much security as this one had, how had "they" gotten in to do this in the first place? *What in the hell is going on here? Something is way wrong with this entire gig. I'll give it one last sweep, see if I can find anything that'll point me to Harry, and then hightail it back to the office to—*

Humph froze when he heard the door squeak on its hinge, his thoughts stopped midway through. He was almost startled enough to drop the face he had glamoured on. Slowly, he turned around to face whoever was there. The man standing in the doorway, obviously drunk, was a perfect match for Harry Somerfield. Mid-thirties, boy-ishly handsome with a hint of sleaze, tailored casual suit, and a bottle of high-end liquor in hand completed the picture.

"Uh, are you with housekeeping?" Harry slurred, so drunk that he was momentarily oblivious to the fact that his expensive hotel room had been trashed.

Humph was about to offer a witty one-liner when he noticed two red dots circling over Harry's breast pocket. Reacting without both-ering to think about it, Humph dove for Harry, tackling the drunk in a rough bear hug. Two lasers stitched the door and the wall that Harry had been standing in front of, cutting lazy lines into them and setting them on fire. The lasers stopped just as quickly and silently.

Two, snipers—maybe more. I gotta figure out how many shaved monkeys are in this equation. Harry had started struggling underneath him, mumbling about paying his tab. Humph roughly shoved his head against the floor. The targeting lasers started up again, sweep-ing the walls of the room, looking for victims. Things immediate-ly took a turn for the worse; at the end of the hall past the open door, Humph saw two lugs in suits round the corner. Upon spotting Humph and Harry, both began to reach inside their jackets; guess-ing that they weren't fumbling for their room keys, Humph reached out and slammed the now fully engulfed door shut. "Stay low if you want your head to stay attached to your shoulders!" He started to drag Harry bodily to some cover while keeping himself as low to the floor as possible; there was an overturned table near the wall with the window. Getting behind the table wouldn't give them much cover, but they'd be close enough to the wall to avoid the snipers. One problem at a time.

Humph had just enough time to reach into his uniform and retrieve the Webley-Fosbery revolver and peer around the edge of the table before the flaming door was kicked in. Both of the lugs had some very nasty pistols in their hands, and were scanning the room.

Somewhere in the back of his mind, part of him was face-palming. *Burning hells. "Two guys bust through the door, guns blazing ...." When I catch whoever is writing my life, I'm going to feed him his liver.* The Boggart waited until one of them was distracted, talking to someone on the other end of the earpiece that he was wearing. Humph leaned out around the right side of the table, leveling the heavy revolver dead center at the thug's chest before squeezing off two rounds. The thug crumpled while his partner dove for cover. Then the thug got back up, shooting as he ducked behind a pillar. "Damn it! Bastards have body armor. I don't have the right bullets for this. Shitfire!" The table that Humph and Harry were hiding behind was starting to get chipped away; the thugs were methodical, if nothing else, and were working from the top to the bottom of the table with their shots.

Harry had finally started to come to; Humph found that gunfire often had a sobering effect on most beings. "W-what the hell! Who are you? Why are those guys shooting at us? Where's sec—" The Boggart smacked Harry, hard, to shut him up.

"They're trying to kill us. There are snipers outside, so we can't jump out onto the fire escape. This table isn't going to last much longer; once it goes, we're going to get turned into Swiss cheese. Any other questions?"

Harry gulped, and then nodded. "Yes. What the hell are you going to do about it!"

That's actually not a bad question. They couldn't stay here much longer; the two goons were getting cocky now, and had come out of cover to advance on the table, still firing. They were decently trained; communicating and making sure that one was covering the other when someone had to reload. Any move that Humph made would probably get him shot. He could hide in his pocket watch, but then

Harry was certainly dead meat; these guys clearly wanted both of them dead. Pocket watch … got it! He fished the pocket watch out of the borrowed uniform, then chucked it hard over what was left of the top of the table. *I hope it went far enough, otherwise this'll have turned out to be a very bad idea.* He waited a heartbeat, went to the Nowhere-Space, and immediately came out of it again centered on the watch. Both of the goons were now in front of him, still working on the table with their expensive guns. Unceremoniously, Humph raised his revolver and planted a lead slug in the back of each of their heads. The goons fell to the floor like puppets with the strings cut, no time to react before they were already dead.

"Time to beat feet, Mr. Somerfield!" The snipers hadn't cut him down; they must've been confused by what had just happened. Humph knew that wouldn't last, however. He ran full tilt toward the table, ducking at the last second; a laser beam cut through the air an inch above his left ear. Humph expended the last two shots from the revolver in the general direction of the snipers; hopefully it'd give them something to think about. Without missing a beat he grabbed Harry by the collar and dragged him toward the remains of the doorway; both snipers had finally wised up and were firing in concert again.

It was all that Humph could do to keep Harry upright and moving, half dragging and half carrying him down the hallway. All the gunfire might have sobered up his head somewhat, but the rest of his body was still very drunk. Amazingly, he hadn't dropped the bottle that he had been carrying. *Time to figure out an exit strategy. I've got to get this guy back to the office and lose this heat. Why the hell haven't the security alarms gone off?* There were two most-likely answers to that: either someone had bribed hotel security to look the other way, or someone had hacked the hotel's system. Either explanation meant money, and a lot of it; places like this one didn't get cracked cheaply. This whole deal was stinking more and more the deeper he stepped in it. At least he wouldn't have to contend with innocents stepping into the line of fire. The soundproofing in this joint was world-class. You could probably set a nuke off in the hall and no one in the rooms would hear it. They reached the elevators after what seemed like ages; Humph had to use one hand to keep

Harry from toppling over while he punched the elevator controls with the grip of the revolver. Thankfully, you didn't need a key to call an elevator from this floor, the assumption being that anyone up here was supposed to be.

Those snipers wouldn't have been sitting idle; there was, without a doubt, going to be a reception committee waiting for both of them. Humph punched in the service floor; lobby was sure to be a no-go, even if the hired goons weren't there. Hotel staff were usually funny about having their customers getting dragged out by strange beings. Once the doors closed, he threw Harry up against the wall of the elevator, lifting him up by the lapels on what had once been a very expensive jacket, before all the burn marks and tears.

"Spill it, pal. What's going on? Who has a hard-on for you bad enough to send a squad of guns to grease both of us?" Humph gave him a light slap to help bring him around, instructional rather than punitive. Harry just stared at him with his mouth a little open and his eyes bulging a little.

"I—I—I—" Harry stammered. Not exactly useful. And the elevator was in "express" mode, heading straight to the service level without stopping at any other floors. The doors were going to open in a second—

Just as he thought that, the elevator slowed and stopped, and the doors whooshed smoothly open. The sight they revealed was not a pleasant one: two out-of-breath thugs in suits, standing right at the entrance of the elevator clear as day. There was a beat where everyone just stared at each other; then everything happened at once. Both thugs started to reach for their weapons. Humph spun around, still holding onto Harry's jacket, and threw the playboy at the thugs. Reflexively, they caught him, one of them dropping his weapon in the process. Just as quickly, Humph was on them; he was out of bullets, so he pistol-whipped the one on the right, catching him in the temple. The other was trying to shove Harry off when Humph kicked his knee out; the man fell to the floor with a squeal of pain before he was silenced with a second kick to his chin. Both thugs were out, at least for a few moments. He kicked the one he had pistol-whipped a few times; partly just to make sure he stayed down, and partly out of annoyance.

Harry had collapsed in a messy pile on the floor, still babbling about how he didn't know what was going on. *Dumb bastard is in shock. Can't say I blame him too much.*

Humph had a sudden flash as he manhandled Harry up off the floor. These goons hadn't been prepared for his reflexes or his strength. What did that mean? Boggarts such as himself weren't nearly as numerous as some other Paras were, so there wasn't much recognition by the average Joe. By nature his kind were solitary, and usually were tied to one place.

Well if they didn't know what he was capable of before, they were probably figuring it out now. Better take advantage of the fact while he still had an advantage. Rather than try and get Harry to move under his own power, Humph heaved the playboy over his shoulders in a fireman's carry position, and sprinted for the back door. There were a few startled waitstaff and other hotel employees about, but he was moving too fast and didn't look like he would brook any opposition. Having the Webley-Fosbery tucked into his waistband certainly didn't hurt that impression.

Ever the cautious one, Humph had left a rented cargo-pod about half a block away in an alley. Sometimes renting from Hire-A-Heap paid off, especially when you were trying to be inconspicuous; the risks you took with the vehicle in question having a motor powered by anemic hamsters were offset by the fact that it was invisible and no one wanted to jack it. Not worth the time or effort. The only change to the egg-shaped carrier since he'd left it was that the inevitable wag had written "Wash Me" in the dirt on the side.

The pod responded to the proximity of the key in his pocket by sliding open the cargo door. A malfunction—it was the driver door that was supposed to pop—but one that served his purpose better right now. He heaved Harry inside, the playboy still as limp as if he was the one that had been coldcocked, and wrenched the driver door open.

Humph changed his face again as he climbed into the driver's seat. Another one of his standbys, meant to look like any regular schmoe—easily forgettable. He also shrugged off the stolen uniform jacket, opting to throw it in the back on top of Harry. "Stay down and out of sight," he growled as he plugged the key into the dash-socket. The van thought about that key for a lot longer than he would have liked, despite having recognized it to open the door for him, but finally, and reluctantly started. "Warning," said the robotic voice from the dash. "We are in a noncontrolled accessway. Vehicles will not be under auto-control."

"No shit, Sherlock," the Boggart snarled under his breath, and hit the accelerator. The pod responded sluggishly, but did move out. At least he'd fit in with every other driver in these alleys; they all drove like madmen once off the traffic grid. Deliveries had to be made and every second you were late cost credits off your take-home pay. Three more pods sped toward him and scraped past him, just barely not hitting the wall. One rode his tail for a moment, and as soon as the way was clear, squeaked past him and accelerated. Humph wished he had that one right now.

The Boggart keyed his comm unit; it was set to call the office on auto-dial. The line rang for a good two minutes before he cut the connection. *Not good. Skinny Jim always picks up by the third ring, no exceptions. That means the office is a no-go.* He had to think fast, now; find someplace to stash the mark and collect his thoughts. He didn't have Jim and Fred to op for him, which was bad; he'd be flying blind.

You worked for years without a partner, he reminded himself. *Alright, then, let's do it.* Yanking the cyclic around and peeling down an intersecting alley, he pummeled his brain for an alternate safe house.

It was close to an hour later before Humph had found the right spot to hole up in. He had driven around for awhile, mostly at random, before he parked; hopefully no one that was paying attention would think that there was any pattern to what he was doing and get a direction off of him. As stealthily as possible, he had climbed under the cargo-pod, poking around in its guts and desperately hoping the hover system wouldn't give out; if it did, his troubles would be over, permanently. After burning himself twice and getting a nice shock from an exposed wire, he had found what he was looking for: the GPS locator that the rental company used to keep track of its fleet. It hadn't been enabled yet; usually they only did that if there was suspicion that the vehicle had been stolen, or if the law came with a warrant. Still, Humph didn't want to take any chances, so he removed it without completely busting it. There was a parked taxi not too far away; the driver was off duty or otherwise occupied. A few more minutes of jerry-rigging, and the locator was now affixed to the frame of the cab. If anyone did start looking for his ride, they'd have to chase the cab around for a while before they figured out the game; it might buy him a little time.

With that chore out of the way, Humph took a circuitous route to the safe house. In all actuality it was more like a safe closet, barely big enough for the bed, sink, vidscreen, and toilet. If two people wanted to pass each other, it would be a tight fit even with both turning their shoulders. Comfort wasn't why he had rented it, though; it was cheap, and in a part of town where keeping your mouth shut was often part of a long-term survival strategy. Paying in cash and slipping a couple hundred extra to the building super sealed the deal; discretion, aided by another forgettable face and a fake name.

Stashing the van-pod down the street, Humph resigned himself to lugging Harry to the apartment. Across the street and up three flights of stairs. *My day keeps getting better and better.* If anyone asked, he figured that he could get away with saying that he was helping his friend who had drunk too much to get home. It would even be partly true, after all. Harry was drunk, and had passed out. Around here, he imagined that it wouldn't be an uncommon sight. After an agonizing climb, he had finally managed to get Harry to the apartment, plop him on the bed, lock all of the security devices on the door, and slump to the cheap carpeting next to the sink. He was almost desperately grateful that if he needed to—and he probably would—he could retreat to his watch to escape Harry. And Harry's snoring. Harry was a world-class snorer. And somehow still had that bottle clenched in his paw; empty now, probably poured out in their flight from the hotel.

The Boggart sat there for a few minutes, staring at the wall and catching his breath. The adrenaline had finally worn off, and he felt like he was another couple of hundred years older. Tiredly, he fumbled under the sink until his fingers wrapped around a roughly cylindrical object. *Thanks be for small favors.* A small bottle of single malt scotch was taped and stashed under the sink. Uncorking it with his teeth, Humph took a belt from it. And then another. In a few moments, the bottle was half empty, but the Boggart didn't even feel a buzz, just a marginal relaxation and warmth spreading from his middle outward. Adrenaline—or whatever it was in his system that passed for it—had eaten most of the effect. *Now I can think.*

The absolute last thing that the Boggart expected was for the landline phone to ring. It took him a moment, but he realized that it wasn't his comm unit. That's when the stab of fear hit him, for the first time. It was the phone line for the safe house; all these rooms had an old-fashioned phone, the sort of arrangement that someone who didn't want his conversations out on the airwaves to be picked up by anyone with the proper equipment appreciated. No one, not even Jim and Fred, had this number. The line kept ringing, persistently. Slowly, the Boggart picked up the receiver for it, his mouth dry before he breathed, "Hello?"

"Hello, Mr. Boggart."

Humph put some steel in his voice. "Who is this?"

"I represent parties that are interested in offering you a one-time-only deal. It will not be repeated after this communication, and there will be no junctures for future communication." The voice had been run through an anonymizer. Every possible inflection had been taken out. Robots sounded more human than this.

"What's the deal?" Caution was in order here. Whoever it was had somehow tracked him down and knew where he was and that he had Harry. That in and of itself was no mean feat; Humph was pretty damned good at what he did, and no one should have been able to find him here at this safe house. Which meant whoever it was probably had the ability to do whatever he said he could do.

"Give us Mr. Somerfield. You'll be able to walk away from this, free and clear, and be given a very large remuneration for your troubles thus far."

Humph was silent for a moment, weighing the offer. "And if I don't give him to you?"

"The alternative will be ... unpleasant."

That means they'll kill me. Humph thought it through. The kid was nothing to him; he didn't know him, and it wasn't like he owed him anything, much less his life. Whoever was after the kid was serious about getting him; they were willing to kill, but also willing to throw large bundles of money at the problem if that's what it took. This case had already turned out to be more of a headache than it was worth; if he took this deal and whoever was offering it kept their end of it, he could get away clean with a stack of cash. It was a good play; even if the other side didn't honor their arrangement, he still had a better shot of living through the situation if he didn't have the kid around.

There was another voice, no less clear, that told him he wasn't going to take the deal. These pricks had tried to kill him, as a matter of course. Humph usually didn't let little things like that slide. Attempts on his life pissed him off, if nothing else. It was bad for business, too; no use letting it get around that just anyone could decide to take him down. The more he thought about it, the more he decided that he wanted to find out why someone had figured bumping him off was a good idea. Besides, he had taken a job; he'd signed on the proverbial dotted line, accepted the first payment. Once he was bought, it was a point of honor with him to stay bought. He wasn't just "a Boggart," he was "*The* Boggart" for a damned good reason; when he took a job, it got done, no matter what.

"The answer is no."

"Very well." The line disconnected with a click.

The Boggart sat there wondering if he had just made a huge mistake; in any case, it was too late now. He was going to have to follow this line to the end.

He tried the office again. Nada. A very, very bad sign. A sign that the Boggart and his firm had both been set up. He turned on the vidscreen, keeping the volume low, and keyed in the Crime Channel, which showed rolling live reports of criminal activity based on your area. Immediately he knew that all of his fears were justified.

"... a heinous deed has taken place not more than two hours ago. We're here at the scene where the police are busy interviewing witnesses and sending in crime-scene investigators. It appears that we have another in the latest rash of Para-on-Human violence; a local Boggart has been implicated in the kidnapping of one

Harry Somerfield, the heir to Somerfield Botanicals. From what our sources have divulged, the Boggart in question stormed Mr. Somerfield's room, killing two of his security detail and subduing two others before abducting him. Police state that the office which is the Boggart's only known address has been raided, but there was no sign of where the Boggart, Mr. Somerfield, or any accomplices are. Police ask for the help of the community for any information—"

Humph shut off the vidscreen in disgust. *Well, fuck.* There was no doubt about it now; he was being framed, and the setup had maybe been in place from the get-go, somehow. This sort of frame-job didn't just happen in the blink of an eye; a not-so-insignificant amount of prep work had gone into this. Those goons had been trying to kill both of them, not to mention the snipers that had done their level best to make mincemeat out of Harry from the opener; no way were they part of any "security detail." The newsfeed didn't bode well for Fred and Jim, either; if the cops had them, it would have said so. They were probably either dead or taken by whoever was behind this cluster. Maybe, maybe, they had gotten away, but if they had, they were in the wind and might as well be dead, for all the help they would be; the "lifeguard's rule" of "you have to save yourself first" was one all three of them knew well. Everything was swirling around in his mind, and the Boggart was getting more and more pissed off with each passing second. *It's time for some goddamned answers.* He took another quaff of whiskey, then stood up and stomped over to the bed. Harry was just starting to come to.

The Boggart roughly yanked Harry up, pinning him against the wall. He caught movement in the corner of his eye, and leaned out of the way as Harry swung the empty bottle at his head. He swatted it out of the playboy's grasp, then gave him another light slap. "Only one sheet in the wind's eye instead of all three now, huh? It's time to talk, Harry."

Harry's eyes went wide as they focused on Humph's face. "Hey, waitaminute! Who are you? Where'd the other guy go? Are you one of the guys trying to kill me?"

Humph realized he was wearing a different face than the one that Harry had met him wearing. *Whoops. Well, this ought to finish sobering him up.* He smiled ... and then allowed his face to show, dropping the

157

glamour. In the time it takes to blink an eye, Harry went from looking at the face of a boringly average human male to one that had a slightly feral cast, was black as coal, partially covered with short bristly fur, and had very sharp teeth in its smile. "Hi there, Harry. I'm the guy that saved your bacon back at the hotel. Meet the real me."

Harry's knees buckled; he only remained standing because Humph was holding him against the wall. "W-who are you? Why w-were you after me?"

"My name is Humphrey; just call me Humph. I was hired to find you by a tight-ass named Bevins; he seems to be under the impression that your mother cares about your half-in-the-bag ass and wants you back." He let one hand off of Harry, putting up his index finger with the claw at the end of it rather close to Harry's nose. "Now that we're properly introduced, I've got some questions for you, Harold. I'm tired and more than a little pissed off, so I'd strongly suggest that you answer truthfully and quickly."

Harry, eyes still bugged wide-open and glued on the tip of Humph's claw, nodded vigorously.

"Good. I'm glad that we understand each other. First things first: do you know those goons in the suits, the ones that were trying to shuffle both of us off this mortal coil?" Harry shook his head, meeting Humph's eyes. "All right. Do you have any clue as to why somebody would want to kill you?" Harry gulped audibly and shook his head again. "Strike one, asshole." Humph slammed him against the wall, hard, and then brought the claw back up. "It's your neck on the line, get it, jerk? More importantly, it's my ass, too. And I'm not in any particularly big hurry to get scragged. So, let's try this again. Why are there some heavily armed lugs trying to kill us?"

Harry shook his head again, holding his hands up in front of himself defensively. "Honest, I don't know! I don't know why somebody would want me dead!"

"Then why are you on the run, chump?"

"On the run?" Harry looked at him quizzically. "I'm not on the run. Who told you that?"

Humph pushed him back up against the wall again. "I'm asking the questions right now. If you're not on the run, why the prepaid cred cards, switching hotels, and all the trouble?"

Harry started shaking like a leaf in the wind, and tried to make appeasing gestures with trembling hands. "All right, all right, take it easy. It's just kind of my thing. With that moron Bevins always snooping around for Mother, it's hard for a guy like me to have fun. Especially my kind of fun." He shrugged, looking sheepish. "So I sneak out a couple of times a month to go slumming. I use those cards and stuff to keep Bevins from reporting back exactly what I'm spending my money on; I'd get cut off if Mother knew that I was still doing it. As for the hotels, a lot of the establishments on this wretched mudball are rather draconian when it comes to their policy on escorts—"

"Okay, save it. I don't need all of the gory details on what you do between the sheets." There's something more to this, there has to be. I've gotta keep digging. "You're a rich kid, so kidnapping and ransom might've been a good fit if it weren't for the fact that they were trying to carve you up the same as me, earlier. And this is too elaborate of a setup if someone was just trying to bump you off as part of a corporate rivalry deal. You must have pissed someone off somewhere down the line. Welched on a bet, or more than one? Got debts? Hit on the wrong man's girl?"

"Seriously, I don't know! The worst trouble I've been in is getting thrown in the drunk tank a few times and wrecking a few hotel rooms!"

The Boggart frowned. Something had to start adding up. "What about Bevins? He's got a part in this, somehow. He hired me, set me on you. Someone would have to know that he did that, then get the cops to go along with the frame job. That takes time and money."

Harry looked around, searching for how to answer when his face went still; something had clicked for him. "Oh, god. They found out. That contemptuous bastard found out." He was talking to himself at this point. "But no, there's no way Mother would ever ... would she? Let him kill me?"

Humph shook Harry. "Would you like to share with the class, sport? I don't like being held in suspense."

He looked at Humph again, his jaw somewhere in the vicinity of his ankles. "I—I stole. From the company. Well, one of the companies; just a small branch that no one pays attention to. I thought that no one would notice."

"You were skimming from your mother's company?"

"Hey, I've got needs! And Mother could cut off my allowance any time she feels like it. It was just for some extra walking-around money, honest!"

Humph sighed heavily. "Here's what's going to happen. I'm going to let go of you, and you're going to sit down on the bed and behave. You're not going to do something stupid like try and run, right? It'd turn out painful for you and exhausting for me. Know this: people in this neighborhood ignore screams on general principle. Okay?" Harry looked longingly at the door, but then nodded in resignation. Humph relaxed his grip on him, and he gloomily plodded the two steps over to the foot of the bed, sitting down hard. Humph took two steps of his own over to the sink, sitting down next to it and retrieving the bottle of single malt. He took a long pull from it and waited for several long moments before he started speaking. "So, let me put all of this together. You're unhappy with whatever exorbitant amount of money that you get from your ma, so you start stealing a little extra on the side. Bevins finds out, tells her, and waits for you to go on one of your little trips. He hires me under the pretense of finding you to bring home, while he sets up an ambush to kill us both and pin the blame on me. That sound like the size of things?" He took another drink before passing the bottle to Harry. Harry shrugged disconsolately before accepting the whiskey.

"I don't think Mother would ever try to have me killed. She's been disappointed in me before, but this …."

"No, there's something more to this. I don't buy it; it's too much trouble for a punk like you, especially for what would probably be a trifling amount to your sort. How much did you steal, anyways?"

Harry swallowed a mouthful of whiskey, coughing roughly. "Just a couple of mil. It was for kicks, mostly."

"Yeah, that's not enough for this kind of trouble. There's something else going on." He held his hand out for the bottle, taking another drink. "I knew I shouldn't have taken this damned job; however hard up we were for money before, we sure as shit are worse off now."

They sat there in silence for a long time, passing the bottle back and forth between the two of them. Harry was the first one to speak, almost sheepish. "So … Humph, right?" The Boggart nodded. "What are you going to do?"

Humph took another long drink, finishing off the bottle. "My office is torn up. Both of my partners are either dead, snatched by the goons, or on the run. You and I have all sorts of trouble on our heels, from cops with itchy trigger fingers to thugs in suits with expensive toys. And we have next to jack and shit in creds or other resources." He stood up, dropping the empty bottle in the sink. "I aim to get to the bottom of this barrel of crap, and figure out who exactly dipped me in it. The who and the why of it, Harry. And you're going to help me." He held out his hand. "And to start with, you can hand over your wallet."

So far as resources went, things were looking up. One compartment of Harry's wallet was stuffed with prepaid credit keys; when the Boggart asked why there were so many, he had just shrugged and said, "When they get down to a couple hundred, I just stash them in the pocket and forget about them unless I need to pay a cab. Then I just give him the whole chip. Easier that way."

Everything besides the cash wasn't looking so hot. Humph only had a couple of disguises with him, all still in the cargo-pod. He could scrounge and come up with stuff on the fly if he had to, but he usually liked to have more options, especially if he was going to be heading into unknown territory. He didn't have any of his usual array of gadgets that might help him out, either: stuff that Jim and Fred had bought off the shelf or doctored up on their own. Humph was used to working without them, but some of those gizmos could be mighty handy. His silver knuckles were still in his coat; you never knew when you'd be running into trouble involving Weres. Lastly, there was the ammunition for his revolver. He only had two speed loaders on him for the Webley-Fosbery—one that was regular plain-Jane hollow points, while the others were specialty rounds. Humph had personally hand loaded that last set; he called them "all-sorts" bullets. "They have a little bit of something for everyone." These loads came in handy when he was dealing with some of the more exotic denizens of this universe. There was a little ammo stored at the hideout, but they probably wouldn't be able to buy much ammo while on the run; all of the government-owned gun shops would be on the lookout for them, and everyone else would be looking at the two of them like they were steak dinner, due to the reward that was no doubt attached for turning them in. Well, Humph, anyway. For Harry … well, if Humph's gut instinct was right, there was a bounty on Harry, not a reward. That'd be something for headhunters, though; maybe a few dirty cops moonlighting as button men thrown in for variety.

And they were going to have to get out of here pretty quickly. It was unlikely that the goons after Harry would mount a daylight raid on this place, but the clock was ticking.

He counted up the credit keys again. Must be nice to be rich. Humph had an application on his comm unit that let him scan keys for the total still on them; it was useful in his line of work. And Harry was an even bigger chump than Humph had thought. Most of those keys had, not a couple hundred, but a couple thousand. Harry must have left a lot of satisfied cabbies in his wake. That would pay for a lot of low-rent rooms, food-cart meals, and transport. He wondered if Harry had ever been on commuter transit. And if he could be trusted to keep his trap shut about the heat, the smell, and the crowding.

Well, for now, they still had the cargo-pod. After he knew what they had to work with—and Humph had confiscated most of the keys so even if Harry pulled a runner and got away, the Boggart would still have some resources—it was on to the next stage. Because they couldn't sit in this room, eating roach-coach meals and staring at the vidscreen, forever. Sooner rather than later, Harry would get over being scared of the Boggart, and start bitching because he'd never been in a capsule hotel before. And after about an hour of the rich bastard's whining, Humph probably would kill him.

Humph had gone through his address book—he was old-fashioned, actually kept his contacts in a little, physical notebook, though it was digital storage rather than paper pages—about twenty times before he finally decided which favor he was going to call in. After a good long ponder, and checking things as best he could without triggering any alerts, he decided that it was probably safe to use the cargo-pod one last time. He'd have to ditch it after that though. Harry balked at the prospect of riding in it again; apparently he had been sick in it during their first trip. *Tough luck, Harry.* Humph made the concession of placing some old newspapers on top of the mess before he shoved Harry in. He then changed faces again before starting the cantankerous vehicle up.

He left it three blocks from the destination, and Harry was beginning to look decidedly put out by the fact that he was expected to walk. He kept his mouth shut, though, which was showing more smarts than the Boggart expected out of him. It might have been because the few denizens of the area that they passed looked as mean and dangerous as Humph—and a good half of them were Paras. Furs, mainly, identifiable by their tribal-motif clothing, themed to their species: leather, spikes, and chains, most of it easily removable in case they Were'd out. The duo stayed to the alleys as much as possible, with Humph trailing Harry to keep an eye on him until they reached the last gulf of empty space between them and their destination: the back door of the Beau Bayou Club.

It was clearly a happening night; Humph could see the tail end of the line to get into the club, even from all the way over where they were. Looking both ways down the street, he spent several minutes scrutinizing the area for any stakeouts or other surveillance. Getting careless at any point could get him killed in a hurry. Harry, too. And he needed Harry alive if he wanted even a slim chance of figuring this mess out. Either Harry was the best bald-faced liar in the world (doubtful), able to keep his facade up while three-fourths drunk and entirely beaten up (even more doubtful) or he was more important than he appeared. In the Boggart's world, that usually meant he knew something. Information—the right information—was usually a thousand times more valuable than money, and the easiest way to get rid of information was to kill all of the people that possessed it.

Satisfied that they weren't going to be immediately surrounded and gunned down as soon as they crossed the street, Humph motioned for Harry to follow him. They walked casually across the street, staying a few feet apart. Humph's senses were on high alert for even the slightest thing out of the ordinary. They reached the back door without incident. There was one thing out of place, however; a surveillance camera was panning back and forth over the top of the door. Once they got close, it stopped, then zoomed in on Humph. *Hmm. He must be getting paranoid in his old age.*

Now we see if my old code still works. It had been a long time since he'd used the back door of the Beau Bayou, and back then it had been because of a dame. Still, the dame hadn't been his, the affair had been resolved thanks to his intervention to the satisfaction of all parties, so ....

He punched in the numbers, and heard the hum and the click of the electronic lock on the door opening. The Boggart ushered Harry in, closing the door behind them. They were in darkness for a few moments before Humph took Harry by the arm and started leading him down the dim hallway they had found themselves in. There was faint red lighting as they moved forward, the smell of spicy food, and loud music thumping through the walls. At the end of the hallway was a large black door; it had a life-sized embossed skeleton in a top hat on it. Humph turned to Harry. "Whatever happens on the other side of this door, you stick close to me. Got it?" Harry nodded. Then he nearly jumped out of his skin when the skeleton talked.

"Who's your date, Boggart? Not your usual fare." The skeleton shifted in the door, and uttered a dry chuckle. "Never pictured you as a switch-hitter."

"Can it, Happy, otherwise I'll make a xylophone out of your rib cage." They waited for a few tense moments. "Well, are you gonna let us in?"

The skeleton seemed to grin wider. "Password, please?"

"For the love of—" Humph fumed. "You're pretty humerus, Happy."

Harry looked from the Boggart to the skeleton with a vaguely disgusted expression. "Seriously? A bone pun?"

The skeleton cackled; it sounded like a bad wind chime with all of its ribs clacking together. "You and your girlfriend can pass, Boggart. But watch out; they'll eat your date alive in there. Got some bad actors for customers tonight."

The door opened by itself. Given its skeletal passenger, it might have been expected to creak ominously, but it was silent—the kind of silence only a lot of money can buy. The loud, thumping music stopped a second or two after the door closed behind them, giving way to something more subdued. The Boggart very much doubted that Harry would have identified either piece—the first had been a loud, brassy number in the New Orleans jazz tradition; the second was also jazz, but cool Chicago-style. Not that one customer in a hundred would know the difference, nor that you'd have risked getting stoned to death in a New Orleans jazz club for playing Chicago tunes. The Boggart opened another door at the end of the hallway, and they walked into the club proper.

It was dark. Most of the lighting was from flickering pseudo-candles on the tables. Overhead, the ceiling had been done with a real-to-life nightscape, showing more stars than you would ever see on an overcast New Orleans night. The walls were made to look like rough timber, as if this was a jazz joint from about the turn of the twentieth century. The rest of the lighting wasn't coming from any obvious source, but pools of red radiance as dark as blood splashed across everything. They started to pick their way through the crowd, weaving up to the bar. And what a crowd it was; Happy wasn't kidding when he warned that some of the patrons might fancy eating Harry alive.

Most obvious were the Fangs and Furs; some of the latter actually wore the teeth and claws of vanquished rivals as trophies. But there were some truly strange Paras that were regulars at this club as well; they edged past a table where a human-headed, lion-bodied Androsphinx was sipping a mint julep and discussing something with a Jersey Devil. A Bigfoot loomed over the end of one of the three bars around the room. A gorgeous woman in a flowing white dress and blonde hair down to her ankles smiled at Harry, and the Boggart had to grab his elbow and shake it before he did something stupid. The next moment, though, his own good sense—or what passed for it—kicked in, as the woman turned away, revealing that her body was hollow from the rear, as if she was only half of a display mannequin, which was certainly enough weirdness to make Harry back off even if he didn't know what that meant.

The regular customers of the Beau Bayou were ... the deadly sorts of Paras. Most of them were kept in check by the legal system ... or by being careful where they picked their victims. They all came here originally for different reasons, but kept coming back for the same one; whatever you wanted, you could probably find, buy, or arrange to have stolen at the Beau Bayou. There were Norms here, too—the usual assortment of Fang and Fur groupies, who wisely chose to stay close to whomever they were fawning over. But there were others, as well; anyone that might have dealings with Paras that wouldn't bear the light of day was here, wheeling and dealing with everyone else.

And then there was the bartender at the main bar—the one that the Bigfoot was bookending. As tall as the Bigfoot or a fully wolfed out Were, the Rougarou had a heavily muscled humanoid torso, humanoid hands ending in claws, the head of a wolf, and literally glowing red eyes. He had a beard as well, neatly braided and finished off with a gold ring, and a very expensive silk brocade vest over a red silk shirt. Presumably he was wearing equally expensive trousers as well, but his lower half was hidden by the bar. Probably just as well. The Boggart really did not want to know whether or not he was wearing pants.

The Rougarou noticed Humph and Harry as they reached the bar, stomping over after refilling the Bigfoot's bowling-ball-sized goblet. "Humph, long time no see." Humph knew that the bartender had an extremely rare and ridiculously expensive anti-glamour charm, which was how he was able to recognize any previous but englamored customer on sight. He sniffed, then looked over at Harry. "Who's the appetizer?"

"Nice to see you, too, Alphonse. And he's a client. Where's—"

Humph—and nearly everyone else in the club—stopped in the middle of what they were doing and looked toward the stage. A new song had begun; this one had a singer who had just begun vocalizing. Now every head was turned her way.

She was as blonde as the hollow woman had been, with her long hair done up loosely on the top of her head in a way that somehow made Humph's fingers itch to find the pins that held it in place and let it fall down around her. Big blue eyes that should have looked innocent, and instead looked sleepily sensuous dominated a heart-shaped face. Her neck was a long ivory sweep, her body, in a tight-fitting black beaded gown, was made of curves, and she moved like the wind on the water as she sang.

Humph couldn't have said what she was singing—blues, maybe. He didn't recognize the song, and any way the song was irrelevant compared to the singing. Her voice was like velvet, or cream with a touch of whiskey, and the words didn't matter at all. Every word held an unspoken promise, and he knew everyone else was hearing the same promise that he was. Of course they did. This was a Lorelei—the German version of a Siren—and although she wasn't luring men to their deaths on the rocks of her river, there were still plenty of rocks to run aground on if you tried to make her hold good to the promise the melody was holding just out of reach.

Her eyes moved slowly over the crowd, until she reached the part where the Boggart and his charge were standing. And her eyes passed over Harry as if he wasn't there and locked with Humph's.

For a moment it felt as if he had grabbed live wires in either hand.

Then the song ended, the moment passed, and she dropped her gaze before starting another number. Everyone in the club waited a few heartbeats before they resumed what they had been doing. A few threw wistful or irritated looks over at Humph; clearly something had happened and they felt cheated that it had happened to him but not them.

He shook himself out of it. The spell, or whatever the hell it was, was over. He tried to look around the crowd to see the singer, but everyone was suddenly in the way. Harry tugged at his arm impatiently; a couple of the patrons were starting to leer at him, licking their chops. Humph turned back to Alphonse, still feeling slightly inebriated from the last song. "Anyways, where's the boss? I need words with him."

Alphonse had his lips curled up in a wicked grin; maybe it was just the only way that he could smile, but Humph still hated it. "He's working the crowd; got some new customers in tonight and he wants to make sure they feel at home." The grin broadened. "But not so much at home that they get out of hand, if you know what I mean." He pointed the glass that he was cleaning over Humph's shoulder; he turned to look, and there was the man of the hour himself.

Jeanpaul Beausolei had owned the Beau Bayou for as long as anyone on-planet could remember. It seemed that he and the club had just sprung up one day, and been a landmark for this part of Mildred ever since. He styled himself as a retired voodoo priest; no one had really tried to challenge that claim. At least, no one that had lived to talk about it afterward. He had a theatrical personality—or at least a theatrical persona—and themed his in-public look to match his bar. It didn't hurt that he was almost eight feet tall, either. If he was a Para, he wasn't a sort that the Boggart recognized, and he hadn't revealed what sort he was. On the other hand, if he wasn't a Para, the Boggart wasn't sure how he had managed to keep the Bayou going without incident all these years. A lot of Paras still respected sheer might; he with the biggest fangs and claws and the willingness to use them ruled.

Making his way genially through the crowd was a dusky-skinned, apparently human man; his natural height was exaggerated by the tall and flawless black-silk top hat he wore, complete with a silk ribbon rose tacked to the hatband. Beneath the hat, he was bald. The hat was matched with a silk tuxedo, also black, the sort with a cutaway jacket and tails. But under the jacket, instead of the usual white tux shirt, was a vest brocaded with skulls and a blood-red shirt with a ruffled jabot. The ruffled cuffs of the shirt peeked out from the end of the jacket's sleeves. Jeanpaul carried a cane matched to his height that appeared to have a carved snake coiled up its length. That was only an appearance; the snake was real, and alive, and had been known to slither up the cane and down Jeanpaul's hand to partake of his drink.

And when he turned his head, just right, to just the perfect angle, it looked as if there was nothing but a skull where his face ought to be. The Boggart had never been able to work out if that was a magical illusion, some sort of hologram, or a hint at Jeanpaul's real nature; it served to creep damn near everyone out, however, which he suspected was its sole purpose.

Currently he had two Nymph waitresses with flowers in their hair hanging on either arm—goblet of wine in one hand, his cane in the other. Evidently he wasn't interested in sharing with his snake tonight. He was flamboyantly entertaining a mixed group of Paras and Norms, all of whom seemed enraptured with his every word. This went on for several minutes, with Jeanpaul bouncing from clique to clique, keeping everyone happy and feeling like they were special guests.

He really does know how to work a room, I'll give him that much.

Not once during his circuit did Jeanpaul come near or even acknowledge that Humph and Harry were there. Humph went ahead and ordered a couple of drinks for them; he hardly touched his, instead looking around for the singer again. Finally, when Jeanpaul was done schmoozing, he sent the two waitresses scurrying off while he retired to the back room. Less than a minute later a very tired-looking Satyr, another one of the waitstaff, approached them.

"Mr. Beausolei would like it if you two gentlemen would share a drink in his office, if you please." The Boggart knew that was an order framed as a request, even if Harry was oblivious to the fact. Not for the first time, Humph wondered how Harry had survived as long as he had without losing life, a limb, or at least teeth. *Fortuna favet fatuis, I guess.* Or maybe it was the insulating cocoon that money wrapped around the rich. They followed the Satyr through the crowd toward the back; Harry stepped on a few toes, hooves, and other unidentifiable appendages on the way, much to the displeasure of their owners. They came to the door, where the Satyr turned and left them. It opened, this one again doing so without the apparent help of anyone. Jeanpaul was seated at a large, polished ebony desk; his frame made it seem like a toy in comparison. He gestured for them to come inside, with the door shutting firmly behind. For a moment, Humph was disturbingly reminded of a certain "interview" with a Wendigo that had taken place in a similar setting.

"Why lookie what have come to me humble establishment, but Mister Boggie himself! Been an age, has it not?"

"You know that you sound like you're half-Jamaican out there, Paulie. Layin' it on a bit thick tonight, aren't you?" Humph softened the criticism with a lopsided smile.

Jeanpaul smiled even wider. "Half of the rubes out there wouldn't know a New Orleans native if one was crawling up their leg and gnawing on them. How've you been, Humph?" The thick accent was gone now; Jeanpaul's voice was deeper and mellow, with just a tinge of the American South in it.

"Been better." Jeanpaul reacted to this statement by reaching under his desk, pulling out two glasses full of ice, and placing them across from the Boggart and Harry. Next to come from under the desk was an unlabeled bottle of dark, viscous liquid, which he poured for both of them. Humph's nose told him it was Paulie's privately made rum—made as it had been in the Caribbean centuries ago, from sugarcane molasses.

"You don't say? Been a long time since you last made the news. Now you're all that anyone can talk about. If you were wearing your own face out there, I have no doubt that some nasty so-and-so's would be very happy to sell your whereabouts in the time it'd take you to blink." He held up a hand. "No need to worry about anything from my staff; they know which side their bread is buttered on. No one will go out to cause you any trouble, not here."

"Good to see that some things never change. Things have become … complicated, for me. I didn't kidnap this lump. Well, not technically, at least." Harry looked up from the rum, waving shyly to Jeanpaul. "The newsfeed is being doctored. I'll let you draw your own conclusions about how deep I am in it."

Jeanpaul appraised both of them. "You'd need a really tall ladder just to climb to the bottom of the shit barrel that the two of you are in right now." He paused, turning his head. "That's why you're here, right?"

Humph nodded. "That's about the size of it, Paulie. I need some breathing room; I figure getting off-planet will help with that, give me some room to move and try to figure this mess out." He sipped his rum, jerking a thumb over to Harry. "There's something bad surrounding ol' Harold here, and I'm caught in it whether I like it or not. You're just about the only person I know that can get both of us off this rock without tipping things to the bulls."

"You're right about that, Humph. You've made more than your fair share of enemies over the years; there are a lot of beings out there that would love to see you crash and burn in the worst way. You don't think this is that, do you? Someone settling old scores?"

He shook his head, swirling the rum a little in his glass as he thought. "No, it doesn't fit. There's a lot easier and messier ways to get that done, and this doesn't have the fingerprints of any of the usual suspects. Besides, why involve the rich kid in it? That complicates things way too much. On the other hand, if you figure I was set up to be the fall guy for taking the rich kid out of the picture, it all makes way too much sense." The Boggart finished his rum, setting the empty glass down on the desk. "What do you think, Paulie? All debts are paid if you can help me out of this jam."

Jeanpaul had brought his snake-cane over, allowing it to drink a little from his glass. "Your 'client' there is going along with all of this?"

Harry started to speak up before Humph cut him off. "He doesn't have any choice in the matter. He's as good as dead on his own; the lad is really like a babe in the woods. Besides, I have need of him. Only way that I'm going to be able to get to the bottom of things is using him."

"Fair enough." He looked at both of them, pondering the situation. "Very well, you've convinced me, ol' buddy. It isn't going to be easy, but I think we can work something out. I know a guy that runs a trans-orbital garbage scow for a service. Something that'll get you off of dirtside, and will bypass a lot of the usual checks and searches." He leaned back in his chair. "Meanwhile, you relax. I'll have the kitchen send in a meal. Just let Jeanpaul do the heavy lifting."

"Thanks for this, Paulie. I meant it when I said we're square after this is done—"

The Boggart stopped halfway through his sentence. From the main room, he could hear that the band had stopped playing. There was shouting and other sounds of a commotion out there, and that sick feeling had returned to his stomach.

Jeanpaul frowned, and took a firm grip on his cane. "Well, drat. They're a mite early."

The Boggart stared daggers at the club owner. "You goddamned rat. You've sold me out."

"Economics, Humph. It was you or my bar, and there's no way I'm letting anyone take my bar." He spread his hands, looking apologetic. "Just the way it is." *Someone's leaning on Jeanpaul? That ... has never happened before.*

Humph turned to the door for a moment, reaching for his revolver. "Forget what I said about scores, Paulie, 'cause now I owe you big—" When he turned back, Jeanpaul was gone, vanished into thin air. *Slippery bastard.*

Harry had dropped his glass, his eyes as big as saucers. "What are we going to do? There's no way out of this room except for the way we came in!"

"We can't stay here, that much is for certain. Come on, and keep your head down. It sounds like it's going to be messy out there." Humph thought for a moment, making sure that his revolver was loaded; the regular hollow points would have to do. He went for the door, opening it slightly. What he saw looked like the inside of a prison riot, or an insane asylum. *All right, Boggart. Whatever you do, don't shoot any cops.* Right now he was just the easy target for a lazy investigator. If he shot a cop or worse, killed one, there was no place in the 'verse far enough away for him to hide. Cops were really persistent when it came to tracking down and "dealing" with those that had killed one of their own. They were the biggest and baddest gang out there, when you got right down to it, and their style of retribution wasn't exactly a short or pretty process.

The first thing that stood out was that there were a lot of cops. And more were trying to pour in through the front door. Everyone else in the place was either scrambling for an exit or fighting with the cops. The latter group must have thought that they were the ones that the police had come for, and this wasn't the sort of demographic that was accustomed to backing down from a fight. The Weres were sticking together; some had partially wolfed out, and were moving as small Packs as they descended on targets. A few of the cops were also Weres, so whenever the two groups met a furball took place. The band was mostly cowering behind their instruments, the singer nowhere in sight. The Jersey Devil was running around, screaming wildly, and generally being in the way. Some of the Fangs had escaped, while others saw this as an opportune time to get some "fresh food" off the books, going after other patrons and cops alike.

Through all of this violence and bloodshed the Bigfoot was still at the end of the bar, drinking disconsolately. A bottle flew through the air and exploded on the door just above the Boggart's head. *Bar looks good right about now.* Ducking low and making sure that Harry followed him, Humph dashed over to the bar, diving behind it. Alphonse was still there; any time someone was thrown over the counter, he grabbed them and threw them right back. He looked like he was having a merry old time. After grabbing a cop and a Were in each hand and throwing them back into the fray, he looked down long enough to notice the duo. "Humph! Having fun yet?"

"What're you smiling about, you damned jackal?" Humph peeked over the edge, trying to look for a way out that wouldn't involve having to kill anyone.

"Because after this is all over with, I have to clean the joint up. And after a fracas like this, there's always lots of spilled blood." Alphonse licked his lips in anticipation, clearly savoring the meal that he would get later. "Sometimes, there are even body parts. And here I was, feeling sorry for myself because I forgot to pack a lunch."

He grabbed Alphonse by the wrist, hard, to get his attention. "Did you know that Paulie was setting me up?"

Alphonse sneered, jerking his arm away. "Please. You're assuming he'd tell any of the staff the time of day, much less that he was about to feed someone like you to the sharks. We're all mushrooms here, Boggart. He keeps us in the dark and feeds us bullshit."

Humph waited a beat, then decided he believed the bartender. He turned to Harry, grabbing him by the collar. "We're going to try for the back door. Don't get lost in this mess; if you do, you might end up on Alphonse's plate. Got it?"

Harry nodded emphatically.

"Let's do it." Humph led the way, staying low. He shoved and kicked his way through, knocking a few hysterical Were groupies down here, bumping "into" the back of the hollow woman there. And it was a damn good thing that he was another Para, because he could feel her magic trying to suck him in, to integrate a mortal soul into her body. He wrenched himself away. Another narrow miss from a swung bottle, followed by a direct hit to the back of his head from a flying one.

"Sonofabitch!" The pain startled him more than anything, but it was enough; his glamour dropped right as he came face-to-face with a cop. The cop's eyes went wide with recognition. Shit. The cop was the first to react; he had a truncheon and apparently knew how to use it. He swung hard and fast for Humph, missing his jaw by an inch. Humph closed the distance; any blows the cop would be able to land would have that much less power that way. The cop responded by backing up and swinging wide, forcing the Boggart back. This exchange went on for a few more beats until the Boggart ducked one roundhouse swing; instead of connecting with the Boggart's temple as the cop had intended, it smashed into the nose of an already blood-crazy Fang. A trickle of blood escaped the Fang's nose as he calmly turned his head to look at the cop; he then shrieked and leapt upon the poor bastard. As the Fang sank his teeth into the cop's neck, three of the cop's compatriots piled on the Fang, hosing the whole area down with garlic spray and using wooden truncheons on the Fang's head. The anti-Para press was going to have a field day with this entire story.

Humph moved on; it was slow going. The club had been packed before the cops barged in, and the fighting wasn't helping matters. Harry was still in tow, however. Humph tried to keep from becoming entangled in any scraps, but a very pissed-off-looking Gargoyle wasn't having any of it. He had been keeping a space around himself relatively clear by thrashing his tail and knocking over anyone that got too close. Harry, too busy looking over his shoulder at another part of the fray, stepped on the Gargoyle's tail, causing it to howl in rage. The Gargoyle was ready to take Harry's head off when Humph stepped in; the Para focused his ire on the new target. Humph didn't want to give him any time to work up a head of steam, so he swept out one of his legs, hoping to topple him. The Gargoyle simply used his tail to keep himself upright, looking vicious and smug. Humph, feeling exasperated, kicked the Gargoyle square in the chest, sending it tumbling backward into a table. The table had been occupied by a party of Cyclopes, who had been staying out of the affray and laughing at everyone else. They weren't laughing any more, and they piled on the Gargoyle with fists swinging.

When Humph checked over his shoulder for Harry he had to do a double take before he confirmed that Harry was gone. He stood up to his full height—what little there was of it—searching for the playboy in the surging crowd. There! Harry was almost to the back door, but had run afoul of a bloodied Were. The Were was partially wolfed out, and was backing Harry up to the wall. Humph gave up all pretenses of sneaking through the crowd, running and dodging toward Harry. A cop got in his way, swinging a haymaker at Humph's jaw. He ducked the swing, spun the cop with the momentum of it, and then rabbit-punched him for his trouble before shoving him away. A few steps later a mook with a switchblade tried to take a stab at him; Humph caught the palooka's wrist under his armpit, then used his free hand to break the man's elbow upward. As the mook was screaming, Humph worked his arm over his shoulder and then threw him backward; from the sound of it, he didn't land comfortably. Another few steps and Humph came up short to avoid a rolling furball of Weres, cops and customers both. Then he was at the back door; the bloodied Were had Harry pinned to the wall by his throat, getting ready to disembowel him with his other paw. Harry's eyes were bugged out and his face was red; he spotted Humph, though, and flailed his arms frantically for him to help.

"Hey, sunshine." The Were turned his head just in time to catch a jab augmented with silver knuckles to his brow. The Were went down instantly, his lights turned out; Harry went down with him in a messy pile, gasping for breath as the Were's grip loosened. Humph gathered Harry up, grabbing the doorknob for the back exit. "Almost there, Harry. Let's get out of here." The Boggart flung the door open.

The hallway was filled with cops, all of whom looked decidedly annoyed.

Happy cackled, and without missing a beat said, "And, behind door number three: an ass whooping!"

Humph slammed the door, then looked to Harry. "We can't go through there." Almost immediately he heard the cops on the other side pounding on the door, ignoring Happy's muffled objections. Humph searched frantically for someplace to run to; there wasn't anywhere. The front door was still plugged by cops; even if he donned a new face with his glamour, they'd be able to recognize Harry. Happy's door started splintering behind him. Out of time. He grabbed Harry and started dragging him toward the bandstand; it was closer than the bar and was as good of a place as any at the moment. They were halfway there when they heard the back door finally come down.

"There he is!"

"Shoot him! Get him now!"

The gunfire was extraordinarily loud in the confines of the club. A few patrons and even cops went down from the fusillade. Humph threw Harry and then dove behind the meager cover of the bandstand. Everyone else except for the most blood-crazed and die-hard of the club patrons hit the deck as well. *This is it. No way out; can't shoot our way out, and once they get us it won't be too long before they hand us over to the goons. Or maybe they won't bother and will just put two in the back of my head while I'm "resisting" or "escaping."* He could hide in his watch, but only if he somehow managed to pass it off to someone else or hide it, since the cops would no doubt be sweeping the entire club for any evidence.

Harry was whimpering next to him. "Sorry, kid. We're out of cards to play this hand." *To hell with it.* He grabbed the top slide of the revolver, pulling it back and cocking the cylinder and hammer; going down swinging was better than buying the farm on his knees. He was about to vault over the edge of the bandstand and meet his fate when he heard something slam open behind him. Whirling around and bringing his revolver to bear, Humph was met with those same electric-blue eyes from before. The singer. Her hair was done up in a simple bun, and she was out of her black beaded dress and into simple working clothes. But he was damned if she still didn't look like the stuff dreams and dark deals were made of.

"Well, come on! We don't have all day!" She grabbed at Harry's leg, and started to pull him in through the trapdoor she had appeared out of. Humph stuffed his pistol in his belt and helped her. As soon as they were all through, she slammed the small door shut and threw the latch. From the main club Humph could still hear the Jersey Devil screaming and the gunfire picking up. They were in a cramped and musty understage area, intersected with support beams, the lighting intermittent and harsh.

"Come on!" the singer said urgently, tugging on Humph's arm. He suppressed a sneeze and dodged around a tangled mess of old music stands, following her toward what looked in the shadows like a blank wall. Harry complied with being dragged along, happy enough to just be alive at that moment. The blank wall wasn't, however, just a simple wall; it was a metal door painted the same color as the concrete wall. She opened it into a service tunnel that was, if anything, less welcoming than the understage.

"Service entrance," she explained, "For the musicians and their instruments and things. Sometimes JeanPaul has a magician in. The stage kind. That's what the trapdoor is for. This place was a club a long, long time before JeanPaul got his greasy mitts on it." By that point they were all the way at the end of the tunnel, and she stopped and put her ear to the door, waving a hand at him. He supposed she wanted him to shut up, so he obeyed. *This broad has moxie, alright.*

"Sounds clear. My pod's out there, I always leave it at this entrance. It saves hassle at the back door." She shoved on the bar to open the door; it did so with a reluctant scrape of metal on concrete. Humph grabbed her by her elbow, holding her back while he scanned the street. He could see the red and blue of squad-car lights playing against the buildings, but he could tell it was from around the corner. "Looks clear."

The trio quickly made their way to the pod; Humph cut in front of the singer when they got to the driver's-side door. "I'm driving, you give me directions." She looked like she wanted to protest, but decided against it after biting her bottom lip and thinking on it for a moment.

They spent the next half hour in tense silence—Humph making sure that they weren't followed as he did his best to follow the singer's initial directions and hurry without standing out in traffic. The last thing that they needed was to get pulled over. Harry was somehow managing to be quiet. Maybe the idiot had finally gotten some sense knocked into him. Circling the area where the singer had directed them to, Humph realized that it was a storage facility; one of the big-box ones that rented out individual units. Lots of security to keep undesirables out. The singer supplied a passcode and flashed an ID to one of the gate guards. Just like that, they were in. They parked the pod in the lot, which was mostly empty, and entered the building. A short walk, an elevator ride, and a few twists and turns brought them to the unit that she was apparently paying for.

"Inside, quick." She pressed her hand to a biometric reader and then punched in another string of characters to a keypad; the door rattled up, and the three of them shuffled inside. It was simple: a small cot, a net station, and a half-sized fridge were the only furnishings. Piled against the back wall were some crates and trunks. "Home sweet home, as they say," the singer offered with an apologetic smile.

They just stood there for a moment, everyone feeling awkward. Harry, surprisingly, was the first to talk. "Uh, shall I fix something to drink for everyone?" He went over to the fridge, opening it. "Oh, yeah, we've got some things to work with here." Humph nodded absently to him, and the singer did the same; they kept their eyes locked on each other.

"So. Are you going to tell me who you are, or am I going to have to guess?" The singer stood there with her fists on her hips, appraising the Boggart. "I'm guessing that the dustup back there was over you and pretty boy here, judging by the way those cops were coming after you. Did Jeanpaul sell you out for money or something?"

He held up a hand. "Before we get into that, I think introductions are in order. First, I'm Humphrey."

She blinked. "You're a Boggart. Humphrey B—"

"Yeah, yeah. I'm a private investigator. The sap behind me is Harry Somerfield, son of my latest client. I was hired to find him. That's where this whole can of worms got opened up."

She gave him a quizzical look. "But if you were hired to find him, why was everyone after you?"

"Exactly the right question to ask. Some sort of frame-up is what I think; they're saying I kidnapped him. Had to deal with some goons when I found him, and they were clearly looking to snuff him." He sat down, sighing. "What about you? What's your name, and why did you help us?"

"My name's Lori." It was her turn to look embarrassed.

"Lori the Lorelei—"

"Hey, don't blame me, I went for most of my life without a name!" She flushed angrily. "It's not my fault the first human to snare me had no imagination whatsoever!"

Humph chuckled. "I feel your pain, darling. Still, why did you help us out? I'm guessing that you were free and clear of the club pretty soon after the ruckus started."

Her flush deepened. "It was the Imp. I mean, it was the spell the Imp used. I mean—it's a long story."

Humph looked around; Harry pushed a drink into both of their hands. "I think we've got time." He took a long draught from it; it was a rather good martini. He suspected that Harry had quite a bit of experience making his own drinks, from whenever he'd been kicked out of whatever establishment he'd worn out his welcome in on any given day. "The beginning is usually the best place to start from."

"The rat bastard that snared me sold me to Jeanpaul. I might have been able to escape from the wretched human, but Jeanpaul ..." she shuddered. She took a sip of her martini before continuing. "Whatever you think you know about him, I can tell you that you are probably only scratching the surface. Anyway, he bound me to him—and as nearly as I can tell it was only so he would always have a singer for that club of his. He loves that place more than anything or anyone."

"That's your answer as to why Jeanpaul sold us out; someone got to him, threatened the club if he didn't turn us over." He motioned with his drink for her to keep going.

"So one night, I bailed out an Imp that was short the cash to pay his tab. I felt sorry for the little guy, and he's from the same part of Old Earth as I am, but more than that, I was pretty sure that an Imp would be able to get around Jeanpaul's binding and break me free. He was drunk—or maybe desperate enough—to agree. He was about to face the wrath of Alphonse, after all." She sighed. "But what I forgot was that an Imp can't ever do anything in a straightforward manner."

Humph had dealt with Imps before; they were wily as hell, and horrible at parties. "What's the twist? How'd the mischievous little bastard sucker you?"

"After he worked the magic and I freed him from his obligation, he told me that the binding wouldn't actually break until I met someone who would bring more trouble into my life than I'd already had. At that point, I didn't care; I just wanted out from under Jeanpaul's thumb. But nothing happened for weeks. I figured that the little rotter had conned me. Then you walked into the bar." She gave him another full stare with those luminous blue eyes, and Humph got another jolt. "See what I mean?"

It was everything he could do to keep from stroking her face right then and telling her that everything was going to be all right. He fought down the urge and finished his martini to brace himself. "Well, darling, I hate to say it, but the Imp did one over on you. Big time. Trouble does not even begin to describe what I brought with me. I'm in a world of hurt right now, and I don't rightly know who put me there. Or why, for that matter." His jaw tightened, and he ground his teeth unconsciously. "But I'm going to figure it out."

Harry sat down between the two of them, grinning and holding his own martini. "Don't worry, miss. With my intrepid companion here, we're sure to figure this out in no time." He leaned in closer, shouldering Humph out of the way slightly. "So, where back on Old Earth are you from again, doll?"

She sighed, and tried to lean to see around him to Humph. "Germany is what you'd call it. Anyways—"

"Ah, Fraulein! How in the world did you ever come to be on this miserable little rock?" He leaned in her way again, sipping his martini.

"It's complicated," she said as she tried to look to Humph again. He had leaned back at this point, watching the show unfold to its inevitable conclusion, which he had already guessed. "So—"

"Come now, it can't be that bad, can it? Tell me your life story, beautiful, and I'll give you the world." Harry had turned the charm up all the way at this point. Humph felt like warning him for half a second, and then decided he'd enjoy just watching the train wreck more.

Lori looked him straight in the eye. "Fine. I used to use my voice and my powers to lure men to horrible, tortured deaths on craggy rocks, and I enjoyed doing it too, until a sorcerer captured me, then sold me to a voodoo priest who bound me to his soul. Satisfied?" Harry looked at her closely, saw that she wasn't making a joke, gulped, finished his drink in one slug, and then stood up.

"I, um ... I think I need a refresher. Anyone else?"

Humph was chuckling to himself. "I'm fine." He leaned forward again, smiling. "Got that out of your system, princess? He'll just be at it again once his goldfish memory resets, y'know."

"They never learn," she sighed. "What's our next move? My plan was to hop a freighter off of this rock to parts unknown—anywhere that Jeanpaul wouldn't be able to find me."

But Humph shook his head at that. "Can't leave the planet, not anymore. For starters, the bulls will no doubt already have every station monitored, and all the spaceports. If they're not running interdiction on all outgoing transports, I'd be very surprised. Jeanpaul, the rat bastard, might've had the resources to sneak us out, but he's obviously not an option anymore. Secondly, this is where the mess started. If I'm going to figure out how to get clear of it, it'll be here that I find the information I'm lookin' for."

"I don't imagine that we can sit in this storage unit forever." She glanced over at Harry. "The booze will run out soon enough, and then I might actually kill that poor sucker."

He had to chuckle at that. This was certainly his kind of woman. "Fair enough. First thing we need is a little breathing room; this part of town has become mighty crowded, fast." He sat thinking for a few moments, taking another sip of his drink. "We're going to need you to work a little of your magic, Lori. And we're going to have to skip town. Are you up for that?"

She chewed her lip, then raised her glass. "As we used to say in the old days, in for a penny, in for a pound. We're stuck together now."

And, predictably, a little more liquid courage had given Harry back his aplomb, or at least, his chutzpah. "Any man would like being stuck to you, gorgeous," he leered. "Want to try it out for size?"

"Sure. I need something unimpressive to mount to my wall." She leered back. "Are you volunteering? Darling?"

It took some convincing to get Harry and Lori to go along with it, but Humph had come up with a semiworkable plan. Lori, being the only one out of all of them that didn't yet have her face plastered on every wanted notice on the planet, would be their "front man" for the time being. First order of business was to get outfitted, literally. She went out and bought them some new clothes. Harry's suit was tatters at that point, and Humph needed something besides coveralls and a trench coat. Some button-down shirts, nice slacks, and comfortable shoes for both of them; nice enough to swim between middle and upper class in a pinch, but not so expensive that they stood out. Lori had a small wardrobe already, but got herself a few dresses, tops, and other necessities anyway.

The next part required a bit of subterfuge. Humph knew they wouldn't be able to get off-planet; if the cops hadn't already been watching for them to escape that way, which was unlikely, they certainly would be now. Jeanpaul had probably divulged everything about their meeting to the cops or whoever had gotten to him. *There'll be a settling of accounts on that one, Paulie. Bet your bones, you rotten fink.* Still, he could use that to his advantage. He and Lori started trolling the bars near the spaceport until they found one particularly disreputable establishment; it didn't seem to have a name, only a sign that said "Cantina" above the door. After spending some time studying the crowd, Humph found their marks: a scruffy-looking freighter captain and his Yeti copilot. Lori worked her magic on both of them, and soon they were ready to eat out of her palm. No one else in the bar seemed to notice, or care. She probably wasn't the first of her kind to come a-hunting around here, and for the most part, the Sirens, the Loreleis, and the other mesmerizing types did tend to stick to fleecing their targets rather than killing them outright. Any sufficiently talented Norm hooker could do that sort of "magic"—the fleecing, that is, not the killing.

Using a script that Humph had made her memorize, she convinced the captain and his copilot that she was in need of help, and that they were her only hope. First she convinced them that they needed to take her and a couple of friends to a port on the other side of the planet; she was fleeing a jealous ex-boyfriend, and couldn't use regular transportation. Second, that they needed to spin a yarn for any cops that they happened to come across after they left the Hub; that they had taken on passengers, a Boggart and a human that fit Humph and Harry's descriptions, and dropped them at a random station. Hopefully that would keep the authorities chasing their tails, and off of Humph's scent. Her magic worked perfectly on the inebriated pair; they were already enamored with her before she started, and the magic itself would last for days. Plenty of time for the Boggart, Harry, and Lori to be far away when it wore off.

Gathering up Harry and their meager possessions, they were off with the captain. The flight was short, only about four hours. The primary advantage was that in-atmosphere flights didn't have to be registered the same way as launches off-planet were—no paper trail to link back to where the trio were heading. Humph dozed for most of it, while Lori was left to fend off the advances of Harry and the Yeti; occasionally Humph would wake up long enough to caution Harry against pissing off the copilot too much. Yetis weren't exactly known for their gentle dispositions. Lori actually seemed more amused by the situation than anything. This might have been the first time in a long time that she'd been at liberty to tell someone no. Humph didn't like to think what else that JeanPaul had had her doing besides singing. Because if he thought about it too much, he'd have to put JeanPaul on the top of his personal Bucket List. *In Paulie's case, meaning the short list of people I beat to death with a bucket full of cement, starting at the feet and working my way up. And if he ain't just a tall bastard.*

Once they had landed and concluded a tearful farewell—Humph had never seen a Yeti cry before (it was, in a word, disturbing)—the trio set off to find a place to start plotting their next move. The port was more of the same as the rest of the planet, but grimier. To put things into perspective, JeanPaul's establishment had rested on the periphery of a zone like this, slightly on the higher end. This area had everything together, jam-packed and stacked on top of itself. Factories and power plants were nestled right next to pleasure districts and gun shops, with casinos and churches just around the corner. The ports were the real face of Planet Mildred, and this was the perfect place for them to disappear into for awhile.

Humph picked an out-of-the-way flophouse; he had Lori pay in advance for a one-week rental room. A few extra bills slipped to the clerk was pretty much required; places like this one housed those on the lam as often as they did transients and factory workers. Only she and Harry walked in; Harry's face was buried in bags that he was carrying for Lori. Humph, meanwhile, rode along via his pocket watch, which he had temporarily entrusted to the Siren. When they were finally settled in the cramped room, Humph started to get to work. Using a cheap, disposable comm unit he started to put feelers out to some of his more trusted contacts. He needed more information on Harry's company, Somerfield Botanicals, the various subsidiaries and other connected businesses. He also needed to know if anyone was making big moves in order to find Harry; someone with a lot of resources was after him, and that sort of influence was hard to hide effectively.

The only thing left to do was wait. He had sent out the messages as securely as he could; unfortunately, he wasn't as good at cybersecurity as Fred. It would take a bit of time for any responses to come back. This left a lot of time to kill in the flophouse room. Harry kept hitting on Lori. Humph had to give him some credit for persistence. Lori continued to shoot Harry down, but each setback seemed to embolden him rather than dissuade him. That didn't really surprise Humph; he doubted that the word "no" was something that Harry had heard very often in his privileged existence.

What did surprise him, however, was when Lori started making passes at him.

Subtle passes. Probably so subtle Harry didn't even notice them, and thought he was free and clear to navigate. Then again, court-ship among Paras tended to have little nuances involving magic that Norms wouldn't see.

Like the little tendrils that looked like golden dust that Lori kept throwing off in his direction. Or the distinctly magical gleam in her eyes when she glanced at him. And the undertones of her voice when she spoke to him—undertones that told him, in essence, "I could use my power on you if I chose, but I choose not to, so you know this is real and not a compulsion." All this read "I am really, really interested in hooking up with you" in Para-language. This was dangerous. Paras and Norms loved ... differently. Paras experienced wild changes in emotion that could only be described as hyper-bipolar, running to deep longings and passion that could burn deep in a being's heart for millennia. After all, in the old days it might be a hundred years before you encountered a potential mate. Or longer. You'd better be able to hold to affection for at least that long.

There were several other problems with this courtship, of course. How much of this was actually due to the Imp's spell? He had no idea. Another consideration was Harry. While Harry wasn't exactly high on Humph's list of all-time favorite people, pissing the Norm off and having him stomp out of the room—possibly to blow their cover before Humph could reel him back in—was a pretty bad idea. While it was clearly not going to happen between Harry and Lori, Harry didn't know that.

And then there was Claire ... dear Claire. Parked in the back of his head, smirking at him, and reminding him that he still wasn't "over" her, no matter what he might think. He never "fell" for anyone; it was a rule of his, or it had been. Especially a Norm; he was going to be around for a while, whereas most Norms just ... weren't. Those were the breaks. Claire had been different, and he was still kicking himself for letting her in. Thirty years had never seemed like such a long time until after he met her. Granted, she had turned into a colossal bitch, and a Fang bitch at that. He knew, however, that he was at least partly responsible for who and what she had become; a mixture of pity and heartache always cropped up when he started thinking about her.

And Lori is a Para, not a Norm, a little voice in his mind reminded him. She was dangerous, certainly. A killer of men, Humph had never heard of a Lorelei that wasn't; she had spent hundreds of years doing it, before she was bound. It was her nature. *But you're no different, Boggart. What have you done in your long life? For survival, for kicks, for money?* He was really starting to hate the hell out of that little voice in his mind.

They were sitting in the room, sharing drinks with the vidscreen droning in the background. Humph had been keeping an eye on it for any little bit of intel that he could gleam. Most media outlets were in the pockets of any number of interested parties, but gems of information could still get out every now and again. Then it happened.

"So. How long have you been—" Lori gestured vaguely in a way to suggest *the world* "—out of the broom closet?" She blinked limpid blue eyes at him. "It hasn't been more than a couple of years for me. I never would have thought anyone would have gone looking for one of my kind up that particular obscure Austrian stream. I'd thought I was pretty safe."

Humph mused thoughtfully. "It's been a while." He left it at that, not wanting to tip his hand too much. "Let's just say it was a surprise to the both of us when I got yanked out into the Norm world."

Lori made a face full of distaste. "If I ever get my hands on the bastard that wrote *Summoning and Binding for Dummies* …." Her expression made it clear that what she had in mind was going to be long, involved, and painful.

He raised his glass. "Not so bad, being out in the world, though. They have scotch, after all." Humph drained his glass. "Beats a share of a farmer's crops, at any rate."

"And your farmer didn't brew his own?" She smiled sweetly. "Really, Boggart, you should have found a better class of host."

Humph shook his head. "I never said I was a particularly good Boggart, lady." There were a few moments of comfortable silence, and he felt it again; the urge to throw caution to the wind and go after her. He had to give himself a hard mental shake. It was an effort to stand up and walk over to the bottle on the bed instead of throwing his arms around her. Harry was still passed out on the bed, empty martini glass in his hand. *Nice that someone is able to sleep, at least.*

But when he got up, so did Lori. Before he could turn, she was behind him, close enough so that he could feel her warm breath on the back of his neck. "So ... since Sleeping Ugly is going to be out cold for a while, think we could go somewhere else more ... comfortable ... for a little?" Her voice was a warm, lush purr in his ear; she didn't physically touch him, but he could feel tendrils of her magic twining seductively with his. "I'm sure we could manage something."

Keep it together, Boggart. "Can't do that, sweetheart. This poor sap is my—our—lifeline right now. I'm not letting him out of my sight for more than a minute at a time if I can help it." He stared at his drink for a second, taking a large gulp to steel his resolve. "I might not be a good Boggart, but I like to think I'm at least a passable gumshoe." He could smell the light perfume that she was wearing; it was blue lotus, and was intoxicating on its own. His head was swimming when he finally turned around to face her. Electric-blue eyes locked with his; he wanted to tear himself away from her, to sit down and pass the time quietly, but he found that he couldn't.

"Oh, Boggie," she breathed, moving in a little closer. "He's finished off most of that bottle of gin. He won't be going anywhere for a good long while. Why don't we get to know each other better?" She was almost nose to nose with him. "A whole ... lot ... better?"

His hands started to move of their own volition. He set down his drink, then gently took the back of her neck into the other hand. It felt like time was stopping, and that he was going to fall into her eyes and be lost forever. Their lips were almost touching, uneven and hot breath gracing one another. It was like a scene from *Beauty and the Beast*; he was savage and feral, she was frail and innocent. He closed his eyes, ready to surrender to the inevitable. Everything shattered when his comm unit went off loudly and insistently. Harry bolted upright in bed, still half asleep. "—no, not on the carpet!" He blinked

186

hard a few times, looked around, then remembered where he was. "Uh, the phone's ringing." Humph and Lori quickly stepped back from each other; Humph felt guilty, and he could see the disappointment on Lori's face. *Too damned close, moron. You know better.* Harry was oblivious to the exchange.

Humph picked up the comm unit. It didn't take very long at all for him to see that things were going downhill fast, and picking up speed. Over the course of the next couple of hours, Humph had bad news piled on top of worse news. Most of the contacts that he had reached out to never got back to him. The Harvey Brothers, Mikhail, Rodney the Fence, Small Tony, Big Tony, Señor Leandro, and Whispering Miguel—all of them were silent, and quite a few of them were his most dependable information brokers and snitches. Everyone he did hear from didn't know anything of value. What stood out was that they were all scared. Which was saying something, considering the clout some of them had and the strings that some of them could pull. There was someone out there making big moves, and all of it seemed centered on Humph.

The last of them was Lenny the Lip, who sounded on the edge of a nervous breakdown before the Boggart closed the connection. He sat down on the bed heavily, feeling weary. He had been in the dark on jobs before when a lot was on the line, but this was different. Someone had painted a bull's-eye on his back, and he didn't like it one bit.

Well this wasn't anything that someone who was merely holding a grudge against the Boggart could pull off. It was one thing to have an APB out on him for kidnapping someone that wasn't quite kidnapped. It was quite another to put out word that he was toxic that reached all the way down to every level—and have it believed enough that his sources wouldn't even touch base to say they knew nothing. *Or it could be worse than that—maybe some of them didn't call back because they couldn't; mighty hard to pick up your phone when you're dead.*

"We've got big trouble, dollface," he ruminated, as Lori watched him with a gaze that had gone from seductive to worried as each call came in. "This is either big corporate, or big crime. Or both, sometimes it's hard to tell them apart. That's people that can spend more than you and I will see in a hundred years on five minutes of organizing." His eyes turned to Harry. "In fact, it's probably more than his mommy's company will ever see in a hundred years, and that just doesn't add up. I can't figure how you'd be worth the cost and trouble for all of this. No offense."

Harry spread his hands and grinned magnanimously before taking another sip of his refreshed martini.

Humph's comm unit chirped again. More bad news. It was an unlisted line. Most of his contacts—even the legitimate ones—made use of burner comm units with reusable lines; that way he would know who it was, but it'd be a lot harder for anyone that was paying attention to find out who was calling. He picked it up after a few beeps. "Hello?"

"Hi there, Boggie. I'm going to screw your head off and play golf with your spine for all the trouble you've caused me, you know."

Humph blinked hard as recognition set in. "Claire?" Relief washed over him; she had been in the back of his mind ever since he got the first returned call, and the implications of someone not getting back to him had become clear. To be honest … no matter how his head felt about her, down in the emotions sector, he'd been worried sick about her. Sure, she was pretty well protected by her Nest on that station of hers … but it wasn't that hard for a Norm hit squad to take out a Fang. Especially the kind that had the sort of money that allowed you to build an entry-pod, hide it in the bay of a freighter, pop out when you were docked, go straight to the section of the station you wanted to hit, cut an entry port and dump the squad right in the target's office.

"Yes, it's me, you bastard. What have you done this time?" Humph caught Lori's expression; whatever she was reading in his face, she was not happy about it. In fact, her expression looked a lot like jealousy.

"Not much. Shot a bunch of goons, saved a blue-blood playboy from getting a permanent haircut at the shoulder range, and I've been accused of kidnapping the same."

"Ha fucking ha. Really, what did you do?"

He explained the situation to her from the beginning: the job from Bevins, the hotel, his partners going missing and his office being ransacked, and being on the run. Claire took a few seconds to process everything once he was done. "That doesn't make sense."

"You're telling me, sister. Only thing I can figure it for is a rival corporation or some big-shot criminal enterprise. Problem is, I can't finger anyone that would fit the bill."

"It can't be either one of those. Boggie, I'm on the goddamned lam."

It was his turn to be stunned. "What?" Claire had serious backing, probably more than any other person that he knew. Her operation had grown in the few years since he'd last seen her; the Elders were grooming her for proper leadership, since she was bringing in real money now with all of her ventures. The Elder Fangs pulled a lot of weight; plans and schemes and machinations that stretched into the century range to see the result, information networks that rivaled those of governments, and more money than God. *Could they be behind this?* The implications made his stomach lurch hard a few degrees to port. It didn't seem likely; he didn't know if he felt that way because of the scarcity of evidence or if it was because he simply didn't want to believe that this whole mess was that far-reaching.

"I got your message a few days ago. I put it off since I was busy. A pesky business rival needed some reeducation; a girl has to have her hobbies, after all. Anyways, once I got back to my station, I started digging into your little problem from what scant information you provided me. A few hours later, everything went straight into Hell's own crapper; we lost our communications, my accounts were frozen, and then the station was attacked! I barely made it out in one piece; as far as I know, no one else did. I've been on the dodge ever since."

"Holy hell, Claire. If I had known—"

"Damn right if you had known! Whatever fucking trouble you're in, I'm in now too. I'm telling you, Boggie, I don't want any part of it! At first I thought it was one of the other Clans making a move; it wasn't. This was different, at least outwardly; whoever is doing this is well trained, well funded, and going after anyone and anything with a connection to you. They're burning all of your bridges and trying to run you into the ground, Boggie."

His mind was swimming with all of this new information, trying to process it. "Look, Claire, tell me where you are. We can figure this out—"

"Stop right there. I'm on the run, and I'm staying that way until this is over, Boggie. I'm not going to be the grist for the mill in this goddamned escapade of yours. I took a big enough chance just calling you, and I only did that to see if you knew anything that could help me. Fat lot of good it did me. Whatever shit you got yourself into, you can get yourself out of. Good luck." With that she closed the connection. And if she was smart—which she was—she ditched the comm she'd just made the call with somewhere in deep space, before course correcting for a tangential trajectory. He wasn't sure, but he thought that he had heard just a trace of concern. He could have just as well been imagining it.

Well. That was … festive. "Huh." So Claire was on the run. Whoever was after him was making sure that he had no one to turn to and nowhere safe to hide. This was beginning to look and feel a lot bigger than he thought even five minutes ago. But who could have the juice to pull all of this off, and stay in the shadows while they were doing it?

"Well?" Lori was sitting on the bed next to Harry now, her arms crossed in front of her chest and her expression icy. "What did she have to say?"

"That someone shut down and attacked her station right after she started poking at our anthill. She's a Fang Nest Mistress and until a few hours ago, she owned a deep-space station. So you tell me what that means." Humph hadn't intended to be quite so point-blank—except that if Lori was going to get all pissy over another woman, that needed to be burnt off at the root, right now. They didn't have any time for that sort of thing; this was a survival situation. "Harry, do you have any idea who could pull all of this off? It can't be your mother or the company, can it?"

Harry shook his head, his brow screwed up in concentration. "I really can't, Humph. We're just a cosmetics company; we've got our rivals, sure, but no one that would have the sort of scratch to go to these lengths to just rub me out." He rubbed the back of his neck, then grinned. "I mean, I am pretty awesome when you get down to it, but it's not like I'm vital to the company or anything. Bumping me off wouldn't hurt things with our board; hell, some of our investors might even throw a party. Especially ol' what's-her-name … never did forgive me for that trip to Mars with her daughter ....." He snort-ed. "And never would believe me when I said it was Brittany's idea."

Lori stood up; her arms were still crossed defensively across her chest, but at least she didn't look like someone had just kicked her dog. Actually she looked scared. "Pauly never let slip who had leaned on him; he didn't really share much information with the hired help. I can't really think of who it would be myself; I'm not exactly an experienced member of the criminal underground, after all." She looked back and forth between Harry and Humph. "Well? What do we do now?"

There was a very loud bang from the front of the flophouse, where the check-in desk was. They were all startled by the sound, but Humph immediately knew what it was. Breaching charges. *How could they have found us, again? Scratch that. How could they have found us so soon?* He immediately set to work, gathering up the essentials, kicking Harry in the ass, and pushing both Harry and Lori toward the door. There were more explosions: flash-bangs, then gunshots. Whoever was raiding this place, they weren't interested in taking prisoners. The rest of the residents of the flophouse had the same idea as Humph and company—get the hell out of Dodge. The hallway was packed with screaming beings, Para and Norm alike. Humph was in the rear, with Harry between him and Lori. Every-one was tripping over each other, stampeding toward the back door. Humph and his crew were by no means the only ones with reasons to run from the law in this joint.

After a lot of noise, elbows, and stepped-on toes, they were out the back door and into the cool night air with the first lot of escapees from the flophouse to fight their way into the open. They didn't so much stumble out as tumble out, barely managing to stay upright. Humph had taken the precaution of keeping them a little back, so they didn't run straight into the arms of whatever dragnet had been set up outside all of the exits. Floodlights came on within seconds of them emerging from the building, blinding everyone. The gun-fire started almost immediately after, cutting down the first rank of people in front of them. Humph shoved Lori and Harry hard to the right, diving after them. He felt something akin to a heavy punch hit his left side, followed by searing pain. They all landed in a pile, behind what looked like a burnt-out transport. Everyone from the flophouse was still piling out, being pushed from behind by the raid team right into the gunfire. There was a lot of screaming; the hot, thick scent of blood that wasn't his hit his nose. Right on top of that was the burned-pork reek of lethal laser wounds. It was a slaughter. No warning, no demand for surrender or quarter given; this was a sweeper team, and they were going to kill everyone that they saw. They might not even be human. Bots were not supposed to be armed, ever, but everyone knew that just as Asimov's Third Law was an old joke, anyone with enough money could shrug off the fine if he was found with a garage full of war-bots.

"We're pinned down," Humph gasped out. The pain was working its way up his side; he glanced down and saw that he was definitely bleeding freely. It was a gunshot, not a laser blast; if he had been tagged by a laser, there'd be less blood and a hell of a lot more pain. At least there was that—no major organs had been hit either, but he was still going to have problems if they didn't get out of here and stop the bleeding soon. He probed the wound, felt that the pocket had torn through, and panic shot through him; his pocket watch was gone. It must've been shot away. If he couldn't find it, he was dead. As a Boggart, he was tied to it; he couldn't go too far away from it, otherwise he'd be instantly transported back to it. He felt himself getting dizzy. He staunched his wound with his hand, mumbling about his watch and needing to punch a way out. Lori shouted something to Harry; all sound except the screams of the dying and the gunfire was starting to fade out.

Things were going dark around the edges of his vision; Humph knew he was going to pass out soon. Lori had disappeared. Had she left them? Had she ever been with them in the first place? Harry was shouting something, trying to keep him awake. Then his face swam in front of Humph's vision; Harry was smiling, flashing his perfect teeth. How could he be smiling? How dare the little punk smile? Harry patted Humph on the shoulder, and then ran into the kill zone. He jumped over bodies, bullets kicking up flecks of concrete and dust all around his feet, impacting all of the surfaces around him as he made his mad dash. He stopped right in the center of everything; there were still a couple dozen people scrambling to find cover before being cut down. Harry calmly bent down, picked something off the ground, and then ran back to where Humph was propped up against the burnt vehicle. The bastard was still smiling.

"Hey, you dropped this, partner." Humph stared at him incredulously for a few seconds before he looked at what Harry was holding up—Humph's pocket watch, smeared with a little bit of blood but otherwise intact. "Every man needs to keep a good watch." Humph blinked for a few seconds, took the watch, pocketed it, and then promptly passed out.

The Boggart woke up in stages. At first he could only register pain; it wasn't sharp and immediate like before, but dull and throbbing, distant. Next there were sounds; he eventually recognized them as voices, Harry and Lori's. *Everyone made it out. How? Where are we?* The last was his vision; he had passed out a few more times before he finally came to fully. He recognized the ceiling: the interior of a modular transport ship. Hundreds of thousands of them were mass-produced every year, to the same specs by different manufacturers.

His first thought was to panic, since if they were off-planet they had just posted a huge red arrow pointing right at themselves. No way they could have gotten on board a ship without someone IDing them. And every ship leaving this system was being searched, that much he was sure of this late in the game. Anyone that could afford a strike team that could take out a Fang station could afford damn near anything, up to and including buying off the planetary police. And after all, he was wanted for kidnapping. It would be a small stretch for him to be "killed in the course of resisting arrest," or some other convenient fiction.

Something was off … the ship didn't have any power. There was no hum from the atmospherics, no lighting other than a cheap hand torch turned into a lamp; he recognized one of Lori's scarves draped over the top of it, diffusing the illumination. He looked around, and soon realized they weren't in space—the large, gaping hole covered with a tarp at the aft of the ship was a pretty big indicator. Harry was close by, sitting on an empty storage crate. "Hey, you're awake!"

"Where?" Humph tried to speak more, but the single word was the only thing he could croak out. He was dehydrated, at least partially from all the blood loss.

"Lori found it. Old spaceship graveyard. We dragged you here, and she started to patch you up a little." He pointed down to Humph's side; there was a crude, but clean, bandage over his wound. "She'll be back soon; once she is, it's my turn to try and find some stuff to hold us over here." Harry shook his head. "You should have seen her, partner. When we were pinned down back in town, she didn't run out on us. She just slinked up to a couple of the goons—you know ffffhow she can strut—and whispered something to them. They put down their guns, just like that! Then she—" He stopped short, shuddering. "Well, she picked up a piece of glass, and just like that, opened their throats. Both of them were smiling when she did it, too. Creeped me out a little bit, I'll tell you."

Humph coughed. "Kid, she's a Lorelei. That's what they do. Lure in men, cut their throats. We're damn lucky she happens to want our throats intact." He wasn't sure if the warning was going to take—the kid was as sharp as a bowling ball sometimes—but he would have felt guilty if he didn't at least try.

There were footsteps outside. Lori swept the tarp aside, standing in the ragged entrance. "Well, look who lived through the day. Hiya, handsome." Harry was about to start speaking, thinking she was talking to him, but stopped himself short with a sheepish chuckle when he realized she was addressing the Boggart.

"Hiya yourself. Looks like I owe both of you; I'm not terribly comfortable with that." He was feeling a little bit better. Lori or Harry must've given him pain meds at some point when they were stitching him up.

"Get us out of this mess with our skins intact, and I think we'll be able to call it even." She stepped into the shuttle, walking over and handing him a bottle of water. "Got a few things from a guard shack at the entrance of this dump. It's not much; Harry's going to need to go out soon to see if there's something he can pick up. Figured it would be better to rotate who goes out, limit our exposure that way."

Belatedly, Humph remembered the handful of prepaid credit chips he'd taken from Harry. Grunting with effort, he reached into his pocket to see if they were still there.

They were. Blood-crusted, but intact. He started to chuckle. Because "blood-crusted" would have raised another enormous red arrow if he'd been human, and his DNA was on file like every other human. The law mandating that DNA be on permanent file went all the way back to the twenty-first century. But he wasn't, and given that having a portion of a magic-being's blood meant you could control said being, there were even laws making sure no one ever got the chance to put what passed for their DNA on file. Part of the weekly "housekeeping" chores the Boggart did for himself and the agency was to run a cyber-magical routine making certain if anyone had gotten a speck of blood, their data was well and truly scrambled. Harry could pass those cards with impunity, and no DNA-sniffer would get a whiff of the Boggart.

"Here," he croaked. "Wash 'em off. Lori, rough the kid up a little so he looks like he belongs around here. Harry, think you can act like a drunk? Not a sloppy drunk, just a little happy."

Harry grinned. "I think I can manage it; I've been practicing for most of my adult life."

He thought for a moment. "Then there's bound to be liquor stores all over this part of town. Find the ones with food. Buy booze and grab food as if it's an afterthought, like the wife sent you out for some and you're taking the chance to get yourself another bottle. Don't buy too much at any one place. When I say too much, I mean, you buy the cheapest, smallest bottle, and maybe 20 creds worth of sundries over that. Got me?"

"Got it!" Lori broke out a compact of makeup, then proceeded to get Harry in character; smudges of grease, dirt, and a few applications of her stock of beauty products got him looking the part. Disreputable and cheap—Harry finished the disguise with the proper swagger of someone with a decent buzz on. Once he was gone, Lori took up a seat on the makeshift bed.

"How're you feeling?" She laid a hand tenderly on his arm. He propped himself up with some effort; the pain in his side ramped up a little, but he was able to bite it back.

"I'll live. Thanks again, by the way. Let's not make it a habit, you saving my rear." This was an uncomfortable position for him to be in, in a lot of ways. Usually when it came to women, he was the one doing the saving. Or at least, when there was saving needing to be done, Claire notwithstanding. And now he owed Lori. He didn't like owing anyone anything. He'd gotten where he was by amassing unspecified-favors-to-be-paid-later, not by being in the position of having to pay one out. Then there was Lori herself. A Lorelei. A species not known for their warm hearts. How much of this supposed attraction she had for him was acting, how much was due to the geas, and how much was real?

"I know it's probably ironic of me to ask this, but I don't suppose you happen to have any more water in that sack?" He chuckled weakly. "You being a Water creature and all that."

"First thing I thought of, since you were going to be dehydrated." She got up ... and every movement of every inch of her was seductive as she walked away from him ... fished another bottle out of the sack, and swayed her way back. "I also found where there's a clean tap; I can refill these so don't go all manly on me and crush them."

They sat quietly for a few minutes as he sipped at the water. Lori watched him the entire time, and Humph did his best to avoid her gaze, occupying himself with his thoughts. Lori was the first one to break the silence.

"We shouldn't be here," she said. "I don't mean here, here. I mean messed up with these damn humans."

"It's kind of their galaxy now, darlin'. We're just living in it."

She sniffed. "Oh yes. They're the 'normals.' We're the ones that— aren't. Humans always have been trouble, right from the time they started to put thoughts together in their little ape-brains. And they can't see anything without wanting to use it, own it, exploit it, or run over the top of it. Look what they've done to you and me! We were minding our own business, never causing any trouble, and then— bam. Geased. Used. Enslaved."

"You're going to learn to get over it sometime, kid. Shit happens, then you deal with it." He sighed. "I've been out in the world a lot longer than you have, so maybe it's just that. But you can't hold onto that kind of hate; there's no money in it, for starters. Besides, it's not like our kind is exactly blameless in the annals of history. There's a reason that Norms have stories about the Bogeyman, Boggarts, and even little Siren Frauleins. That reason isn't particularly cheery, but you already knew that, didn't you? If you're preaching revolution, you've got the wrong Boggart."

Suddenly, and without warning, he missed his partners. If Skinny Jim and Fred had been here ... he'd have had not one, but two foils to fend off Lori. He'd have had someone to keep an eye on Harry at all times. Skinny Jim didn't even sleep; he'd have had someone he could trust to stand watch while everyone else did.

He'd gone decades without having partners; he'd always been convinced he didn't need them, didn't need anyone, and now look. A handful of months with those two lugs cluttering up the office and he felt crippled by their absence. *Is this what it's like for Norms?*

And where were they? Were they even still alive? Or—at least, what passed for alive in Jim's case? He'd always been told that Paras who worked together for a long time or had some sort of bond could at least tell when something Bad and Permanent had happened to each other, but he'd never been in the position to find out. Mostly he had put that down to an old wives' tale; more than a few Paras got caught up in their own bullshit and myths. Now he hoped that it wasn't. Still, it was better if Jim and Fred were in the wind or taking dirt naps than in the clutches of whoever the hell was after him, that much he was certain of.

Lori pressed on, undaunted. "Fine, fine. I'll put away the placards and slogans. But more immediately ... shouldn't we ditch Harry? If we didn't have to worry about him, we could disappear, lose ourselves out there. We've got enough money to get by, at least for awhile." She laid a hand on his arm. "We could run away together, Humph."

The Boggart stared into her eyes for several long moments, searching for how to answer. "The thought has crossed my mind, more than once. The kid is a stone around our necks sometimes; he just doesn't know how to walk on our side of the tracks." He paused before continuing—he thought he had heard something outside, but quickly dismissed it. "Despite that, he's been starting to pull his weight. If he hadn't managed to snag my watch back at the flophouse, you'd be short one Boggart. Even though he'd more than likely be toast without me, he still stuck his neck out in a way that not a lot of beings would've for an old PI."

"So that's it?" He could tell that Lori knew she was defeated, but still harbored some hope that he would change his mind.

"It is." He had to be firm with her, to stamp this notion out once and for all. "The kid is all right, despite being a spoilt nincompoop. We need him as much as he needs us, if we're going to get to the bottom of this and come out of it alive. Besides, even if we did ditch him, we're in it too deep now; whoever is after us will keep coming after us until we're dead. That's what my gut says on this one; whenever I start going against my gut feelings is when shit goes sideways on me."

She let out her breath in a long hiss that reminded him that some people claimed the Sirens and Loreleis were somehow serpentine in nature. "I never got involved in anything this twisted before," she admitted, finally. "My kind are pretty straightforward, if we like you, we like you, if we don't, you're dead. And there wasn't a lot that Paulie wanted out of me but singing and simple seduction; he never let me in on any of his complicated schemes. I guess I had better stop trying to ride on my own instinct and follow yours."

The Boggart relaxed. The last thing he needed right now was a recalcitrant Lorelei on his hands. She was a great asset ... and she would have left a serious hole in his planning if she decided to cut her losses and leave them. "Thanks, Lori. I need you on my side to help me figure out how we're going to get out of this pickle. Now, what's taking Harry so long?"

Lori shrugged, taking a sip from his bottle of water. That sick feeling in his stomach came back. Humph debated internally, then started gathering up gear. He checked the revolver, made sure it was still fully loaded. "I'm going to head out, see if I can find what's taking Harry so long. I've got a bad feeling for some reason." That part caught her attention; concern creased her brow. "If I'm not back in three hours, take the money and disappear. No guarantees, but you might be able to slip off alone if you're careful."

"Don't count on me doing anything that sensible," she retorted. "Let's hope this time your gut is wrong." She grabbed him by the ears and kissed him, releasing him again quickly. Then she slipped off into the bowels of the old derelict; he hoped she had herself a hiding place or a back exit or something down there in the darkness. He didn't waste any more time; he started off out of the hole in the craft, his pace quickening as he oriented himself in the ship grave-yard. He broke into a full-on sprint when he heard a commotion on the edge of the lot; it was near one of the entrances, between the lot and an adjoining street. Humph stopped short of the exit, quickly catching his breath and steadying himself before he carefully peered around the corner of the wreck he was hiding behind. He drank in the details immediately: Harry, shouting obscenities, and being manhandled by two hired guns in suits into an all-black and tagless transport before having a black bag roughly pulled over his head. The suits followed him in, slamming the doors shut after them. But the vehicle did not immediately speed off. Maybe they figured there hadn't been anyone watching them. Or maybe they needed to secure Harry a bit more before they moved.

I've got to move fast; if they take off and get into traffic, I'll never be able to find them again. Humph put on one of his standby disguise faces; he made sure it was one of the ones he hadn't used in quite a while, just to be safe. He quickly ran a few dozen yards along the fence and away from the transport before he found a hole in the enclosure big enough for him to slip through. *Shit! It's taking off!* The transport was just starting to lift off the ground, readying to join the air traffic. Humph looked around frantically, then ran out into the street to stop a passing aircar; he was almost run over for his trouble twice before one, a junker that looked like it was on its last legs, stopped for him. The driver was a Norm male, and was less than happy with the Boggart. "Fuckin' idiot! Tryin' to get yourself kill—" Humph had gone around to the driver's side, punched the man in the jaw, and ripped him out of the vehicle before he could finish his sentence or properly react. He slammed the door and scanned for the transport. There! It had already lifted off and was moving to merge with traffic; luckily, this wasn't his first time performing a tail, and he knew all the tricks. Tails were a lot easier—and safer—with multiple vehicles, but he didn't need any with this bunch; they didn't seem at all concerned that someone might be following them. Still, he played it cautious—the last thing he needed was to tip his hand and turn this into a proper chase.

Or worse, end up with them chasing him. Whatever happened, he needed to get Harry back, alive. Thoughts raced through his mind as he followed the transport: did Lori feed Harry to the wolves, tip off the goons to get rid of him? *Would she do that to save her own neck? Is she doing that to me now, that final kiss to seal my fate?* Loreleis ... they were all about themselves. Well, that was what he'd heard, anyway. All Paras that used fascination as a weapon were cold. He supposed it came as part of the territory; how else could you stand to lure someone in, seduce him, then off him, up close and personal, yet oh so impersonal?

It wasn't long until they arrived at their destination; it was a medium-sized warehouse, buried in one of the more run-down industrial sections. The transport went into landing mode and parked in front of the entrance. Since the traffic wasn't as sparse in this part of town, Humph flew past, then turned a corner a block down before parking himself.

"This could get messy," he muttered. He hated going in cold, not knowing the strength of the opposition, the layout of the building, or any of the other numerous little details that could kill or save him. But this time the Boggart didn't have any choice; checking and readying his revolver one final time, he started walking toward the warehouse. His destination was the rear door, maybe loading docks if the place had them; with any luck, the security there wouldn't be as heavy as the front door. His single best hope was that Harry's captors had no idea there was still any opposition left.

He rounded the corner, then found his way next to a trash-can fire that was burning unattended. Humph pretended to warm his hands as he studied the rear of the building; it didn't appear that there was any external security. No cameras, sensors, or guards, at least that he could make out. Maybe they had to set this place up in a hurry. *Or maybe they're not planning on sticking around all that long. Either way, I need to get in there and get out with Harry, the sooner the better.* He made his way slowly over to the warehouse door, crossing the street and trying to look like just another bum down on his luck, stopping to peek inside dumpsters and trash cans—at least, the ones that weren't on fire. Once he reached the door, he did a very quick check on it; not even so much as an alarm appeared to be hooked up to it, just a simple lock. It took him a few minutes of working at the lock with his picks, but he finally cracked it. Slowly, he opened the door, then slipped inside, closing it behind him. He had just enough time to place the picks back into his pocket with his watch when he heard a voice from behind.

"Put your hands up and turn around slowly, or you're a dead man."

Shit. Humph grabbed his watch, then complied with the demands, raising his hands and turning around slowly. He was greeted with the muzzle of a rather mean-looking shock-gun being held by a rather mean-looking guard. One squeeze of the firing stud, and the Boggart would either be incapacitated or fried to a crisp.

"Please, mister, I was just hungry an' lookin' for food! Don't kill me!" He whispered urgently, then proffered his watch. "Here, take this! It's the only thing of value I have, I swear!" He dropped the watch, then kicked it with his boot so that it slid behind the guard.

"Shut up, and keep your hands where I can see them." The guard reached for his radio, then blinked hard; the trespasser had disappeared before his eyes. He didn't feel a thing when Humph clubbed him over the back of the head with the butt of his revolver. Humph caught the man as he slumped to the floor, setting him down gently. He checked for a pulse; there was none. That's the thing about getting hit in the head; if it's hard enough to knock you out for any significant amount of time, it's also probably hard enough to damn near kill you. Tough break. Humph had a quick burst of inspiration. He stripped the man down, putting on his uniform: a simple black jumpsuit and a load-bearing vest with tactical gear. To complete the look, he changed his face to that of the guard's, scooping up his shock-gun.

"Thanks," Humph said as he wedged the dead guard's body between a couple of shipping crates; hopefully no one would be able to easily stumble upon him there. There was something incredibly pathetic about the whole little scene—one poor idiot, dead in his underwear, crammed into a space full of dust and mouse turds. *Helluva way to end your life.*

Shit, he probably deserved it. No time to ponder it now. He did his level best to act casual; he needed to put off the vibe that he belonged here, after all. It took him less than a minute to get to the center of the room through the labyrinth of shipping containers. Humph didn't like what he saw—there was a cleared space in the middle of the room, with Harry tied to a chair with the black hood still over his head. There were two suits standing in front of him, arms crossed in front of their chests and smug grins on their lips. Three more guards were spread out in the open space, all of them with shock-guns; probably more elsewhere in the warehouse. Harry was saying something, but Humph couldn't make it out, so he walked closer.

"… you bastards just wait! You're going to regret the day you ever, ever laid a hand on me. My mother is going to make your lives hell!"

The suit on the right casually leaned forward and slapped Harry through the hood, hard. "Whatever you say, pretty boy. Just wait until the boss gets here, then we'll see how much you feel like issuing threats that your ass can't cash." The suit checked his watch, then chuckled. "In fact, he ought to be here in just a couple of minutes."

There were too many guards for Humph to fry before he'd get fried in return; they weren't grouped close enough together to get all of them in one blast, at least without hitting Harry in the process. He had to come up with something fast; whoever this boss was that the suit was talking about, Humph was pretty sure he wouldn't be alone when he arrived. He kept walking closer, then found what he was looking for. Keeping his shock-gun ready but trying to be discreet, he strolled up to a control panel and started to quickly punch in commands. The suit that had slapped Harry took notice.

"Hey! Simmons, you're supposed to be patrolling your sector of the perimeter. What do you think you're doing?"

"Redecorating." Humph mashed a final button. Machinery whirred to life overhead as a crane activated with a hum, swinging down and then flailing crazily. It struck a stack of containers, sending them toppling over; the topmost one crushed one of the guards as the others scattered. The suit looked back to Humph, disbelief being replaced by rage just before he caught a blast from the shock-gun; he burst into flame, jerking wildly with the voltage. The other suit and one of the guards managed to dive out of the way of the shot, scrambling for cover from the falling shipping containers and the shock-gun. Humph ran over to Harry, who was squirming in his seat from all the loud crashing and weapons fire. He grabbed Harry, tearing the hood off. "Hold still!"

"Don't kill me!" Harry started squirming harder.

Humph took a second, then dropped his glamour in annoyance, revealing his true face. "It's me, dumbass! Hold still so I can cut the rope!" He extended his claws, then started sawing at the rope around Harry's wrists.

"Humph? Humph! You came to save me? How'd you find me?" With a final cut, Harry's hands came free.

"Fewer questions, more running! Let's go!"

The shipping containers were still being knocked over as the crane followed the erratic and conflicting instructions Humph had programmed into it. The guards and the suit were starting to recover. Humph sent a blast from the shock-gun their way, even though they were outside of its pitifully short range; it'd give them something to think about at any rate. He grabbed Harry by the arm and then shoved him toward the exit. Both of them started running, skidding to stops and dodging as crates and containers rained down all around them. Fortunately the same falling objects were making life just as difficult for their pursuers. It was pandemonium; between running herd on Harry, dodging the falling crates, and occasionally shooting over his shoulder to dissuade their pursuers, Humph had his hands full. One guard ran into their path; Harry actually gut-punched him, shoving him out of the way before continuing his dash. At some point—Humph didn't even remember how—he picked up a second shock-gun.

The exit suddenly loomed in front of them, salvation for at least a few moments. Humph could still hear shouting and barked orders from behind them over the din. He and Harry both burst through the warehouse door one after the other.

"What now? We can't lead them back to Lori!" *Kid is actually starting to use his head. If we live through this, he might actually be worth his salt.*

"Here!" Humph reached into his belt, pulled out the revolver, and thrust it into Harry's hands. "Go hide behind that dumpster on the other side of the street, I'll be right there!" Humph had to work fast. He fished out a torsion wrench from his lock-pick kit and jammed it into the emitter of one of the shock-guns. Then he keyed the firing stud, using the grip from the other shock-gun to keep it depressed; the shock-gun started to emit an insistent whine that was growing in intensity with each passing second. Humph set the jerry-rigged guns down gingerly, then sprinted as hard and fast as he could over to the dumpster that Harry was hiding behind. Harry startled for a half-second before he recognized Humph. "Gimme the gun!" Harry handed the heavy revolver to the Boggart; Humph took very careful aim at the shock-guns, and waited.

Seconds later, the door to the warehouse burst open. The remaining suit and at least two of the surviving guards were there, guns at the ready. Humph couldn't help but grin as he fired the revolver; the Webley-Fosbery was an old, accurate gun, and it struck true. The bullet hit the power pack of the jammed shock-gun, breaching it; both guns exploded brilliantly. The blast was enough to momentarily blind Humph and knock him onto his ass. When he was able to right himself, he and Harry peered over the edge of the dumpster at the same time. Where the suit, guards, and door used to be was now only a ragged, smoldering hole the size of an aircar.

"How the hell did you do that?" Harry's jaw hung open in awe of the impromptu destruction. "I mean, finding me and then the thing with the crane and blowing up the guns?"

Humph shrugged, helping Harry to his feet as he stood up. "Just winged it, kid. It ain't exactly my first rodeo. C'mon, we need to get out of here before the 'boss' shows up." They hoofed it to where Humph's stolen aircar was still waiting; there was some fresh graffiti on it, a quick one-color tag of what looked like a gang sign, but otherwise it looked undisturbed. Once they were in the air, Humph made sure not to beeline straight back to the ship graveyard; still, they had to hurry. The clock was ticking and if Lori actually did what she was supposed to, she'd be in the wind in the next half an hour. He had some questions for her, if his suspicions had any merit.

"Why'd you come after me?" Harry had a look on his face like a puppy that had been caught rummaging in the garbage.

"What are you talking about," Humph asked, annoyed. "Why wouldn't I?"

"Well … I overheard you and Lori. Talking about ditching me and running off. I figured that you didn't want me around anymore;

she sure doesn't." He looked down at the floorboards. "So I made a call, or tried to. Those guys in the suits grabbed me right after, and you know the rest."

Humph couldn't take his hands off the controls to smack himself—or Harry—in the head, but at that moment, he dearly wanted to. "Aw good Christ, kid ..." he groaned. "Look, I tried to explain. Lemme try it again, this time you're sober, maybe you'll get it. Three things. One: you're stuck with me, I'm stuck with you, because whatever is going on around here, it's gonna take both of us to figure out enough to get these bastards off us. Whoever they are, they're huge. Whatever it is you somehow got yourself into, it's huge. They killed an entire Fang space station just to keep us from getting help. But that means somehow, something we know or can figure out is dangerous to them. You got that part?"

Slowly, Harry nodded.

"Okay. Two: Lori is a Lorelei. At best, they're cold bitches, and she has a real hard case against Norms. Don't worry about her; it's better if neither of us is involved with her, anyways. That dame is trouble with a capital T; if anything's true, that most certainly is."

"Yeah, I suppose. What's the last thing?"

"The last thing is we haven't been paid yet. And the job ain't done till the Boggart gets paid. Right, partner?" Humph turned to give Harry the full-on toothy grin, Boggart style.

Harry returned the grin, his spirits evidently lifted. "You got it, partner."

The pair arrived back at the ship graveyard after taking a circuitous route; Humph was a lot more careful than the goons that had nabbed Harry, and was continually checking to make sure that they weren't being followed. They ditched the stolen aircar and the guard's uniform several blocks away and continued on foot, just to be sure. Finally they made it back to the ship they had set up sanctuary in; Humph could see light very faintly past the edges of the tarp. When they were less than half a dozen paces away, Lori stepped out. She instantly looked alarmed.

"Stop!"

It was too late. Before either of them could react, the ground gave way under Harry's feet; flailing around, he hooked Humph's collar, dragging the Boggart down after him. They both landed in a very uncomfortable pile at the bottom of the hole. *At least there aren't any spikes. Or saw blades. Or snakes. Or all of the above.*

"Ow," Humph croaked out. The hole was about six-feet deep, and hastily dug; the corners had been squared, though, so whoever had dug the trap at least knew what they were doing.

"You're sitting on my chest and you weigh a ton!" Harry was somewhere underneath him; it took them a few moments to untangle their arms and legs, stand up, and dust off.

"Lori, you mind telling me what the hell is going on?" Humph was in no mood for this nonsense; they didn't have time to be screwing around, since the goons could show back up here and take them all out in short order. He looked up—Lori was peering over the edge of the hole. Then her face was joined by two more; one rather desiccated, the other slowly changing from fur-covered to average Norm-looking. "Sonofabitch."

"Really, the first thing you can think to say to me after all of this is a dog joke? You're losing your touch, boss." Fred was scratching his chin as the last of the fur receded, his face now back to its usual unremarkable self.

"Well, we've always known I had the brains in this operation. Get it? Huh, get it?" Skinny Jim had the "helmet" from his bot suit under one arm, elbowing Fred with the other.

"If you two jokers are done, I'd very much like to get out of this hole. Today. Right now."

"It's the boss, alright. Bitch, bitch, bitch," Skinny Jim quipped, reaching down and throwing Humph the end of a rope. "I swear, here we are, turning up, protecting his fair damsel, fortifying the castle, and all he can think is to complain."

Humph hauled himself out, and offered Harry a hand to help him scramble up the dirt wall. "Glad to see you idiots," he said gruffly. "Damn it, I thought you might have gotten fragged when I couldn't raise you."

"Aww, see now? He cares!" Skinny Jim clapped the bot head back on. "You weren't nearly as hard to keep track of, boss. Whoever is behind this really didn't give a rat's ass about us, you and pretty boy there were who they wanted. All we had to do is get to Fred's hideout, and sit tight, and watch the news."

Fred nodded solemnly. "Once we saw where all the shit was going down, we knew you had to be in the middle of it. We got the general loc, then I sniffed you out. Took awhile; the ol' nose is a bit off after a century of smelling Deadheads. Anyways, tracked you here from the flophouse where all the killing got done. Water Witch here gave us the rundown, then told us you'd gone after the kid, so we hunkered down to wait."

"I've got one other question." Humph looked back to see Harry climbing out of the pit. "Why dig the hole?"

Both of them shrugged. "We were bored, and it seemed like the thing to do." Jim hooked a thumb back at Fred. "Besides, someone had to bury their treats." There was a light clang as Fred slapped the back of Jim's helmet.

"Well, can't argue with that. Next time, don't let me fall in it."

"What, you don't like looking up to us?"

Fred snickered. "He's already short enough for that, Jim."

"I wonder if a dog and a real robot would be any less annoying than you two. Probably make less of a mess."

"But they wouldn't dig holes nearly as good."

Harry joined the circle, still dusting himself off. "Harry Somerfield, I present to you the rest of Boggart, Barkes, and Bot: Fred and Skinny Jim, respectively." After the introductions and handshaking—Harry was somewhat reluctant to shake hands with a Reboot at first—was over, Humph instructed everyone to gather up what little there was in the shuttle; they had to get out of the area and find a new place to hunker down and plot their next move.

"Way ahead of ya, boss. But, I'll warn you," Jim said. "It's not the Ritz."

"More like the 'fritz,'" Fred admitted.

"What's that supposed to mean?" Humph asked, raising an eyebrow.

"You'll see when you get there."

It looked like a World War II bunker. Literally. Superficially, at least, it didn't look as if there was a single piece of modern tech in it—or at least, hadn't been brought in by someone else. Right now, the light was being supplied by portable lamps. Living conditions were pretty basic. Six metal-frame bunk beds bolted to the floor had been made up with surgical precision, and Humph was damn sure the linens were some form of military surplus. They just had that look to them. There was a kitchen area with a stove that apparently ran on fuel cells, a couple of metal tables also bolted to the floor. There was a bathroom at one of the far ends with an incinerating toilet and a water-recycling shower. The bunker looked as if someone had welded spaceship hull plates together into a pair of square tubes, put the thing together in the form of an X, and buried the whole thing. Most of it was taken up with storage: food in the form of concentrates, water, other supplies.

"The hell," said Humph, once he'd climbed down the ladder and surveyed the place. "How in the name of all things dark and dangerous did you find this place?"

"Bought it," Fred said. "For cash. Furs never trust Norms, this is a standard bug-out bunker you can pick up on the black market virtually everywhere there's a planet. Well, we don't call 'em bug-out bunkers, we call 'em emergency Dens. We make sure they're off the grid and off the radar. Some Furs even go so far as to hand dig their Dens, or put 'em in cave systems." He pointed to a single thin wire running up the wall, and from there, up the access tube with its ladder that led to what looked like a standard city-utility hatch. "That's our sole connection to the outside. I found a planetary data-node and wired into it. Otherwise, we could bolt the hatch and not come out for a year if we didn't feel like it. That's how Furs can go missing for years, decades at a time."

Humph whistled. "I like how you think," he said.

Lori dropped down onto one of the bunks. "It's more comfortable than it looks!" she said, with a look of surprise.

"Standard ship mattresses. We figure on hibernating if we have to go under. Saves consumables." Fred went over to the stove and fired it up, emptying a couple of pouches into a pot and adding water. "You don't want to hibernate on a bad mattress."

"I don't suppose—" Lori began.

Fred nodded toward the storage. "One size fits most T-shirts and pants. Hot water in the shower module."

Lori got up quickly and headed for the storage crates. Clean clothing clutched to her chest, she edged past them and disappeared into the bathroom. Humph sniffed appreciatively. Maybe the stuff in that pan was also some form of military ration, but after the last several days, it smelled like a gourmet dream.

Lori came back out some time later, hair wet and bound up on the top of her head, face innocent of makeup, just as the food was ready. Fred divided it equally among all of them except for Jim, who waved at the bowls and said, "I ate already." Humph wasn't going to argue or inquire as to how Jim had eaten, instead he dug into whatever-it-was—some sort of casserole—and damn near licked the bowl clean. He noticed that neither Lori nor Harry were any more fastidious than he was about doing the same. They hadn't gone hungry, but the adrenaline had rendered them all famished. Fred passed around coffee, or what passed for coffee, when they were all about halfway through.

"Short story," Fred said, collecting the bowls and stacking them in the little sink. "We got about two minutes' warning before all hell broke loose on the office. And that was only because they cut off all our comm just before they hit. We used the emergency exit, headed for one of the safe houses, discovered it wasn't so safe after all, and I declared FUBAR and hauled Jim here. All we did was monitor what was going on after that. Sorry, boss, but the best thing we could do was not to go after you, but to disappear. We needed to drop completely out of sight first and let them figure we'd bailed on you."

Humph nodded. This couldn't have been Skinny Jim's plan, but it made perfect sense for Fred. The Fangs had reverted to their old medieval arrogance after the Great Uncloseting, but the Furs, it seemed, had retained a lot of their old paranoia. Good thing they had.

"That's where I started tracking you," Skinny Jim said. "I bet it isn't going to shock you in the least to hear that most of the people after you aren't law enforcement."

Lori had already curled up on a bottom bunk, but wasn't looking sleepy. Humph stayed where he was, in the metal chair. It wasn't comfortable, but he wanted to keep a little distance between himself and the Lorelei. "I was beginning to think along those lines, yeah," he admitted.

Harry had hoisted himself up into a top bunk, and was watching them all like a superfan following the ball at a tennis match.

"If anything, the law was reacting to what was going on after the fact," Jim continued, pulling his bothead off and putting it on the table. "Take the raid on JeanPaul's place. That wasn't cops. The cops only showed up after the shooting started. Radio chatter started and they were pissed, then suddenly the radio chatter stopped dead, and the only thing that came over the freqs was an order to withdraw."

Humph nodded. That fit in with a growing suspicion in his mind. He turned to Harry. "Okay, kid," he said, gruffly. "Spill me some beans. Who'd you call when you bugged out on us and those goons grabbed you?"

"My mother," Harry said, sheepishly. "Or—actually the head of company security." He frowned, then, thinking. "Or, actually, I tried. It was the right number, but I didn't recognize the voice of the person I talked to. He cut me off and told me to stay put, and it wasn't more than a minute later that those thugs turned up and—"

"And I saw the rest." Humph cut him off. He patted his jacket, then retrieved a cigar; the last one in his case.

"Not down here, boss; don't want to tax the ventilation system any more than we have to."

He shook his head. "Naw, I'm not going to smoke it, just chew the hell out of it while I think. This entire mess has more twists and turns than a Medusa on a bad hair day."

"Well," Jim said, after a very long pause. "Elephant in the room. I can't think of any multiplanetary business that can push local law enforcement around the way we've been seeing. I very much doubt even the Mafias or Tongs could do it. So, that leaves us with—?" Jim had learned to signal a lot with his voice alone, since what was left of his face didn't have hardly any expression to speak of.

"What, Feds?" Fred shook his head. "How does that make sense? We're not exactly all that high on anyone's wanted list, at least before this fiasco started. Whoever these goons are, they seem to want Harry, but for what? He's just a rich kid with too little sense." He held up his hands. "No offense."

"None taken," Harry replied.

"Anyways, we're all small-time in the grand scheme of things. And even if it were the Feds, which ones? Planetary? Earth-gov? One of the alliances out on the rim?"

"Fred, you and me, we watched a lot of old vids and movies. I know Humph has. When it isn't who you are that's dangerous, it's what you know." Jim tapped his metal-encased finger on Harry's head for emphasis. "And that's doubly true when you don't know what you know. When you were in the right place at the wrong time, for instance."

Humph stopped chewing on his cigar to speak. "I've been thinking on that. I don't think it's anything that any of us know; we've dug up stuff for all sorts, and hell knows that we've trudged through enough crap to maybe get a whiff of something we shouldn't have. But it's nothing earth-shattering; if it was, we'd have been able to suss it out by now." He looked at everyone in the group before settling on Harry. "Which leaves just one person that this could be about, though it doesn't make much sense."

Harry put up his hands in frustration. "We've been over that, though. I really don't know anything, nothing that could bring this kind of trouble."

There was silence for a few moments. Humph jabbed his stogie in the direction of Jim. "While you two have been off the radar, have you been keeping at the digging I told you to do for this gig before it blew up in our faces?"

"That's a 10-4 chief," Jim replied. "Incentive and boredom, don'cha know. Harry has been a very naughty boy, haven't you, Harry?"

"Well, yeah. I already told Humph about all of that, though. Sure, I was embezzling, but that's small potatoes, right?"

"That alone isn't enough to draw down this kind of thunder, that's for sure. There's something else to it, though."

"When is a raven like a writing desk?" Fred said, suddenly, as if something struck him out of the blue.

"I have not been smoking the Caterpillar's hookah, nor eating and drinking things that say Eat Me and Drink Me," Lori put in, crossly. "And my name isn't Alice."

"The point of that riddle, because it was nonsense, was to make children try and figure out a way that a raven could be like a writing desk," Fred explained. "Turn the reasoning around. We're sitting here assuming that there was nothing Harry could possibly have gotten into to bring this kind of attention down on him. Turn it around. Assume there must have been something he did, and start looking for it from the back end."

Humph turned in his seat, looking to Fred and Jim. "Did anything stick out to you two when you were digging around Harry's misadventures in economics?"

"Why did you pick Nightshade Ltd. to plunder?" Jim asked Harry.

The playboy shrugged. "Same reason I picked all of the others; it was small, isolated from the rest of the company, not really involved in most of our day-to-day activities. I figured that no one would notice if some money went missing; just shuffle it all around to make it disappear. Hell, if the banks can do it, I could, too." He frowned. "Why do you ask?"

"Because if I were an auditor, I'd be pulling in the CFO and everyone in the chain down for interviews right now," Jim said with authority. "I could tell what meddling was you—you're crude and unsophisticated, and you left fingerprints all over what you stole. It's the five or six other people in there that I'd be worrying about. For a little company it's drawing outside resources all out of proportion to its size, and they aren't coming from the main firm, either. Then those resources disappear. I found not two sets of books, but four. There's property on one of those sets of books that doesn't appear on the public books, or any of the other two sets. That property is eating a lot of utilities, and I mean a lot, the kind of power-draw that used to signal someone was running a drug-greenhouse. That ringing a bell?"

Humph felt his jaw dropping. He had taken Skinny Jim's word for it when the Zombie had claimed he'd been a bookkeeper for the mob in life … he'd had no idea that the Reboot had been that kind of bookkeeper. This was Fed-level forensic accounting! "That sounds like a lead to me. Right now we don't have any other moves to play; we don't have enough to go public and expect to live, and getting off-planet isn't exactly the safest bet either. Whoever is doing this has reach."

Lori sat up from the bed, alert. "What're you thinking of doing, Humph?"

"I'm tired of being on the defensive, always running from whoever these bastards are. I think it's time to take the fight to them, to get proactive." He stood up, replacing his cigar and chewing on it as he talked. "I say we raid the damned place that Jim found, see what we can see."

There wasn't a lot of privacy in the bunker, but Skinny Jim and Fred had either gotten a lot more sensitive to Humph's body language or they'd figured out something was going on between Humph and the Lorelei some other way. In either case, they both pulled Harry into an intense interrogation about Nightshade Ltd. around the kitchen table, giving Humph a chance to get down into the end of one of the storage arms on the excuse of looking for some firepower.

"No need to sneak around, Lori. I know you're there." He turned around to find her standing at the entrance of the storage arm, hand against the frame. Even in a generic shirt and trousers, she still looked enticing.

"You're not going to let me come with you, are you?" she said, although the way she said it, it was more like a statement than a question.

"You're right, I'm not." Humph crossed his arms in front of his chest, readying himself; he knew that this wasn't going to be an easy conversation. "You've been a trooper so far, Lori; you've saved my hide, and that's something I don't take lightly. So I'm going to save yours; you need to get clear of this while you still can. We're going to be causing a lot more trouble, and that means we'll have more trouble heading our way, likely. That ought to give you a better shot of getting safe, while they focus on us."

"What if I don't want to get safe?" she countered. "I know Loreleis don't have the best reputation in the world, Boggart, but we're not all bad. I never killed anyone I didn't have to. If we get out of this, I could be a lot of help to you—"

"You already said the key word, darlin', 'if' we get out of this. We're all way out of our league on this thing; getting by on dumb luck—especially in Harry's case—and dirty tricks are the only reasons we've all stayed in one piece so far. I don't imagine that our lucky streak is going to last much longer, especially since we're probably about to poke the Tiger with a stick."

She moved closer. "So? Shouldn't you use everything and everyone you've got? I just found you, Boggart. I don't want to lose you. I don't let many people get close to me, much less this close."

The Boggart could already see the tendrils of her magic seeking him out, trying to caress him. "People that get that close to me don't have the best track record, Lori. I've left enough bodies in my wake; I really don't need another person I'm close to added to that number."

"It's not just your decision, Boggart. It's mine, too." She had him penned in the end of the tunnel now. It was obvious that she wasn't going to just sit back and take what he planned. Not without an argument … maybe a fight.

"Damned if it is your decision!" He angrily took a step forward, but Lori held her ground. "I'm not going to let you throw your life away trying to help us."

"Let? Let? I was making my own decisions thousands of years ago, Boggart! What makes you think I'm going to sit still and let you treat me like a caveman with his hand wrapped in my hair?" She blocked his way with her hands on her hips. "Admit it, Boggart! You're just afraid—afraid of me. Afraid that if you admit you have feelings for me, every bit of your control over things is going to go flying out the window!"

"All right! I am afraid of that! I do care about you, you silly little girl. A helluva lot." He was fuming, and had to take a breath to calm himself. "I'm afraid with you around when this gets worse than it already is, I won't be thinking clearly. I'll be too worried about you, wondering if you're safe. And I need every bit of attention for what's to come—if I don't have it, we're all dead even surer than we probably already are." He took a final step forward, leaving less than a foot between them as he took her by the arms. "If I know you're safe, away from this, maybe, just maybe we'll get out of it. Probably not, but it's still a shot." Being this close to her was maddening; her magic was mingling with his, and he could feel her breath against his neck and chest as he looked into her eyes.

She looked up into his face, and for once, he didn't see a single trace of guile about her. "This isn't the geas, Boggie. I know what it feels like to be manipulated by magic. You're the first man in a thousand years to get to me. I don't want to lose that."

"Then do this one thing for me, Lori. Get out of here, run, hide and be safe. I won't be much good to you if I'm dead."

"And how do I find you again?" she asked, her eyes filling with tears.

She wanted comfort and that was the one thing he couldn't give her. He never made promises, even implied promises, that he couldn't keep. "We'll just have to see, kiddo." He kissed her—softly at first, then more urgently. And, of course, the kiss was interrupted by a polite cough from the other part of the bunker.

"Boss, if we're going to make a run, we need to decide if it's now or later. And if it's now, we need to plan." Fred's voice echoed from far enough away that it was obvious he wasn't within eyeshot of them …

… now. No telling but what he hadn't gotten a full view of the clinch. *I don't know whether to kick the tar out of that fleabag or buy him a case of scotch for interrupting.* Humph and Lori separated; she was still wiping tears from her eyes and trying to smile.

"If I could shoot … or turn invisible … or pick locks …" she said, her voice thick with tears.

"I'd still want you to run, to find someplace safe. This is just how it has to be, Lori." He caressed her cheek, then thought better of it and let his hand fall away with some reluctance. "Get together the cash we have leftover on the cards. Jim ought to be able to arrange something for you while Fred and I are on this little mission." He chuckled lightly, looking down at his feet. "I imagine that you can take care of yourself pretty well, if anything comes up. You're a survivor."

Before he could say anything else that he might regret, he pushed her gently aside and called out to Fred. "Now. They don't know we know about Nightshade. And they don't know you two hooked up with us. We hit them while we still have some pretenses at surprise." It took every bit of his resolve but he edged past Lori and back to the main module.

The first thing they needed was a vehicle. Amazingly there were half a dozen in the ship graveyard that only needed a couple of parts to get running. Some quick cannibalization by Fred and they had another beater-transport, virtually invisible. Some clever get-arounds by Jim and they even renewed one of the tags, so they wouldn't even be stopped, registering the thing to the graveyard. It would be a nice little present to their involuntary hosts if they all survived this.

Now it was the Boggart and Fred in the transport, and a single burner phone. Lori, Harry, and Jim were hunkered down in the bunker with only the data-node-hack running. The Boggart didn't know what their plans were if everything went to hell, and he didn't want to know. *Makes for less that someone can beat out of us later.* He just hoped that Lori was gone by the time he got back; he didn't want to have to go through another emotional goodbye. Twice in one century was over his limit already.

Nightshade, Ltd., was housed in a neat, antiseptically clean research park, full of little companies just like it, all in identical white buildings finished with a shiny ceramcoat—which alone would tell the knowledgeable that what was going on here was something biochem or tech in nature. If something went terribly wrong, the building could be tented, fumed, and hosed down. With or without victims still inside.

And that was … interesting. Because this was supposed to be a cosmetics researcher. So … why put it in a Biohazard level 4 rated park?

"What do you think we're going to find in there, boss?" Fred had been uncharacteristically fidgety on their ride over. He knew what the stakes were, and how low their chances of success were. It said a lot about him that he decided to come along despite that. Humph just hoped that his friend's loyalty wouldn't be the death of him.

"Hopefully something that'll give us an out, something to get free of this mess. If we can't get our hands on that, we're sunk."

Their plan was simple; that way, fewer things could go wrong with it. The downside was that if anything went wrong, they were probably going to end up dead—or worse. They were going to sneak in as a delivery crew—coveralls, some dollies with boxes loaded with really heavy parts and things that looked like expensive machines borrowed from the yard, and the transport completed the picture. Bullshit their way in the front door, and move as fast and stealthily as they could until they found some dirt. They were sitting in the transport outside of Nightshade Ltd. Humph took a moment to look over at Fred. "Are you ready for this, partner?"

"Yeah, I'll be fine." He looked anything but fine; Humph tossed his flask into Fred's lap, grinning as he put on one of his disguise faces. This one was of a dockside bartender he had met centuries ago, back on Earth—boxed-in ears, a flat nose, and darkened eyes completed the picture, just another beaten-down laborer.

"Never leave home without it," he said, pointing to the flask. "Take a nip, and then we're on." Fred did so, downing quite a bit more than a nip of the whiskey before handing the flask back to Humph. With that, both of them exited the transport and started unloading the boxes. They affected their best "worn out and ready for happy hour" expressions as they trundled up to the entrance of the building.

Long ago, firms had figured out that having a bored, minimum-wage guard on the door was actually more effective than having a sophisticated, AI run security check-in. And cheaper too. A few too many incidents with bots letting in people just like Fred and the Boggart, and incinerating legitimate, unexpected deliveries, had led to going retro. As advanced as bot tech was, there was still something to be said for a living element somewhere in the decision making, though Humph had heard rumors and conspiracy theories about some places experimenting with cyborgs and other gruesome inventions, fusing living beings with machines. As expected, waiting at a desk at the loading dock was a guy that looked like a tired basset hound, with the telltale whiff of whiskey about him, behind a little white desk with a rack of monitors on it. An old-timer like him was perfect for a gig like this—just there to collect a paycheck, too jaded and exhausted to ask too many questions other than, "When's lunch?" Just another piece of the puzzle.

"Delivery for Lab 3," Fred said, as the guard waved them forward. It was a gamble, guessing at their "destination," but it paid off this time. Places like this weren't usually big on creatively named rooms. The guard took a box cutter and opened Fred's container, and the exhaustion in his face was pathetic. He knew that if the delivery was for a specific lab, that lab expected it to be there in the morning. He also knew there was no one to get it there but him ....

"Buddy, you look beat. We'll haul this shit in for you, if you want," the Boggart offered. "Us little guys gotta look out for each other."

The guard's face brightened. "Thanks, bud. I got a herniated disk, and you know those damn insurance companies, they won't do nothin' about it until I'm crippled. I get off in about five minutes, and all I wanna do is lay down."

The Boggart had been counting on that. Counting on the fact that the human guard would probably be replaced by a simple locked-and-warded door after hours, and counted on the fact that showing up five minutes before second-shift change would guarantee them at least an hour of undisturbed snooping. Their timing was truly a piece of luck, one of the few they'd had during this entire fiasco. "Ain't that the truth. Take a load off, just point us where we need to go." The guard gave them a generalized layout of the facility: where the administrative level was, engineering, and the labs. At the end of the description, he handed them both generic-looking name tags.

"Wear these from this point on, if you don't want to get zapped. You'll see what I mean." With that, they were buzzed through the doors into the main facility. The first thing that struck both Fred and Humph was how … average the facility was. It looked like the inside of any other office building—people in cubicles, at desks in offices, and no one paying them very much mind at all. There were security cameras in all of the usual places. There wasn't any sort of oppressive, totalitarian feel to the place. It was boring. *Maybe this is how evil, Norm evil, really looks: mundane.*

All of that changed once they reached the labs. The hallway they had turned down ended abruptly with two very solid doors; they looked like blast doors from a distance, and Humph confirmed it once they were closer. The really scary thing about the hallway were the two security bots that manned the entrance.

But the bots didn't even power up as they approached, and the doors opened silently for them. Some sort of passive scanning, probably; judging from the cannons affixed to the bots, Humph surmised that he and Fred would've been little more than scorch marks if they weren't wearing the badges that the guard had given them. The doors stood open, waiting for them to pass; the bots stood watch, still no indicator that they were even active. The hallway beyond was pristine: gleaming white on white, with the faint smell of medical antiseptic, the kind of smell that hospitals always seemed to have. They didn't see anyone for what felt like ages—just more hallways, all the exact same. Most of the doors they passed by were unmarked; several were marked "Storage," and more than a few of those were plastered with warnings about the contents.

Boggart spotted a door marked "Lab 3," and on impulse, pushed his dolly toward it. The door opened before he reached it, and Fred followed him. "What're we doing?" Fred hissed.

"I figured whatever you needed to do, you could probably do from the lab," the Boggart replied. "No? I figured outside the labs, the computers are probably kept from accessing the lab stuff, but I bet there's no such security keeping one lab from looking at another's work." He looked for a storage closet, found one, and opened the door, shoving his box inside. Chances were, no one would even look at the boxes for a week. Maybe more, given how much dust was in here and how barren the shelves were. He took Fred's dolly from him, and did the same with Fred's box. Fred was giving him a stare that said *How the hell did you figure that out?*

"I'm smarter than I look," Boggart said, and wiggled his fingers at Fred. "Make with the computer magic."

"We'll have to get into the lab proper, use one of those computers. It's going to be a closed network, otherwise we could have Jim help us out remotely. This place looks pretty secure, so no chance of a signal getting out of here, at least undetected." Fred reached into his coveralls, retrieving a data pad and a few other little gizmos—tools of the trade for the experienced hacker.

"Let's get to it; I don't imagine we'll have much time once we start messing around in the lab proper."

The pair exited the storage closet, still pushing their dollies. The lab itself was open, with various technicians working at their stations; none of them seemed to pay much attention to the two workers as they made their way around. Past some thick glass was a clean room, complete with airlock. It was a tidy little operation, a place for everything and everything in its place. Humph found what he was looking for—a terminal off to the side, obstructed by some lab equipment.

"Do your thing, furbag. Get whatever you can, and then we're out of here."

Fred immediately set to working. He plugged some of the smaller gadgets into ports on the terminal, then hooked his data pad up to it as well. Humph was keeping one eye on Fred's progress, with the other on the technicians. One thing he had noticed about this lab was that there weren't any cameras here. At all. That was strange, and he didn't like it one bit. It took a few minutes before he got any indication from Fred.

"Humph, this is bad."

"No kidding, we need to get moving." Some of the technicians had noticed the two of them, and were starting to stare in-between their tasks.

"No, I mean this is all bad here. I'm getting next to nothing."

Humph bent down, hovering over Fred's shoulder. "What the hell do you mean, nothing? We didn't get this far to leave empty-handed, damn it!" His voice was a harsh whisper; he had to keep scanning the room, as the technicians were now starting to talk amongst themselves.

"I mean, there's stuff here, but none of it is very useful. At least, the stuff that I can get to." He pressed a finger to the viewscreen, indicating what he was talking about. "We've got references to a lot of data, but very little concrete stuff. 'Population densities,' 'dispersal patterns,' 'delivery vectors,' 'patients,' and so on. Shipping manifests, some supply lists that I can't make much sense out of. But that's all I'm getting; everything else is behind encryption and firewalls that I'm not equipped to get past. Not even Jim could, I don't think."

"What the hell are you saying, then, Fred?"

"I'm trying to say that this is military grade, Humph. There's no way that I'm cracking it. Hacking isn't like in the vids; for anything other than basic stuff, it can take weeks. Months even."

Military grade? "What the hell is protection that heavy doing in a cosmetics lab?" he whispered, feeling a cold knot in his gut. "Download what you can. Grab something that looks like it needs moving and let's get out of here."

He headed for a stack of what were obviously empty boxes and shoved his dolly under them. One of the technicians was walking toward them.

"Excuse me, could I have a word with you two?"

"No need, chum, we're on our way out. Thanks, though." Fred and Humph quickly exited the lab, hoping that would be the end of it. They were what Humph thought was halfway out of that part of the facility when the announcement came:

"Security to Labs, sector 3, please."

"That's our cue, exit stage right." Humph cursed under his breath. Then he looked around. "Wait, where is our exit?"

Fred looked over to Humph. "I thought you knew the way out?"

"Goddamnit, we're lost." He searched for a sign, anything. "Screw it, we've got to keep moving. If I say run, don't hesitate; just hoof it." They started quick walking down the nearest hallway; it was maddening trying to find the way out, since all of the hallways looked nearly identical. Finally they turned down one hallway that was different from the rest; through a different set of security doors, it was interspaced with clear walls every ten feet or so. "We'll use this as a reference point if we have to. Let's keep going—" Humph noticed that Fred had stopped in front of one of the clear walls. "Fred, what's going on?" He regretted the question a moment later when he saw what was on the other side of the wall. He abandoned the dolly to walk over beside Fred.

"These aren't rooms … they're cages." Fred's voice was low, and taking on a low, bestial rumble more and more with every word he spoke. Inside the cages there were dozens of Weres, some caught in mid-transition—every kind of Were, from Bears to the big Cats, though mostly Wolves. And all of them were recently dead, and horribly so. Splotchy skin, fur gone in huge patches, red lesions, and too much blood spread around were the common features. Some looked like they had torn their own throats out. The entire scene was awful, and almost caused Humph's gorge to rise. "It's all the cleaner and antiseptic; I couldn't smell 'em. Weres can always tell when our dead are around …."

"Fred … we've got to go." He gently placed a hand on the Werewolf's shoulder; Fred spun on him, fury and tears masking his eyes.

"Whoever did this … these bastards have to pay for this."

Humph shook his head slowly. "Now's not the time. We need to survive if we're going to make sense of this, make it right. Okay?"

Fred didn't answer him; his eyes were back on all the dead Weres. Humph grabbed him by the arm. "We're leaving." Fred jerked his arm away, then started down the hallway at a trot. Humph sighed, then started running after his partner to catch up.

He had the sinking feeling that Fred was not listening to him—that the Fur had an agenda of his own at this point, and he wasn't going to listen to anything. Still, they were able to avoid security; they had passed a few bewildered technicians in lab coats, but no one else. Humph mentally cursed when he realized that he had left the dolly behind. Things started to look slightly more familiar as they progressed; Humph recognized a smudge on one of the storage doors they passed. "We're getting close, Fred. Once we get to the front, act natural—hey!"

Fred veered off down a corridor, one that actually had a little sign with an arrow on it. Engineering and Maintenance. Now ... that could be a good way to get out, since most maintenance areas almost always have their own doors. But Humph had the feeling that getting out wasn't on Fred's mind right now.

Humph was fast, but Fred was faster; there wasn't any way he could compete with the Were's supernatural speed. Humph almost lost him a few times, and had to guess at several intersections about which way to take. He reached a terminus for a hallway, two service doors that were still swinging from Fred's passage. Humph pushed through the doors. "Fred, we don't have time for this shit! Whatever security this place has is going to be coming down on us any second—what the hell are you doing?"

Fred was at a control console, typing so fast his hands were a blur. "Thought so. Standard Home Services' security protocol. I can frack this up in my sleep." Fred finished at the console, then began pulling levers, flipping switches, and performing all sorts of other seemingly arcane actions at different panels and control stations. Red warning lights flashed and alarms went off, then went dead and silenced. "That bought us some time." Fred extended his claws on one hand, using them to puncture the tops of several barrels before kicking them over. He then retrieved a lighter from his pocket, flicking it on after several tries. He carefully set the lighter on the ground, then turned to Humph. "We should run, before the fumes reach the flame."

"What've you done?" Humph was staring at the scene in front of him, uncomprehending.

"No time, I'll tell you on the way!" Now it was his turn to drag Humph away. They were through the doors and less than a dozen paces down the hallway when they heard a muffled whumph, followed by what Humph judged to be the sound of a moderately sized explosion. He chanced a look over his shoulder to see flames spilling out of the room they had just been in.

"Mind explaining before I twist your head off of your shoulders?"

"Futzed the climate control, fire suppression systems, and a few other key systems. The actual labs are locked down, but that won't save them; that little fire I started back there is going to spread unimpeded through the ventilation. Probably a lot of toxic fumes, too. That means they won't be able to put the fire out themselves and the fire services will be called. They'll never be able to cover it all up once you get three or four fire companies and a swath of reporters showing up." He smiled, looking over to Humph as they jogged. "I used to be an engineer, y'know."

"You're goddamned crazy, Fred! Ever think that your little stunt might get us killed in the course of things?"

"No worries, boss. We're almost home free." They turned a corner to find the blast doors; beyond was the less secure sections of the building, and the exit. Humph sighed in relief, shaking his head. Any sense of a breather ended once they were through the doors; two out-of-breath security guards, younger and better equipped than the old-timer at the loading dock desk, were there to greet them.

Everyone was still for half a heartbeat. Fred was the first to start talking. "Thank god you two are here! There are a couple of maniacs loose in the building!" He was walking toward them, arms spread wide. Humph followed his lead. *If we can get close enough, we can take them out before they have a chance to—*

Both guards went for their weapons simultaneously.

—do that.

Fred was closer, and rushed forward to grab the first guard in a bear hug, pinning the guard's arms to his sides and preventing him from raising his gun. Humph kicked the second guard's pistol out of his hand just before he was about to turn it on Fred.

The guard reacted instantly, switching his attention to the more immediate threat. He flicked out a collapsible baton, readying himself. Humph moved forward, extending his claws; he had to stay inside of the guard's swing, otherwise he'd be sporting broken bones at best. And these guys obviously knew how to handle Paras. The guard was good; he backed up, swinging in tight arcs to keep Humph from getting too close. Humph caught Fred and the other guard still struggling from the corner of his eye; they had rolled forward into the hallway, and the guard was trying to get on top of Fred and pin his arms to the floor with his knees. Humph made a split-second decision, turned, and kicked at the guard Fred was fighting; he flinched away at the last second, causing the kick to take him in the shoulder instead of his temple.

That gave the second guard the opportunity he'd been looking for; he lunged, bringing the baton down on Humph's left forearm. Luckily, it was a glancing blow since the guard had overextended himself, but it still drove nearly all of the sensation—save for overwhelming pain—from Humph's arm. *Hope it was worth it, bought Fred some time, maybe.* For now, he had to focus on his own attacker; the guard was pressing his advantage, trying to catch Humph on his arm again, soften him up for the finish. Humph ducked under one swing that the guard misjudged, going wide; the Boggart used his good arm to shove the guard in the back, sending him face-first into a wall. He tried to unholster the revolver, but the guard had recovered enough to kick him squarely in the side, causing him to fumble and send the gun clattering to the floor.

"I'm getting sick of this shit!" These guys definitely had been trained against Paras. They weren't making most of the usual Norm mistakes. Humph threw himself at the guard just as the guard was springing off of the wall; they met in the middle of the hallway, colliding hard enough to almost drive the wind out of Humph's lungs. He tried to claw the bastard's kidneys out, but the uniform the man was wearing wasn't giving—some sort of tear-resistant armor, at the very least. Whoever the bastards were behind all of this, they trained and equipped their goons to deal with Para powers. Humph didn't have time to process the new information; the guard was at his throat again. The fight went to the floor, both of them trying to get a few good hits on the other. Humph heard more, then he saw Fred wolf out; he didn't know how much good that was going to do. The hallway was too cramped with all four of them wrestling around. Humph reared a fist back to punch his guard, only to accidentally smash his fist into Fred's nose. The blow elicited an angry snarl from the Were, but he kept fighting.

The guard was good, too damned good; he flipped his legs around, changing the center of gravity for the both of them. From there, he was able to slip under and around Humph, flipping him over. At that point, the guard was over top of Humph; the Boggart barely had time to catch the guard's wrists as a knife came down toward his throat. *Where the hell did he get that from?* The guard was putting his full weight down, trying to drive the knife through the Boggart's voice box and into the vicinity of his spine. Humph noticed, in one of those surreal moments of clarity that happen when adrenaline starts flowing, that the guard's ID badge was hanging from his lapel. Taking a chance, Humph used one hand to rip the badge off, while working one of his legs between them until he had a foot braced against the man's belly. The knife was moving down, centimeter by centimeter.

"Fred! Throw your guy, now!" With a final burst of effort, Humph kicked the guard off of him; a testament to the man's reflexes, he landed on his feet, already in a fighting stance. He didn't have tunnel vision, either; the guard was able to catch his colleague as Fred, reluctant to miss an opportunity to savage a deserving opponent but still cognizant enough to follow his partner's instructions, threw the other guard. Somehow, as he passed, the Boggart snagged his ID off his shirt too. Both guards retrieved their firearms, aiming at Fred and Humph as they got to their feet.

"Hands in the air, now!" Both guards had self-satisfied smirks on their faces; even consummate professionals can get full of themselves after getting the drop on an opponent.

"Whatever you say, pal." Humph complied, looking over to Fred; the Were's features were returning to normal.

"I hope you know what the hell you're doing, dumbass," Fred sneered. His expression immediately changed when they heard the ultrasonic whine of an energy weapon powering up behind them. The smirks the guards had disappeared.

225

"I do—now duck!"

They both threw themselves to the floor; Humph shut his eyes and covered his head, and Fred followed suit. No sooner had they hit the floor than both of them felt intense heat on their backs, and smelled the unmistakable acrid tang of ozonating air, accompanied by what sounded like a very sharp and electrical *zat!* When they looked up, where the two guards used to be there were two vaguely humanoid shapes burnt black, along with a very dark smear against the floor and wall. Upon closer inspection, the bodies looked more like piles of heavily burnt wood, although they stank of burned meat.

Humph stood up, nursing his injured forearm. Over his shoulder, the security bots were settling back down into inactivity. Fred looked at him, uncomprehending.

"Never leave home without your plastic," Humph said, holding up the ID badges of the guards. "Let's get out of here. Now."

Understanding dawned on Fred's face. "You've got it, boss. My fire should start in earnest any—"

There was a muffled whumph in the distance. Alarms were going off, but … it seemed haphazard, as if they were only local. Then there was a bigger whumph, and the two of them felt a pressure wave pass through the corridor. The security bots came to life again, and headed in the direction of maintenance.

And all down the corridor, doors began springing open on their own, and people began pouring into the corridor. Fred found a knot of people in lab coats and joined them; Humph did the same, but not before scooping up his revolver and surreptitiously reholstering it.

There was a kind of stuttering blat from whatever they were using for a speaker system, and finally the real alarms kicked on. Humph guessed that someone had triggered it from the security desk manually. More security bots were pressed against the wall, edging their way back toward the direction of the fire, contrary to the streams of increasingly panicking workers. When they reached the entrance, Humph noticed the elderly security guard standing next to his desk, looking bewildered. On an impulse he couldn't have explained, Humph grabbed him by the collar and dragged him out the exit with everyone else. The smoke was really starting to pour out of the doors

226

in huge billowing, acrid clouds; some of the windows farther back in the facility had flames visible through them.

The crowd of lab technicians and office workers had gathered out in front of the building, and were milling around. "What happened?" The security guard was shaking his head slowly, looking back at the inferno that had been his job just minutes ago.

"Sorry, old timer. Time to look for a new gig." Humph looked for Fred in the crowd; the Were was already by an aircar that had stopped, the owner having exited his vehicle to gaze at the fire. One thing that never went to waste in a neighborhood like this was the opportunity to enjoy a good building fire, especially if it wasn't your building. Humph wove his way through the crowd, sparing a final glance over his shoulder as he reached the aircar and Fred. The old timer was pointing at him insistently. *Uh oh.*

"Those two! Somebody stop them!" The old security guard was shouting loud enough for the on-site security to hear over the noise of the crowd. Humph noticed with dismay that they all turned to focus their collective attention on him and Fred; they all started to move toward the pair, with one talking urgently into a comm device.

"Like you said, boss, it's time to go!" Fred hopped into the passenger side of the aircar, slamming the door behind him. Humph followed suit on the opposite side; the original owner finally noticed what was happening, but only had time to futilely pound on the driver's-side window before the vehicle lurched into the sky. "Think we got away clean?"

"Not a chance. Our luck has been shit lately."

"Well ... there's this much. No way they can cover up all those bodies in the back room once the fire service gets there." Fred's face was fixed in a snarl.

"You're an optimist, Fred. I'm not putting anything past the bunch of bastards that want us dead. You saw that shit in there; they're doing something to kill Weres. Chemical? Biological?" Humph shook his head. "That's beyond serious; that sort of research carries the death penalty, never mind using test subjects like that."

The rattle of bullets pinging off the roof of the aircar interrupted any further speculation. One of the rounds that penetrated passed close enough to whisper past Humph's cheek; Fred wasn't as lucky, with a round hitting him in the shoulder.

"Fuck!" He frantically started digging at the wound, using two claws to pull the slug out; it was sizzling with his blood on it. "Silver! They aren't playing around, boss." With the silver removed, his wound started to close up, the process sped up by his supernatural healing. "What's the plan now?"

Humph took out his revolver and tossed it into Fred's lap. "Shoot back, damn it! I'll try to lose them. Don't lean out too far, though; it's a long way to the ground."

Humph wondered if their pursuers might be more careful about their shots if there were more civilians around. That was an evil thought, yes. But he was no angel, and after seeing those piled-up bodies back at the lab, he knew for a fact that it was back to the bad old days, of Para versus Norm, at least in someone's eyes, and that same someone was behind whoever was pulling the trigger now. *Time to play dirty. Just the way I like it.*

He arced the car around, heading away from the industrial area and straight into residential. Ideally it would have been expensive, exclusive residential, but there wasn't much of that around on Mildred. Common-block high-rises, whose grimy exterior reminded him of long-ago days in Chicago, would have to do. The nice thing was that a lot of those high-rises were parked really close together. There was room for an aircar, but not much more.

Oh, what I wouldn't give for a dragon wingman about now. Fred punched out the glass of the window behind him, then leaned out of the door with one arm wrapped around the post, firing carefully. "I hope you got more ammo for this thing, boss," he snarled into the wind. His face was half feral now, probably adrenaline.

"Cantrip," Humph shouted back. "Self-replacing slug in the last chamber. Just a plain-Jane lead slug, though."

"They're fracking Norms. Lead'll frack 'em up just fine." Fred really was in a rage. "Die, you murderous bastards!" Fred plugged away with the revolver, emptying it at the pursuing aircar as it swooped down behind them. When he finally reached the last chamber, he held out his hand for reloads; Humph quickly handed him three speed loaders, dividing his attention between that and driving. Even with the cantrip, it was more convenient and faster to use reloads instead of having to manually rotate the cylinder to reach the last chamber every time. At the rate that Fred was burning through the ammunition, it wouldn't be long before he had to resort to the cantrip to keep shooting.

Humph spotted just what he was looking for: two high-rises with a narrow passage between them. Someone was about to get a show. The passage was big enough for the aircar—barely. He had no idea about the size of what was behind him.

More bullets pinged off the vehicle, as their pursuers realized where he was heading. "Pull your head in!" he yelled at Fred, who did a quick look ahead and pulled in faster than a turtle taking shelter. Then they were in the slot.

To Humph's acute disappointment, there was no boom behind them of the pursuit vehicle hitting one or both walls. Instead he caught a glimpse of them pulling straight up just short of the slot.

Well that would gain them a little time and distance ....

To cement that, he dove as he exited, doing a dance around shorter buildings at about the three-story-height level. The more he could confuse their pursuers when they came back down and around the high-rise, the better.

"Where'd you learn to fly like this?" Fred shouted over the wind rushing through the broken-out windows. He leaned out slightly to look behind them, watching for pursuit.

"World War II. Long story."

"You'll have to tell it to me some—look out!" Fred barely had time to duck fully back into the car before the pursuit vehicle slammed into them from above, partially crumpling the roof.

So, they were swapping out bullets for ramming. In theory that was less hazardous for the innocent bystanders. In practice though, an aircar on fire hitting an apartment block would not be good for anyone. *Maybe they're as fed up with this chase business as I am; if they get a good hit on us in the works of this jalopy, we're landing—hard.* The thought was punctuated with another jarring crash as the security car rammed them again, trying to force them to the ground; with the buildings on either side, there wasn't very much room to maneuver.

229

It seemed that the same potential disaster had finally occurred to the other pilots—or maybe whoever was controlling them had figured out that a fiery crash into the side of a heavily occupied building was going to become a nightmare nothing could cover up. The two security cars were maneuvering to force Humph and Fred to the ground. Presumably it wouldn't matter if they crashed, as long as they didn't take anyone with them.

Now what Humph had to do instead of dodging bullets was to dodge in and out of the spaces between the apartment buildings so that only one of the aircars could get on top of him at any one time. His goal was to get above them; two could play their game, and if he could force one of them into the ground, the odds would even up.

Their handicap was that this was a civilian car. Theirs … weren't. Armoring, heavier and with no speed limiters. He had to do a lot with braking. Fortunately, he'd learned his craft on prop planes, which were a lot less forgiving than these glorified shuttles. He'd done dogfighting, for real, with machine guns stitching their way across his wings. They'd likely only trained on simulators.

He got his chance when he managed to brake unexpectedly and dart upward, while he and one of the two security cars were in another slot between two buildings. There was no place for the security car to go. He dropped down on top of it like a rock, and accelerated, forcing it down before the pilot had time to react. This wasn't the sort of thing you got with simulator training. The two of them powered toward a parking lot, and the heavier engine on the security car was not able to prevail against the weight of two cars, the force Humph was applying and pitiless gravity. At the last possible second, Humph pulled their car up. The engine screamed for mercy but obeyed. It was too late for the security car; all that armor was too much. The security car made a barely controlled crash, skidding across the paved area rather than slamming into it. But it couldn't avoid the knot of parked cars ahead of it, and it did slam into them in a shower of glass and metal fragments.

One down. One to go. "Fred, is there any way for you to get the civilian limiters off this thing?" he shouted over the wind roaring in through the broken windows. If they could disable the limiters, it would open up Humph's options for speed and maneuverability; by law, all civilian and commercial aircars were made virtually idiotproof to keep the airways from becoming free-for-all destruction derbies.

"Not unless you want to die in a horrible crash," Fred replied, snarling at the mess of crashed cars and the wobbly figures pulling themselves out of the security car. "It requires being on the ground and powered down, you big dope. And even if it didn't, I'm not climbing out on the hood right now, thanks."

Well so much for that idea. This last security car wasn't taking any chances with Humph, and this chase couldn't go on forever. Sooner or later—probably sooner—they'd get backup or be able to ground the aircar, and that would be all she wrote. He couldn't hightail back to the others; leading whoever was pulling the strings on this game back to Harry would get all of them killed, and not all that pleasantly or quickly. Humph made a snap decision, then started peeling his jacket off.

"I'm going to try something. It probably won't work, but it's our only shot." He handed the jacket to Fred, focusing on driving while he talked. "Once I get low, you've gotta bail; find cover. My jacket has the last of the reloads for the pistol. No matter what happens, get back to the others. They've gotta know about what we found in that lab. I'm betting you and Jim can figure out ways to get it out to the Furs at least, if not the rest of the semicivilized universe. Got that?"

"Yeah, boss, but ... what the hell are you going to try?"

"Something incredibly stupid. Par for the course, right?"

"At least you're consistent, boss." Fred bundled the jacket up, tucking it under his arm. Checking the revolver a final time to make sure it was ready, he nodded to Humph. "I'm set, boss."

Fred was, at heart, an engineer, not an action hero. Humph was going to have to give him instructions for this. "When I'm close enough to the ground and going slow enough that you think you can survive it, I want you to jump out, roll, and get under cover." He glanced over at Fred. "You might want to wolf out for that."

"But—"

"Don't argue, just do it." With one eye on the sky, Humph dove for the deck and began maneuvering around obstacles among the buildings. Fred went half-Wolf rather than full Wolf, but everything Humph knew about Furs told him that would give him just about all of the healing ability of the fully lupine form and none of the disadvantages. Fred didn't bother opening what was left of the door; he just kicked it off its hinges, grabbed the A and B pillars, and poised on the edge. He must have spotted a good opening as Humph streaked down an alley, just above a lot of dumpsters laden with what looked like industrial stuff. One second he was there in the doorframe, the next, he was gone.

"Here goes nothing," Humph muttered, gunning the throttle.

Fred landed hard, trying to roll with the impact and failing. The result was that after tumbling over trash and broken crap he ground to a halt, the last foot of it on his face. He hardly felt the road rash, though; with the adrenaline and being partially wolfed out, he was back up on his feet and dashing for cover immediately. A dumpster that was still smoldering from being used as an impromptu burn-pit was the first thing that he found; he thudded his back against the side of it, crouching down.

Humph had laid on some extra speed after swooping back into the air, but he was coming to the end of the alley. There wasn't going to be any room left to run, soon. Fred first heard, then saw the pursuing aircar as it zoomed overhead. He did his best to work his way into a corner between the dumpster and the wall it was nestled against; the last thing he needed was for one of the security goons in that car to fill him with more precious metal. *C'mon, boss, whatever you're going to pull out of your sleeve, now's the time.*

As if answering Fred's call, Humph fishtailed the aircar at the very end of the alley; it was close enough that he could clearly see sparks lighting off of the rear of the vehicle as it scraped against concrete. As soon as he was righted, Humph floored the aircar; the engine whined in protest, but obediently responded and was going its maximum speed within seconds. The security aircar matched speed, facing the hopeless charge. Fred cried out wordlessly, jumping up and lining up Humph's Webley-Fosbery with the aircar; it felt as if it weighed a ton, and that he was moving in slow motion. He knew what was going to happen, and he had to do something, anything, to stop it. It was already too late, however; both cars were well out of range of the revolver, at least with how bad Fred's aim was. All Fred could do was watch as the two vehicles hurtled toward each other. At the last second, the security car tried to swerve out of the way, but there was nowhere to go in the alley. The aircars impacted with a sickening and too-loud crunch, immediately followed by the percussive beat and pressure wave from an explosion as their engines and fuel tanks detonated.

Harry paced around the bunker restlessly. He had been ignoring Lori almost completely since Humph and Fred had left. She had stayed in the main compartment, watching the entrance and waiting. Jim was still busy, working on something at his computer terminal. Whenever Harry tried to ask him a question, the Zombie simply replied with a grunt or a single word. They were all nervous, and were doing their best to hide it with varying levels of success. He desperately wanted to be doing something other than sitting around in this warren. He couldn't even seem to think in this hole. The lighting or just the tight spaces or Lori sitting there sort of distracting him, something was sapping his ability to concentrate, to make himself useful. *If only I could get a latte, or some room service. Maybe one of my suits. That'd clear my head.*

This entire episode had almost driven him to his wits' end; if he wasn't being dragged somewhere, he was being shot at. If he wasn't being shot at, he was running. If he wasn't running, he was hiding, and so on. It was enough to cause any sensible and sophisticated person to go insane. Despite all of that, he was starting to get into what he saw as the spirit of things. This was an adventure; not one of the lame, bought-and-paid-for trips that some of the more eccentric guests at the parties he attended would brag about. Holidays where they shot renowned and dangerous game on very carefully cultivated and sanitized hunting preserves, or "adventure cruises," sailing or flying into situations like planetary storms or massive volcanic eruptions that gave the illusion of peril but where no one was in danger of so much as a hangnail. This was real. They could all be caught and killed at any moment, and he was at the center of it. In one of his rare moments of clarity, Harry realized that he was probably the happiest he had been in a long time, never mind the fact that a well-equipped and well-funded group of merciless killers wanted to turn him to dust.

When this is over .... Well that was the question, wasn't it? It might be over with him dead, but if it wasn't, what was he going to do with the rest of his life? This was the first time he'd ever been this close to Paras for this long, and he kind of liked it. They were more real than any of his so-called friends. If he went back to his old sort of life ... *I'll be bored out of my skull.*

Before Harry could ponder that line of thought any further, he heard the telltale screech of the exterior hatch opening. Harry and Lori looked at each other, then to Jim. None of them had heard the passcode they had all agreed on for anyone reentering the bunker. There was a quick scramble for weapons, everyone trying to be as quiet as possible; Jim had thrown his helmet on and picked up a pipe, while Lori had produced a long knife seemingly from thin air. Harry twisted around, unable to find anything, and then stood in the center of the room, with a deer-in-the-headlights look plastered on his face.

Jim took pity on him and threw a broom at him just as the footfalls reached the inner door. Harry fumbled with the broom, sending it twirling in the air as he tried to get a grip on it. The final hatch swung open. It wasn't a squad of mercenaries with guns at the ready. Just Fred, looking a little worse for wear but otherwise fine.

The tension in the room broke, with Harry the first one to speak. "Holy crap, Fred. Way to give a body a scare, huh?" He bent down to pick up the broom, leaning on it and doing his best to strike a manly pose. "I mean, we were prepared for any sort of violent encounter, but still, you mustn't enter so abruptly and without announcing yourself—wouldn't want the women to faint, right?" He grinned, looking back to Jim. The Zombie had removed his helmet, setting it down on the desk in front of him. Once Harry saw the stricken gaze on Jim's emaciated face, his own expression soon fell.

"Fred," Jim said slowly, something strange in his voice. "Where's Humph?"

"Gone," was the only thing that Fred could manage to say. He was holding what looked like Humph's jacket; Harry's gaze drifted down to the revolver stuck into Fred's waistband. He heard a

234

slight rustling of fabric on fabric behind him. When he turned around, Lori was already walking toward the door, the few things she owned in her bag. Her face was a mask of tears, but she was walking determinedly.

"Lori, please, just wait—" She silently pushed past Harry, then Fred, and then she was gone out the door without a single word. Just like that, just as suddenly and irrevocably as Humph, Lori was now gone. Harry knew that she wouldn't be back, no matter how much he wished for it. He decided that maybe he didn't like this adventure business all that much after all.

The three of them were silent for a long time, as if they were frozen in place where they each stood in the bunker. The thought floated through Harry's mind that maybe if they were still enough, time would freeze too, maybe turn back and then Humph would still be alive.

"… the main thing is to get it all out to the Fur Dens," Fred said, for about the fifth time. "After that, we try and get it to the Fang Nests. We let them work the media, there are enough of them that whoever this is won't be able to stop them all."

Inside information? Wishful thinking? Skinny Jim wasn't sure which … but he did figure this much, "whoever" was behind all of this, they were probably betting that now that their ragtag band of brothers had discovered just what was being covered up, and had gotten footage of it (which he had, via the spy cam he'd glued into Fred's hair right at the hairline), they'd go straight to the media themselves. So Fred's plan made perfect sense.

Harry wasn't buying it, though. It was too easy, too perfect. Something they could have conceivably done awhile ago. Before Humph had … gone. Fred was repeating himself too much, as if he was trying to convince himself a little too hard as much as the rest of them. They were silent in the aircar for some time, all of them uncomfortable and distinctly aware of it. Harry cleared his throat twice before speaking. "I know that we're not going to spill the story, not the way you two are talking about." The long pause when neither Fred nor Jim denied the statement seemed to bolster

Harry, shore up his courage. "You're going to trade me in to save yourselves, aren't you?"

The Adjudicator was satisfied with himself. He had a real name, of course, but his own egomania sometimes overflowed into reality; most of his underlings were just as ruthless as he was, but few of them dared to call him anything other than by his self-styled title for fear of what he would do to them. He was a cruel man, a sadist, and only took joy when someone else was submitting to his will. Pain, terror, and violence were his favorite and most-used tools. Paired with that willingness to inflict hurt into the world was a cunning intelligence, cold and sharp. Without his mind he would have been just an average bully; someone to watch out for, but easily lost in multitudes. But he wasn't the average bully; he was able to hide his cruelties, his excesses. His career afforded him all the opportunities he could ever want to kill and maim, all of it sanctioned and generously funded. It was good to be a government man.

This job was no different, really, than the dozens he'd had before it. Someone had done something or found something that they shouldn't have; they had become an impediment to the smooth workings of the machine, and thus had to be removed. That's where the Adjudicator came in—to turn the handle and grind whoever was between the gears. This time, it was a minor socialite: one Harry Somerfield. He was connected, but no one was above being dealt with when it came to the Adjudicator and those whose interests he protected. Mr. Somerfield had enlisted some help along the way; minor annoyances like that sometimes happened with a job, but that was part of the fun. The chase was part of what kept the Adjudicator hungry and interested; flushing his quarry out, and the attendant violence, all sated his bloodlust little by little until the very end.

It seemed that the end was fast approaching for Mr. Somerfield. Two of his compatriots had sold him out, and were now on their way to deliver the playboy in exchange for their lives. It always came down to something like this, with this sort of scum—begging and pleading, giving each other up for even a few more minutes of their pathetic lives. He had been hoping that he would be able to run down the entire mangy lot; seeing the realization on their faces when their little "deal" would prove futile would be almost as satisfying. Their naiveté was almost funny. After the little stunt they had pulled at the production lab, and then, the number of his underlings they'd taken out in that chase, how could they think that they'd ever be allowed to live? *You don't fuck with the government; we're here to fuck with you.*

The Adjudicator didn't waste much time pondering the concerns of soon-to-be-dead freaks; they would arrive soon enough, and then the real fun could begin. The only question that remained was how long he would take to kill them; such things had to be done with a measure of artistry to really be enjoyed.

This was not Fred's favorite part of Mildred. Even fully wolfed out, he never came here unless he was forced to.

Sunset City Recreational Park—well, the name was apt if you considered that the place had been "sunsetted" years ago. Another victim in a long line of budget cuts, it was not situated in a commercially advantageous spot, so Sunset City—a subdivision comprised of mostly low-income high-rises inhabited by low-income renters—had neither sold the land nor bothered to maintain it. The original plan had probably been for a "wilderness" style park combined with a big, grassy commons and other amenities, along the lines of Central Park in New York City on Old Earth. Now the grassy commons was waist-high in weeds, the trails among the dense trees were the hunting grounds of predators with two, four, and six legs, the ballparks could only be discerned by the remains of chain-link fences full of blown trash, and the entire eighty-acre site gave off the aura of something just after an apocalypse, poisoned and abused nature struggling to reclaim the landscape. Fred knew of some Packs who hunted here recreationally … they would never say what it was that they hunted, and he never asked. Suffice it to say that anyone here after dark was probably someone who would not be missed.

Jim and Fred had Harry sandwiched in between them as they waded through weeds and garbage to what had been a band shell. Well, it was still a band shell; plascreet was hard to destroy with anything less than a pocket nuke or specialized construction equipment. But it had been stripped of anything that could be sold or just pried off, so the doors on either side where musicians would have entered and exited were open holes like a pair of gouged-out eyes. And it had been graffitied up as far as anyone could reach, and then a little higher. Someone had been ambitious and brought a rope or a ladder … or else the rumors of Were-apes were real, and they liked to tag buildings.

In the half-light of near dusk, the selection of dark-suited men waiting on the plascreet stage looked even more out of place than they might have in full light. In daylight, they could have been mistaken for a group of entrepreneurs examining the area for potential, or even city officials surveying the damage. But now, so close to dark, there was no reason for anyone dressed as they were to be in a place this dangerous.

Unless these wolves in sheep's clothing happened to be even more dangerous than the killers that called this place their territory.

Dead center in front of the congregation was the apparent leader; he was in a suit just like the rest, though his was plainly more expensive and actually tailored. He could have been anywhere between his late twenties and early fifties; he had a timeless look to him, and by all common aesthetic standards should have been attractive, or at the very least, ordinary. There was something … off about him, however. Maybe it was something about the eyes, or the constant half-smile he always had on his face. It was a strange sort of vibe, unwholesome, like the feeling one would get from being around a convicted but unrepentant child molester.

Harry hung his head, listlessly being led on. Jim and Fred exchanged a look with each other before they continued toward the waiting team, coming up about fifty paces short of the stage before the leader spoke.

"That'll be far enough, gentlemen." The sound was carried easily by the acoustics of the stage, and none of them were forced to shout as they talked. The leader kept his hands behind his back as he talked, looking down on the trio, still smirking. "You," he nodded to Jim, "can remove that helmet, if you like. I don't believe that there'll be any need to keep up appearances here."

Jim let go of Harry's arm to use both hands, removing his helmet. None of the suited goons on the stage seemed to be surprised to see that he was a Reboot. "You sure seem to know a lot about us."

"It's my job to find out such things. And to find people once they've been … misplaced."

Fred took a step forward. "We've fulfilled our end of the bargain. We've brought Harry to you. In exchange, we get to walk away from this. That's our deal."

"That is what was discussed." The leader raised a hand; the men behind him all produced compact and rather dangerous-looking weapons on command, aiming them directly at the trio.

Fred's hackles raised, and he started to slowly unsheathe his claws, the beginning stage of him wolfing out. "What the hell is this?"

"The arrangement that we discussed, whereby you go free in exchange for turning over Harry Somerfield to us, is predicated upon, first, us actually needing to let you go. Most importantly, however, it assumes you actually have Harry Somerfield. Which you clearly do not."

Fred literally jumped, he was so startled. "What in hell are you talking about?" he demanded. "He's right here!" And with that, he shoved Harry forward, making him stumble a little.

"Drop the act, please. It's starting to get pathetic." The head goon—Fred could only think of him as that—lifted his lip in a sneer. Fred looked back at Harry, distraught. This was all falling apart! This wasn't in the plan! Now what was he going to do?

"It's okay, Fred." Harry stood up straighter, looking into the leader's eyes. "There's more to this guy than meets the eye." As he spoke, he walked forward a few paces. His features started to change; his face darkened, he shrunk and became more compact and wiry, and short, bristly black hair sprouted on the exposed parts of his body. Once he was done, he was Harry no more. Humph planted his fists on his hips, sizing up the goons. "How'd you know, if I may ask?"

The leader tapped the side of his head with a finger. "Having money affords one all the best toys; even ones that can pierce your glamour." He started forward a few steps, still smiling. "To be honest, we thought you were dead in the collision. I didn't know that you were alive until your friends came strolling along with you in tow, instead of Mr. Somerfield." The leader sounded mildly impressed. "My turn to ask how you managed that. If I may?"

Humph held up his pocket watch. "You have your tricks, I have mine. Slipped this into a jacket that I gave Fred right before he bailed out. Effectively teleported to it right before the collision; that way it looks like I got crushed on all the cameras. Figured it'd give us an edge, you thinking I was dead." The leader watched Humph replace the pocket watch, still smirking.

"It would have been a good deception, had it worked. But to what end?"

Humph shrugged. "Couldn't let you have the kid. He's dumb, and out of his league, but he doesn't deserve what you bastards were going to do to him. Plus," Humph leaned forward slightly, "I figured I could twist your head off and shove it up your ass, if I could just get close enough."

"Very cute, Mr. Boggart." The leader was allowing a tinge of annoyance to creep into his voice. "None of you are going to leave here alive, you know. If you'd like the small mercy of dying quicker than the others, I do suggest you tell me where Mr. Somerfield is."

Humph thought for a moment. "First, I've got to know something." The leader waved his hand for Humph to continue. "Why Weres? Why go after them? What the hell did the Fur set ever do to you? Piss on your shrubs?" *Keep monologuing, you rat fuck, and I'll waltz right up and gut you where you stand.* Humph continued to slowly walk forward, keeping his hands at his sides and his posture nonthreatening.

The leader laughed; it was a sharp, mean sound without any real mirth in it. "You really have no clue how far off the beaten path you've stumbled, Mr. Boggart. The Weres are just a small part of things. A sideshow for the main attraction, the big event. In time—"

Floodlights suddenly hit the leader, his men on the stage, and Humph. Everyone looked around, shielding their eyes. Humph detected a flash of panic spread across the leader's face; things were finally not going according to plan for him, instead of not for everyone else.

About damn time.

"This is the MPPF. Throw down your weapons and remain where you are. Anyone that attempts to flee or resist will be engaged immediately with lethal force. This is your only warning." Then Humph saw them: at least four specialized aircars, huge ones, painted solid black. Ah the glory of fully stealthed aircars. Nothing to give them away until they were all in place and there was nowhere to run to and nowhere to hide. They didn't have any markings, and dozens of troops in tactical gear were rappelling out of the open doors. Good move, that; kept the aircars as overhead support while the troops piled onto the ground. Humph approved; this was the first time he was actually happy to see the cops.

"Kill them, kill them all!" The leader of the goons shouted furiously at his men, pulling out his own sidearm. Then the shooting began—the goons, the leader, and the newly arrived troops.

Skinny Jim jammed his helmet back on; at that point, Humph knew, he was the next thing to invulnerable in his robot shell. He might look like a battered old bot, but that chassis was from an industrial model and was hardened against damn near anything. Fred wasted no time, and wolfed out partly; that would take care of ordinary projectiles and even direct-energy weapons up to a point, but not silver. Humph was the one that was the most vulnerable.

But he was also the one that was the most angry.

Both of his partners charged forward toward the goons—it was time for payback, time for blood on the ground. Humph looked for the leader; he was still standing out in the open, firing at the aircars. When he stopped to reload, both of them locked eyes. Humph unholstered the old Webley-Fosbery from under Harry's rumpled suit jacket, and ran toward the leader. The bastard wasn't smiling anymore. Just as Humph raised his revolver, the leader turned to run, darting between his men with bullets and energy blasts hitting the ground around him.

I am not letting this son of a bitch get away!

The Boggart ran after the leader, his legs pumping hard and driving him forward as fast as they could carry him.

Some of the goons tried to stop him, tried to run interference for their boss. He shot the first one squarely in the face, not even breaking stride. The second one stepped in front of his path; a backhanded pistol strike to his orbital socket sent the man down to the ground, maybe dead. Humph vaulted over the body, still following the leader. Off to the side of the fighting, he saw Jim knock down two goons, messily kicking in their heads after they were sent sprawling to the ground. Energy blasts and bullets ricocheted off of his robot shell, with some of the shots getting sent off wildly, one of them striking a goon square in the back. In the back of his mind, he found himself marveling; when he'd first hooked up with these two, he would never have dreamed of seeing the Reboot wade into a fight like this. Fred—well, the guy might be an engineer, but he was also a Fur—a tough Loner at that—and Furs, no matter what they had been before they were Turned, were scrappers. But a Reboot? Normally they won—back when they were still hostile—by sheer overwhelming numbers. And that had been back when they weren't manual labor, and had to kill for their food. You just didn't picture them duking it out, Boggart-style.

He emptied the rest of his revolver's cylinder into the gut of a suited goon that had grabbed hold of his shoulder, costing him precious steps and time. He turned, trying to catch up with the leader; he had to get him. If that bastard got away, this would never be over. He got a glimpse of the leader sprinting down a side path, and took off after him. Just as he was about to reach the beginning of the path, four goons, all with their guns trained on him, closed ranks, blocking him off from his quarry.

Humph raised his revolver, pulling the trigger—*click*. He hadn't had time to reload, and he couldn't cock the mechanism and pull the trigger fast enough to get to the last cylinder again for the cantrip to kick in; at least not enough times to take out all four of the goons. They were about to cut him down when an inhuman howl split the sky, cutting through the noise of the melee. A large auburn blur bathed in silver light slammed into all four of the goons, dragging them screaming to the ground. Fred—he was in full form, centered in the middle of a moonglow-spot trained on him from one of the aircars—had the men pinned down, and was literally tearing them apart before Humph's eyes. This wasn't the half-form he could take at will. This was the Monster in the Dark, the fully feral beast for whom killing was as easy as breathing. Easier. His victims really never had a chance.

They weren't dying quietly. The Werewolf's head came up, gore dripping from his muzzle. Humph saw a glimmer of intelligence behind those canine eyes, and what he would have sworn was a wink; with that, the Were was back up and looking for more victims. Humph had heard of the spotlights, restricted to law enforcement, but he'd never seen what happened when one hit a Fur until now. The difference between a moonspot and a real full moon was that the Fur in question would keep his human brain rather than going completely mindless and bestial. How they managed that, Humph had no idea. *I'm going to owe Fred a case of scotch for that save. Business first, though.* Humph ran down the path, doggedly following the leader.

The path was overgrown, with branches hanging down from trees and bushes growing out into the middle from the edges. The leader of the goons would wait at some of the twists and turns, shooting at Humph when he came into view; Humph had had time to reload at this point, and shot back. He took his time, lining up his sights and squeezing the trigger. During the last exchange, he saw his round take the leader in the knee; a spurt of blood and the man's cry of pain confirmed the wound. The leader kept stumbling down the path, fumbling with his pistol and cursing. Humph slowed down, from a trot to finally walking, as he followed the blood on the ground. The path terminated at a stone arch bridge; it must have been part of a scenic overlook for the river it crossed over, which ended with a gentle waterfall to the left. The leader paused on the bridge, still trying to reload his sidearm. Finally he jammed the magazine home, raising the pistol; Humph did the same, firing once. The bullet caught the leader in his shoulder, causing him to drop his pistol and fall back over the edge of the bridge. He landed with a small splash in the river which wasn't anything more than ornamental. He came out of the water gasping and floundering toward the waterfall—not dead yet, evidently. Humph followed him, still unhurried; when he reached the bridge, he walked around it and into the river. The water wasn't very deep even at the center, maybe a foot at most.

The leader reached the waterfall, then struggled to stand up; there wasn't anywhere else for him to go. The waterfall fell onto a shallow artificial lake, which was thickly overgrown and green with algae from lack of care. There were jagged rocks at the bottom of the waterfall, nearly forty feet down. He turned to face Humph, clutching his shoulder. "You goddamned mongrel!" Spittle leaked down his chin as he shouted. "You think this is the end? You think that killing me is going to change anything, anything at all?" Humph holstered his pistol as he trudged through the water. He walked right up to the leader, staring him in the eyes right up until he plunged his claws into the man's belly.

"No, I don't think it'll bring back all of my friends that you've murdered, or change anything else that has happened. But killing you is too damned satisfying to pass up." He dug the claws in farther, twisting to the side and upward, the fabric of the man's shirt and suit bunching up in between Humph's knuckles. The leader's eyes bulged out of his skull, his mouth ringed in a silent "oh" of agony. Humph used his free hand to shove the leader, hard, pulling him off of Humph's claws and sending him over the edge of the waterfall. There was a loud clap as he hit the rocks below.

Humph looked over the edge. The man wasn't moving, wasn't breathing. Still.

The Boggart selected a good-sized rock from the ornamental boulders in the stream. Fortunately, they hadn't been cemented into place. He picked it up with a grunt, walked carefully to the edge of the waterfall, aimed, and threw.

It landed with a wet smack on the human's head.

No sooner had it done so, than there was movement in the underbrush. First one, then a second, then a third and a fourth Ghoul crept out from cover on all fours. In a moment there was nothing of the body to be seen beneath the feeding Ghouls. Humph didn't bother to watch any further, opting to wash the blood off of his hands in the river before walking back to the path. "Now there's no chance of seeing that prick again. Rot in hell, asshole."

"I don't get it," said Harry, as he handed Humph a double scotch. "What the hell were they after?"

"Captain Monologue didn't get to finish," Humph replied, taking his first sip and savoring it. "And once the fighting started, and he knew the jig was up, well, you wouldn't have gotten anything out of him with pliers and razor blades. At least, nothing useful."

He'd seen the type before, and although he wasn't going to let Harry in on the full deal, he recognized a government goon when he saw one. Even if the Chief Suit hadn't been conditioned to a fare-thee-well to resist torture and other interrogation techniques—and Humph strongly doubted that he hadn't been—he'd probably been implanted with a remote device to eliminate him if he was "compromised." Probably without his knowledge, during something like minor surgery or dental work, long, long before he ever reached the position he'd held. The man himself had said it; someone was playing a long game.

The less Harry knew about this, the better off Harry was. He'd done all right for a green kid, but they'd had crap-tons of luck on their side. The playboy would be no match even for one of The Suit's underlings, much less whoever had been pulling The Suit's strings. All the same, he'd come through for them. When Harry thought he was being sold out so that Jim and Fred could save their own hides, he was actually being taken to meet the still-alive-and-pissed-off Humph so that they could make a switch. Humph impersonating Harry would give him enough time to get back to his mother; with her seeing him alive and hearing the story straight from him, they figured that she could pull some strings and maybe get them out of the jam. Mrs. Somerfield had, and then some. Humph could only guess how. It could be that renegade lab massacring Furs wasn't the only time the firm had done business with the government. Or it could be Mrs. Somerfield just happened to have some powerful pals. You never know when an old college friend is going to come in handy.

After Humph had given the hard goodbye to the head goon, he had made his way back to the stage where the bulk of the fighting had taken place. By the time he got back, everything was just about said and done; Fred was back to Norm and wrapped in a blanket due to his clothes being shredded. Jim was doing his best deaf-mute impression next to Fred, pretending to only respond to Fred's voice like a real bot would. None of the goons were alive; between Fred, Jim, and the late arrivals, not a single one of them had made it. Humph suspected that the "cops" had performed a few executions when no one was looking. He had taken a chance and talked to the one that seemed to be in charge. The Boggart had dealt with all sorts of law enforcement over the years, for various reasons. One thing he was sure of was that that guy was not a cop. On the other hand, Fred hadn't been the only Fur on the ground in that crew, every one of those aircars had a moonspot and there had been at least four others in the wrecking crew besides Fred. So at least they were Para-friendly. When he hazarded asking the Norm who he worked for, the man only smiled sadly and said, "You wouldn't have heard of us."

After that, everything went as Humph had expected. Everyone was told to shut up, and forget ever being there. The warrant for Humph's arrest was dropped, and everything was swept under the rug. Fred was not happy about it, at all, and understandably so. Humph had been able to talk him out of going public with info of what went down. From what Jim had been able to piece together after the fact, once the office was back in working order, was that it was some sort of rogue chapter of government that was carrying out someone's pet project. Mr. Bevins had brokered the deal, using his influence to set up the lab using Somerfield Botanicals as a front. He'd also been the one to discover that Harry was embezzling, and things had spiraled out of control from there. Bevins was still missing, so far as any of them knew; scooped up by the "good" government guys, on the run, or dead. None of them particularly cared at that point, they were too tired. Beyond that they knew nothing, and frankly they were fine with that. Digging any deeper would've probably brought the same sort of trouble back down on their heads, only this time they wouldn't have as good of a chance of coming out alive. They'd been assured by the Norm in charge of the strike team that "those parties responsible will be dealt with," and his tone left no room for interpreting how final it would be.

Harry had come by the office this last time to see how everything looked; at his insistence, he'd had his mother pay to help BB&B set up shop again. After all, it was the least she could do for saving her darling baby boy, and so on, yada yada yada. She wasn't particularly enthused when she had heard about the exploits that Humph had put her son through, but she had acquiesced in the end. Harry was looking like his old self, save for the fact that he wasn't falling-down drunk now. Something had changed in him during their time on the run; Humph definitely liked the new Harry. He was maybe half an idiot, but he wasn't the stuck-up and annoying rich boy he had been.

"Boggart ... why in hell did you let a gorgeous gal like Lori walk out thinking you were dead?" he finally blurted, proving that he was at least still half an idiot. "She was crazy about you!"

Fred cleared his throat and Jim shifted uncomfortably in his seat; both of them were looking intently into their drinks—Jim's only being for show and politeness, of course—too embarrassed to correct Harry. Humph was quiet for a long while, finally sighing and finishing his drink before he spoke.

"I could cop out and say that I wanted to keep her safe. But that'd only be half the answer, Harry." Humph held out his glass; dutifully, Harry refilled it, keeping his eyes on Humph, interested in what he was going to say. "The bottom line is, her and me, it'd never work. Guys like me are always stepping in the shit, riding the ragged edge, and coming away bloody. Dames like her ... they move up, and get what they want. Can't have two ends of a rope pulling in different directions, Harry; the rope snaps, eventually." Humph sounded like he was trying to convince himself as much as he was trying to convince the others.

"Well, that might be so." Harry thought for a few moments. "But she wanted you."

Humph laughed, mirthlessly. "Yeah, but I was never Mister Right. Only Mister Right Now. You live as long as I have, you finally figure that out."

It was Harry's turn to finish his drink; he set the glass down, hard, after he was done. "I think you're wrong, Humph. Even The Boggart has to let himself be happy once in a while."

Fred looked ostentatiously at his watch. "Harry, we gotta leave now if we're gonna get you to that fancy soiree. Traffic around that art gallery is gonna be murder."

Harry grumbled something about being forced into being respectable and the company face man, but Humph could tell he wasn't all that displeased. A word with Mummy Dear about how keeping the kid on a short leash with no responsibilities was ruining him seemed to have done some good.

"Go on, you two. Make sure you're seen but not seen. We can use more bodyguarding gigs." Humph waved them off, and the three departed with relief on both sides of the conversation. Fred flicked the lights off, leaving only the single light that hung over Humph's desk on.

Humph opened his desk drawer and pulled out one of the earrings Lori had worn onstage for her singing gig at Paulie's club. It was just costume jewelry, not expensive. She'd lost it, hooked into his jacket during the brawl and their flight from the bar. He'd meant to return it ….

He stared at it for a very long time.

He still could ….

Then he jumped as the phone rang. "Boggart, Barkes, and Bot," he answered, and listened for a moment. "Yeah, we can do that job …."

He poured another scotch and lit up a stogie. The smoke curled around the room, a single shaft of light from the overhead lamp playing through the swirls. "… for the right price."

PART FOUR

THE SOMNAMBULIST WALTZ

This was an easy, *cushy* gig, no two ways about it. Easy: keep eyes on the client's suspected-to-be-wayward husband. Cushy: on board a luxury cruise ship to nowhere, or rather, out to a star that was currently tearing a gas giant apart, orbit awhile for the view, and then back to port again. I mean, a *cruise ship*. Even when I'd been alive I'd never been able to afford a cruise. And this was the sort of boat I couldn't even afford to look at vids of.

It would have been even better if I'd been able to enjoy the same amenities my partners did: the buffets, the restaurants, the spa, the beds (which, I was told, had controls so you could alter the gravity local to the bed, and sleep six inches above the blankets if you chose). But hey, there were still the entertainment venues, which were lavish, and people-watching, which we were supposed to do anyway.

That I couldn't enjoy the buffets, spa, and beds wasn't because my partners were dicks. But hey you know that. I've gotten into why intelligent Reboots are feared and hunted, Norms and Paras, and all that before—look it up. And call me Skinny Jim, everyone else does.

Now, before I get any further into this story, let me describe our setting. We were on the *Wayfaring Stranger,* the aforementioned cruise ship to nowhere. She was actually never supposed to be a ship in the first place. She was supposed to be a city-sized climate-controlled shipping warehouse in near-planet orbit, so she's basically a giant cube. I don't know whose brilliant idea this was, but it was a dud, and the builders went bankrupt before they could finish her.

But a spacefaring ship doesn't have to be any particular shape these days, and someone else, whose ideas were a little less bankruptcy-inclined, figured out that there was a lot of money to be made in the idea from the pre-spaceflight days of *cruises*. Especially cruises that will guarantee you a luxe environment. It was probably a Fang; they're pretty clever that way, always a nose for making cabbage and living the high life. So they picked up the hulk for a song, refitted it with everything you could possibly want in a vacation, picked an unusual destination that didn't require shuttling passengers to a planet surface for a once-in-a-lifetime experience, in this case a dying star system circling a black hole, and commenced making bank deposits.

This was the *Wayfaring Stranger*'s tenth trip out and back to this particular stellar spectacle, with "repositioning cruises" between each trip, where the owners would fill her up with folks who wanted a luxury one-way trip from Planet A to B. That way they could legit advertise, once they got to the new orbital spaceport, that it *would* be a unique experience for that system.

She had everything a city would have that you'd want, and nothing that you didn't want, like, say, slums. Unless you counted the crew quarters as slums. Mind you, even the crew quarters weren't bad, even if they were spartan. With a cube the size of a city, there was no lack of space, so it wasn't as if the crew was living in steerage conditions. They were merely in the buffer zone between the working parts of the ship and the paying customers.

There were segregated sectors just for families, for singles, for "adventurous singles," for couples, for kids on their own. That's right, you could dump Junior in his age-restricted section and enjoy several weeks of child-free bliss while you downed all the booze you could stand, the way Old Earthers used to send their kids to summer camp. She even had special sections for Furs, Fangs, and "Other," Paras like Humph, and, because they thought of *everything*, a "xenophobic" section if you didn't want to ever encounter anything during the trip that wasn't a pure human. Ah, *homo sapiens*, no one has ever lost money catering to prejudice. Paras and Norms, and plenty of hate to go around on both sides. Mercenary that I am, I have to admire someone making money selling what most creatures engage in for free, and actually making moolah at it.

There were of, course, no "aliens." So far, intelligent life outside of Old Earth—and the Paranormals and Norms that inhabited it—had yet to be found. There were lots of theories why, but so far, no evidence. Personally, I went with the "intelligence is statistically improbable" version. Anything else is just too depressing, or terrifying, depending on how you look at it.

We landed this gig, and many others like it, courtesy of Harry Sommerville. You remember Harry—young, dumb, richer than Croesus, but not a bad guy in the end. And, way out of the norm for one of our clients, he'd actually learned a few hard lessons from the escapade we bailed him out of. Harry had lots of friends, plenty of them were women, and one of those women was afraid her husband was doing the usual. Well, as Humph would say, when a dame got that feeling, most of the time it was right. But when a dame moves in Harry Sommerville's circles … things get more complicated and expensive, prenups are often involved, and it's never a quick visit to a divorce lawyer. *Plus ça change, plus ça même chose*; it had been just like that back when I was still alive. The numbers were just higher now, and measured in creds, not dollars.

Another thing that never seems to change is that no matter how glamorous a job is on paper, it's always the nasty drudge work that gets it done at the end of the day. As the resident drudge in a can, that meant me, working my bony ass off in a Tiki Bar in the "adventurous singles" part of the ship. I had been scrubbing floors, polishing brass railings and doorknobs, and getting bumped into by drunken cruise-goers for that entire day, all just to keep my "eyes" (mostly, in this case, an array of sensors and surveillance devices installed covertly all over my suit's helmet) on our mark.

"Y'missed a spot." That was Fred.

"Is 'Spot' your girlfriend's pet name, Fido?" I countered. As much as a Reboot can love anything, I love Fred. He's a great partner. Has been ever since we bailed each other out from under the pointy-nailed thumbs of that bunch of asshat Fangs running our ship, back when we still worked for the company.

Don't ever tell him I said that. He'd get all sappy, and he's enough of a sap already.

"All twenty of them," he retorted, gazing soulfully into his scotch. "You still missed *that* spot, though."

"To quote, 'Bite my shiny metal ass,' hairball."

Fred was posted up on the other side of the room, doing his level best to hold up the bar with a passable—some would even say "natural"—drunkard's lean. Judging by the number of empty glasses that had formed a constellation around his posting, Fred was a method actor. Even with a Para's, especially a Were's, constitution, it was an impressive amount of alcohol.

"Could be worse, Jim," Humph piped in through their shared comms. "You could be getting your ass pinched every five minutes by anything in this room with a pulse. This bunch isn't 'bi-curious,' they're 'I'll try everything in the house.'"

"At least you're getting tipped for it. Me, I'm furniture."

Humph had chosen—his prerogative, as the boss of our coterie's little enterprise—to take the "floater" position; a stolen uniform, one of his usual faces, and he instantly blended in as a waiter. With ships this big, and the high turnover rate among the sections—protection for the crew from some of the rapacious harpies, Para and Norm—the crew would be used to new unknown faces cycling through and out of jobs all the time. This allowed him to constantly move in and out, and get as close to the target as he wanted. It was pretty slick, and for Humph it was old hat.

As you know, Humph is a Boggart. Shape-shifter extraordinaire with a taste for good scotch, cheap bourbon, and crazy dames. Even as flawed as the old devil was, I still respected him. When Fred and I were on the run, and he had every reason in the world to turn us in for a hefty reward from the company, he decided to take a chance on us. Took us in, helped Fred cook up the idea on how to hide my identity, and taught us the ropes about PI work. A rare being, without a doubt; there wasn't much "Para solidarity" back in the old days, and, like as not, every creature with—or without—a heartbeat would screw you over to get ahead. Not Humphrey Boggart, though. About the only person that Humph screwed over—and over, and over—was himself.

"Eyes up," Humph whispered over the comms.

I heard him before I saw him. That wheezy, annoying laugh, which we had a sample of from a recorded conversation from the client. The system in my suit ID'd the laugh and the cam pointing in his direction fed to my HUD. And there he was. Richard Burgess, "investment banker," playing with Daddy's money like the millions of other birds just like him.

Those dweebs hadn't changed much from when I'd been alive either. Whatever sort of suit was "in," they all wore it, in slight variations of color and weave-pattern. This year it was a one-piece, like an ultra-designer jumpsuit, with a shirt and tie under it. Whatever sort of haircut was in, they all wore it. This year the mullet—even when I was still alive, it was before my time—was back in. Most of them were Caucasian—I don't know why. You can change your skin color these days along with everything else, so maybe it was another fad. "Dick" was in a light blue-gray model, with a brown mullet with—I kid you not—artificial sun streaks in it.

"Jeez, do these guys come from a factory?" I muttered in my suit, trying to split my attention between scraping gum out of the carpet and tracking our target.

"Gods above and below forbid that they start producing the bastards *industrially*," Fred responded, downing the rest of his drink while keeping an eye trained on Mr. Burgess.

Dickie wheezed again, I suppose at the joke of one of his companions, who, sadly for us, were another pair of idiots just like him. And the body language was all wrong for Dickie or his new best friends being switch-hitters, so that was out too. Sometimes, spy jobs like this were easy; the goofs were so obvious, it was surprising that their partners ever paid anyone to investigate what the entire world knew about already. Dickie, however, was careful. After I had hacked into the cruise ship's network—and by hacked I mean I just waited until someone left a computer unlocked while they took a visit to the john—we had found out his suite number and promptly broke in. A few well-placed bugs, and it was booze o'clock while we waited for him to screw up, right? Not Dickie. He never brought whoever he was seeing back to his room, and seemingly didn't meet with them all that often in public. Hell, when I had scrubbed his financials, a preliminary look anyway, all I found was the usual amount of embezzling and a frankly pedestrian drug habit. No second apartment rented out in his name for the mistress, no obvious gifts, no nothin'.

That meant that instead of relaxing and enjoying the sights, we actually had to work for this one. So, we waited, and watched, for when Dickie would have to meet his special lady friend. The wife—our client—had assured us that his side girl would be here with him. Either he'd slip up and meet her in the open, or we'd follow him to her room and bug it after the fact. In the end, it all amounted to billable hours, and after Harry Sommerville's wild ride, our rates were astronomical just to keep our workload manageable. The upper crust had a lot of dirty laundry, and we were just the creatures to capitalize on it.

Dick checked his watch; the ultrarich had gone through the cyborg fad with the rest of humanity, but found cybernetics gauche, at least for now, and now the twentieth century was "in." Through my sensors, I spotted a tiny smile curl his lips, different from the too-wide grin that had been pasted on his face between chugging drinks. *I'd bet my remaining toes that's our cue,* I thought, a death-rictus grin growing on my own mug.

"Alistair, Fraser, it's been a gas, but I need to freshen up a bit," Dickie said, tapping the side of his nose. "I'll catch you both on the executive-class bar in a few hours. And don't you bastards try and weasel out, neither!" Dickie slapped both men on their backs, and they responded with a chorus of insults and forced-humor threats. Dickie walked backward, flipping them off, before he turned on his heel and walked quickly toward the entryway.

"Jim," Humph's voice growled through the comms. "You got him on the camera system?"

"Done and done, boss," I replied. A space tub this big, there were literally hundreds of access points where someone could patch into the security system. Now, on professional installations, there are sensors and all sorts of pain-in-the-ass access control that either prevents someone from doing that, or at the very least alerts security personnel when a panel is being accessed. Well, on the *Wayfaring Stranger*, they'd gone a bit cheap in some areas. It was a retrofit, so it made sense that there'd be stuff that would be missed or even kludged together. In any case, the equipment we'd brought in to connect to the security feeds hadn't been cheap, and would probably need to be left in place so as not to tip anyone off, but that all just got added to the bill, in the end.

I keyed up Dickie Boy on my helmet's display; he was definitely moving with a purpose in the direction of the suites for this section.

"Tail him. I know you have him on your scopes, but—"

"I know, I know. 'Tech is great, but use your eyes to see.' It ain't our first day, boss." Humph had mostly become used to all of the technical know-how that Fred and I had brought to his trade, and he was a fair hand himself at quite a bit of it. At the end of the day, though, he only really trusted his own senses, especially when it came to the job. Old habits, and old Paras, die hard. I stood up, holstered my gum scraper, and made for the bot service access. Luckily, Bots moved a lot more "natural" now than back when I was still alive; trying to imitate a jerky, jittery robot would've been enough to make me top myself after the first week in this tin can.

Following Dickie wasn't particularly hard; the bot service access-ways allowed bots to get pretty much anywhere that wasn't restricted in the ship, bypassing a lot of the interior structures to make travel quicker. They reminded me of the pathways that us Reboots had to use on the old Para exploration ships, if only a lot cleaner; not as much rubbed off gunk and bits of body all over the place. Dim light—there actually had to be *some* light because the crew used these hallways too on rare occasions—bare metal floors, walls, and ceilings, but all of it covered with a thick coating of a gray, rubbery some-thing to keep any of the customers from hearing immersion-break-ing noises. I kept Dickie on my scopes, mirroring his movements at a fair distance; I could've stayed in lockstep with him, but if he made any sudden direction changes, I would've had to come up short and backtrack. Another lucky thing, there wasn't any real surveillance or security in these access hallways; just tracking for the bots, which I spoofed to get in and out, but otherwise kept switched off. There were Reboots on this ship, of course—there were still Reboots ev-erywhere—but they worked well away from places where the paying customers and even most of the crew would ever see them, so climb-ing out of my tin long johns to join them for surveillance purposes was not even remotely feasible.

257

The layout here was actually logical: guest hall, rooms that guests would want to be in, then "back alley" rooms that guests would want to be in, and passageway again, just like a big city on Old Earth. That meant I could not only stay on my target's tail at all times with a room between us, but if for some reason I had to get to him, I theoretically could, because I had access to the back doors to all those rooms we were passing. They were visible in here, but invisible on the guest side—you didn't want guests wandering around where they shouldn't be, making mischief.

I was all but certain my target was heading for the euphemistically named "theme rooms"—which were a very upscale version of a no-tell motel—in the "adventurous singles" area. If there was a kink with a name, there was a room for it in there, and you could reserve them for fifteen minutes to a full twenty-four hours. Well, this would explain why he'd never brought his current hottie to his official suite; he was meeting her there.

But then he headed straight for something I had not expected at all.

"Boss!" I hissed. "He's heading for Fang Central!"

Sure enough, just as I said that, he stepped into a pod on a podway that went only one place: the terminal in *La Ville Des Delices Sombres.*

Someday someone will give me a good explanation for why the Fangs seem to delight in naming their Nests and stations in Old Earth French. It wasn't as if more than a handful of them understood it. Then again, overusing French fit in with the trashy faux-elegance a lot of Fangs affected.

"Don't lose him!" Humph hissed in tones that suggested he would very much have liked to shout, but he was in a public place.

"On it, boss. There's only one terminal for that podway. I can beat him there."

Oh, the bliss of being on a cruise ship. No one paying was ever in a hurry here. The pod was going to cradle Dickie and trundle him along in a sweet haze of light endorphin-mist at a pace a toddler could have matched. Meanwhile, I could take the hired help's express version of the same thing. Gentle, it was not; what it lacked in comfort it made up for in utility and speed. I got slammed around in a tube barely big enough to hold me for about a full minute, no more. By the time Dickie was assisted out of his pod by his seat at the *Delices Sombres* terminal, I was scrubbing the floor there. Despite the analgesic gas in his transport pod, Dickie looked surprisingly clear and confident. Eager, even. *Pay dirt. This has to be where he has his side piece stashed.*

If we were in Were territory, I would've been worried that my scent—even sealed in the suit with plenty of air fresheners and scrubbers—might've been picked up by the supernatural sense of smell of some Fur. Fangs had nearly as good of a sense of smell ... but they were so self-involved, that unless it was fresh blood, they didn't give a demon's tail.

I'd been in the Fang section on our initial recon, when Humph and Fred were keeping track of Dickie, or Dickie was verifiably asleep in his own suite. Fred had done the Furs, and Humph the Others, but someone needed to know the full layout, and neither of them would have been welcome among the Fangs; between anti-glamour fields and the inherent hatred between Fangs and Furs, I was the only one that could feasibly get into that section, personally. So ... here's the thing. Every time the Fangs set up a Nest, *someone* on top decides what the decor is going to be like. So the whole Nest has a uniform look. And this time, that *someone* had decided that since this was a cruise ship, their Nest had to look like Mardi Gras in New Orleans at night, on LSD and steroids. So the base color of everything was black. Every other color was the fluorescent version of itself. Lots of fake New Orleans buildings with balconies with white wrought iron and plants and fake cobblestone streets interrupted by the occasional mansion set back a little from the rest by a tiny garden with the obligatory fountain, except the fountain was spouting a different flavor of Hurricane instead of water. And the "street" (corridor) was not only full of the paying passengers, but costumed role-players, some of whom were Fangs, and the rest of whom were not crew, but the human Renfields from the Fang Nest. Every once in a while a scaled-down Mardi Gras float cruised by, the three or four riders tossing worthless trinkets and candy. Overhead, the ceiling showed a cloudless, moonless night sky.

Party Central, filtered through Hell and smacked alongside the head before a drink was pressed into its hand. It was gaudy, even by

Fang standards. If drugs still did anything to me, I would've wanted a few downers just then, if only to balance out the harshness of the section.

"I'm on him. This place is going to be a mess if he starts moving through the crowd for long."

"Everyone is so high there, just move through them." Humph paused for a moment. "Avoid the Fangs, though."

"Uppity bastiches don't like getting their outfits ruffled," Fred added, more than a little subvocal growl tagged onto the end of his sentence.

"And don't use the botways. We don't know what they have back there," Humph added. Which was sound good sense, and something I hadn't considered. Fangs, as similar as they were weird to other Paras, did some things drastically different. Anything in the public eye was all about appearances, so it was squeaky clean. But what they had stashed behind the walls? Anyone's guess, and not something a Reboot like yours truly wanted to discover, alone and unarmed.

So far though, Dickie was just standing there, bright-eyed and bushy-tailed, and out of traffic. Clearly waiting for someone.

And then, in the middle distance down the main drag the crowd of mostly Renfields began parting. I couldn't see the reason the crowd was parting until the last of the toadies cleared away between us.

I was not aware I knew that many cusswords—in such colorful combinations and languages—until they began spilling out. But my vocabulary was nothing compared to Humph, who must have switched his data-cuff to my camera view. I didn't know any ancient Celtic, but I was pretty sure whatever Humph was saying was not fit for church.

Because it was Claire. Humph's one-time Norm paramour, who after getting her poor heart broken, had run off and gotten Turned to try to win Humph back. A Fang for eternity, with nothing but time to nurse and savor grudges. And she headed straight for Dickie, oiling her way across the floor toward him in a way that left no doubt that she was who he had been waiting for.

Unlike her surroundings, she was dressed tastefully, but in a style that corroborated that she was a Fang, and a high-ranker at that. Ankle-length black pencil skirt, slit to the knee, not the thigh, lined with fuchsia. Single-button black suit jacket, cut to the millimeter to her figure, also lined with fuchsia. Low-cut fuchsia blouse under that. Little black hat-thing with a bit of feather and a bit of veil tilted coquettishly over her right eyebrow. I think women call that thing a "fascinator." High-heeled matte-black pumps. The one change was her hair. It had been short. Fang hair does not grow. Now, however, it was a straight black waterfall down to her ass. So it was either a wig or extensions, and good ones.

The last time any of us had heard from Claire, she had been wishing a painful death upon Humph and was on the run from her unlife, with everything that she had worked for a burning cinder because of our investigation into Harry. The people that had wanted Harry dead, well, they didn't mind turning anyone and everyone near to Humph into collateral damage. Clearly, she'd been able to do well enough for herself in the intervening period. That said, I could only guess at what sort of hell would be raised should she find out that Humph was on this tub with her.

I amped up my mic so that all of us on comms could hear them talking.

"… babe, you don't know how happy I am to see you—"

Claire gently placed a single finger over Dickie's lips, shushing him. "Doll, I know. You don't have to say anything. Let's get somewhere more … comfortable, shall we?"

"Jim," Humph's voice came over my comms, his words clipped. "Don't lose them. No matter what."

"I've got 'em, boss, I've got 'em. Going quiet until I have more to report."

Humph had to be *seething* on his end of the connection. This was a fly in the ointment, a wrinkle in the bedsheets, a dump in the punch bowl. While our class of clientele had gone up a few notches, most of the jobs were the same sort we'd always taken on. But things had been going relatively well for a while; the money rolled in, and we spent it. It made a bit of sense that we were past due for a wallop, and brother, Claire was it. No matter what happened, that skirt always seemed to come crashing back into Humph's life, or he into her unlife.

Following the couple through the surging crowd alternated between frustrating and maddening. A bubble seemed to form around

261

her and Dickie where the crowd would part to gawk and fawn, which immediately collapsed after she was far enough away. I couldn't get too close, otherwise I'd be pretty easy to spot for anyone who cared to notice, and far enough away to be covered, I was always getting sandwiched when the crowd came back together. Claire was clearly feeding off of all of the attention. She was trying to be discreet … but not that discreet. Dickie was absorbed in Claire; I could've probably flicked him on the ear, and his hand would've remained firmly clamped to her waist and his eyes fixed on her smiling profile.

Poor bastard is head over heels. For a Fang. Poor, dumb *bastard,* I thought, as yet another reveler dinged their shin on my suit's leg. Just like that, though, we had reached the end of this section. I spotted Claire and Dickie's retreating forms pass through a doorway, back into the ship proper. It'd be a trick following them without the crowd or a bot hallway for cover, but I'd had plenty of practice, at this point.

I also had a trick up my sleeve—or rather a trick Fred enabled on the shell he'd got me. This bot-hull had what was called a "livery" coat—some kind of skin that could change colors and patterns instantly. So just before I broke from the crowd I changed it from the drab service-bot colors to the color and pattern of the local Nest's high-ranking personal bots. A lot of Fangs prefer bots to Reboots; they have about the same level of "intelligence," and bots, when appropriately decorated, are more attractive, if a lot more expensive. But then, for Fangs, a bit of conspicuous consumption comes with the territory. In more ways than one, sometimes.

So, now even if Claire had spotted me, she shouldn't make me for a tail, and she wouldn't take the chance of pissing off a higher-ranking Fang than she was by accosting someone else's bot. Me, I was counting on the arrogance of Fangs to not trouble themselves to know the actual number of bots in their inventory, or to personalize them. In the end, either someone above—or a lot of someones below—liked me, because Claire and Dickie reached their destination without either them or someone else spotting or stopping me. It was a large suite, and took up about as much space as five of the regular, more pedestrian suites put together, judging from what the ship layout said.

"Boss, I think we're at the room. Marking it down on the map," I whispered inside of my helmet. A few keystrokes, and the room was highlighted for Humph and Fred on our local net.

"Good job, Jim. Get out of there, casual like. Hanging around is only liable to get you found out; there's no such thing as an idle bot on a ship like this." Judging from Humph's tone, he had managed to calm himself, somewhat. At least he was able to put aside his personal feelings for a while and focus on the job. Which was, of course, *Dick*, not Claire. We needed dirt on Dick, and Claire was just the unexpected twist. The sooner we got the goods and off of this tub, the better. Claire was trouble; Claire and Humph? Disaster, dressed to the nines in blood and guts.

So I reminded the boss of the job, as I passed them unlocking the suite door, moving like a bot with a place to be. "We need the goods on Dick, and these aren't by-the-hour pads. I bet this is where she's hanging her hat for the whole trip."

"Passenger manifest says she is," Fred replied. I'm not bad at hacking, but he's a genius; got a real talent for it. "This should be …" he paused and I mentally cursed him, hoping he wasn't going to jinx us. "… possible to get our equipment into and out of. Looks like the management's in the habit of sending random gift baskets to these high rollers. All I need to do is figure out what they put into a gift basket for a Fang that doesn't eat fruit and chocolate."

"They put that sort of stuff in there, along with multivitamins and supplements. For their 'donors,'" Humph added after a pause. "Gotta keep the livestock in good shape and happy. Well the good news is that'll be on the expense account. The bad news is if it ain't cigars and booze, I can't tell the good from the bad."

"Leave that to me, boss," Fred said cheerfully. Maybe it was forced cheer; he knew as well as I did that the boss was getting eaten up by this revelation. "The nose always knows. All we have to do is wait for them to go back out to dinner."

The Boggart was rattled, but the last thing he wanted was for his partners to know it. Although truth to tell, they probably knew anyway. He and Claire had so much baggage between them that it needed its own train car. He had no idea if she was friend, foe, or fried chicken. The last time he'd had any contact with her—he'd inadvertently been the indirect cause of her losing her entire space station. But for some reason she'd taken just long enough to get a burner phone and let him know just how badly he was screwed. She didn't have to do that, though admittedly she did also let him have both barrels of her vexation. She'd probably have been better off if she'd just gone into the wind. *And if she really hated me, she would've fed those goons some info, maybe even something they could've used. Might've kept her station, too.*

On the other hand, maybe she'd wanted an ace up her sleeve, because she knew if he somehow survived all that mess, he would be in her debt; either from the loss, for not turning him in, or more likely both. And maybe getting revenge on the people that wrecked her station and her livelihood—undeadlihood?—was worth more than getting revenge on him, and she knew if anyone could pull that off, it would be him.

Whatever, he owed her, big-time. He didn't have any space stations in his back pocket, but he had no doubt that Claire would call in that favor somehow. He never did have much history of getting away clean, at least in the long run.

"Boss, you've been chewing on that cigar stub for the last two minutes. We're clear here, and they've actually left the hotel. Are you still good to go?"

Jim's voice over his comm shocked him back to the task at hand. Jim was in charge of watching for Claire and her mark to leave, via the hotel's security cams. With some swiped credentials from Jim, some reprogramming from Fred, and a little bit of luck, Humph had managed to gain access to the ship's "smart dumbwaiter" system through a maintenance access point. Understandably, it was behind lock and key; all sorts of evil could be moved through the dumbwaiters. Anything from pranks to bombs or poison gas. Getting caught in here, even with his PI credentials from Mildred, would mean *beaucoup* trouble for him and the boys. Worse, the job would probably be completely blown. *First rule of being a detective for hire: don't get captured. Second rule: always get paid.*

Humph took a deep breath and held it before he pressed the keypass to the reader. A click and a beep, and the door unlocked, instead of sounding alarms that would've brought very angry men in uniforms down upon his head. He let out his breath, moving quickly into the room, before he shut the door firmly behind himself.

"I'm in. Once I'm riding the watch, I'm going to be pretty useless until I get to the room. You sure the tricks will work?"

"Hey, they have on every job before this," Jim said.

"What about that one time on—" Fred interjected over the comms.

"Doesn't count," Jim cut him off. "They sold me bunk goods. Anyways, boss, it'll work. Promise you my dinner if it don't."

Humph rolled his eyes. *Jim eats fungus "brains." Besides the only dinner I'll be having if this screws up will either be lead, or jail food. Honestly, I'd prefer the lead.* He pulled out his pocket watch—the one object in this world that he was bound to, through ancient magics—and placed it in the gift basket he'd smuggled to that point. Gently, he placed it underneath some of the baubles. While he was "in" his watch—in reality, the "Other," in-between space just outside of ... well, reality—he'd have limited senses about his surroundings. If the dumbwaiter system took him to, say, an incinerator ... it'd be bye-bye Boggart, and Fred and Jim would have to change the sign on the office door. Probably after they had raided his desk for the good scotch and stogies.

"Time to get it over with." Humph placed the basket into the intake for the dumbwaiter; this access room—more of a closet—only had one small intake and one output port, and was only really meant for maintenance and testing. He programmed in the room number for Claire's suite, waited for the doors to close on the intake, and then ... he was Nowhere Space. Time passed somewhat the same while he was stuck in the in-between dimension that his watch was connected to, but it was ... weird. A bit pliable, and played hell with his senses if he spent too long inside of it. He could feel the watch *moving*, though, which was a good sign. Now he just hoped that Jim and Fred's countermeasures would hold up. Ships like this invested in actually decent anti-Gremlin defenses; top-paid mages to keep the little buggers from unscrewing things or snipping wires or chewing on circuit boards. The other half of things was the real, physical security; anti-intrusion sensors to prevent precisely the sort of "attack" that Humph was carrying out. Jim had given Humph a trinket that would hide him, at least for a little bit before the crystal powering it burned out, and Fred had given him a gizmo that would scramble the more mundane security until its programming adapted. He had roughly two minutes to get through the dumbwaiter system, get into the room, plant the surveillance camera and its transmitter, and get back out of both the room *and* the dumbwaiter. It was going to take crackerjack timing.

Humph "felt" the watch come to a stop. It had to be at the room; if the sensors or the Gremlin alarms had gone off, he'd have been ejected to space, more than like, to boil in the ship's drive cone. *Fortune favors the bold* …. With a thought, he popped out of the No-where-Space and back into reality.

Well now. Although the color scheme was in dark red, black, and a muted gray that could have passed for weathered bone, it didn't scream *I am a high-level Fang* the way most of the high-roller Vamps had their pads decked out. It reminded Humph not of a Nest but of a really expensive early 21st-century hotel suite. The lines were all clean, there was no clutter, there was no gilt or gold plating—in fact everything that was metal was in gunmetal, not gilded or shiny chrome. But you could tell without even touching anything that it was all made from the most expensive materials and in the most expensive fashion possible. There were holo-windows for the claustrophobic that showed, not haunted moors or decrepit castles, but moonlight over the ocean and moonlight over Castle Neuschwanstein. Interesting touch that; the holos probably doubled as Fur defense—those that didn't have the discipline Fred had would probably wolf out at the mere image of a full moon.

Claire's taste has improved since she lost the station, The Tenderloin, Humph mused. That, or she'd picked this suite at random; he thought the former more likely, with how particular Fangs got about where they slept. He couldn't afford any more time admiring the digs; he was on the clock, and the penalty for failure would be more than a little embarrassing, if not extremely painful. He went back to the gift basket, and lifted out the camera and its transmitter; it would patch into a secure line that the cruise ship used, since there was no way they'd be able to get a signal all the way from Claire's suite to their room. Although it made his skin crawl, he left his pocket watch in the basket; if he needed to port out in a flaming hurry, he could jump back to the watch.

Now, where to place the damn camera ... there! Since the floor plan for the suite was open, he picked a corner that overlooked the bed, the couch, and the kitchenette counter; all potential, ahem, locations for "romance."

Humph went to place the camera—a dirt simple, self-embedding job—when he felt himself start, then come up short. *What in all the hells?* His throat was tight, and his stomach was in a knot. It took him a moment, but then he realized what the hell was the matter; Claire ... in the arms of another man. The thought of it, and the soon-to-be reality of, actually *bothered* him.

Oh, for the love of.... It was absurd, of course. He had dumped her, and decades ago, at that! Dames came and went, especially in this business. Back then especially, he had torn a swath through several planets' populations of the fairer sex. Claire had been something else, to be sure ... but that was the problem, wasn't it? He was a Boggart, and she had been a Norm. Not made to last together, either by some higher-being's design, or the grinding twists of fate. How could it not have ended in tears? Or worse. Boredom. Resentment. Hate. He'd either seen or heard of too many of these "romances" that ended up with the Norm hating and envying what they once loved, and the Para bored with Norm sameness, or resenting being tied to something that was doomed to age and die in the blink of a Para eye. It wasn't like in the romance-holos, where the doomed couple somehow made it work. So ... he had broken it off. Claire had broken as a result, and ultimately became a Fang. Humph knew that, of all the horrible, damnable things that he was responsible for in his long life, that act was probably the one thing out of all of them that guaranteed him a hot, cramped spot in Hell.

"Boss! One of the help got past me without my catching her! She's on her way, I saw the work invoice!" Fred's voice was strident; he didn't get rattled easy, so this was a big problem. Even getting *seen* by one of the crew in here would blow the entire gig; the room would get swept down to its constituent molecules, and all of the expense and planning for this job would be down the tubes.

Shitfire!

Humph tapped the camera into place with the transmitter, then immediately dropped to the floor and went flat, rolling behind a divan just as the lock of the door clicked open.

From here, all he could see was shoes and ankles. Slim, cocoa-colored ankles. Sensible shoes that matched the color of the "hotel" livery. (This wasn't a real hotel, obviously, but the ship's owners were invested in making sure that every different level of accommodation gave the impression of being a separate entity. It was all part of the fantasy.) Brisk, yet somehow delicate movements.

There was a gentle, but persistent "alert" tone coming from just where the ankles were—just as Jim said, "She just got a ping to pick up a gift basket. When she leaves to collect it, you'll have about two minutes to place the cam and move to the watch so I can get you out."

Damn camera's already in place, Deadhead, Humph cursed. If Jim had forgotten to put batteries in it, he'd be paying for Humph's drinks for a long, long time. The room was all open floor plan, with only a few pieces of furniture for him to hide behind. His mind scrambled for a way out of this; it would be a second before she would be at an angle in the room where she could see him, and he'd be cooked. He didn't belong there, and she'd know it instantly. *Think, damn you, think! Wait, that's it!* Humph didn't belong there ... so he made it so that he did.

Humph burst up from behind the divan, mumbling and blinking, his ever-present flask in his right hand. He sputtered, took a few deep breaths, and then turned to look at the crewmate.

It was impossible to tell her ethnicity; only that her complexion matched her ankles and her hair was bronze and put up on the top of her head in a tight bun. The kind where all the hair was scraped back into the knot in a way that made his own scalp ache in sympathy. Her uniform of tailored jacket and skirt in black with scarlet piping fitted to a slim figure, and her features were delicate, with large eyes that were now wide with shock. In her arms was a gift basket identical to the one in the dumbwaiter.

"Room service?" Humph slurred his words, and swayed gently on his feet. There was a reason why the crewmate's eyes were only wide with surprise, and not fear; he wasn't wearing "his" face, with its pitch-black fur, dark eyes, and *sharp* teeth. Instead, he was wearing Dickie's face, perfect Day-Glo teeth, skin, and with the hair sticking up at every possible angle, as if he had fallen asleep drunk on the floor, wallowed around until he got himself wedged under the couch, and passed out there. He looked down at himself, and the janitor uniform that he was wearing. "How the hell did I end up in this thing?"

Humph didn't wait for a reply, instead swiveling his head toward the gift basket in the dumbwaiter. "Ah, reloads!" He did a convincing stumble toward the dumbwaiter, weaving his way between the furniture, intentionally bumping a shin into a footstool and cursing at it, before colliding solidly with the wall that held the chute system. He reached into the basket, keeping his back to the woman, while he quickly slipped the pocket watch and both of the gizmos the boys had provided him with into one of the janitor overall's pockets. He snatched a bottle of good booze from the basket with his left hand, and then whirled around, flask and bottle both raised. "Success!"

The crewmate had taken several steps toward him, and her expression had changed. Something strange ... suspicion? No, not that. More like—never mind. It wasn't suspicion, that was all that counted. *Clock's ticking, no time to ponder.* "Just leave that one on ... well, leave it on something, m'kay? Back to the ... yeah, the Big Easy!" Humph puffed up his chest, then marched to the door, correcting his course a couple of times as he tried to pretend to be drunk, pretending to be sober. He expertly opened the door with his flask hand using only his pinkie and ring fingers, then slipped through the opening before shutting it securely behind him. He had to keep up the drunk act, but whenever he got near where there were security devices, he lifted both the flask *and* the bottle to his mouth, hopefully obscuring enough of his face so that any bored security tech wouldn't try to run a match and find that Dickie was in two places at once.

It was an agonizing stumble to where Fred was waiting for Humph, just off the main concourse of rooms, standing guard by a service elevator. He changed his face back to the janitor, and dropped the bottle to his side while he stowed his flask.

"When I say run interference, I don't mean to stand around with your thumb up your ass. I nearly got made," Humph said, letting some of his annoyance come through. All the booze he'd had to chug to get this far had also loosened up his tongue a bit, otherwise he might not have said anything at all. He didn't like to snap at Fred or Jim; bad for morale, and he didn't want to be that kind of boss.

"Boss, I swear, I don't know how she got past me. My nose never lies, and I never got a whiff of her. If it weren't for the work-order screen … well, shit, I don't want to think about it."

"C'mon, we need to get gone. And I need a shower. I smell like a distillery. So, in other words, wonderful."

"Want me to order some QuickSober to the room?" Fred asked helpfully.

"No. Why ruin a victory snatched from the jaws of defeat with sobriety? I might've had to have left this bottle there."

"That would have been a tragedy," Fred agreed. "Leaving behind a full bottle of Glen McMorris? Worse than a tragedy. A crime. Dick doesn't deserve it."

"War crime, on some planets, to waste good scotch on bad people." Humph patted his pocket. "Near-miss or not, we're due a celebration. We can monitor that cam from our suite."

"Sure, rub it in," Jim said in his ear. "Me, the only one of us that can't drink and is going to be doing all the work."

"Could be worse," Humph said, taking a swig from his flask as the lift started moving. "You could actually be a bot. Oh, the witty banter we'd miss out on, then. Not to mention the bitching."

"Leave the bitching to Fred," Jim said. "He's the one equipped for it."

Like I said, it was a real cushy job, and with it, came a real cushy suite. Three bedrooms, three baths, a big common living area, with an order-in setup where a kitchenette would have been. The client hadn't balked at the third room, and a good thing; in a lot of our contracts, at least nowadays, Humph stipulated that "the Bot gets a room." That puzzled some folks, but this client was a whale, and didn't even blink at the upcharge. The common living area had a stocked bar, and so far the client hadn't objected to Fred and Humph using it. Well, abusing it like it was a rented mule would be more accurate; those boys did like their booze. Since I wasn't actually using the bedroom as a place to sleep, we had the full security suite set up in there, with a feed to the vidscreen in the main room. Normally we traveled lighter on the gear, but we weren't footing the shipping costs on this one, so the boss had said to bring it all.

Alas, there is nothing that gets me buzzed anymore, and brains or brain fungus is just fuel, so my only alcoholic entertainment came from watching them.

"You did not, you lying goat! And they let you *get away* with it?" Fred shook his head incredulously, hard enough to slosh the drink in his raised glass.

"Well, you gotta understand. I did still have the gun, so's they didn't have all that much choice in the matter!"

Tonight's episode was on war stories; Humph from getting off of Earth after the Great Uncloseting and how he got into the PI business, and Fred about his time as a Lone Wolf. I'd heard a lot of these stories before, and part of the entertainment was trying to gauge how much of what either of my partners said was complete bull. It helped to beat back the monotony of looking at the security feeds, and waiting for our mark to make his appearance and give up the goods. I'd volunteered for this part of the gig; if there was one thing that Reboots were good at, it was monotonous tasks. There was also the question of having Humph watching the cameras as Dickie got up to no good with Claire. Humph was doing what he could—namely, drink himself blind—to hide how shook up he was, but I could tell. Some hurts just didn't fade; the bruises just turned a different shade. Having him busy when the deed was done also kept him from potentially shooting my equipment; I liked my setup, thank you very much.

I was lost in thought, listening to Fred retelling a tale about the time he got caught on a Pack's turf, and had to take on ten—no, thirty!—of the Packmates, all by himself, when it occurred to me that I ought to check the clock. *Well, shit ... they're late.* We'd been tracking Dickie, and before we had found out where he had been meeting up with Claire, we'd clocked his departure for his evening of fun at around the same time, every night. The man was like a Swiss watch; same time, every night, after laughing it up with his chucklehead almost-clones in the executive-class bar, he'd head to the Big Easy section of the Fang wing, meet the side piece that turned out to be Claire, and they'd retreat back to someplace—that we now knew was her suite—for that evening's entertainment. No real reason to do all the work of trying to track both of them constantly, when we knew where they'd end up; besides, we only had cameras set up in that one suite, so it's not like we'd be getting what we came for if they decided to elope to a broom closet somewhere to knock boots.

So last night, after we planted the bug, he and Claire had parted rather than coming back to Claire's suite. Claire had gone to sleep somewhere else—typical for Fangs, who never slept except in highly defended lockers. Dickie slept about three hours, downed his usual morning cocktail of uppers, and went out on his usual prowl. We expected pay dirt just before dinnertime.

"So then, I had one in a headlock, and was grabbing the other by his—"

"Yo, boss, Fred. Something's up," I said, interrupting Fred right before he got to the juicy part of his story.

Humph instantly went from drunk and jovial ... to still pretty drunk, but at least he was paying attention. "Jim, whaddya got? Are they in the room?"

I'll give it to the boss; he did his damndest to say all of that with a straight face. Not a hint of anger ... 'cept for his eyes. He wasn't wearing a Norm face, just his regular scary-as-hell Boggart mug, and those ink-dark eyes flashed for a second when he said "they."

"No, that's just it, boss. They aren't. Actually, way past due. Either they're not following their pattern, and why wouldn't they, or something's wrong."

Humph mulled that over. "Stay here, and keep your peepers on the monitors." He glanced over at Fred. "Put a pot of coffee on and take a mule's dose of QuickSober; we're going to go find our boy." Fred pouted, downed the last of his drink, and then sullenly got up and trudged over to the dining area to brew some coffee.

Me, I had already assumed the worst, and had set my computer to scan all the ship's personnel channels, looking for security alerts.

Humph was actually in the process of swallowing his QuickSo-ber—a first, at least in recent memory—when I got a hit, from the area of Big Easy where they'd stacked a bunch of "Mardi Gras Ball-rooms" like a warren of Habitrail cubes. Those were supposed to be closed except for reserved events. The "Mardi Gras Balls" held every night in these things are such clusters that once the last celebrant has left the scene, they have to be closed and hosed down with industrial antiseptics, then given time to air out. This one had a theme of a graveyard, and there was a crowd in there of hotel staff, a crowd that should not have been there. I flipped the security cam to the main screen and yelled "Boss! Security alert!"

Humph zipped up his jumpsuit and was already running for the door. "Talk me on over comms, Fred, you're the tail!"

"On it, boss!" Fred and I yelled in unison. Fred was out the door a split-second after Humph.

I kept my attention split between following the two of them on the monitors, scanning for Dickie, and trying to see what the commotion in the ballroom was about. I had a sinking feeling in the shriveled husk that used to be my stomach. There were too many people, and it was impossible to get a look at what they were crowd-ing around, but judging from the shocked faces, it wasn't a puppy. *Well, maybe a dead puppy* ....

Humph got there just behind the official "house security manag-er" for the Big Easy—IE, the chief house "detective," someone who was supposed to track down lost kids, missing drunks, and handle anything that was past the pay grade of his security detail. Which, being Fang-hired, were pretty good, as the Fangs have a vested inter-est in keeping things squeaky-clean and above-age consensual. But as the crowd parted and I saw what was lying there, and I saw the look on the detective's face, I knew for a fact that even if he was as good as the Fang-hired security, he was totally out of his depth right now. Because lying in a crumpled heap as though he had collapsed and died instantly, was our dear little Dickie.

Humph was pissed. The first thing he had felt had been shock, with a smear of nausea from the still-working QuickSober. This wasn't the first mark of his to turn up dead, but it was the first one that had a connection to Claire. His mind had immediately raced to, *"Oh gods, Claire, what have you done now?"* before he'd forced himself to tamp those thoughts down. No, Claire was much too careful to leave a body out in the open like this, or even to kill prey at all. Wasn't she? Granted, she'd gone through hard times since losing her station, but they couldn't have been so hard as to make her sloppy ... could they have been?

"Holy shit, boss," Fred's whisper came in over the comms. He was stationed just outside the room, in an intersection, faking smoking so that he could watch everyone entering and leaving the room. And, if things truly went all the way to Hell, he could charge in and save Humph's hide; such was the nature of being the "tail" man. "Is that him?"

"Yeah, it's him," Humph replied, covering his mouth as if to cough, so as not to alert anyone that he was talking on a private line. "Going to get closer. Keep your eyes peeled."

"On it," Fred said, then clicked off.

Humph pushed his way through the crowd until he was at the inner circle. There was a ring of uniformed security personnel keeping everyone from getting too close, and one old, tired-looking chap who kept on rubbing at the stubble on his jaw and grimacing. He was wearing a beat-up suit to match his beat-up face; pinned on the suit was a badge, "Ship's Detective," that looked like it came out of a cereal box. He looked like he was contemplating whether this job was really worth whatever he was pulling down in pay for it, and if resigning might be a good play.

Now, Humph could work this one of two ways. He could lie low and work around this guy, or take the chance that he'd grab onto Humph like the lifesaver he actually was. Humph was still debating which of the two paths he'd choose when the old man looked up and straight into his eyes. The poor old sap looked like a dying deer. That clinched it.

"Jim, what's the dick's name?" he subvocalized.

"Kevin Blackstone. Retired from Central City PD on planet Urso in the S-79 system about fifteen years ago with an inadequate pension."

"And about three heartbeats away from retiring from the living, by the looks of it. You're a champ." He dropped his "face," pulled out his ID and PI credentials, and approached Detective Blackstone with both held out. "Detective Blackstone? I'm Humphrey Boggart, I was working a case involving the deceased, and I wonder if I could give you any help?"

The poor sap lit up as if Humph had just offered him the keys to heaven. Still, some loyalty to procedure caused him to check himself. "Oh! Yes, yes, of course. But, eh, first I'll need to check your name and papers. Policy."

"Of course," Humph said, handing over his credentials. All of the crewmates—and even some of the security—were whispering to each other, presumably about Humph's arrival and "unmasking." After a few perfunctory calls to the central security room, Blackstone handed back Humph's IDs and let out an audible sigh.

"Okay," he said, trying and failing to hide his relief. "We should ..." Blackstone trailed off, his eyes flitting to Humph.

"Get your security to log all the names of these people, and then get them out of here. Who found the body? Are they still here?"

"Yes! I got them sequestered, over in that corner there, sitting down," Blackstone said, gesturing to a table in the far corner of the ballroom. A Norm couple, both of whom looked distressed, were sitting and holding each other while a security guard glowered at them with his arms crossed in front of his chest.

"Right," Humph said. "Get the room clear, then back everyone off of the body. You, too," Humph added. "I'm going to talk with them. And get a forensic unit in here." He didn't wait for a reply as he marched off toward the Norm couple.

Humph, using the recorder function on his pocket comm, interviewed the couple. They were almost entirely useless. Newlyweds, and drunk as skunks; they had been having a good time, enjoying the Big Easy section, when they stumbled into the ballroom. Found the body, then immediately ran for help. They didn't get near Dickie, and didn't touch anything; even drunk and shook up, about the only thing they appeared to be handsy with was each other. *All the best party drugs on this tub, and being near death does that to some people.* One thing that did stick out to Humph was that they had found the door unlocked. Usually, places like this ballroom would be locked down, since there was stuff that could be broken or stolen; a lot of cruise ships would leave unimportant or empty rooms unlocked, since there was nowhere for thieves to go on a sealed ship, anyway. This one was access controlled, though, precisely to keep amorous sorts like the newlyweds out, and requiring the place get hosed down again.

Once Humph was done with the couple, he had the security guard send them back off to the party outside; they were more than happy to put the ballroom in their rearview mirror. "Detective Blackstone," Humph said, looking back over the transcription of his recording as he approached the older Norm, "ballroom like this is normally locked up, isn't it?"

Blackstone shook his head, uncomprehending … and then his eyes grew wide at something from behind Humph. Humph was just about to clear leather on the holster inside of his jumpsuit when he whirled around. Standing directly behind him, as if by magic—and maybe it was, though teleportation wasn't all that common or easy—was quite possibly the smallest, angriest Vamp that Humph had ever seen. Quickly, he seated the ancient Webley-Fosbery revolver back in its holster.

"Blackstone, you *imbecile* … what dump have you taken in my lap this time?" This Fang was … well, different. He came barely chest-high on Humph, had dark hair with a widow's peak, was cartoon-ishly thin, and was dressed in bright scarlet, head to toe—in the style that, back in Old Earth's 1980s was called "New Romantic"—a velvet suit coat with tails, brass buttons, and brocade lapels, a match-ing brocade waistcoat underneath that, and a scarlet silk shirt with ruffles at the collar under that, with tight scarlet pants and scarlet boots. He glanced at Humph briefly.

The hangdog ship's detective looked from the Fang, to Humph; the plaintive whine in that look couldn't have been more obvious if Blackstone had put up a neon billboard. Humph, with a sigh, pro-duced his credentials again, holding them up between Blackstone and whoever this Vamp was supposed to be.

"Humphrey Boggart—"

"You can't be serious," the Vamp interrupted with a sneer.

"Didn't pick it. You know how that goes—Summoner picks the name, and we're stuck with it. I'm a PI, and the vic over there is my current case. You are …" Humph trailed off, waiting for the Vamp.

"Pierre Bergeron, Deck Manager," the Vamp finished, curtly. "Why is your case lying dead on *my* ballroom floor?"

"Trying to figure that out presently, Mr. Bergeron," Humph said, ignoring the increasingly peevish tone that the Fang was laying on. Humph suspected that the diminutive deck manager got at least a majority of the enjoyment from his profession by harrying and bossing people around and making them squirm. Poor Blackstone probably was a favorite whipping boy for the Fang; he was just too perfect of a pushover target. "Is this room normally locked?"

"Of course."

"And who has access?"

"Pretty much the entire crew; it's necessary, with how much use we get out of these rooms, set up, tear down, and so forth. Now listen, I need—"

"Any records of who comes in and out? Access control, a log system for key cards, or the like?" He couldn't let the Fang take control of the conversation, otherwise he'd get stonewalled and learn nothing. Better to put his foot down now.

"What?" Pierre came up short—no pun intended. "No, too many people in and out, it'd be a mountain of logs. Listen, what authority do you even have here?"

Humph dangled his PI credentials in front of Pierre's face again. "You've got a ship death, and no clue on how it happened, as yet. Since I'm certified and bonded out of Mildred—"

"Oh, hells, you're from that dump?"

"—and the victim was the object of my current investigation, I've got cause. And I cleared it with your ship's detective, so it's all wrapped up with a bow."

Pierre looked like a pot that was about to boil over, he was fuming so much. After trying to stare down Humph—difficult, from his vantage point—he finally threw his hands up. "Fine! Whatever you need, *detective*. We're happy to cooperate to bring all of this to a swift resolution, and all of that claptrap."

"Great," Humph said. "Now, I need to get a look at the body. Blackstone," he looked to the detective, whose relief vanished upon being the center of attention again. "Did you manage to get that forensic equipment sent up?"

"Oh, no. We don't have anything like that on board."

Humph's jaw didn't quite hit the floor, and he did his best to recover quickly. "Okay ... well, do you have a ship wizard or mage? I'll settle for a hedge witch, at this point." Despite the expensive security guards, and all the glitz and glamour of the cruise, it seemed that they had cut corners in a few spots. It made a kind of sense; anything serious enough to really need a forensic unit, they could probably just dock at an appropriately civilized world and send a request down.

"We have a ship wizard, alright," Pierre said with a huff. "But you won't like him; we sure as hell don't."

"I'll need him, regardless," Humph said. "Also, we'll need to lock down this ballroom after I'm done; no one in, no one out."

"But you can't! We have an event in here in just under two hours!" Pierre was on the verge of shrieking, and looked about ready to pop a vein.

"Tough luck; you'll have to reschedule or move it to a different room. Crime scene takes precedence." Humph glanced over at the detective for confirmation, and to his surprise, the guy stiffened his spine and stared Pierre down.

"You want to deal with Mildred's cops when we get back, Bergeron? You *know* how they like to pile fines on when you don't follow procedure. Hell, I heard they once impounded an entire flotilla over a missing form." In addition to the revenue-motivated nature of Mildred's law-enforcement apparatus, it was also known for throwing Were cops at problems that needed to be pounded into the ground like a tent peg. Which, in their view, was most things.

And that reminder, it seemed, was all Bergeron needed to deflate. This whole ship wasn't owned by Fangs, it was owned by a consortium. And that consortium would not hesitate to flush the entire Nest here down the vacuum-toilet if the actions of one of its members—Bergeron—caused the entire ship to be tied up on Mildred. And he knew it.

"Fine, just be *quick* with this nonsense. I'll call the wizard; then he's *your* problem," Pierre said, turning on his heel and digging out a pocket comm.

Humph shrugged, sighing to himself. *I ought to be cashing a check and getting drunk right now. Well, more drunk.* He strolled over to the body, bumming a pair of disposable gloves off of one of the security guards, who handed them over with a brief nod. Security, undoubtedly, had to deal with some less-than-pleasant items, persons, and excretions in their work. First, he set to taking pictures from every conceivable angle with his own pocket comm; all of the images would get fed back to Jim in their suite, so he could examine and study them later. When that was done, Humph shifted his hands so that they didn't have sharp claws or bristly hair before he pulled the gloves on, then squatted next to the body. "Let's see what we got."

Dickie was in a heap; from the way he was crumpled, Humph didn't think he had been dumped here. He was wearing an athletic jumpsuit; stylish, and made to look good as leisure wear. The gray-white material had obvious, large sweat stains, and Humph's nose definitely picked up on the acrid scent of strenuous exertion. Heedful not to touch any more material than he had to, he lifted up sections of clothing to examine Dickie's skin. There weren't any marks or other indications of him being injured or forced in some way. A check of his pockets revealed nothing too spectacular: a pocket comm with a cracked screen, a room fob key, some gambling tokens and receipts, and a cartridge of breath spray. A security guard had preemptively tracked down an evidence bag, and had it ready for Humph to deposit all of the items in it.

Humph crouch-walked over to where Dickie's head laid against the floor. He pulled down the dead man's eyelids, smelled near his mouth, and checked inside of it. Only a slight stink of booze, and no swelling or discoloration anywhere that Humph could see. Humph pulled the skin in a pinch at the back of the hand. It stayed pinched. So—severe dehydration. He didn't look poisoned, or drugged any more than any other person on the cruise ship was. Humph scratched his head with the heel of a gloved hand, then looked around. There were a number of black marks on the floor all around the body, in about a thirty-foot circle. They were too random and chaotic to be sigils or runes, at least any that Humph had seen before. Digging a small knife out of one of his pockets, he scraped up a bit of it; it looked and smelled like rubber. *Maybe he was kicking around while ... what? Someone dragged him across a third of the ballroom? Naw, can't be it. Besides, no marks on the neck. Huh. Unless the perp stripped him and reclothed him, that lets out Fangs letting the instincts off the leash. That doesn't stick, either; they reclothed him in his own sweat-soaked jumpsuit? Since when would a Fang ever do that?*

There was a loud bang from one set of doors, and Humph snapped his head around to look. A truly ancient Norm, wearing a truly awful orange-and-green Aloha shirt, tan board shorts, and an incredibly exasperated expression stomped across the ballroom until he was towering over Humph with his hands on his fists.

"Well? Whatcha need?"

Humph tilted his head to the side. "You are ...."

"Irked. I was in the middle of something when Tiny Teeth over there interrupted me with something urgent. You can call me Gerhardt Fritz, Ship Wizard."

Humph leaned to the side to peer around Fritz at Blackstone, who looked apologetic ... but not that much. *He's probably had a bellyful of this old goat already; happy enough to pawn him off on me.*

"I need some forensic magic done on this body. Anything you could tell me would be helpful. Do you have any psychometry spells or rituals?"

"Ha! What do I look like, one'a them fancy city wizards? Hell no, that stuff costs money, and is a pain in the ass. Staff!" He shouted over his shoulder; a visibly upset crew member ran up, carrying a slender, gnarled piece of wood. It was ugly and old, so it fit its owner like a glove. Gerhardt snatched the staff from the crew member, making shoo'ing motions at everyone. "Back now, let a professional have room to work!"

Sighing, Humph stood up, and moved out of range of Gerhardt's magic and wrath. The wizened Norm began circling the body, drawing symbols in the air. With each one, he tapped his staff, and the previously invisible symbol would suddenly glow in midair. After the second pass, he began to eye Humph critically ... a look that Humph had come to know too well from magic users. *Old bastard wants to bind me to his service. Boggarts can be all sorts of "useful" for the unscrupulous wizard or mage ... and that usually means gross and illegal.*

"Don't even think about it," Humph growled, jutting his chin toward the body. "Keep working."

Gerhardt snorted at that and went back to the ritual. A couple of minutes later, he finished, invoking some power or another, and clapped his hands above his head before bringing the staff down on the floor, hard. A rune flashed above the body, and Gerhardt studied it intently for a solid minute before Humph cleared his throat to get the wizard's attention.

"Hrm? Oh. Your body here died from exhaustion. No poison, no wounds, just got himself too worked up and his heart gave out. Young fellers these days, no sense of proportion or pacing themselves. There was some sort of magic in here, too."

"Well, what kind? What was the effect?"

"Hell if I know," Gerhardt said, throwing his arms wide and shrugging. "Now, 'bout my fee …."

"Not my problem," Humph said, handing the metaphorical ball back to Blackstone and the Fang. "I should think any *fees* would be covered in the company's generous retainer anyway."

The Fang actually gave him a subtle nod at that, and rounded on Gerhardt, clearly happy to have someone to bully at last. Humph turned to Blackstone. "Dying of exhaustion in the middle of an empty ballroom? And magic involved?" Blackstone pulled on his lower lip. "That just—" Humph knew what he wanted to say. Blackstone *wanted* to call this a "natural" death and shove it under the rug. But what was left of his conscience wouldn't let him.

And besides that, it would be Humph's problem to track down, now, wouldn't it?

Pierre finished reading the wizard the riot act, and sent him away to drown his sorrows. "Well!" he said briskly, actually rubbing his hands together. "Exhaustion! That settles it, natural death, now—"

"No you don't," Humph and Blackstone said together. Blackstone glanced at Humph. Humph sighed.

"If it had been exhaustion in an orgy room, or the gym, or running laps in the corridor, and there was no magic involved, Mildred PD would buy it. But this? They won't, and neither do we," Humph said, pulling Blackstone in whether he liked it or not with the "we." "They'll take one look at the death certificate and you're going to be explaining to the company why they have to cancel the next three trips out and back while Mildred PD shakes the place down."

Pierre looked like he wanted to vamp out and drain Humph … or break down into bloody tears. In the end, he settled for growling and throwing his hands up. "Just figure this out, damn it! With celerity! That means *fast*, you up-jumped Gnome, okay!" Pierre stalked out of the room, cursing in what passed for rather bad French.

If that's the last I ever see of that Fang, I'll say some extra prayers to whatever gods make it happen, Humph thought. He gathered up Dickie's possessions, and left instructions with Blackstone to get the body on ice—if they didn't have a morgue, then a meat locker would work—and keep the room sealed off, no matter what Pierre said. Humph needed a drink and some time to get his noodle working on this. Fred and Jim, too; the more heads involved, the better. Just as Humph reached the entrance that he'd used before, his comm chirped.

"Boss, you won't like this. The bereaved just showed up and is about to get in there."

The "bereaved"? Surely he doesn't mean—aw, shit.

Humph opened the door and managed to take one step before Karen Burgess slapped him, hard, across the cheek.

She was a salute to expensive bad taste from the tiny teal space-ship resting in her expensive teal hair to the tip of her teal design-er toes. Harmonizing shades of teal covered every part of her that was not bare skin, and that included the irises of her eyes. The little spaceship was another piece of expensive display consumption; it was a gadget she could use to guide herself around the ship without needing to look at signs or maps. She merely had to say where she wanted to go, the thing would lift off from her head, hover about a foot above the crowd and no more than three feet from her, and show her the way to go. When she got there, it would settle back down into her hair.

"I hired you to find out who he was sleeping with!" she shrieked. *"Not to let him end up dead!"*

Humph's face still stung something fierce from the slap, but he resisted the urge to bring a hand up to massage his cheek. He quickly studied Karen for a moment before responding. There was plenty of anger there, sure, but nothing that even looked like sadness. No smudged makeup, no tear streaks, nothing. Either she was a tough

282

cookie, covering and delaying any of the waterworks with rage, or not all that broken up that her philanderous husband was heading toward room temperature.

"Mrs. Burgess, the job was to discover who your husband was sleeping with, yes. And I believe I have done that. I was in the process of obtaining direct evidence, and constant observation of your husband wasn't possible at the time that I was doing that." A small lie; Humph had gotten lazy after the camera and transmitter were in place in Claire's room, and he'd screwed up by drowning his thoughts about Claire with a bottle instead of keeping a tail on Dickie. "I have to ask, ma'am; what are you doing here? I specifically said that you weren't to be aboard this ship while I conducted my investigation, since it could foul things up."

"Yes, whatever. You're not the boss of me, I'm the one that employed *you*," Karen fumed, pointing a perfectly manicured finger dead at Humph's chest. Humph imagined that if she had a rapier instead of a several-hundred-credit nail job, she would've tried to skewer him. "Now how did he die? Can you tell me that at least, Mr. Boggart?"

Humph licked his lips. *This is going to suck.* "Preliminary examination seems to indicate that he died of exhaustion. But right now, we don't know *how* he died."

It was hard for Humph to tell through all the layers of expensive makeup, but he was pretty sure that Karen's face started to glow red. "What the hell do you mean? You just said that he died of exhaustion!"

"Yes," Humph nodded, chancing a quick glance back to the ballroom doors.

Karen searched his eyes for several seconds, waiting for Humph to continue. He waited until he thought she was about ready to explode if he delayed any longer, then decided to short-circuit the tantrum.

"From what evidence we have, he died from exhaustion. But ... we don't know *how* he got into a position to die from it. Why'd he come to this ballroom? Why wasn't he following his normal schedule? Was he with anyone else in here? And, the biggest question, is what caused him to get exhausted enough for his body to give out?"

"What does all of that *mean!*" She screamed the last word, close enough to Humph's face that he was able to get a good look at her flawless teeth.

"It means that there are a lot of really weird things about him dying here, and now. Could be they all have simple explanations, and it's just bad luck." He shrugged. "Or it could be murder."

The implications hit Karen a heartbeat later, and she blinked. She was deep breathing; in Humph's estimate, it was an entirely calculated move. She probably was deciding she'd said too much in that scream; too much, and not enough. She was probably realizing that in front of a ballroom full of witnesses, she had not looked like a bereaved spouse—she'd acted like a woman full of rage yelling at her divorce lawyer.

And he literally saw her make a tiny, almost imperceptible shrug, as if she was saying to herself, "Too late now."

Humph wanted to press the advantage, trying to see if he could catch her on the back foot. After many, many years of questioning people, it was one of his favorite tactics; the more worked up they were, and the bigger the shock, the harder it was for them to come up with lies or stick to their stories. He didn't have much reason—that wasn't to say *none at all*—to suspect Karen of anything, but at this point leveraging conversations was almost reflex for the Boggart.

"Mrs. Burgess, I'm forced to ask again. Why are you on this ship, when I made it clear that it could jeopardize my investigation?"

"I needed a vacation," she said flatly. "This hulk is the size of a small planet. I know Dick's tastes, and I knew I could keep clear of any cesspits he decided to frolic in. I've been in Spa-La-City the entire time."

That was a pat answer if Humph had ever heard one. It was plausible enough, though, to potentially pass the "sniff test." Either she was a great liar, or it was the honest truth. Even if she wasn't trying to put something past him, there was a massive elephant in the room, which he thought she had probably already seen when he said the "m" word. Nevertheless, now he had to say it. He pitched his voice low. "You do realize that you're going to be number one on the list of suspects because you're here, and the ship's law enforcement is going to be in a hurry to throw you under the bus and get this case out of their hair. Right?" He narrowed his eyes, watching her *very* closely. Maybe saying it out loud would be enough to make it reality for her, and rattle something loose.

But her first reaction was not what he'd expected. She touched her data-cuff; his chimed and he glanced at it. It was the firm's payoff registering to their account. Before he could react to that, she was doing something else, and an offer came up.

Find out who did this and clear my name. The offer was four times what the price to find Dickie's paramour had been.

Now this put him between a rock and a hard place. Take it, and it meant he was going after Claire, personally. She was the last one to see Dickie, after all, so she was involved no matter what. No way to keep her out of it and call it an investigation, even by Humph's admittedly murky standards. Refuse it—give the excuse that he was in charge of the investigation, say—and it meant that she'd be going after *him*, with all the resources she had, and he'd still be going after Claire, personally. Potentially anyone she found to hire on this boat could find or manufacture enough circumstantial evidence that *he* would end up the prime suspect. It was a bum deal no matter what ... so Humph figured that getting a solid chunk of change to do what he was already planning on doing was better than not.

"Jim," he said under his breath. "Accept that for us." Then he raised his voice so everyone could hear him, and said, "If you have no objections or somewhere you need to be, why don't we just get all the preliminary questions your presence on the ship raised out of the way right now?"

This time the shrug was visible to everyone. "Nothing I can't reschedule. Are you—"

But he was already turning to Blackstone. "Detective, would you care to interview the victim's wife at this time?"

Blackstone clearly saw what was going on. Humph had a conflict of interest, since he'd been stalking the deceased on behalf of Karen. All kinds of ugly could be implied if *he* interviewed her. But Blackstone? No problem. And it didn't matter if the crime was shoplifting or murder, all suspect interviews were somewhat alike, and Blackstone must have done a couple thousand by this point in his career. Humph had just handed him a relatively easy slice of murder-pie, one that would confirm in the eyes of outsiders that Blackstone had taken charge, and that Humph was staying on the up-and-up.

"Would you come this way, Mrs. Burgess?" the old man said immediately. "I think there's a private room over here—" And he discretely took Karen's elbow and led her toward the back of the room.

Which was a little macabre, since the place was decked out to look like a clearing in the middle of a Louisiana graveyard, and it looked like he was leading her into a mausoleum. The holo-walls on this room were really *good*. It would have been even more convincing if someone—probably Blackstone—hadn't ordered the lights to be brought up to full in here.

Huh, Humph thought, taking a closer look, then walking up to the part of the ballroom where tables were set up among the graves. *It's not all holos and fakes.* Because either they had paid a freaking fortune for a stonecutter, or they'd found someone willing to look the other way while they looted a graveyard. That wasn't all that hard to do back on Old Earth. Old graveyards in what had been small towns were often abandoned, especially after they had disgorged their contents as Reboots. And these stones and the wrought iron were *old*, the inscriptions worn away to mere suggestions.

Not a moment after Blackstone had ushered Karen into privacy for her interview, someone from the ship's hospital turned up with a gurney and a body bag. At this point Humph had taken all the vids he thought he'd need, and gave them the go-ahead to bag the body up and store it in cryo. It was a particularly nice touch, he thought, that after collecting the dearly departed, they left as they had come via the service passages. Heaven forbid the guests should be reminded that there was anything more important than making sure they wrung every last picosecond of pleasure out of their trip.

By the time Blackstone finished with Karen, the ballroom was empty. There wasn't much more to do. Blackstone escorted Karen to the door, then came back to stand next to Humph, hands in his pockets, looking down at the spot where the late Dick had been.

"Not exactly in mourning," Blackstone observed.

"Yeah, but also not thrilled with this," Humph replied. "Things were rolling along nicely on schedule. I was about to get hard evidence, she'd invoke the prenup, and she'd have walked away with a hefty payday, and everything would have been nice and tidy in a month, max. Now? It's ugly and messy and I'll bet the prenup didn't allow for one of the parties being murdered. Unless we catch a break this could stretch on for a year or more."

Blackstone sucked on his lower lip. "Looked it up while I was discussing things with her. Mildred law puts a hold on the assets of an unsolved murder. Survivors get what the court decides is an 'adequate maintenance allowance.' Supposed to prevent spouses killing each other and kids killing parents."

"Did she know that?" Humph wanted to know. Blackstone nodded. *Well, that accounts for the slap.* Karen's idea of an "adequate maintenance allowance" was probably nothing like what the probate court would think was enough.

Humph mulled that bit over. Karen knowing about Mildred law could mean a few things. One, that she was the sort of person that read the fine print on everything. They existed, but Humph had never known any stuck-up heiresses that fit that type; they have *people* for *that*, don't you know. Two, folks that were looking at *all* of their options, even the unsavory and potentially illegal kind. He'd only ever met Karen twice; once on Mildred to take the job and get the particulars that he needed on poor, dead Dickie, and just moments ago when she'd barged into the room and slapped him. Was she the murdering variety of wife? Maybe, but knowing the law and having a lousy husband weren't enough to definitively make her the culprit. Not to mention, there was still the question of *how* someone had killed him. That part in particular was aggravating Humph. A half dozen stab wounds, a bullet hole, hells, even a bloody hammer or piece of rope; nasty ways to go, but he understood them. Unfortunately, there were a lot of weirder ways to buy the farm in the wider 'verse.

And Dickie found himself one that's going to be a royal pain in my ass, Humph thought, chagrined.

"What else did she have to say?"

Blackstone looked over his shoulder quickly before turning back to Humph. "I think she was lying."

"How do you figure?"

"Well," he said, sighing as he rubbed his head, "she gave the same line about being here on vacation. Okay, fair enough, right? I start going through the other standard questions, getting her

287

whereabouts—she was in a spa session when she got the alert about Dickie, and that checks out with receipts and such—when she started getting agitated-like, looking at the body."

"Upset?" Humph offered.

"I'd say more eminently pissed off. She said she wanted to 'throw it all in that bastard's face.' I'm guessing whatever, erm, 'evidence' you were going to present her with." Blackstone looked to the floor to try to hide his obvious embarrassment. A lot of real cops, even retired ones, were uncomfortable with PIs, and some of the more distasteful jobs they often took. Like this one. "She was mad that he was dead, because now she never would be able to give him a piece of her mind about his philandering. But it didn't ring true, and I can't put my finger on why. Kind of …."

"Go on, Blackstone," Humph prompted. "Kind of like what?"

"I don't know. Kind of like she was acting more pissed off than she really was." He shrugged. "She froze me out after that, just boilerplate answers for the rest of the boilerplate questions. Sorry, Mr. Boggart."

Humph shook his head, putting a hand on the taller man's shoulder. "No, that's all right, Blackstone. You did good. Besides, you were doing me a solid, too; her being my client, wouldn't do for me to look like I was coaching her. Though if anything comes of this, you might have to give testimony on it."

Blackstone's moment of pride deflated just as quickly as it had arrived, and was replaced with that same hangdog resignation. "Yeah, I figured. It's okay. Done it plenty of times before. Just a pain, going to court anymore."

"Make a recorded deposition right now while your mind is fresh," Humph urged. "Do it every time we get more information in this case. Chances are they'll accept that." And chances were, they would. This guy lived on a cruise ship, and the odds of him being anywhere near Mildred when and if a trial came up were nil. No one was going to fly a fast courier out to wherever the ship was, pick him up, pay for his expenses on Mildred during the trial, and fly him back.

With that, Humph officially ran out of anything concrete to go on … save for one thing. "Blackstone, if you'll excuse me for a moment." The elder detective nodded once, then set about taking

Humph's advice and making his recorded depositions. Humph keyed his comm unit, bringing up the work channel. "Okay, gents. We've got our work cut out for us on this one. So much for an easy gig."

"The only 'stiff' I wanted out of this job had 'drink' attached to it," Fred grumbled.

"What's next, boss?" Jim, in contrast to Fred, sounded excited. Eager, even. *Gods, I hope that isn't the start of a trend.*

"You two are going to work, immediately. Jim, you're on Dickie's financials. Dig through all of the stuff we already have, then look for anything we might have missed initially. If there's anything that could point to someone or screams 'motive,' I want it. Fred, you're going to link up with Blackstone; I'll send him a message to let him know you're coming. Comb through every security-cam feed you can get. Try to track Dickie's movements, see if there's anyone that made a pass at him, anything unusual. Something happened in that ballroom, and it is as sure as I am pretty that it wasn't any sort of 'natural causes.'"

"What're you going to be doing?" Fred had already left the hallway, on his way to meet Blackstone in the ballroom.

"Something stupid. I'm going to go speak with Claire."

Jim and Fred went on—at length—about how colossally stupid Humph's idea was. He had a conflict of interest, for obvious reasons; his prior relationship with Claire, his current strained "relationship" in the sense that she probably wanted to use his guts for harp strings, and that he was being paid by the wife of her dead paramour.

"Couldn't that, oh, I don't know, screw up things in a court?" Jim had said over the comm.

"We're PIs, Jim, not actual cops. We're not here angling for a conviction anymore; we're here to see that our client is cleared. If we stumble across the killer, bully for the cops at the end of the line who get to take all the credit. We've been paid, and we're doing a job."

"And that's all it is, right boss? Just the job?" Fred hadn't been as vocal in his objections to having Claire questioned, merely suggesting that either Humph have Blackstone do it, or at least wait for Fred, so that he could do it. Barring all of that, to wait so that the Were could back Humph up. Still, the implication was there; Humph was letting Claire cloud his judgment and that was bad business.

"Just the job. Executive decision, too. So, both of you quit yammering, and get to work. Ping me if you get something, and I'll ring if I need anything. Humph, signing off." He switched his comm unit to standby with a little more force than he had intended.

Both of his partners were right, of course. This was dumb on a level that Humph rarely achieved. All of their problems with what he was doing were spot on, and he ought to have heeded their advice. Ought to have, but wasn't going to. The money for this job didn't matter, beyond the fact that it bound their firm to Karen and doing what they could to help her. If she turned out to be the one that had killed her husband, those were the breaks, and he already had the money in the firm's account; turning her over to the real cops was about the only thing he could do at that point. In truth, Humph didn't care overly what had really happened to Dickie, beyond curiosity and annoyance at someone complicating his day. What he really cared about was ....

Well, what do you care about, idiot?

It couldn't be Claire. Humph had shut that part of his heart down himself, and paid for it, even though it was probably what was best for everyone involved. Or so he'd told himself. Looking back, maybe it had just been what was best for him. Claire would probably agree with that. If he didn't care about Claire, then why was he putting himself out in front like this, forcing things so that he had to be face-to-face with her? Did he want to confront her, give her a piece of his mind? Did he really think that she might've had something to do with Dickie's death? He couldn't make sense of it, especially with the fast-attack headache that was currently hitting his head with repeated bombing runs. QuickSober also came with a quick hangover, and all the joy that those entailed.

This time, Humph didn't need to rely on subterfuge to get to Claire's suite; Blackstone had already messaged that Humph had full run of the ship in the course of the investigation, and that anyone that gave him guff was to be directed to the ship's detective. It was good that the old Norm was starting to find his spine; he'd probably need it a lot more before this case was over.

Humph raised his fist to bang on the door, but hesitated, opting to wrap his knuckles on it instead.

"Come in," came the languid response. Humph steeled himself for whatever was ahead, and opened the door.

Well, score one for the classics. Either this was Claire's idea of juicing her victim up, or Dick had had unguessed-of depths when it came to his tastes.

Strike that. This was Claire's idea. She was done up like a 1950s pinup girl, complete with stockings with seams up the back and a garter belt. The only thing striking the odd chord was her fuchsia hair; a magnificent temp job, but not permanent; so the black waterfall earlier had been a wig. She was arranged decoratively on the sofa and it was clear she had been expecting Dick—or maybe some other sucker. She sure as hell wasn't expecting Humph, that much was plain.

The bemused smile that Claire had been wearing for whoever Humph was supposed to have been shifted, and her eyes widened. Humph had known her long enough that, even though she had become an expert in hiding what she was really feeling—what little *that* was anymore—she couldn't fully hide from him. There was genuine shock, then a flit of delight, which was quickly replaced with a white-hot flash of fury, before it all settled into another mask of exasperated boredom.

"Well, if it isn't Trouble. What disaster are you dragging along behind you this time?" she asked. Her tart question, or whatever follow-up rejoinder she was preparing, died on her lips when she saw the cast of Humph's face. Her mask fell, too; she could sense and see how serious Humph was, and that meant that whatever he was there for was the worst kind of trouble. She swung her legs off of the sofa so that she could sit up straight. "Whatever it is, I didn't do it," she said, looking dead into Humph's eyes.

"How can you be so sure, if you don't even know what I'm here about?" Humph couldn't tell if she was being honest; she didn't seem to be dissembling, and the whirlwind of emotions she had just gone through had seemed genuine enough. But Claire was a Fang, and deception was like fine wine to their kind.

She wasted no time. "Fix yourself a drink, and tell me the bad news, *after* you tell me why you're on this ship." Her composure was back, and he had to give the old girl credit, she recovered like a champ. None of the false bravery and bluster of Karen, using anger to hide how shit-scared she was. Claire was a real, dyed-in-the-wool survivor. If nothing else at all, he could admire her for that.

"On a job," Humph rumbled as he slowly made his way over to a drink cart. Picking up a decanter, he uncorked it and sniffed the contents; *really* good scotch, even better than the stuff in the gift basket they had put together. Unable to resist, he poured two stiff fingers of the booze into a matching crystal glass, and took a long drag, savoring it.

"That much is obvious, *dear*." There were knives in that last word as Claire swiveled to lean against one arm of the sofa, crossing her legs. "You never were much of one for vacations or relaxing, were you?" Her tone was arch, and Humph could feel her studying him intently, looking for anything she could use. Always a game of brinksmanship with her.

"Investigating a Romeo out on a debauch, away from his 'loving' wife," Humph said by way of reply.

"Your profession has always been such a grimy one, you know," she declared. "Chasing down losers for those desperate enough to pay you. Though, maybe it's a case of sending one to catch one, perhaps?"

But then, and he could actually see her put two and two together, she tensed. She held up her hand. "Wait, don't tell me. Dick Burgess." Her jaw hardened, and her eyes took on an almost feral sheen. "Don't tell me that you've been spying on me, for that harridan of a woman." More words unsaid. *That you're spying on me, taking money to do it, after everything else that you've done to me.*

He shrugged, taking a slug of his drink to stretch things out a bit more. "I never know who the 'Jezebel' is until I catch the Romeo in the act. And that was yesterday, too late to back out of the deal. And as of today ...."

Claire's eyes searched his for a moment, her lips pursing as she tried to get him to crack and spill something. When he didn't, she spoke slowly. "Something has happened. This isn't a social call after you've already taken what you *needed*, come here to gloat and wave your sordid goods in my face, is it?"

"Dick's taking a dirt nap, kid," he said it flatly and impersonally. "Dead as human kindness. And it looks like homicide. The House Dick doesn't know you're the Other Woman, *yet*, but he's going to find out, and when he does, your Fang friends are going to all pretend they never heard of you." He finished his drink and kept himself from pouring another by sheer strength of will. "So where were you last night? You weren't here."

Claire looked at him with the sort of contempt an owner would have for their dog, right after it took a dump on a shag carpet. "Why are you always bringing me messes, hmm? Never a payday, never good news, never—" Claire stopped herself short, shaking her head. He could guess what she had wanted to say, before her pride had stopped her. *An apology.*

"I live a charmed life. Now, where were you? Were you with Dick? When did you last see him?" He pointed the empty glass at Claire with each question, taking a step toward her.

Claire waved a hand dismissively. "Sometime late yesterday, I don't know when. Watching a clock wasn't very high on my list of priorities at the time. As for where ..." her voice trailed off as her eyes swung over to the bed. Humph felt something in his chest twinge, *hard*, and he almost dropped the glass. Squeezing it harder, he stomped over to the decanter with leaden feet, pouring himself a full drink. Claire was still studying him, her eyes narrowed.

Humph swallowed half of the drink in a gulp that left him teary-eyed, wiping his mouth with the hirsute back of his free hand. "And after that?"

A small, cruel smile curled the edge of Claire's lips. "To my private room, to rest. You're actually *bothered* by this, aren't you?"

Humph counted himself lucky that Boggarts didn't really blush. "Do you have anyone that can corroborate that?"

Claire had found his weak spot, however, and wasn't going to go on without twisting the knife. "You mean was I screwing anyone else after I got done with Dickie? No, Humphie, I wasn't." Her eyes bored into him, smelling blood in the water. "Is that what gets you hot under the collar? Knowing that I was bedding someone else?" She looked around the room, as if a thought had just occurred to her. "Do you like watching it? Are there dirty little cameras in here? That's how you knew right where my room was, maybe … you've been here before? My, I didn't know you were so *cosmopolitan* when it came to the bedroom. If only that had been the case when we shared one, hmm?"

That was finally too much for Humph. "Shut the hell up, bitch!" To Claire's credit, she didn't start or recoil at the outburst, though her amused expression had vanished, replaced with something colder. "Your target—I assume he was some kind of mark—was murdered and you're at the top of the list, or will be, as the prime suspect! And you're just damn lucky that the House Dick here hasn't figured out who you are yet! And sooner or later, if he doesn't, I *have to* tell him! Start taking this seriously, and forget about us for one godsdamned minute, would you?"

Humph knew it had been the wrong thing to say as soon as the words left his mouth, but he couldn't stop himself. Whether it was something that had been brewing for too long, or all of the high-end scotch, he couldn't say.

"Forget?" She breathed the word, keeping her eyes locked on his. Her chin tilted downward, so that she was looking up at him, and Humph felt like she was building up to a truly epic scream. "About *us?"* Then she surprised the Boggart, by throwing her head back and laughed, a full, throaty sound that was completely unlike Claire. When she was finished, there was a glimmer to Claire's eyes that hadn't been there before. "How could I *ever* forget, Humph? About any of it?" Claire stood up preternaturally quickly, crossing half the distance between them before Humph could even blink. He almost dropped the glass for a second time as his right hand reflexively twitched toward his holstered gun. Claire stood there, unnaturally still. Humph breathed hard, and Claire didn't breathe at all. "After everything, I couldn't forget about you if I tried, Boggart. I remember all of it, from the beginning. Ours, together, and its end … then my *real* beginning. Every time I've thought that you were nothing but a bad memory, you've always come out of the woodwork to screw up my life all over again. Maybe *that* is what really does it for you, huh?" Humph knew what was going on with Claire's eyes, now. They were tears; bloody ones, the only sort that Fangs could produce. A single tear escaped, rolling down Claire's perfect, porcelain cheek

like a crimson reminder of everything she had lost and everything she was now forced to be. "Maybe you're the real Vampire. Feeding on the misery of everyone around you, and making more when there isn't enough."

Humph hadn't known what he had expected, but *that* certainly hadn't been part of it. Slowly, he set his glass of scotch, half-finished, down on the serving table. He never took his eyes off Claire, the way one didn't stop watching a cornered, feral animal. "Claire," he said, keeping his tone even in direct opposition to how he felt. "You need to lawyer up, *now*, before the Fang Nest on this station dries up whatever credit lines you have. I have to follow this all the way through. I can't—"

"You *can't*," Claire interrupted, the last word nothing but venom. "I'm tired of what you can't do, Humph. What you can do is leave my *fucking* room, right now."

There was dead silence in the room, and a single heartbeat that seemed to stretch into eternity for Humph. Underneath all of the fire, indignation, and rage that Claire was displaying … was pain. So much of it, that it broke Humph's heart all over again. He had the strongest urge to rush over to Claire, hold her in his arms, and tell her that everything would be okay. But then that moment passed, and without a word, he swept out of the room and back into the hallway, slamming the door behind him. He paused in the hallway, trying to will his blood pressure to drop and for his heart to quit hammering in his chest.

Stupid, stupid, stupid! He had utterly screwed that encounter up, and maybe any chance he had to get anything useful out of Claire at all. Why? He'd interviewed countless witnesses, suspects, and leads during his many years as a PI. Why had he let her control the dialogue, kept on letting her get away with needling him and turning the conversation back to the personal? And yelling at her … *Gods, what an idiot mistake!* He couldn't have done worse if he'd tried, he was sure of that. Now, she knew that Dickie was dead, and that she was on the suspect list. If she really did ice the poor fool—which Humph, even after that "interview," still had zero idea if she really was responsible or not—then she now knew that she was being investigated. If Fred had bungled an interview that badly, Humph would've been tempted to fire him on the spot, or demote him to cleaning the office. Why had he messed it all up with Claire?

Maybe because you know that you deserve everything she said, a tiny, evil voice in the back of his mind said. *Because all of what she said is true in the end, and you can't deny it anymore.* Humph's head was throbbing, and he couldn't grit his teeth hard enough to ignore it or that malicious devil plaguing his conscience.

So get your mind back on the job, moron, he told himself. That, after all, was the important thing, the *only* important thing. Clear the client. Get paid. Get out. Get the next job. He could cry into his scotch about Claire later, after he was back on Mildred and off of this tub.

Humph didn't feel convinced, but it would have to do. He couldn't stand in the hallway outside of her room forever, wondering where it all went wrong. Humph took a deep breath, and was about to march back to the elevators when he noticed the bellhop.

Now, bellhops are generally *strong*, but ever since lifting and hauling assistance became cheap enough every fleabag hotel could afford to have liftcarts for their ten-credit-a-night patrons—bellhops weren't the bantam-weight prizefighters they used to be. So Humph was more than a little surprised to see someone muscled up moving the cart down the hall. And he was even more surprised to see that the guy moved like a martial artist. There was an economy to his movements that the untrained just didn't have. Humph, having trained in pretty much every martial art he could find a teacher for, would know. He wasn't exactly trying to make time with the cart, either, and for a bellhop, time is money. In fact, if Humph were to put a name on the way the guy was moving, it was "dawdling."

And just as he came to that conclusion, even though he didn't spot the moment the guy realized he'd been made, the "bellhop" abandoned his charge and dashed for the exit.

"Shit!"

Like a dog that can't help but chase a moving hover car, Humph's instincts couldn't help but run after someone that ran from him like a perp. The bastard was *fast*, but so was Humph. The hallways in this section were long, and though the fake bellhop had a decent lead on Humph, he couldn't break line of sight by taking a turn down a different hallway for long enough to lose Humph.

The Boggart's legs pumped mechanically, and his head felt like it was going to explode into a cloud of red confetti, but he kept up the pursuit. The bellhop rounded another corner, and immediately there was a loud crash. Humph came up to the corner a second later, but took it cautiously; getting nailed with something because he was overeager was not something he was keen on experiencing, especially with his growing headache.

Around the corner were a set of double doors, still swaying on their hinges, and Humph could smell a smorgasbord of aromas. *The kitchens for this level.* Through two porthole windows in the doors, he could see the retreating form of the fake bellhop, pushing cooks and assistants out of the way in his mad dash, with a growing amount of debris scattering to the floor from his flight. Humph pushed through the doors, jumping over the clutter on the floors and dodging around the shouting kitchen staff as he pursued. The bellhop juked to the left after passing a prep table, and Humph lost sight of him. It was sheer dumb luck that Humph slipped on some food detritus and slid onto the floor; the bellhop had grabbed a pot of boiling *something*, and had been poised to douse Humph with it. Instead, his aim was high, and it splattered against the wall instead of in Humph's face. The bellhop cursed, and took off running again. Humph cursed as well, fumbling as he righted himself, and once again gave chase.

A dizzying array of service halls followed, and Humph was beginning to regret all the scotch he had downed. He wasn't yet winded, but he certainly felt his stomach turning sour. Another bang as the bellhop turned a corner, this time followed by screams and very feminine screeches of displeasure.

It was too late for him to stop. He crashed through the same doors to find himself in the middle of the "Ladies Only" pool of this "hotel's" feature presentation.

The Roman Baths of Cleopatra's Villa. And if he'd been in the position to sightsee, it would have been quite a sight—a pretty accurate reproduction of a set of ancient Roman baths. This was a "Ladies Only" *calderium*, a big, hot pool that was just about tit-deep on the *highly* attractive and leggy gals currently standing and shrieking impotently at the first intruder. The *calderium*, as was appropriate, was surrounded by massage benches, most of those had been occupied at the time of intrusion, and the lithe, nude Furies who'd been getting their aches rubbed out had backed the guy he'd been chasing into an inescapable corner and were pelting him with everything they could get their hands on. It was only the fact that every one of the gals sported lavender hair on their heads and not so much as an occupied follicle elsewhere on their bodies, that they were nearly identical in height and weight, and that they were all uniformly attractive in a similar mold that something in the back of his mind recognized them as the hotel's showgirls. They must have been enjoying their day off until this moment, and they were not happy about the situation.

The fake bellhop took a shiatsu stone to the brow; that, apparently, was enough for him, as he ran toward the group and pasted the offending showgirl right on her nose with a mean right jab. She crumpled, holding her ruined face, as the others screamed and started slapping at him. He pushed through them, scattering any that got too close with a raised fist. That's when he turned right into Humph's answering right hook. It was a good shot, and probably would've laid out most folks that weren't expecting it. The bellhop took it on the jaw like a champ, though, and spun with the hit. He quickly shook his head to clear it, then settled into a low fighting stance when Humph came into focus for him.

"Listen," Humph started, holding his hands up, palms out. "I've got the beginning of a real bad hangover, and—"

He never had a chance to finish, as the fake bellhop surged toward him. It was on pure reflex that Humph was able to deflect the first two punches, swatting them away with his open hands and ducking to the right with a quick step. *Okay, so the asshole doesn't want to talk. Maybe a few lumps will change his attitude.* Though he didn't acknowledge it right then, a not-so-small part of him relished the idea of beating the snot out of this guy. For starters, the creep had socked one of the showgirls; bad form and low, if nothing else. And he'd made Humph run; he hadn't been lying about the hangover, as the headache was really ramping up to be titanic. But, the real reason he was happy about laying hands on this chump was that he was still pissed off about Claire. Working out that aggression on the bellhop's hide wouldn't change that, but it would take his mind off of it for at least a short while.

Not content to leave the attack unanswered, Humph replied in kind, feinting an overhand punch with his left, then ducking back low and to the right again to work the Norm's ribs with three quick shots. The Norm was good. He recovered immediately, and tried to repay Humph with a solid knee to his face; the Boggart twisted at the last second, taking the knee to his upper right bicep before he retreated. The Norm kept advancing, though, and Humph had to block more lightning-fast jabs and uppercuts. One strike got through, and a white-hot flash of pain seared Humph's left cheek; the bellhop had tried to blind him, clawing at his eye, but had only managed to score the dark flesh underneath it.

Okay, jerk. Two can play at that game.

Humph unsheathed his own claws, and drove the Norm back with several wide, sweeping swings. The first had caught the Norm off guard, and torn through his likely stolen uniform and found the ribs underneath, eliciting a gasp from the man. He may have had sharp nails, but they were no match for Humph's natural weapons. He pulled a push dagger, seemingly from thin air, and started for Humph's midsection with it. While the small blade probably wouldn't kill Humph unless it hit something truly vital, he still didn't want any holes poked in his own hide. He backed up as quickly as the bellhop came for him, knocking massage tables and chairs out of the way. Luckily, all of the showgirls had either retreated to the walls of the *calderium*, or had fled the room entirely.

The fake bellhop's front foot found a puddle of water on the tile floor during a stutter-step in his advance, and he slipped forward as his footing failed, overstretched with his latest lunge. Humph seized the man's arm with both hands, letting his claws dig deep into the meat of the Norm's forearm. A twist and a chop to the wrist, and the punch dagger flew from the Norm's grasp before it clattered and skittered along the floor into one of the pools. The man cried out in pain, but slithered his way out of Humph's grasp. The next thing that Humph saw were stars, followed by a nova-blossom of pain on top of his skull.

Damn, that was fast! The man had pulled off a blisteringly quick and well-aimed axe kick, catching Humph with his guard down. That had created enough room between the two of them for the Norm to examine his bloodied forearm. He quickly looked at Humph, and his eyes tracked to the only exit—behind Humph. Something changed, and the Norm squinted with some new determination. Humph felt it before it happened; the Norm pulled open the uniform jacket, reaching with his strong hand, in that universal motion that said, "I've got a gun, and I'm going to use it on you, *jack*." There was just enough distance between them that with the Norm's speed, Humph wouldn't be able to arrest his draw stroke in time, and there was zero cover. Diving into the pool would just limit his mobility, and he might crack his skull on the bottom of it, it was so shallow. The Norm was just about to clear his jacket when Humph's hand, on an instinct of its own, fished out his pocket watch and dropped it. Humph ported to it before it got close to hitting the ground. Time being odd in the Nowhere-Space of the watch, he waited for what he thought would translate to a split-second back in the Real, and then ported back in … this time behind the Norm. Reaching under the man's outstretched arm, he slashed at the wrist and fingers that were holding the gun; shocked by the injury, the man gasped and dropped the weapon. Then Humph kicked the man in the balls with all the force that he could muster.

The Norm had vomited after he had crumpled to the wet floor, cradling his undoubtedly sore balls. Humph bent down to pick up his watch and the handgun that the man had dropped. A hold-out pistol of decent enough quality, and more than enough gun to kill Humph if the Norm had managed to land a shot.

"Y'know, I'm pretty sure that the cruise doesn't issue these to staff. You and me, we're—"

"FREEZE! DROP THE WEAPON, NOW!"

Humph, lacking a meaningful response, looked up. Good on the girls for calling security. D minus for timing on the security's part. A handful of large, uniformed men were all crammed in the doorway, pointing equally large and uniform weapons directly at Humph. It must've been quite the scene; a bloodied Boggart, menacing an injured bellhop, while nude showgirls shrieked and yelled in the background.

And then, before anyone else could move, one of the girls leapt forward and smacked the rent-a-cop up alongside his head. "Not *him*, stupid!" she shouted—and she had one impressive set of lungs. "*Him!*" and she pointed to the downed bellhop.

What could've been a very painful, and very deadly, cluster got cleared up when Blackstone arrived, red-faced and out of breath. The security guards didn't shoot Humph, and instead clapped security cuffs on the fake bellhop, who they then *confirmed* was fake. It took a while, but eventually the Norm copped to everything. He was a PI, or at least working for one, just like Humph. His boss—who no one could reach—had tasked him with snooping on Claire, and he had picked up a uniform from the ship's laundry, easy as could be. Truth be told, that's exactly how Humph had gotten several different uniforms to blend in with the crew, though he didn't inform Blackstone of this. Apparently, Karen hadn't fully trusted Humph or his firm, and had hired some unofficial "backup." If one failed, the other still had a shot of picking up the slack, or so went the logic as the hired gun explained it. He had run when Humph spotted him, because he suspected *Humph* of maybe being the killer; it wasn't every day that a Norm saw a Boggart, and Humph's appearance was mighty frightening if he was in a bad mood.

And there it was, all out in the literally naked open. Claire's link to Dick Burgess. Humph had been hoping he'd get a *little* more time before that bombshell came out, but the gods hated him, evidently, and were determined to get their maximum of screwing-Humph-over entertainment.

Blackstone waited until the security guards had hauled the other Norm off to the ship's brig, very much against the protests of the supposed PI.

Blackstone sighed, and rubbed his pate. He'd managed to get his color under control, even if the heat of the *calderium* kept him sweating. "We're booking him for assault with a deadly weapon, battery, and a few other things. Someone will come pick him up, or they won't. He ain't the problem, though," Blackstone said, leveling a stare at Humph.

"The Other Woman, Claire. Yeah, I know." Blackstone shrugged, waiting. Humph sighed, picking at a bandage that one of the security personnel had applied to his cheek. "She was part of my investigation. Before Dickie died, I mean. And ... there's history there. I know her." Humph laid out everything that he knew so far; there wasn't much point in playing things close to the vest with Blackstone, since he needed the Norm's good graces to get anything done. When Humph finished, Blackstone shook his head slowly, mulling it over before he spoke again.

"You know all of that, taken together, buggers the entire mess good and hard, right?"

"I do," Humph breathed, nodding. "Listen, Blackstone. I need a solid on this. Give me some time to sort things out. There's more to this, what with the second PI firm, and Karen. And there isn't anything concrete to tie Claire to Dickie's death."

"Nothing concrete, you're right. All circumstantial. But that lug with the karate moves was right, too. You're in close to the same boat as the Fang." Humph's hangover headache had matured into a world-class skull-splitter, with the thug's kick to his dome only helping to amplify it, so it took a few moments for him to follow. Humph knew Claire, had history with her. Sure, it was dumb luck that the job landed in his lap. But he gets on the case, sees that it's *Claire* ... and gets jealous. Offs poor, dead Dickie in a fit of jealous rage—

"Only problem with that theory is I have a solid alibi with t—one witness and the security feed on our suite to prove I was being a good little PI and minding my client's business at the time." He'd almost let slip, albeit only a bit, about Jim. Still, the combination of Fred and the security feed ought to be enough to hold up to a court's critical eye. "And there's still the question of *how* I killed the dumb bastard, what without touching him at all."

"That's fine. But it still means you ought to be off this case, at the minimum. And that's not even counting about how Mildred cops and due process ain't exactly well acquainted. Could be they just lock everyone up and sort things out from there."

"And if I can't crack this thing by the time we get back to port, they'll do that and you don't lose anything." Humph had no idea how his brain was managing to work at this point, but at least it was, and the old man seemed to be inclined to listen. "Meanwhile, you've still got me, and that's two sets—*three* sets, counting my partner—of trained eyes on this that you'd otherwise have to take on alone."

Blackstone was between a rock and a hard place. No matter what he chose, it was a risk. Finally, he decided. "Keep on tracking it down. But if it comes right down to it, and I gotta go up before a judge, I'm going to have to cover my ass, first. I'm too old and too broke for anything else."

Humph clapped a hand on the detective's shoulder. "I owe you, Blackstone." He stepped past the older Norm toward the exit.

"What's your next move?"

Humph turned, rubbing the back of his neck. "First, get something for this headache, and a hot shower after that. Then, start looking for more pieces. Comm's on if you need me."

Both Fred and Jim were waiting for Humph back at their cabin. Fred wore a worried expression, and Jim … was unreadable as always, with his death's head rictus grin, though Humph could swear he picked up an air of disapproval from the Reboot.

"Before you even say it for the thousandth time, *yes*, I *know*, that was dumb. I'm not in the mood, and my head is killing me. Just give me what you've found," Humph said as unzipped the top of his jumpsuit. Fred was ready with a bag of ice wrapped with a cloth, which Humph gratefully accepted and pressed to his forehead.

"Well, after looking at Dickie's financials again, some creative accounting, boss," Jim replied. "Two outgoing streams. One was pretty easy to unravel; turns out to have been high-end designer goods, gifts without a doubt …" Jim let that hang. *Gifts for Claire, Dickie's side sweetness.* "But there's a discrepancy. Some of those gifts were things that a Fang would just have no use for. I gotta wonder if our horndog was cheating on Claire too."

Humph groaned. Because … *of course* Dick had been fooling around with another woman, not just Claire. He prayed to anything that would listen that it was just the one other woman and Claire, and not half the phone book. It would only make sense for the gods to inflict him with a case that had a dozen suspects running around. But Jim was continuing.

"The other was just cash withdrawals, which doesn't make a lot of sense on this boat, unless his side-side-piece was asking for cash presents. There's not much in these all-inclusive cruises to spend cash on. Besides, the amounts seem … well, too large for that. Big chunks of credits, from what I can see. And while Dickie wasn't the brightest bulb, even I don't see him throwing a bunch of cash at some stripper that he fell in love with."

That part was odd. There were plenty of reasons for someone to pull cash in odd amounts, and most of them involved hiding why you were taking it out and where you were putting it. Money laundering, some of the vanishingly small still-illegal variety of drugs, or setting up a nest egg in case you had to bail ship, maybe. Humph leaned over Jim's armored shoulder, reading the screen as the Reboot scrolled through the tagged account.

"A lot of these are over the cap," Humph said, referring to the fixed amount that, if a withdrawal or deposit is made that meets or exceeds that number, automatically flags the transaction for the bank and, by extension, the government. If Dickie had been trying to launder the money, or hide some away in case he went to divorce court, he did a crap job of it. Which, for an investment banker, didn't make a lot of sense. Even if he wasn't an accountant, such as Jim was in his previous life, he'd have had the good sense to not leave things so obvious, in any case.

"Right you are, which makes it even weirder. Haven't been able to pin down why he was taking it all out. Not yet, at least."

"Keep on it," Humph said, standing up and stretching. His back popped in several places, and an uncomfortable amount of those pops were accompanied by lightning bolts of pain. "Fred, what'd you get on your end?"

The Were shook his head, holding up a small data drive. "Less than Jim did, boss." Fred sped through the footage that he'd bothered to record, all of it featuring Dickie. "This is all from just after we bugged the suite where he'd been meeting up with Claire. He went back to his room—not the suite that we had under surveillance— alone. Emerged a short time later, and instead of meeting up with his pals on the executive level like he always has, he beelined it to the level with the Mardi Gras scene and the ballroom where he was found. No cameras inside the ballroom, and none on the entrances for the ballroom itself, just for the level. So far as I can see, he was in his room alone, traveled alone, and went into the ballroom alone."

Humph chewed on that. "Which means that whoever—or whatever—killed him was either in his room, in the ballroom, or otherwise met him at the ballroom."

"And we still don't know what exactly wore him out enough to kill him," Jim added. "Helluva murder weapon, whatever it was."

Blast it all! Humph kept himself from slamming a fist into the table that held the monitor by grinding his teeth instead. He had at *least* another potential suspect, a *third* woman that Dickie was involved with, which was good and bad at the same time. Good, in that it could possibly clear Claire and Karen of being the killer, and bad in that he had zero ideas on who it could be, since none of their surveillance had turned up any other female—or male, for that matter—romantic liaisons for Dickie. They still didn't have much to go on for how Dickie died, or if he was alone when it happened. Humph *wanted* a drink, and needed an actual forensics kit, about four other detectives, and a month to untangle this ball of bullshit. Instead, he had an over-the-hill ship wizard, an equally over-the-hill ship's detective, and his two partners. Oh, and a limited time before they returned to port, and Mildred's finest were loosed upon the whole lot of them. Humph had the sudden urge to commandeer an escape pod and hope for the best.

"What's the next move, boss?"

Fred and Jim looked at Humph expectantly. If he had still been solo, running a firm of one, he might've cut his losses and run from the entire mess. As things stood, he couldn't do that. He'd already been paid, and Fred and Jim looked to him to make the good calls, or at least to make confident ones. And there was still Claire ... if he took off now, he didn't favor her chances with the Mildred detectives or their leg-breakers.

"Keep on retracing our body's steps, see what we can shake loose. That means his personal cabin. Going to go there, toss it, hopefully find something that'll lead us to the next thing, and so on."

"I'll stick with you on this one, boss. You can't cut our paychecks if you're dead," Fred offered. Humph nodded his assent.

"I can maybe try to track down where some of those withdrawals were done," Jim rasped. "If I can get eyes on the locations where the ones that happened on the ship, might be able to figure out what he was doing with the money."

"Good plan," Humph replied. Drinking and resting seemed like a wonderful idea, but he just didn't have the time for it, nor the shower he wanted. He settled for changing into his "working" wardrobe: fedora, trench coat, a well-worn suit, and some comfortable shoes. And, as always, his revolver ... with just the right bullets, for whatever might come.

Dickie's room turned out to be just as cookie cutter as the dead man had been. To be sure, it was a *very* nice room, afforded with all the amenities an executive-level guest could expect. The suite that Karen's money had bought as part of "expenses" was close, but not quite up to this level of decadence. Still, it felt ... well, *boring*, to Humph. While the sheets were clean and expensive, and the carpet didn't have any mysterious smells or stains, he couldn't shake the feeling that there wasn't any character to how it was done up. Maybe the feeling was just a product of his lifestyle over the many long years of his life, and the parade of dive bars, greasy spoons, and grubby social clubs that he'd spent most of them in. Not to mention the eclectic decor of all of the no-tell motels he'd been in and out of over the years. As such, he didn't have any reservation about thoroughly tossing the place; any damage would go on the bill or get eaten by the cruise line.

Even after slicing into the walls, dismantling the bed and all of its comfort-inducing contraptions, and fishing in the toilet tank, they'd turned up only a few scant traces of anything. While Humph was only a lowly PI, and didn't have the resources of a real dirtside police department, he had the next best thing: Fred. The Were's supernatural sense of smell had helped on more than a few cases, but here, it was proving to be fairly useless.

"Don't know if this place has been hit by a maid service or what, boss, but there ain't nothing here that the ol' schnoz is picking up."

"We'll have to get in touch with Blackstone, see if there's a schedule for the maids. Maybe we'll get lucky, and one of them has something we can go off of for this case stuffed in a garbage bag," Humph replied, scratching the back of his head. He was starting to run out of ideas on where to go next. In the room, they'd found some gambling receipts, another gift basket that still had most of its complimentary goodies, and … a white flower. A real one, and still fresh.

Normally, the last item wouldn't have elicited much attention from Humph. Hotels and cruises like this one always had tons of prop items scattered about, to show exactly how high-end and special they were compared to all the other ultraexpensive relaxation and entertainment options in the galaxy. But usually, such things— especially in a place as garish and in-your-face as this cruise ship was—were done *big*, with zero ambiguity as to what message they were trying to send. The flower, all alone, was simple, almost elegant; for that alone, it stuck out.

He'd found it lying across the foot of the bed, like a prop for a glamour shot, and it didn't even have one of those bits of nearly invisible water-film wrapped around the cut stem to keep it alive.

Humph, lacking anything else to go on, pointed to the flower last. "You get anything off of that?"

Fred shrugged. "Common lily, grown somewhere with real dirt but fake light, been around the ship, and handled both by a woman and our dead target."

Even though it didn't seem like much, that level of detail still unnerved Humph a little bit; even as a Para himself, there were things among the occult, paranormal, and Fae that just weirded him the hell out.

"Can you narrow down where in the ship it's been?"

Fred shook his head. "Don't think so. It's got a little bit of everything on it, if you know what I mean. Nothing really 'jumps out,' nothing distinct that I could use to give you a more precise location. Now the woman," he said, picking up the flower. "If I got close enough to her, same room or something, I'm pretty sure I could pick her out."

"Well, in that case, we just need to get you into a room with the, what, half a million guests and staff that this boat has on it?" They might as well drop a few credits on some lottery tickets, while they were at it. Even if they could manage to *somehow* sort through the entire roster—bloody unlikely, in no small part because of how disagreeable partiers could be when someone pumped the brakes on their fun—they just didn't have the time. As soon as they got to port in orbit above Mildred, the PD would take over ... and that's when heads got busted and someone took the rap for Dickie's murder.

"Sorry, boss." Fred looked down at the space between his shoes for a few seconds before speaking again. "So, uh ... what now?"

Humph sighed. *'Hell if I know' won't cut it; Fred and Jim need me to be decisive.* "Let's walk the murder scene again, and the area around it on that deck. A second pass might give some new perspective on it. And, who knows? Maybe we'll get lucky, and you'll get a whiff of the mystery woman that handled the tulip."

"Lily, boss."

"Whatever." Humph was halfway to the door when he felt more than he heard that Fred was lingering behind. He turned to see the Were bending over to pick up the gift basket. "Really?"

"Hey, free swag is free swag. And it's not like Dickie is going to make use of it."

"Fine. But you look ridiculous. Like you already mugged Red Riding Hood, and you're making off with her basket for snacks later." Fred had, of course, gone human form. Were for the purposes of using his nose. Now he looked as sheepish as his lupine head would allow.

Yet again, Humph was at an impasse. He had next to no clues to go on, and time was still running out. The trip back to their suite was uneventful; Fred had changed his face back to fully human in the nick of time, as there had been a bellboy coming down the hall just as they'd left Dickie's room. Even if the staff were accustomed to Paras, a partially wolfed out Were was a sight. They dropped off the gambling receipts and the flower with Jim, while Fred made quick work of rifling through the gift basket. Jim looked expectantly at Humph, and Fred picked up on the vibe quickly enough. *What now, boss?* Humph cleared his throat, and was prepared to utter the dreaded words—"I've got zero damned idea on what to do next, other than interview every passenger,"—when his comm chimed. Thankful for the brief respite so that he could gather his thoughts, he answered, though he kept the relief out of his voice. "This is the Boggart, go."

"Blackstone here," the older man said, and immediately Humph knew something was up from the clipped way he spoke. "That mug that you knocked around, the one that said he was a PI? Well, someone broke him out of the brig. Roughed up some of the security boys pretty good; a couple of them are in surgery right now, in the medical bay."

"Shit. We were hoping someone would turn up to claim him ... just not like this."

"Yeah, no kidding," Blackstone said with a sigh. "We put out a quiet alert to the entire ship; just staff and security, don't want to freak out the passengers. If they turn up—"

"You'll let me know," Humph finished. "Thanks, Blackstone. I'll let you know if we get anything on this end. Humph out."

The others were still looking at Humph, waiting for him to tell them what was going on. He filled them in, to a chorus of swearing.

"So ..." Fred said, trailing off intentionally.

"So we go visit the Widow Burgess," Humph said, surprisingly himself a little with the certainty in his voice. "She hired whoever probably busted the goon out of the ship's lockup. Maybe she'll give us something to help track them down. They might've stumbled on something with Dickie that can lead us to the next thing; only way we'll know is if we can put hands to 'em." Both of his partners nodded at that. While Jim's expressions were hard to interpret, Humph was sure that both of them looked more confident, energized. *It's amazing what a little leadership and a little less boozing can accomplish,* he thought, chagrined. "You're with me, Fred. Jim, you're—"

"—on research duty, I got it," the Reboot said, picking up and waving the gambling receipts. "I'll keep my other eye on the cameras and see if I can find our karate goon."

Fred waited until he and Humph were in the lift to speak. "Why'dya think the other PI went through the trouble to bust his guy out? I mean, it's drawing a lot of heat down on himself, ain't it?"

"Dunno," Humph said. "Maybe he needed him before we hit Mildred space. Or maybe there's a clock that we're not seeing. Seems

309

like something that someone desperate would do. And desperate folks are dangerous."

"And if we run into them?"

Humph let the question hang for a moment. "Then we do so like a freight train. I've already had one of these mugs try to shoot at me. I don't fancy doing it again."

The various themed sections of this tub were given very specific names. "Paris in the Springtime," for instance, was very different from Karen's section, "Paris in Fashion Week." Instead of re-creations of romantic walks and museums, this part of the ship had three things in it: "hotels" (each of which was named and themed for famous Parisian hotels, but which fundamentally were identical except for decor), restaurants and bistros (no bars here as such), and "boutiques." The latter were all named for famous designers like Dior, Chanel, Wang, and Choo—not that Humph would have recognized any of them without being told—and created copies of said designer's famous clothing. All mixed up. All times, all styles. This created a certain ... weird effect ... when Humph looked in the display windows of a designer whose "house" had been relatively long lived—1858–1954, for instance—and you saw enormous Victorian ball gowns displayed next to 1940s "war rationing" suits and dresses.

And no mistake about it, this part of the ship was *all* about the clothing. You could buy it if you wanted, you could merely try it on and have yourself a bunch of ultra-glam display shots or a life-sized portrait made, or you could sit at as many runway shows as you could stand and simply watch the fabric parade by you.

He would have thought, relic of the past as he was, that the population of this part of the ship would favor women. But no. It seemed equally split.

Then again, he found his own gaze drifting as the stunning faces and spectacular figures of the show models intercepted it. *Guess it's not hard to find something to look at around here ....*

Karen's digs were at "Le Metropolitan," a hotel that looked like it had been built some time in the late 1800s. Supposedly every window was actually a holoscreen that played out the exact view you'd get from that window of the actual hotel in Paris at exactly this time of day and year. So if you "looked out" right now, you wouldn't see the street—or Humph and Fred. That suited him just fine. If he'd had a nickel for every time a gig had gone sour because someone looked out of a window at the wrong time, he'd be able to afford a berth on this boat all on his own. Then again, Old Earth nickels went for a lot, nowadays.

The key to not getting pinched by local security was almost always to move briskly and look like you knew where you were going. If you looked like you belonged, everyone assumed that you did. So he and Fred got into the elevator and went up to the tenth floor where the ultra-luxe suites with their distinctive round windows were. This was by no means the priciest suite in the ship. It wasn't even the most expensive in "Fashion Week." But it was a cut above the one Claire shared with the late Dickie.

The elevator opened onto a hallway done in beige carpeting and white-on-white brocade wallpaper, with little touches of gold everywhere. Karen's suite was halfway down the hall on the right. And as they approached the door, Humph's supernatural hearing picked up voices. Even past the hotel's noise dampening construction, he could tell that they were *angry*. Fred had perked up, his hearing several orders of magnitude above Humph's.

"Boss?"

"Got your iron on you?" Humph reached to sweep his trench coat aside, revealing his own revolver.

"Never leave home without it," Fred said.

"Good. Don't plug 'em unless I do. If this is who I think it is, we need these humps still breathing. Got it?"

"Who's kickin' the door, you or me?"

"You, I'm old."

Fred grumbled as he moved to the side of the door controls. Holding up his pocket comm, he unlocked a special service compartment. Several dimly glowing buttons shone through in the hallway's gloomy ambiance. "Okay, I hit the emergency override, this thing is going to open pretty much immediately. I'm through first, going right."

"And I'm going left. If anyone makes a run for the door, you get in their way."

"Why me, this time?"

" 'Cause you can turn into a ten-foot-tall roadblock of fur, teeth, and claws. I'm a speed bump, at best. Besides, privileges of seniority in the firm." Fred frowned at that, then nodded. Humph did one final check, making sure his Webley was at the ready, then gave Fred the "go ahead" nod. The Were pushed the button, and the pneumatic door violently cycled into its frame. Fred was through the portal in a blur, and Humph followed on his heels. Humph immediately pivoted left, his hand on his revolver as he scanned to make sure the corner was clear, as Fred did the same on the opposite side. They both quickly swiveled back to the center of the room, and were greeted with three shocked faces.

The one sitting down on the edge of a divan was the Widow Burgess. Menacing over her, an accusatory finger still thrust at her face, was a man that Humph didn't recognize. Humph had, however, a lot of acquaintance with his *type*. The high point of his life was in high school, when he was the top athlete—usually football, usually quarterback. But he was never good enough even to get a college scholarship, and generally he ended up selling used autopods, insurance, or in this case at least, getting a job in what was probably a family PI firm that specialized in easy jobs like spousal surveillance. He had once had a glorious mane of golden hair. It had been reduced to a handful of sad strands pulled over the middle of a male-pattern-bald head. Once upon a time, he'd had a six-pack; but despite being in space, gravity had had its way with him, and what had been a chest was now a belly. Actually, his utterly nondescript appearance probably worked well for him in most jobs, but on an expensive cruise ship full of beautiful people, he stood out like the only duck at a swan convention. Hovering close at hand behind him, arms uncovered and flexed, was the martial-artist fake bellhop, now out of his stolen uniform and in a nondescript jumpsuit.

"Keep your hands where we can see 'em, and back away to the wall, now!" Humph made a show of tightening his hand on his revolver, hoping that the men would have the good sense to back down. The last thing he wanted to do was blast them, especially with Karen right there; otherwise, he would've had himself and Fred enter the room with guns drawn. As it was, if he had to get hands-on with the thugs, he didn't want to have to drop his revolver to do it. *Maybe, just maybe, one part of this job will go easy.*

The tension in the air was thicker than day-old soup in a greasy spoon on Mildred, which was saying something. No one said anything, and Humph could tell that the schlubby PI and his assistant were doing their best to remain as motionless as possible. Everyone knew that as soon as the first move was made, all bets were off, and Humph kicked himself for not waiting to get a security team stationed outside for backup. His hope was that if he gave them a minute to think, they'd choose not getting their parts broken over valor.

That hope was shattered when Humph saw, out of the corner of his eye, Fred lick his lips and shift from one foot to another. That was all it took. The PI and his assistant both dove in opposite directions, toward the nearest cover.

It was all Humph could do to yell, "Get down!" and throw himself at the floor before bullets started flying. Somewhere underneath the crescendo of gunfire, Karen was screaming; not hysterical, but incensed. He thought he caught something about her luggage being ruined, but he couldn't be sure. Looking through his feet to the other side of the doorway, he saw Fred. Luckily, the Were had taken the hint and managed not to get any new holes poked into his hide.

"Plan?" he yelled through the din, wincing and ducking as the low counter he was hiding behind splintered from a bullet.

"Take at least one of 'em alive, and don't die doing it!" Humph pulled his revolver, and Fred followed suit. "Empty your gun into the ceiling, keep their heads down! I'll try to pop up behind them, then you rush 'em while I've got 'em distracted!"

Fred blinked at him. "That's a really shit plan, boss!"

"What's new? And don't hit the client!"

Humph's fingers darted into a pocket, fishing out his pocket watch. He figured that if he got near to one of them, the other would be less inclined to shoot. He decided on the PI; he didn't look like much, and if the martial artist got squirrelly, the PI was a bigger shield. Humph checked to see that Fred was ready, his own pistol already braced against the counter and pointed at the ceiling.

Humph sidearmed his pocket watch, sending it skittering along the floor. He kept his eyes on it, to see where it would end up—he had been aiming for behind a grand piano on a dais near the center of the room—when he noticed the martial artist taking aim at the watch as it was slowing to a stop. The lug must've remembered their earlier fight, where Humph had used that trick before. While the magics that tied Humph to the pocket watch made it supernaturally sturdy, he doubted that it could take a round from the mug's gun. Faster than he thought possible, he brought the Webley around the corner of his cover, and unloaded the entire cylinder at the martial artist before the man could get off a single shot. The Norm crumpled backward, his arms going theatrically wide.

Fred, reacting, started shooting. *Time to be stupid.* Humph jumped into the Nowhere-Space of the watch, oriented himself for the room, and then popped back into the Real. He ended up exactly where he wanted to—behind the PI. He swung the butt of the revolver down, hard, aiming for the base of the man's neck, hoping to stun him long enough for Fred to get over and help him subdue the second Norm. To his surprise, the PI twisted in place to turn his upper body to face Humph, and actually *caught* his gun hand by the wrist.

Before he could follow up or wrench his hand free, a big, meaty fist planted itself, *hard*, in his gut. Humph felt the air go out of his lungs, and had the urge to vomit. He managed to ignore his rising gorge, and instead lashed out at the PI. The man, to his credit, kept hold of Humph's wrist, even as Humph's claws scored the man's cheek with the backhanded swipe. Humph attacked again, landing a hit to the ribs, a couple of jabs, and tried to come back over the top with a hammerblow to the elbow of the arm that the PI was holding him with, while the PI was protecting his face with his free hand. Right before Humph connected with the overhand strike, the PI's free hand shot out, catching Humph's left wrist in a crushing grip.

The PI *smiled* at Humph, with blood seeping through his large, yellowing teeth.

"Gotcha."

The headbutt that came a split-second later made stars explode in Humph's vision, and he felt himself reeling. Something had broken—probably his nose, though it was hard to tell through the constellation of pain in his head—and he could feel blood immediately begin to run and dribble onto the top of his chest. With both of his hands locked in the stronger-than-expected hands of the PI, Humph tried to kick at the man's crotch, or bring a leg up to push the two of them apart. Each time, the Norm swung a knee up to block the attack, and punished Humph afterward, with another headbutt or wrenching his arms painfully. Humph managed to dodge getting his faced smashed in, but the headbutts still hit his collarbones and upper shoulder, and one blow was so fierce that Humph felt his knees weaken.

And that, thank the dark little gods, was when ship's security showed up.

"Jesus Christ, you two look like warmed-over shit," observed the Para-paramedic as he swabbed Humph's face. He held up a hand. "Don't make whatever witty comment you were about to, because I've heard them all. I want both of you to check in at the central hospital, or I'll have security lock you up until a Para-doc gets free to come scan you. This is nonnegotiable; you either go on your own two feet, or you get locked up."

"Oh yeah?" Humph snarled, half rising, perfectly ready at this point to butt heads with the medic.

"Yeah." The medic snarled back at him, and shoved him back into the chair. He was a lot stronger than Humph had thought. "I'm the one whose balls are going to be in a vice if one of you two stooges decides to drop dead of something I missed."

"Don't argue with him, boss," Jim advised in his ear.

Fred had shifted back to human so the silver bullet that was still in his shoulder wasn't going to cripple him—but it needed to come out. As Humph was very well aware. And the paramedic didn't have the tools to do that. Humph *could* take it out with just about anything sharp, but he'd make a mess of it, and given that there was a perfectly good state-of-the-art medical facility right here, what would be the point?

"How long is it going to take?" Humph growled, glowering at him.

315

"Less time than it takes for your partner to come down off that shot I gave him." The medic smirked. Does that mean if I call the wagon, you'll get in it without me having to give you one too?"

"You might find some information down there, boss," Jim reminded him.

He sighed.

"I'll take that as a 'yes.' " The paramedic could not quite conceal his satisfaction at having "won" the argument. Before Humph had quite figured out what was happening, the back wall of the room opened up, and what looked like a two-man coffin rolled in. Next thing Humph knew, he and Fred were sealed in the thing—which had no windows—and all that he could tell was that they were moving.

He figured out quickly enough that this capsule-ambulance was shooting along the service corridors at what was probably a high enough speed to be hazardous to anyone outside it. And he figured out why he and Fred weren't being wheeled off through the "streets" as well. First, there were probably all sorts of shortcuts back here, and second, you don't want the happy travelers to get even a hint that it was possible something unpleasant could happen to them here.

In fact, it couldn't have been much more than five minutes later that the coffin-lid opened, and he blinked up at the bright light and faces staring down at them.

"What the hell are you?" asked a graying, heavyset man who looked as if he took as little guff as Humph did, as a colleague helped a sweating Fred out of the other side.

"Boggart. With a concussion, if past experience serves," Humph replied. The doctor flipped a monocle screen down over his left eye, and muttered something Humph couldn't hear under his breath. Instructions for an AI?

"So, you're pretty much bog-standard normal human in most things. Let's get you out of that coffin and into a scanner. What in the name of Dante's Inferno is going on up there?" The standard medical scanner was enough like a bed that Humph was happy to lie down on it. "They're treating us like mushrooms down here."

"Keeping you in the dark and feeding you bullshit?" Humph almost smiled. This guy, he liked.

"Hey boss? This guy's the main ER doc here. I bet if you clue him in, he'll give you what he knows." Jim had a point. And … he was going to have to confide in someone sooner or later.

He made the explanation short and sweet, but before he could finish it, the doc's eyes had narrowed and his jaw hardened. "And they didn't tell you about the *others*, did they?" he demanded.

Humph's own jaw tightened. Which hurt. "Ow! *What* others?" he asked.

"Hold your horses, sheriff," the doc said. "Let me explain a dirty little secret. People die on cruises all the time. Accidents, old age, even a murder or two; the company doesn't like people to know about that, but it's statistically inevitable. This thing's the size of a city, so it has all of the problems of a city except an actual criminal underclass and poverty because we've got bots and Reboots for anything that'd be too low-paying for a sapient to handle. I've been a doc on cruise ships for forty years, so I know what to anticipate. But *this* ship—this is different. Every four weeks or so, like clockwork, I get a stiff in here that as near as I or anyone else can tell died of sheer exhaustion. Except that shouldn't be possible. They're all male, all check in as singles, not elderly either, none of them have any contributing factors, and no one knows what they were doing in the hours before they died. They just turn up dead in their beds. Or at least, on their beds, like they got that far and keeled over. And that bastard Blackwood didn't bother to tell you about them, did he?" The question was obviously rhetorical, because the doc didn't wait for an answer. "He didn't believe me when I said there was something going on!"

"Wait, you said these others all turned up dead in their beds?" Humph asked, as the scanner made polite little noises. "Alone or with someone?"

"Alone as far as anyone can tell," the doc replied. "You can turn your cabin security cams off, of course, and most people do. Most people just turn the cabin security cams off when they arrive, and forget to ever turn them back on again, but the door does keep track of the guests by means of the amenities bracelet on your wrists, and the only one registering is the dead guy whose cabin it is. So all *I* know is the victims were all found alone in their beds when housekeeping shows up in late morning."

"Same part of the ship?" Humph wanted to know.

The doc shook his head. "All over. Only place there hasn't been a vic is the part of the ship where the real high rollers are, the ones that bring their own entourages and guards and never move an inch without 'em."

"Well ain't that a pip." This was certainly information, but it was only making things more complicated.

"I *told* that flatfoot there was more going on!" the doc continued in a growl. "It's got to be Para related, right? Can any of you guys walk through walls?"

"Gremlins, but their deal is stealing little bits of vital tech and wrecking stuff, and besides, the tech crews sweep for them regularly," Humph replied absently. "I've never heard of them offing someone directly. Ever."

Humph was getting a very, very uneasy feeling in his gut. Because there was one thing that, up until this very moment, he'd been sure was absolute, unbreakable gospel. No matter *what* weird critters had gotten dragged out of the shadows when the paranormal suddenly became "normal," there was one class that had never once manifested.

Human spirits.

No ghosts. No angels. And no demons-who-were-former-humans. Reboots didn't count; the vast majority of them were as mindless as planarian worms, and the very few that were like Skinny Jim—well, the unspoken consensus of opinion was that they were soulless, the spirit had fled the mortal realms and left behind nothing but memories. Humph preferred not to think about such things at all, life was already complicated enough. Start asking too many unanswerable questions and you'd either end up as a perpetual philosophy grad student or in a looney bin.

... but what if ....

"You done with me?" He asked the doc.

"Sure thing. You can't have your buddy yet, though, he still needs some work." The doc jerked his head to the side; having gotten at least a dozen injections around the site of the wound, someone was going in after the bullet. Fred's eyes were half-shut, and it looked as if he wasn't feeling anything they were doing to him. He was alert enough to answer though. "I can catch up with you later, boss, if there's someplace you need to be."

"Do that." The doc handed him a little plastic cup with a couple pills in it; he swallowed them dry. "I need to see a man about a dog."

As it happened the office of the ship's wizard was in the same area as the hospital and the rest of the mundane operational parts of the ship, the old goat was actually in it, although the half-empty bottle of gin testified to the fact that he hadn't exactly been doing any work. The old man looked up as he appeared in the doorway and grunted.

"You again?" he said, but without rancor. "What this time?"

Humph helped himself to a glass and a splash from the bottle, although the doc probably would have had a hissy if he'd been there. "What do you know about ghosts?" he asked without preamble.

"No such thing," the wizard replied with authority. "There you go, you can toddle off now."

"What if there were?" he asked. "What if you could get a haunted object? Like in all those old vids, haunted dolls and shit."

The wizard sucked on his bottom lip, a trickle of gin still running down his chin. "Well ... huh. You tell me something. Are there Paras that aren't exactly material? Let's not get into the whole metaphysical crap, just things that don't actually need a physical body."

"Banshees," Humph answered immediately. "I useta know one, before we all got booted out of the broom closet. I guess they'd be—I dunno, energy critters?"

"So ... hmm. Where's this going?" the wizard asked. There was a glitter of something in his eyes as he regarded Humph; inebriation ... or suspicion, maybe?

"Where'd those tombstones in the ballroom come from?" he asked bluntly. "Because those aren't fake. They're old, old enough the inscriptions mostly wore off, but they're real."

"I'm not gonna ask 'and you know this, how, exactly'? Because you Paras—" the old man cocked his head to one side. "You got instincts. How about we find out?"

Before Humph could say anything, the wizard whistled something that sounded like a fragment of a melody. A computer interface holo appeared over his desk. And a girl's head and shoulders manifested on it. She was irresistibly cute and blonde, her hair was in a ponytail on the top of her head, and she was wearing some sort of arrangement of a pillbox hat and scarf, both spangled and pink. "Yes, Master?" she said brightly.

"Access the build records for this boat, Genie," he told the computer. "Where'd the decorations in the Skeleton Krewe Ballroom in Big Easy come from? The tombstones, specifically."

"Working. They were purchased from a dealer on Old Earth in the country of Germany, the city of Düsseldorf."

"And where did *he* get them?"

"Working." It took longer this time, because the computer was probably having to search across a crap-ton of space and access records on Old Earth.

"You're thinking what I'm thinking," Humph stated flatly.

"I wasn't before, but I am now." The wizard scratched his beard. "Still a shit-ton we don't know about you Paras. It's a theory."

"Still a shit-ton we Paras don't know about us Paras. We're not like, one race, y'know. And a lotta us don't exactly get along, either." Humph was actually beginning to like this old goat. He might not be as incompetent as Humph had originally thought. *Just old and tired, and usually has to deal with crap that an apprentice could handle, if the Fangs running this joint would spring for one.*

"I have the answer, Master," the computer said. "They were sourced from a graveyard outside of Düsseldorf that was attached to a convent. The conventional Order died off, the Church sold the property, what was left of the bodies were moved and the headstones purchased by a stone dealer. That was where Pierre Bergeron found them when he was sourcing authentic decorations for Big Easy."

"Good job, Genie, dis—wait. What was the Order?"

Humph had no idea where this was going, but the wizard obviously *did*, so he kept his mouth shut.

"Poor Clares, specifically, a convent that took unwed mothers."

The wizard's lips twisted for a moment, as if he had tasted something bad. "Good job," he repeated. "Dismissed."

The girl tossed her head and giggled. "Oh *thank* you, Master!" she trilled, and disappeared.

"What was that about?" Humph asked.

"Well, I'm what you'd call a student of the history of bad choices," the wizard replied. "That wouldn't be what we modern folks call a *convent*, as such. It was ... more like a prison for girls that had 'disgraced the family.' Combination prison and work farm, you didn't go there because you wanted to, you went there because your family forced you to. Poor Clares were notorious for that—mostly in Ireland, but all over, really. So ... figure you have a whole building full of miserable women, who had their babies taken from them at birth and were forced into what was essentially slave labor combined with *forceful* 'religious instruction.' They tended to die young, hence the graveyard. Now that is a big sucking pile of what we wizardly types call negative energy. There might not be haunts ...."

"But it sure could attract the attention of something like a Banshee, that eats that kinda shit," Humph replied, nodding.

"So, let's go take a walk in the Ballroom and we'll see if my theory is correct." The wizard put the bottle down, took his feet off the desk, and stood up, looking about a hundred percent sharper and more alert than Humph had seen him before. He grabbed a bag from behind the desk and gestured for Humph to follow.

The wizard knew all the "back ways," and it didn't take them long to get there. Humph had expected him to wander around the place for the next couple hours, but again, the wizard surprised him. "This is where I earn my bonus," he said, opened his bag and took out a jar of what looked like glitter. He handed it to Humph. "Don't drop that, and don't open it until I tell you. Gold is cheaper than what's in there."

The room was still sealed off, with security posted at all of the entrances; one look at Humph, and the pair at the first set of doors he and the wizard arrived at opened the doors for them. The wizard surveyed the room, and clapped his hands together, rubbing them vigorously.

"For this next part, I want you to stand back. And don't say a word; breaking my concentration is the sort of thing that has consequences, for the *both* of us. Got it?"

Humph nodded, shifting the jar in his hands. *Let's see what the old coot has up his sleeves.*

For the following half hour, the wizard went to work. Complicated hand gestures where several of his fingers moved in different directions at once, muttered incantations or sung-aloud spells, all manner of contraptions and ingredients pulled from his seemingly bottomless bag, and at one point he even danced—backward. At the end of the half hour, the wizard threw up his hands, then stomped back over to where Humph had been quietly standing.

"Can I talk now?"

"Well, you just did, didn't ya? Go ahead!" The wizard patted his pockets—looking for a flask, probably—and came up empty. His mood, which already seemed low, did not improve at this.

"Did you learn anything?"

"Not a blessed *or* a damned thing!" the wizard half-shouted, throwing up his hands again. "Only one thing left to do. Open the jar. But—ah, keep it pointed toward the center of the room. Not at me, or at your own face."

Humph felt a great deal more wary about the package he'd been holding all this time. Per the wizard's instructions, he opened the jar—at arm's length, facing away from both of them. At first, nothing happened, and he expected the wizard to curse at another dud of a spell, or something similar. Right as Humph was about to look over to the wizard and say something, he felt a tingle in his fingers. The jar, his hands, and the space immediately around them were all vibrating, the air shimmering impossibly. Humph felt like he was simultaneously going to drop the jar, and that he wouldn't be able to let it go, ever. The dueling sensations were maddening, and before he could cry out, the jar released the glittery-substance in a gigantic, swirling tornado. The tornado shot for the ceiling of the ballroom, the glitter surging and whipping up the air in the room, causing chandeliers to sway and the faux mist to dance about the tombstones. With a final flash, the whirlwind descended. All of the glittery-substance settled on the ground ... but not around or on any of the tombstones. Instead, it had found an obelisk, hidden in a corner behind a row of impressive cross monuments.

The jar in Humph's hand wasn't vibrating any longer. Cautiously, he put the lid back on, and handed it back to the wizard. Initially, the wizard was dumbfounded, looking down at the jar. Then he plucked it from Humph's outstretched hand and threw it back over his shoulder, where it collided noisily—but didn't break—on the floor.

The pair walked over to the obelisk; the ventilation system and smoke machines had restored the airflow and mist back to their proper spookiness levels, and the only evidence of the spell—or whatever the hell had been contained in that jar—was the ring of glitter around the obelisk. As Humph grew closer to the obelisk, he could start to see details through the dim lighting. It was carved out of unadorned stone, heavily weathered with age. Well, not completely featureless; there were some vague hints of carvings on one side of it, but they were too faint to make out clearly.

"What we have here," the wizard said, sucking on his teeth, "is an anchor. Much like what you have, I suspect." The wizard's eyes darted from the stone to Humph's pockets briefly.

"An anchor for *what*, though?" If a Para was tied to the obelisk, how much like Humph was it? He was hard to kill, and what's more, his anchoring made him tricky to deal with. Some would say "annoying," as well.

"How the hell should I know? I haven't seen anything like this before, not precisely, anyways."

"Shit," Humph said, rubbing his chin; his jaw and head were still killing him.

"That's about the size of it. And I'll bet you my back teeth that whatever is tied to this hunk of rock—"

"—was in the room when Dickie died," Humph finished for him.

"You aren't as dumb as you look."

"Hold that assessment. We still have to figure out *what* is connected to this anchor, how it killed Dickie—if that's what happened, and the why of it all."

"How do you propose we do that, hmm?"

Humph thought for a moment. "You stay here, keep trying to figure out what sort of Para—or whatever—is tied to the stone. If it's anything like me, it might be able to be drawn back to its anchor."

"We could just destroy the damned thing, too."

"No!" Humph started for a moment, then collected himself. "Not yet. Do that now, and I won't be able to figure this case out, not all the way. That doesn't get my client cleared." *Or Claire, for that matter,* he thought. "Besides, anchors are usually pretty sturdy, due to the magic used in their creation. Even if it weren't already made of rock, it'd be damned tough to destroy."

The wizard chewed on that for a moment. "Fine," he spat, then thrust his chin out at Humph. "What're you going to be doing?"

"Standard gumshoe stuff. Question people that don't want to be questioned."

When the security squad had busted in and saved Fred and Humph's asses, they'd had to kill the PI and his assistant to pull it off. "Imminent threat to life and limb," and all that. Humph couldn't knock them for it, not really; he was alive and able to be pissed off that he couldn't question the lugs. Which begged the question; why was he still tugging on this string with Karen, and the PIs? He had a pretty good hunch that whatever had happened to Dickie had to do with that obelisk; the "why?" and "how" of it were still up in the air. He had a gut feeling, though, that Karen was caught up in things more than she was letting on, and he couldn't shake that feeling. It had something to do with the dead PI, he was sure of that much … but what?

He was half of the way to Karen's suite when his comm buzzed, interrupting his train of thought—an urgent alert. He keyed it, quickly bringing it up to his head. "Humph here, what's up?"

"It's Jim. I've got to get in the back to hide and pretend I'm a service bot; Blackstone is on his way here, and sounds pissed. Fred is hobbling his way back, too—shit, gotta go, boss."

Humph let loose an exquisitely inventive string of curses, and changed direction. Even using all of the service areas and shortcuts he'd picked up during his short stay on the cruise, the mad dash back to his room felt like it took hours. He almost ran past the door to his room, and had to skate to a stop, his lungs burning and his legs aching. He took a few moments to get some air back into his body, then waved the key fob for the door, hoping he looked more composed than he felt. Fred was sitting down; his arm was in a sling, and he looked hung over, but otherwise not in that bad of shape for someone that had been shot that day. Blackstone stood over him, and he did indeed look pissed. Then Humph saw why the old Norm was in such a mood. Sitting in a far chair, her back to the wall and her arms crossed—one wrist secured to the chair arm with a handcuff bracelet—was Claire. If Blackstone was pissed, she was *fuming* with barely concealed rage, a volcano ready to touch off at any second.

"Nice of you to show up," Blackstone growled.

"What's going on?" Humph slid into the room as the room's door shut behind him with a whisper. "What's she doing here?"

"Oh, her? *Your* little complication tried to jump ship."

Humph resisted the urge to laugh, but only just. "Go on."

"I put a security alert on her after our little talk." That earned a withering glare from Claire; if Fangs had had the power to reduce people to cinders with their eyes, Claire would've turned Humph into a steaming pile of ash right then. "So, she took a walkabout from her room, and I had my men intercept her. Next thing I know, they're babbling idiots about the 'beautiful goddess,' and she's almost charmed her way onto a racing pinnace that was docked for the day."

"How did you stop her?" Humph asked.

Blackstone shrugged. "For someone who used to own her own station, she knows crap about dockside. The only way she could have gotten that boat to fly would have been to have found the licensed pilot. It's DNA locked to him and to the owner. You can't override that without a service tech coming in from the builder."

"I *owned* a station and ships, I never *flew* them, human," Claire said through gritted teeth.

"Anyways, that stopped her. I had some men that weren't so susceptible to Fangs put her in irons, and here we are."

"Yeah, about that," Humph said, shaking his head. "*Why* did you bring her *here?*"

"'Cause she's your problem, and I aim to keep it that way. I'm not going to have my men—or worse yet, *me*—get blamed if she gets away somehow, or causes any other trouble. Besides, I imagine you're equipped to handle her."

"*Handle* me?" Claire stood up quickly from the chair, knocking it back; it would've crashed into the wall, if it weren't for the handcuff anchoring it to her. "How dare—"

"Blackstone, this isn't going to work. Lock her in her own room if you have to. And get hold of Bergeron, make her *his* problem. She's a Fang. Make it the Fangs' business."

"No." He crossed his arms. "That would take a lot of explanation and paperwork, and that would put both of us up a creek, wouldn't it? I'm not doing anything else to risk my retirement. Which, until you bunch showed up, was nice and quiet."

"Except for all the dead bodies that kept showing up like clockwork." Blackstone stared at Humph, uncomprehending. "I talked to the Para-paramedic when they took me and Fred in, Blackstone. I *know* that Dickie wasn't the first."

The Norm's eyes went wide, and—moving faster than Humph thought the old man could—crossed the distance and took Humph by the arm, dragging him in close. Humph tried to shake him off, but the ship's detective was surprisingly strong as well as quick.

"You *shut up!*" Blackstone said in a harsh whisper, shooting a glance back at Claire and Fred before meeting Humph's eyes again. "The company *wants* all of that to stay quiet, okay? Is that what you want to hear? Bad for business, blah, blah, blah. That meant keeping you out of the loop."

"And so what if someone had to take a fall, 'cause I didn't have all the information to figure this thing out. Right?" Humph sneered, looking Blackstone up and down. "All to protect your retirement and the company's bottom line, huh?"

"Not. My. Problem." Blackstone gave Humph's arm one final shake before releasing it. "I don't care, I'm not paid to care, and I'm too old and tired to get involved anymore." He jabbed a finger at Claire. "You watch her. Or don't. But it's on you, now. That's what my report will read, when we get to Mildred."

The Norm turned to go. Humph felt the blood thundering in his ears, and his head throbbed even worse than before. There was no way he'd let the old bastard have the last word.

"Blackstone!"

The ship's detective turned back to face Humph, a disgusted and expectant look on his face. Humph looked around for a moment, then found what he needed. He snatched up the gift basket from Dickie's room. "Still some good hooch left in this. Use it. Either to drown your conscience, or 'cause your pension won't let you buy the good stuff. Don't matter to me." In an underhand throw, he tossed it to Blackstone. Perhaps a little too hard, but Humph didn't care anymore. The Norm still caught it, though.

At first, Humph thought that Blackstone was having a stroke. His entire face had gone slack, and his eyes glazed over. *All the devils in hell, I've killed him!*

A moment later, Blackstone was moving again, but like a sleep-walker. He put down the basket and shuffled toward the door.

"Blackstone!" Claire snarled. "What the hell are you do—" her eyes narrowed. "Boggart, he's under a compulsion!"

Well a Fang would know a compulsion when she sees one. And something like this ... would only work on a Norm.

Humph cursed under his breath. He had Claire handcuffed to a chair, Blackstone—well, if this wasn't *part* of the whole mess he'd eat his own hat—and the ship's detective was heading for the door. He needed *everybody* in the same place so he could keep eyes on all of them!

"Fred, snap those cuffs—or the chair arm, if you can't—and follow me. Claire's comin' with us, too."

"And if he can't snap the chair arm?" Claire was already standing, holding up her chained wrist.

"Yours will grow back. You're coming with us, Claire." She pouted at that, but let her arm drop, chain ringing against the expensive wood. Humph was halfway out the door, his attention split between Fred, Claire, and the retreating back of Blackstone farther down the hallway.

To his credit Fred didn't hesitate. He pulled his arm carefully out of the sling, took a deep breath, and wolfed out to his half-and-half form. Humph turned away as he heard the *snap* of the chain breaking and hustled after Blackstone.

It wasn't much of a chase. Blackstone wasn't trying to evade them, and as quick as the old man was, Humph would be surprised if Blackstone could manage a light jog. The compulsion seemed very straightforward; it was taking him somewhere, by the most direct route possible. After they had caught up to him, they didn't need to do more than maintain a brisk walking pace to stay with him.

"Boss, maybe we should, I dunno … stop him?" Fred had fought his arm back into its sling, wincing as he readjusted it.

"Hell no. This is tied to the case, and it's the first major break we've had. We're going to find out where this compulsion leads."

"Aaaaand *how*, pray tell, do you know that this is part of the case? And not any other bit of randomness on this screwed up Love Boat?" Claire had kicked off her shoes somewhere and left them behind; uncharacteristic for her, given her thrifty nature, but Humph wasn't going to argue. She was carrying the snapped bit of chain in her cuffed hand to keep it from jingling too much.

"One of those things that detectives get, or so I'm told. Gut feeling. That basket? Looks like all the other gift baskets that high rollers and fancy types get in their rooms, right? Just one difference. This one came from Dickie's room." Humph glanced over to Claire, grinning. She merely shrugged, and the trio continued to trudge after Blackstone. Though she'd never admit to it, Humph was sure he could sense at least a little curiosity on her part; she wanted to see where all of this was going, too.

They were several levels down and a chunk of ship over—heading back to the leisure and pleasure spaces—when Humph got a call from Jim.

"Kinda in the middle of somethin' here, Jim."

"Yeah, boss, I know. But I found somethin'—"

"Part of Dickie's death?"

"What? Oh, no, I don't think so. It's about his accounts."

"Sit on it until we're done with this. And have your finger on the button to get reinforcements sent to our location, wherever we end up. I've got no clue about what comes next, and I'd perfectly okay with being saved by a bunch of uniforms."

"Okay, boss. You got it." With that, Jim shut down the connection from his end with a beep.

Humph was utterly unsurprised when Blackstone reached Big Easy and headed in the direction of the ballrooms. Taking a chance, he sprinted ahead of the detective, hoping the wizard would still be at the crime scene. He caught him a few steps from the taped-off door.

The old man sighed. "You ag—"

"Heads up, Wiz. Here comes a new development." He flung his hand in the direction of the approaching trio, Blackstone still shuffling along like a sleepwalker, or maybe a Reboot, Claire and Fred trailing.

"What in the ever-loving—"

"He picked up a gift basket that'd been in the vic's room, and *wham*. Turned into La Somnambula."

The wizard's eyes widened. "A compulsion!" He smiled wickedly. "That's a neat little trick, though I don't know how the hell it would've gotten past security."

Humph nodded. "Because it never went past security. It was put on the basket, I bet, by whatever has been in this room, and then taken straight to the vic's room."

"You know, that raises—"

The wizard didn't get a chance to finish. Blackstone made his entrance into the ballroom, the same slack expression on his face. Fred and Claire followed, Fred a few steps behind; if Humph had to guess, Fred was giving a quick notice to the security posted outside to be ready for anything. Blackstone continued walking until he reached the center of the ballroom floor, and then ... stopped.

Humph looked at the others; they were all staring expectantly, either at him or at Blackstone. He swallowed dryly, then cautiously made his way over to stand in front of the elderly Norm. If Blackstone had exploded into confetti right then, Humph thought he'd be prepared for it. Instead, the old man's face still had the dumb, vacant expression of magical compulsion. He waved a hand in front of the man's eyes, snapped his fingers, and even gave Blackstone's shoulder a firm shove; no change.

"Well ... shit."

Humph had raised his hand to motion for Gerhardt to approach when a side door opened; one of the service doors, if Humph's memory served. A door that was *supposed* to be locked. A young woman dressed in a maid's uniform calmly stepped through the opening. Humph had half a mind to warn her off, thinking that she had somehow been turned around while taking care of duties ... and then recognition hit. He never forgot a pair of ankles; they were almost as distinctive as faces as far as he was concerned. A look at her face confirmed it. It was the same maid that he'd almost been caught by in Dickie and Claire's little love suite. The one that had been holding a gift basket, and staring at him with some undefined need while he had worn Dickie's face with his glamour.

"Wha—" That was Blackstone, who started blinking and coming around. "What the hell?"

And the maid crumpled into a heap on the floor.

A mist rose from her body, a silvery mist that throbbed with energy. The mist formed a column, a column that settled into the contours of a body.

A woman. A woman made of silvery, pulsing mist, dressed in a long, filmy gown, with a tiny wreath of white flowers in her hair. Her eyes were closed. She held her arms crossed on her chest, a single lily in each hand. Exactly like the lily he'd found here after Dick's death.

She opened her eyes, and the first thing she saw was—Humph.

Her lips twisted into a snarl.

"*You!*" she said, her voice sounding as if it was coming from an echo chamber. "How *dare* you interfere!"

"I dare a lot, lady," he said, making a subtle sign to Gerhardt and Fred to get out of her line of sight. She was concentrating on him, she was *some* kind of Para, but he got the sense that she was old and ... well, not really used to the modern world. Which made sense if she'd only awakened when her stone was loaded onto the ship and people started coming to this ballroom. That kind tended to be pretty blind, so to speak. Monofocused on their task, whatever it was. Monofocused on what stood directly between them and that task.

His fingers itched for his revolver, but he resisted the urge to grip the butt of the old Webley-Fosbery. Even with his specialty ammunition, he very much doubted that the bullets would do anything to this Para. *'Cept piss it off, maybe. And it already seems plenty pissed. And ... that gives me an idea.*

"Oh, I dare a lot," he said lightly. "So, wench, make yourself useful. Get me a sammich." If he could keep her distracted for long enough, keep her focused on him ... well, his hopes and prayers rested on a winged Fur, a blitzed wizard, and a Fang that wouldn't spit on him if he was on fire. So, he was probably screwed six ways to Sunday.

With a howl worthy of a Banshee, the thing somehow made it-self taller. *"How dare you!"* she shrieked. "I am Myrtha! Queen of the Wilis! And you faithless boors are my prey!"

"Queen, Schmeen," he drawled. "Bring me a beer with that sam-mich while you're at it. And—"

He didn't get any further than that. The thing gestured angrily with one of her lilies, and his throat closed up. And then—

Then he began to dance.

Strain as he might he wasn't in control of so much as his eyelids. The Wili had completely taken over his body. He didn't recognize the dance, at all, but it was … well, if they turned this thing into an Olympic sport, he wouldn't have been surprised. He was hopping and jumping around like an electrified frog. Something medieval. Something German, he guessed. Something that had him dripping sweat and panting in moments. A second later, he had a partner—Blackstone. Blackstone's eyes were fixed in horror and the old man was already gasping. The Wili's laugh rang out, filling the ballroom.

"You danced with tender maidens, beguiled them with your lies, then betrayed them, leaving them to weep amid the ruin of their lives. Now you will dance for me—until you dance with Death itself!"

"Fritz! Do something!" Claire shrieked.

The wizard gave her an answer in the form of action.

With a roar, he raised his arms, and shouted out words Humph didn't understand. But the effect was immediate—he had his body back again, and so did Blackstone. They both dropped to the ground like a couple of understuffed toys. All he could do was hold himself on his knees and pant, while the wizard made complex gestures that raised some kind of magical wind that whipped around the ballroom like a vortex centered on the Wili.

She'd lost her lilies. Her hair whipped around her, the wreath gone askew. She screamed and seemed to try to fight, but whatever she was, she wasn't a magician, and her wild flailing accomplished nothing. Instead, it looked as if something had hold of her and was dragging her, step by step, to that obelisk in the corner of the room. Her screams grew fainter and fainter, the closer she got, until with a final roar, Fritz made a throwing gesture that flung her *into* the obe-lisk, which glowed for a moment with a baleful, red glare, then faded.

The old wizard went to his knee. "Holy crap. I am too old for this," he said. But he sounded pleased.

"So am I," Blackstone wheezed. His face was beet red, and his clothes were soaked through with sweat; Humph had been worried that he might have a heart attack, until he started speaking.

Humph, having finally regained enough of his composure to stand—albeit shakily—shook his head, still breathing hard. "I've got both of you beat, give or take a few centuries." He regarded Gerhardt, his eyes flicking over to the stone. "Is it …?"

"Contained." The ship wizard looked almost smug. "It won't come out of there again until I let it." That same greedy twinkle as when he'd spotted Humph's pocket watch entered his eyes again, and Humph frowned.

"Which you won't. 'Cause we're getting rid of this thing, *pronto*." For emphasis, Humph adjusted his trench coat, allowing his holstered revolver to briefly make an appearance. "Agreed?"

"Oh, fine. You're no fun. No nose for profit, either. A real, live … well, maybe not *live*, per se …."

"Fritz, this thing is going out the airlock," Blackstone said firmly. "Now. Or as soon as I can get a pair of bots here."

Abandoned in deep space? Seemed like a good idea, since they had no idea how to hurt it, much less kill it. And it wasn't as if anyone was going to stop their ship to look at some random floating rock.

"Seconded," said Fred. "The bots are on the way."

The airlock opened on hyperspace, which was exceedingly nauseating to look at, so Humph didn't. Instead he watched as the obelisk slowly drifted out, pushed by the air currents, then, when it reached the interface of shield and hyperspace, suddenly seem to stretch into an impossibly long pencil of stone, then vanish.

He wondered what that trip had felt like to the Wili. Some part of him felt something akin to solidarity with the doomed Para; trapped forever in a stone, floating through the endless, dark void? He wondered if she slept, like he had in the Nowhere Space, or if she was clawing at the metaphysical walls. On the other hand, she had tried to kill him, so it all ended in a wash of "not my problem anymore."

332

Which was good enough, since he still had plenty of problems on his plate. It had taken a couple of hours to get everyone collected, calm, and willing to stop yelling at each other for Humph to lay everything out. While the maid showing up had been the last piece of the puzzle for the Wili, and thus Dickie's death, there had still been all the weirdness with Karen, the second team of PIs, and so forth. Jim—bless his desiccated husk of a heart—had come through on that front. The information he had dug up had to do with Dickie's finances—and not just the official, aboveboard stuff. While it had all been hidden decently enough, Jim's history as a mob bookkeeper back when he didn't eat brains had given him plenty of insight into where dark money went and how it got made.

"Karen had been extorting her own hubbie, using the PIs, to launder some money from a charity fund she's in charge of. All the gambling stuff was tied up into it; that's where all of the weird amounts were coming from, and why it tripped me up initially. Cash, all put through and controlled with the PIs. After she was done pumping Dickie, Karen was going to use all of the infidelity stuff to divorce his ass. Double blackmail, or something."

After having a private conversation with his erstwhile "client," Humph made it clear that he'd keep his trap shut about the whole scheme ... provided that none of the mess from Dickie's death blew back on him, or on Claire. Karen, predictably, was furious, and promised that she'd end his career as a private investigator if it was the last thing she did. In the end, mad as she was, her check still cleared.

What would happen when the ship docked at Mildred and all the funny-money games brought the chickens home to roost? Well, he didn't care.

Bergeron had been nonplussed at the "news" concerning one of the set decorations, and its inconvenient Wili inhabitant. While someone, somewhere had broken some laws—Earth, Mildred, and common sense—no one could figure it out, precisely. But, the cursed stone was gone, and that's all that Bergeron, and by extension the company that owned the cruise ship, cared about. Blackstone, for his part in concealing the other deaths, was going to be let go from the company ... with a *very* healthy severance to cushion the fall. He didn't seem all that put out.

Gerhardt had been the only one not to come out on top. He had whined and moaned the entire time the stone was being transported for disposal, about how much an actual Wili—contained and "safe"—would be worth on the open market. In the end, being spaced with the stone didn't appeal to him, and he had relented.

Humph supposed that the Mildred PD would also lose out. There were no heads left to bust, or at least none that they could get away with busting. There had been enough witnesses to give statements on the events in the ballroom, that there was no question that a mythical Para had been at fault, and no one that they could actually put in irons.

"We'll be blip-casting this back to the Mildred PD," said the Fang who had been in charge of taking all the statements. "Don't concern yourself about repercussions; there won't be any. We're taking care of that."

As he turned away from the closing airlock, Humph suspected that the Mildred PD egos were soothed by a healthy contribution to their pension fund by the cruise ship's parent company, since they didn't bitch nearly as long as usual.

With everyone either appropriately pissed off or paid off, that left only one piece of unfinished business for Humph, and for Boggart, Barkes, and Bot.

Humph, despite not staring out the viewport at hyperspace, had decided to stay and prop up the wall. His flask—brought to him by Jim after all of the details had been sorted out—still had a bit of the high-class scotch that he'd scored from Dickie's suite. He'd been nursing it quietly, mulling over the entire blasted trip in his mind. Every part of him hurt, and he desperately wanted to sleep. But, instead, he waited, eyes unfocused and lost in thought.

"Remember when I said I'd rip out your spine and use it as a nine iron if I ever ran into you again? I may have been a bit mild in my assessment of what I'd want to do." Humph had noticed Claire's perfume long before she spoke; with her preternatural Fang grace, she had been able to slink up to him without making a sound.

"Sounds about right, kid. I can't say that I don't deserve it, either." He didn't dare look at her. The scotch burned a little more than usual when he took another sip.

"Let me make it plain. You are nothing but trouble, Humphrey Boggart. If I ever see your face again—ah, let me rephrase, if I ever see *you*, even wearing a different face—I'm going to shoot first and then run. You only have the power to ruin things, y'know. Other people, other lives, and your own."

"Okay, kiddo." Finally, he mustered the courage to meet her eyes. There wasn't any of the righteous anger there anymore. Just ... sadness. *Pity.*

"You're poison. Maybe it was the fault of whoever bound you, or fate, or whatever. But that doesn't matter anymore, Humph. You own it, now. Stay away from me."

Without another word, and so much as a backward glance, she turned on an immaculate heel and walked away. *Gone forever*, he hoped. For her sake.

Humph heard the shuffle of feet from the opposite direction where Claire had gone, and turned. Fred and Jim.

"Boss ...." Fred started, rubbing the back of his head. His arm was fully healed now, though he still babied it, only extending it slowly as if he was afraid it'd pain him suddenly.

"Save it. It's done. And so are we on this boat. Soon as we get to port, we're going straight back dirtside on Mildred. Space sucks."

"Y'know, that was my line when all of this started, back on the *Cenotaph*," Jim said through his suit's speakers. "But, if I could, I'd still drink to that."

Fred looked askance at Jim. "The *Cenotaph*?"

"No, furball! 'Space Sucks!'"

Humph raised his flask, then clinked it against Jim's helmet. "Space sucks!" He took a long swig, then handed the flask to Fred, who followed suit.

So long as there was good scotch, and beings that needed the truth—well, if you squinted real hard and looked at it from the side—Humph figured that they'd have work. And working was enough for the Boggart, the Barke, and the Bot.